W9-BDN-418

A SHOCKING REVELATION . . .

Julia Larsen felt goose pimples rise all over her body. She gripped the neck of the champagne bottle tighter and looked triumphant now, suddenly realizing what he was saying, they'd gotten the bastard, they knew who did it. "Oh God, did you—?"

"Yes, Julia," answered Jim, the local police chief. "A couple hours ago, we took someone into custody for the murder of your mom and dad."

"Who was it?"

"Julia," Jim Crowley said somberly, "the man I arrested is Matthew Hinson."

No, not Matt. Anyone but Matt, the man she'd trust with her life.

The cork popped out of the bottle. Champagne bubbled up and cascaded down Julia's leg. Then the bottle fell free of her hand and hit the floor as she closed her eyes and felt every last drop of blood drain from her head.

Snow Angel

"A TALE OF OBSESSIVE LOVE RUN NASTILY AMOK."
—*Kirkus Reviews*

**"POWERFUL, COMPELLING . . .
A HIGHLY CHARGED THRILLER
WITH A SURPRISE ENDING."**
—*Tulsa World*

① SIGNET **ⓑ** ONYX

MASTERFUL SUSPENSE NOVELS

☐ **THE TAKEOVER by Stephen W. Frey.** *New York Times* **Bestseller!** Investment banker Andrew Falcon is spearheading the biggest hostile takeover in Wall Street history. But Falcon doesn't realize that he has stumbled onto the secret power of a shadowy organization known only as The Sevens. Now his struggle for survival begins as he tries to outwit his enemies. "Absolutely first-rate!"—James Patterson, author of *Kiss the Girls* (184785—$6.99)

☐ **THE WORLD ON BLOOD by Jonathan Nasaw.** This stylish, super-charged novel of eroticism and suspense gives voice to the hidden side of passion. Not since Anne Rice's *Interview with the Vampire* has the vampire myth been so boldly reimagined. "Sly, wicked . . . charged with suspense."—*San Francisco Chronicle* (186583—$6.99)

☐ **MY SOUL TO KEEP by Judith Hawkes.** Twenty years ago, on a Tennessee mountainside in an abandoned quarry, something happened to nine-year-old Nan Lucas. Trying to start a new life after the collapse of her marriage, Nan returns to Tennessee with her young son, Stephen . . . and to shadowy childhood memories. "A haunting chiller."—*Anniston Star* (184149—$6.99)

☐ **THE DARK BACKWARD by Gregory Hall.** Mary Reynolds had the perfect husband, but now he was suddenly, mysteriously gone. After grief became shock, Mary began to discover how much she did not know about the man who had made her so blissfully happy for so heartbreakingly short a span of time. And what she did not know could kill her. . . . "Dark, riveting, compelling, masterful."—Jeffery Deaver, author of *A Maiden's Grave* (188500—$5.99)

☐ **THE CONDUCTOR by Jerry Kennealy.** When Mary Ariza, a beautiful, savvy lawyer, stops to help a man having a heart attack on the street, she unknowingly marks herself for death. Police Inspector Jack Kordic is thrust into the same nightmare when he discovers a headless, handless corpse floating in the icy Pacific. But what neither of them know is that they are in the path of The Conductor—an international assassin who must commit a crime of unthinkable proportions. (187474—$5.99)

☐ **MATINEE by Sally Kemp.** Monica Foyles keeps one secret escape: Wednesday afternoons at the movies—the scarier the film, the better. But Monica is about to learn that real fear is no fun. For in the dark shadows of the theater a young man is watching her, devising a scenario of his own. (407431—$5.99)

Prices slightly higher in Canada

Buy them at your local bookstore or use this convenient coupon for ordering.

PENGUIN USA
P.O. Box 999 — Dept. #17109
Bergenfield, New Jersey 07621

Please send me the books I have checked above.
I am enclosing $_____ (please add $2.00 to cover postage and handling). Send check or money order (no cash or C.O.D.'s) or charge by Mastercard or VISA (with a $15.00 minimum). Prices and numbers are subject to change without notice.

Card #_____ Exp. Date _____
Signature_____
Name_____
Address_____
City _____ State _____ Zip Code _____

For faster service when ordering by credit card call **1-800-253-6476**

Allow a minimum of 4-6 weeks for delivery. This offer is subject to change without notice.

Snow Angel

Thom Racina

AN ONYX BOOK

ONYX
Published by the Penguin Group
Penguin Books USA Inc., 375 Hudson Street,
New York, New York 10014, U.S.A.
Penguin Books Ltd, 27 Wrights Lane,
London W8 5TZ, England
Penguin Books Australia Ltd,
Ringwood, Victoria, Australia
Penguin Books Canada Ltd, 10 Alcorn Avenue,
Toronto, Ontario, Canada M4V 3B2
Penguin Books (N.Z.) Ltd, 182-190 Wairau Road,
Auckland 10, New Zealand

Penguin Books Ltd, Registered Offices:
Harmondsworth, Middlesex, England

Published by Onyx, an imprint of Dutton Signet,
a division of Penguin Books USA Inc.
Previously published in a Dutton edition.

First Onyx Printing, September, 1997
10 9 8 7 6 5 4 3 2 1

Copyright © Thom Racina, 1996
All rights reserved

Logos courtesy *Enquirer, Mariposa Gazette, Newsweek, Time,* and *Star.*

Ⓑ REGISTERED TRADEMARK—MARCA REGISTRADA

Printed in the United States of America

Without limiting the rights under copyright reserved above, no
part of this publication may be reproduced, stored in or introduced
into a retrieval system, or transmitted, in any form, or by any
means (electronic, mechanical, photocopying, recording, or other-
wise), without the prior written permission of both the copyright
owner and the above publisher of this book.

PUBLISHER'S NOTE
This is a work of fiction. Names, characters, places, and incidents
either are the products of the author's imagination or are used ficti-
tiously, and any resemblance to actual persons, living or dead,
events, or locales is entirely coincidental.

BOOKS ARE AVAILABLE AT QUANTITY DISCOUNTS WHEN USED TO PRO-
MOTE PRODUCTS OR SERVICES. FOR INFORMATION PLEASE WRITE TO
PREMIUM MARKETING DIVISION, PENGUIN BOOKS USA INC., 375
HUDSON STREET, NEW YORK, NY 10014.

If you purchased this book without a cover you should be aware
that this book is stolen property. It was reported as "unsold and
destroyed" to the publisher and neither the author nor the publisher has received any payment for this "stripped book."

For Esther & Frank, my parents,
who are alive and well—thank God!—
and living in Mariposa.

And for John "JB" Breeze,
without whose intriguing idea this book
would never have been written.

Acknowledgments

Writing a novel takes time, and *Snow Angel* was no exception. I want to thank the people who, over the years, helped give it life: Connie Roderick, who read every incarnation, and kept the fire burning. Kathleen Doyle, early believer, champion all the way. George Diskant and Kathy P. Robbins for their early encouragement and editorial input. Fredda Rose, for the brilliant tweak, and Candy Monteiro, for those zingy line changes. Pat Rupp for inspiring the story with her courage. Sherman Magidson for the early legal help. Sharon Benko for the title (and the waterglobe!). Mary Helen Zrenner and Joan Roberts—and Pam, Carole, Shelby, Hildy, Yvonne, Joan, Jane, Marilyn, Pat, Juanita, Cathy, Mary Anne, Maria and Angela—of the Ambassador Clubs at LAX, St. Louis and LaGuardia, for all the upgrades which allowed me to write most of this book in the front cabins on TWA aircraft.

My gratitude also to Trish Wiggins for her insightful suggestions, and to Todd Wiggins for believing in it when no one else did. To my editor, Joe Pittman, for taking the stray manuscript in from the cold, to Michaela Hamilton, for giving it a warm home at Dutton, and to Jane Dystel for adopting it and *me* midstream. And to my dear Susan Feiles for the determined Hollywood ride.

Special thanks to my much-missed friend, Judy Sussman, who didn't live long enough to see it published, but her enthusiasm and encouragement will remain with me forever.

And to Kecky, for being constant, in my work and in my life.

Prologue

U nder his foot, in the snow, a branch snapped. He froze. He was engulfed in the shadow of the house now, atop the ragged slope he'd just climbed. He could see the woman in the kitchen window, and suddenly worried that she could see him. No, he told himself, calm down, it was light in there but dark out here. Yet she was looking up, out—God, had she heard him? His heart skipped a beat. Wait a minute, stupid, the window was double-paned. He, *of all people*, should know that.

He knew a lot about these two. Harry would finish eating dinner about six-thirty, then drift into his hallowed den at about seven-fifteen to watch television. She'd clean the dishes, make a phone call or two, replenish her Dewar's—several times over—and finally join him no later than eight o'clock, settling in for a winter's night. She'd emerge at ten to pop the corn and mix another drink, the one that would eventually send her into oblivion. They'd watch the news till eleven-thirty, sticking around for *Nightline* only if the topic sounded compelling. *Not tonight*, he thought with a surge of omnipotence, *you won't be seeing Koppel tonight*.

What the hell was she doing at the sink for so long? Cleaning dishes this late? Washing her hands? As he strained to his tiptoes, he saw she was pouring liquid from a bottle into some kind of a vase or pitcher. She stood there forever, looking right at him, though he trusted now that there was little danger of her seeing him because the house was ablaze with lights—brighter than a baseball stadium, this place was a vir-tual beacon—and the night was dark, with dense, wet, falling snow to help camouflage his image. She finally turned her back to him. Just in time. He was starting to look like a snowman. He moved closer to the house.

He was just feet away now. His right hand clutched two bulky objects, and he pressed them to his side as he used his left hand to steady himself on the railing. He put his weight on the first step and ascended the deck that surrounded the rear of the structure.

He immediately saw the Christmas decorations, the lights, the candles, the glow of the fire. They disguised this ice palace with music and warmth during the holidays, and it worked; if you sang, "I'll Be Home for Christmas," this was where you'd want to be, with eggnog, carols, good cheer, an abundance of food. And the angels! Angels on high, angels topping the tree, angels proclaiming the birth of Jesus, angels in golden gowns with sugarplum cheeks and glinting trumpets harking sounds of joy. He thought Christmas was the most wonderful time of the year. It was, it also suddenly occurred to him, a very good time to kill someone, because the sheer good spirit of the season would help take the edge off the deed. Yes, he was going to feel *some* guilt. Hell, he wasn't *totally* without feelings. And doing this at Christmas would make it all the more macabre—and *she* would be more vulnerable.

He moved slightly closer to the window and realized from his new vantage point that the woman was actually holding a sprinkling can over brick-sized cakes lined up on the wide island in the center of the room. He'd sat on the end stool several times, sipping her iced lemonade with rosemary sprigs—God, how he loved that taste!—when the weather was warm and the old man wasn't nosing around. Those had been the best times—when the old man wasn't around—because Martha had been different then, caring and motherly and interesting. She had a personality all her own, and he never understood why it seemed to go into remission when her husband neared. Old school rules for the political wife? Truth was, she was lonely up in these hills, he'd sensed that right off, this society dame who was once the belle of the Bay Area. Hell, he'd drink too if he were her.

He'd always believed she moved here only because Harry ordered her to, not because, as she often vigorously put it (as if trying to convince herself), "We really wanted to retire someplace peaceful." Peaceful, my ass, he thought. Her idea of peaceful would have been Palm Beach, where she'd have a charity ball or museum fund-raiser to attend every other night. She was bored silly up here, you couldn't kid him. But she did what the old man wanted. Everyone did what the old man wanted.

Until now.

The wind suddenly whistled through the white-encrusted pines above him, and from down the slope he heard the unmistakable sound of a cow. Perfect. A cow. Mooing at this hideous stone and glass monument to bad taste. He thought it vile that this structure sat in this wilderness. Sure, it seemed that houses were rising on the hills in Mariposa County almost weekly these days, but none so ridiculously grand and ostentatious as this. They'd built it of cedar and glass and rock ("to keep with the surrounding environment," the horse's ass had boasted), but what about all those unnatural architectural angles? What about those soaring ceilings, the pretentious dozen fireplaces, the granite counters Harry had made him change at least fifteen times before he was satisfied— not to mention the eight bedrooms. Some retirement "cottage," as the old bastard had called it in his delusion of being a Vanderbilt. The irony was that it was **this** very house that had begun *his* career and made *his* name. He, who should have been their son-in-law.

He pressed his nose to the icy windowpane and watched her rinse her fingers in the sink, then wipe her hands on the apron tied around her chunky middle. She left the apron on, meaning she'd be back. Then she poured herself another of those toylike cups of coffee from the fancy Italian machine the old man had ordered him to drag home from Italy. But she hesitated near the sink, apparently thinking twice, and finally dumped the black liquid down the drain. *Come on, honey, one for the road!*

She did. She went back to her scotch, pouring a healthy few inches, added her signature one ice cube, and disappeared down the hall. She left all the lights on. Why not? The old geezer had all the money in the world stashed in his den safe, money he had ripped off from the taxpayers of California as he, as the "Great Governor," turned the economy around. California Edison was probably in his pocket through those years. Let the kilowatts burn. And tonight they'd burn a little longer than usual.

When he was sure she was now behind the locked doors of the den—the only room in this cathedral which had no windows—he moved carefully to the back door. This was going to be the first tricky part. He had to unlatch it without a sound. He knew already that the security system wouldn't be on. Harry had boasted about his daughters arriving tonight. He would turn it on only after they showed up. But Harry hadn't said what time the girls were expected; all he needed was to have Julia walk in on this.

He moved away from the window and approached the back door, where he could see the pool across the deck to his left, covered and winterized, dusted with white powder. He set down the bulky objects he was carrying, placing them carefully against the wall just outside the screen. There, perfect; they'd remain here till he needed them. When it was over.

He pulled off his old leather gloves and slid them into his jacket pocket. From the other pocket he withdrew a pair of gray women's stretch gloves, and pulled them on with his teeth till they encased his fingers like a rubber on his dick. Snug. It was like sliding into a second skin, and that would be good, for he had to grip things—he might have to stronghold an arm, a neck; he couldn't slip, not on this mission. He started laughing, recalling the young salesgirl at Macy's in Fresno actually believing they were for his mother. Oh, Mom, what big hands you have! Too bad he had to undo that nice complimentary wrapping she must have worked on for a half hour. Maybe he could use it on something else. Something for Julia? His heart raced.

Now. He pulled out a little metal pin he'd saved

from a put-it-together-yourself chair from Ikea. It curved in a way that it fit easily up into the lock. It took him a moment, but with a twist of his wrist, a little judgment, a little feeling, a little luck, like a safe-cracker spinning the dial, he put his ear to the box, waiting for the telltale click—

Click.

It unlatched. He pushed the door in and with a creaking sound it opened all the way. He silently shook his feet free of snow, vibrating them in the air like a dog after a bath, then stepped inside, gently shutting the door. Putting one foot behind the other, holding his left toe against the heel of the right boot, he stepped out of it. Then he bent down and pulled the left one off with his gloved hands. He stood still and listened like a cat.

He had good ears. He prided himself on his hearing. If his eyes were the focal point of his rugged beauty, his ears were his soul. He could hear—feel?—a deer running through the woods at a hundred yards. He could hear—sense?—rain coming a mile away. He knew now the TV was on in the den, even though the heavy door was closed and the room was too far away. Right on schedule, they were watching their idiotic television sitcoms. And they hadn't a clue.

He took ten steps down the hall and found himself looking into the big kitchen and family room. He could see steam spouting from the dishwasher vents; it had made it to the drying cycle. The red power light was shining on the Gaggia; thoughtfully, he clicked it off. No one would be having a late cup in this house tonight.

He saw a big bowl of nuts of every kind—walnuts, almonds, cashews, chestnuts, pistachios, pignoli. Then the fruitcakes lined up on the table. His stomach rumbled. Never plan a murder on an empty stomach. But why had she left them like this, tempting him to take a bite? He could smell the pungency of liquor suddenly. Ah, that was it, she had just doused them with brandy, that's what was in the sprinkling can. He recalled her doing that on her cooking show on PBS some years back. She was letting the cakes get good and drunk, like herself.

Hurry. No telling when she'd return to wrap them. He walked to the table and stuck his finger in one. It was mushy. He pulled it out. Then he spotted a bright red cherry half-baked into the top of another. He scooped it out with his left index finger and ate it. He loathed fruitcake, but this tasted of booze and chocolate. The booze part was especially inviting. So he picked up the sprinkling can and put his mouth on the spout, lifting it high, letting the brandy trickle down his windpipe. He licked the last drops from the plastic showerhead. The alcohol burned his throat.

Then he moved to the big rock fireplace all decked out with boughs and holly and angels standing guard over blinking white lights, warming himself a little in front of the hot embers. He recalled the day they'd finished building it, how when he'd mortared the last rock into place, Harry slapped him on the back and said, "Son, that's beautiful." Son. *Son!* He supposed it was meant to say that the man really liked him then. But he knew the truth. The governor had hated him from the moment he'd found out about him and his daughter.

He found himself staring at the silly Christmas tree for a moment, that ridiculous tree covered with cats that the old lady gabbed about every year, and then he crouched down, reaching under his soggy pant leg, and withdrew the knife he had taped to his ankle. The blade gleamed in the glow of the fire as he looked at it, studying each side of the shiny sheath. Just like in the movies, he thought, the madman looking at the weapon with insane relish, eyes wild, mouth drooling, eerie music playing in the background, just before he plunges it. *Murder most foul, as in the best it is; but this most foul, strange, and unnatural.* This was just absurd; it was too corny. He wondered if Shakespeare felt the same. Naw. He probably never murdered anyone.

He felt scared suddenly. He didn't do this for a living, after all. Anything could go wrong, and he knew it. He *had* butterflies in his stomach because, quite simply, he had never killed anyone before. What astonished him was not that he could think that, but rather why he hadn't. He certainly had it in him. He was sure of that. He could easily have killed that bully Fred Schlater back in the seventh grade, or that bitch

Lois Nygren, who betrayed him, or the prick who smashed his car two years back. But nobody had ever asked for it the way Harry Radcliffe had today. He'd been pushed. For he was no Ted Bundy, no serial killer who murdered on a whim or imaginary orders from Jesus. He had to have a good reason to take a life.

Or two.

He pulled the ski mask out of his jacket pocket and unrolled it down over his head—like putting a rubber on again, he laughed to himself—adjusting it so he could breathe, so the eye holes were lined up with his baby greens, but man, did it itch. He chuckled again. He could see it now, "Take this, you motherfu—" and he would suddenly sneeze and Harry would kick him in the nuts and it would all be over.

No, he thought emphatically, *no!* His anger burned so hot that his entire body stiffened as he stood up. No, that would never happen. He would succeed. He knew his mission. He was counting on himself to do what he should have done a long time ago, when he had first realized Harry's deceit and treachery. This afternoon he'd finally taken the vow, made the promise. He would rid the planet of this cancer Harry Radcliffe. Then he'd have what he was destined to have. What he deserved. What he should have had long ago. With Harry and the woman gone, no one would stand in his way. Not even Tom Larsen.

He made his way toward the den. Where the hall opened to the immense foyer in the shadow of the entrance doors, there on the big black Bosendorfer sat treasured family photographs, and one of *her*, Julia, the youngest daughter, that he'd never seen before. She was standing on the set of her new show. Holding her Emmy. She looked proud. She had the prettiest smile. The most beautiful breasts that God had ever—

Sobering pain shot through him. *No. Not now. Concentrate on what you're here for.*

He took a few more steps down the hall. And for the first time he noticed little cavorting deer were carved into the wood frame around the den door, that much-talked-about door, the door that had been written up in *House Beautiful* and *The Smithsonian*, a door that, Harry liked to brag, had been ripped off the front of a monastery by William Randolph Hearst himself when he sacked Europe, the door that sealed him off from the rest of the world.

But not for much longer.

He pressed his left ear against the wood. He heard the TV and the drone of the air purifier for the woman's asthma. So far, so good, but now came the second tricky part: getting in without them hearing or seeing him. She would pretty much be in her cups by now, so it was the man he really worried about. A commercial was on, he could hear someone singing about kids' Christmas selections at Mervyns. He'd wait a moment till the program came back on, so they'd be glued to the screen. He reached into his pocket and pulled out a key. The old man, as paranoid as Nixon about his "papers," had installed a door that automatically locked every time it shut, insuring his crap would be protected. There was no way even to set the lock so it would remain open; you lost your key, and you were denied entry. No admittance.

But he'd been smart. He'd had Martha's key copied without either of them knowing. At the time he wasn't quite sure why. But as he stood there touching the door with his gloved hands, now he knew exactly why. And it felt like sex, he thought, or foreplay, or even before that, like when you know the girl is on her way to your place and just the *thought* of her approaching gets you hard. He felt something move inside his corduroys, a sensation somewhere behind his testicles that tingled and made him thrust his crotch forward, as if being led by his penis. He pressed his groin against the cherubs carved into the lower right part of the door. Angels everywhere. He felt a sensual surge. This was getting good.

But, knowing foreplay is all the fun, he turned serious: would the rest go as smoothly as this? He held his breath and slid the key into the lock and started slowly to turn it—

Jesus Christ! He froze. An alarm! A fucking *alarm*, he thought at first, as his heart leaped into his throat. A mini-second later, he realized it was the telephone, rattling there on the hall table, ringing there in the kitchen, echoing several other places in the bowels of the house, countless electronic tones shrilly wailing in distant bedrooms. *The phone. The phone. It's only the phone.* It rang once. It rang twice. It rang a third time. *Answer it in there, in there, stay in there!* he shrieked in his mind, still frozen with the key melting in his hand. If they opened the door now, it was all over. It rang a fourth time—

But it did not ring a fifth.

He took a deep breath. Sweat, a bead of it, actually ran down his nose and dropped to his hand, which sat paralyzed on the door handle. He had nearly shit his pants. He'd thought it was all over. But it was only the phone, and, providentially answering his silent plea, they had taken the call inside the den. *Okay, relax, cool it, calm down.* The only change in his plan was he'd have to wait a little longer. He didn't want to walk in and find them gabbing on the phone, risk someone *hearing* this on the other end. He started to panic again. But how would he know how long it went on? He couldn't hear a conversation above the TV. Would they talk all night?

He thought it through. He'd give them a minute. Then he'd pick up the extension in the hall. If they were still talking, he'd listen. He'd get the gist of it and either wait till it was over, or cut the main wire leading to the house. He knew where it was because he'd supervised the installation himself. He could instantly slice through the wire with his knife, and they'd just think the snow had caused the lines to go down.

He walked back to the foyer, stopped near the

piano, and reached out to the phone on a wobbly table. He sucked in his breath and lifted the handset oh so carefully. It must have clicked even so, because he heard Harry saying, "Honey, you still there?"

A girl's voice. "Yeah, Dad. I'm here. Better hang up before the line goes down, it's crackling with static already." *God, it's her.*

"I heard it too, baby," Harry said.

He listened to the rest of the conversation, stupid stuff, a real waste of time, Harry explaining he couldn't come get them, the kid talking to Nana, who also yakked for a moment about candy, and then he hung up after they did. Julia and her daughter were in Mariposa already. Not good. But they couldn't get to the house. That was very good. The way it was supposed to be. Newly confident that there was no increased time pressure, he walked back to the den door and returned his hand to the key that glistened in the handle like a diamond set in stone. He started the countdown. *One. Two.* Damned bastard, sitting in there thinking he was safe. Fool. *Three. Four.* He had the gall to call *him* a moron? Yes, he'd been a moron to let Harry exile him, to let him destroy what he and Julia had felt for each other, to allow him to hand her over to another—but who was the moron now? The fat fraud sitting with his ass parked in his chair, smug in his security. *I'm right here, Harry, in your goddamned house, under your goddamned nose, right here.* The key had turned a complete circle. *Click. Five!*

He pulled the key out and slipped it back into his pocket. The door silently swung open. And there they sat, backs to him, completely unaware. They didn't even sense the change of air when he slipped in, didn't even notice the fire in the fireplace dance with the fresh bursts of oxygen. They were so interested in the black-and-white movie they were watching they had no idea they were no longer alone. She was eating candy out of a box on her lap, getting fatter, muttering something about going back to her fruitcakes, but absolutely engrossed in the movie. He saw nuns moving in black and white on the screen, and it reminded him of the third grade, when he'd been sent to Catholic school. *Thou shalt not kill.* Like hell.

He took a step onto the thickly padded wool carpet. Like the pads on a cat's paws, silencers. He realized the first thing he needed to do was prop the door open, in case he had to make a fast escape. He didn't move for a split second, his knee pressing against the weight of the door to prop it open, watching the backs of the unsuspecting couple, while his eyes quickly cased the wall to his right. The shelves behind the open door were covered with thick, leather-bound books. He silently reached for a heavy one and set it gently on the carpeting. *Crime and Punishment.* Fitting. It prevented the door from moving. Then he raised the knife into position and took another step toward them.

He was now within a foot of the back of the old

man's chair. Thing was, how to stab him? How could he poke his heart? Through the springs of the chair? Shit. This wasn't Excalibur he was carrying, and though he knew he could manage one good thrust through the left side of his chest, he knew he was no Arthur. Or was it Lancelot? He would need to be in front of him, skewer him in the heart, ripping off his mask with a flourish as he did so, to show the old bastard, before he died, who to remember once he arrived in hell.

But now he had a brilliant revelation: Get *her* first. Yes, force the old man to watch, make him see, make him suffer, let him implode in agony as his devoted wife met her maker in full view.

The fact was, he hadn't really wanted to kill her, but her words this afternoon had changed his mind, when he had his final argument with Harry. That's when she had passed her own death sentence. She had agreed with the asshole. Just a few hours ago, she had betrayed her own daughter. Her words were imprinted on his brain. *"Harry, you're right, I'm disappointed in Julia as well. She must hold onto her marriage, at any cost. She isn't even trying."* Fucking bitch!

Plus, he couldn't be sure that if he let her live she wouldn't finger him. Three sheets to the wind or not, who knew what she'd remember? There could be no witnesses. She'd written her artery-clogging cookbooks, given birth to two overachieving daughters: purpose fulfilled. She was old, fat, and wrinkled. A drunk to boot. Who'd really miss her? Well, Julia, of course, but that would suit his purpose well.

Get her first! Yes, brilliant. But she was cocooned in her matching Barcalounger, and he couldn't stab through that one either, so how to do it? Not that he really had time to consider the options; he was, after all, standing directly behind them at this moment, and it **was either** his extreme good luck or a tribute to the staying power of the movie they were watching that protected him while he made up his mind.

"Harry, is that Barry Fitzgibbons?" Martha suddenly asked. "I always forget."

Her voice shook him. The ski mask seemed to tighten with his facial muscles, and his hand gripped the knife so hard that it started to shake. He could have diced carrots standing still.

"Fitz*gerald*," Harry gruffly corrected her. "Of course that's Barry Fitzgerald. Who do you *think* it is with that accent?"

"I just asked. You always make me sound like some kind of idiot."

"Watch the movie."

You fat fuck, how dare you talk to her like that? He was seething. *You think you rule the world, sitting there in your goddamn chair with the stick shift on the side like some kind of modern-day Caesar—*

His reverie was suddenly cut short by a woman's scream. It was a short, fiery blast, almost like the sound of a shop whistle signaling five o'clock. And he was reasonably sure it wasn't coming from the nuns on the screen.

Harry turned and saw why his wife was suddenly screeching. She was looking over his shoulder, behind him—behind *her*—at the figure of a man with a ski mask over his head and a hunting knife in his right hand. A knife that now plunged directly into the side of her face, about half an inch behind her right eye, severing the plastic side piece of her glasses. He shoved it into her skull so hard that the blade actually poked its tip out her left cheek.

When he pulled the knife out, her hands came up to her face as her whole body toppled forward, doubling over onto the floor, at King Harry's feet, as if either desperately seeking his forgiveness in this, the last moment of her life, or merely trying to hold her face together. Then her hands were covered with red and she whimpered, not the hard-to-breathe sound she sometimes made because of her asthma, but a pitiful moan, so melancholy and so penetrating that it actually rose above the chorus of nuns and school kids on the television set.

Throughout this dance of death, which seemed as if it were happening in slow motion, this unplanned, macabre moment of improvisation, her husband sat unmoving in his chair, his drink slipping silently through his fingers into his lap, landing upside down there, where he had just peed in his pants. He was putty for that moment as he watched his wife collapse to the floor in front of him, blood spurting from her head.

The knife sliced the air in front of Harry's face but did not cut him because he pushed his head back into the pillow of the lounger. Then he tried to stand, but his legs caught in the foot-rest mechanism, allowing the knife to gently slide into his back. He grunted, stiffened straight up, then mustered a surge of energy, the adrenaline rushing, and he leaped—actually leaped, all sixty-eight years and two hundred and forty pounds of him—to the desk and opened a drawer as the crazed man in the ski mask swung at him again. Harry pulled out a gun and shot at the intruder, but at the moment he pulled the trigger, he felt a gushing, burning pain inside his guts and the bullet discharged instead into the person writhing, amidst what seemed like hundreds of pieces of chocolate that had spilled from the box on her lap, on the floor in front of the TV. "My God," he croaked, "Martha. I'm sorry. Martha . . . Jesus!"

Like it matters, asshole. She's dead already.

The intruder was on top of Harry now, knocking him backward against the books on the shelf, toppling him. The knife was raised and Harry Radcliffe, abusive husband, overly protective father, famous fraud, former governor of the state of California, begged, cried out for mercy, for this madman to spare him, please, please, he'd do anything, take his money, take his treasures, take anything, everything.

"I'll take something," the intruder whispered, revealing his voice for the first time.

The flash of recognition in Harry's eyes was instantaneous.

"I'm gonna take *her*," the intruder added, reaching up with his right hand to pull off the ski mask with a flourish.

And it wasn't so much shock that registered on the grizzled old face as it was understanding, cognizance, comprehension; it was as if the old man was saying, *You! You, of course, who else but you?*

But all he really did say was, "Matthew."

Matthew plunged the knife directly through his heart, and Harry Radcliffe died.

He turned to look at the woman. Amazing! She was moaning softly, still somewhat alive. He turned her over and looked at her for a moment, and then slit her throat. She stopped breathing within seconds. He was sorry he'd caused her that much pain.

But the woman's death wasn't his fault, he told himself, not by a long shot. It was the old man's fault, everything was the old man's fault, and now the rage moved from his expression to his entire body, and the focus of his stabbing eyes centered on the gun lying there where it had fallen. He grabbed it and he pumped every bullet it held into the old man's face from a distance of only a few feet, destroying, obliterating it forever.

Then he stood up and tossed the gun aside and

picked up his ski mask and shoved it into his pocket. He looked at himself. His socks were soaked with blood, and his first instinct was to pull them off. But he feared leaving clues if he walked barefoot on the hardwood floors of the hallway. He could see the headlines now: *Toe Prints Reveal Murderer!* No, he wasn't as stupid as the old man thought. So he pulled the slippers off the dead man's feet and pulled them onto his own. They were toasty warm. Should be; good leather, fleece lined. Then he looked around the room, this secret room the old man bragged was safer than the Pentagon, this most private of all private places, and thought to himself that it wasn't as cozy as it was cracked up to be.

But there was more to be done. *Make it look like a robbery, Matt.* He tried to open the safe, which of course he knew he would never be able to do. But he needed to make it seem as though that was the purpose of his visit. Thus, the blood-soaked glove stains gave it the authentic look any sheriff would love. Not that he didn't want the money—that would have been great, he'd have wiped his ass with Harry's money—but it wasn't his purpose in coming tonight. He found the heavy oak rolltop desk locked, but with the help of his knife and a good kick with his heel, he forced open all the desk drawers and rummaged through them—this junk was his precious "papers"?—and finally found twenty-three hundred dollar bills, the brand-new ones he'd seen Art Bagett give Harry that afternoon, all set to go into a stack of money envelopes that said *Happy Holidays* on it, *From Governor & Martha Radcliffe*. He laughed out loud. Not this year, Guv. Then he shoved the bills into his pants with his bloodied gloves. Not into his pants, actually, but down under his belt, into his briefs. He didn't know why. Something about the old fart's money resting next to his still engorged penis seemed somehow fitting.

When he stood straight up, his eyes were struck by a photograph on the bookshelf. Julia and Tom, Julia in her wedding dress, clinging to that wimp asshole she'd married, all starch and respectability in his perfect tuxedo. Julia radiant, happy—oh, she probably thought she was, for that moment at least. *You chose that bastard over me?* His rage was so deep it made his teeth rattle. He flew across the room, slamming his balled fist against the framed picture so hard that it was airborne in a second, a violent projectile that crashed into the wall and landed on the floor, broken, amidst the shards of glass, in someone's blood.

At the back door, he picked his boots off the floor and carried them as he opened the door to the deck. Good, the snow had piled up. His tracks to the door had already been obliterated by new white powder. He reached out into the cold, still standing inside, and grabbed the objects he'd placed against the wall there, attaching them directly to Harry's slippers. He knew once the police found the tracks, he'd be deemed the *Snowshoe Killer*. He sort of liked that. He'd never heard of one before. Then he stepped out, in the snowshoes, into the snow, into the cold, back again into the protection of the night.

The snow was barely falling now, just flurries of white dancing in the moonlight. It was colder, though, much colder. He shivered as he actually felt the still warm blood soaking his pants legs start to cling in a frigid stiffness. He started thinking about a mug of cinnamon hot chocolate, curling up in front of the fire with Maggie . . .

Suddenly, above him, the heavens seemed to light up, and he froze. It was as if a strobe had illuminated the snow clinging to the trees. It went dark, but then it happened again, brilliant lights flashing over the house, from right to left, and he realized it was the lights of a vehicle coming up the steep drive in front. For a split second he wondered who. Neighbors? At this hour? Then his ears picked up the sound of a vehicle he knew well—a four-wheel-drive sheriff's department Blazer. Jesus, why? Had he tripped some kind of silent alarm? He heard the horn blow several times, and that's when he started to run. As fast as he could in the fucking snowshoes.

He left the mountain without again looking back.

PART I

Julia

1

Julia Radcliffe Larsen had no intention of dying young, least of all on a rainswept highway in the middle of California's San Joaquin Valley, but things weren't looking too good. She could feel the balding tires on her ancient TR7 hydroplaning as the wind blew sheets of rain sideways against the windshield. The road was an obstacle course littered with giant loofahs of soggy tumbleweed, and Julia did her best to steer around them. In the passenger seat, her seven-year-old daughter, Molly, held on for dear life. Julia turned and glanced at the little girl's profile in the dappled illumination of oncoming headlights. "Not much farther, honey. Don't worry."

The little girl turned to her. "Liar."

Julia smiled. It was the truth. She squinted at the glass in front of her. "Wish these wipers would wipe for a change."

"I like Daddy's car."

The mention of her husband erased all amusement

from Julia's face. "Yes," she said softly, "and he does too ... it might be the only thing he really cares about."

"What?"

"Nothing. Count gas stations or something."

Julia thought about Tom. And his precious BMW. And his drafting table, from which she believed he might one day have to be surgically removed. She was mentally listing his faults, but she knew what she was really doing, what she was really masking. The pain was just below the surface, even after nine months. Nine whole months! It seemed an eternity—and yet it had passed in a moment.

"Mom?"

"Yes, honey?"

"How can you chew that much gum?"

Julia was blowing a bubble so large it almost touched the steering wheel. She sucked it in.

Molly said, "Dad says gum is against the law in Sing Pore."

"Sing-a-pore. And you don't even know where Singapore is."

"Do too. Dad showed me. If we drive there, they'll put you in jail."

"We're not driving there. We're driving to Nana's. About a hundred and fifty miles to go."

"You say gum rots my teeth."

Julia wondered how to explain. "Since I stopped

smoking, Molly, I . . . well, I guess I've replaced one obsession with another."

Molly said, "Like perfume?"

"Not that kind of obsession. No, it's like when you can't control something and it gets the better of you."

"Like Dad's work?"

"Smart girl."

There was silence for almost a mile. Then Molly, without looking at her mother, said, "Why do you hate Daddy?"

"I don't *hate* Daddy. You know that."

"Why do you sleep on the couch all the time? Nana and Grandpa sleep in the same bed. Aunt Cornelia and Uncle Brad. Marybeth Safransky's mother and—"

"Daddy snores sometimes and I can't sleep, that's all." She knew her daughter wouldn't believe that lie. But she didn't have a better answer. She turned the radio on. She heard a country station. Molly said she wanted to hear the CD of *Beauty and the Beast*. This wasn't Dad's car, Julia again reminded her. "Dad says German cars are the only good cars," Molly asserted.

"Neo-Nazi plot, trust me. See, the Hitler cronies they didn't catch after the war got together and said hey, we'll develop our technology so everyone wants our products, but what we won't tell them is that inside every Mercedes, every BMW, every Krups coffeemaker, every Braun shaver, is a little bomb. They're going to set them all off by remote one day and bring the world to its knees."

"What?"

"Just wait," Julia cautioned, "press that seat-adjust button too many times and ka-boom."

"Mom, I think you've been driving too long."

Julia's newest bubble popped all over the steering wheel. "Thank God this thing *isn't* a Mercedes," she muttered, trying to scrape it off and watch the road at the same time. On the radio, Tanya Tucker was singing about sparrows in a hurricane, an apt image for this night, she thought.

It was getting harder and harder to see through the water that was now taxing the frayed wipers. Molly looked up at her mother and said, out of the blue, "It was raining that day Dad took you to the hospital."

"Yes, it was."

Long pause. Julia had a feeling something was on Molly's mind. She waited. Hoping it wouldn't be what she feared.

Finally, keeping her eyes focused straight ahead, Molly said, "Mom?"

"Yeah, honey?"

"Mom, will I have breasts when I grow up?"

"You know you will." Julia gritted her teeth. She knew what was coming next. For nine months, ever since they had told Molly the night before the surgery, she had expected this question—but not in a car in a rainstorm a few days before Christmas.

Molly said, "Will I get sick and they'll cut it—?"

"No, honey," Julia interrupted, mustering confidence, "you won't lose one."

"But you and Nana—"

Julia cut her short. "You won't lose one, I promise you," she said with authority.

Molly closed her eyes and put her head back, clutched her favorite stuffed animal, a ratty old bear called Mr. Tiddleberk, and said no more.

Julia saw the sign for Merced. "Only about forty-five minutes to go." But the rain came down harder, striking the car like hail. Ominously she whispered, "Rain scares the hell out of me. I always think it means something awful is going to happen."

Molly napped while Julia thought. Hard. She needed someone to talk to, someone who had been there, and she had finally made the determination that she would simply lay her cards on the table and *open up*. Oh, she'd tried to talk to others about it, but all attempts had failed or were in the end unfulfilling. She had talked to the doctors first, and her surgeon in particular recommended a therapy group, which she met with for a few weeks until she could stand the New Age references of the moderator no more. "You're just not *centered*, Julia." Reading *The Celestine Prophecy* was about as far as she could go in the nineties search for spirituality and self-fulfillment. Her fulfillment had been in her work, her love for her husband, her child. Someone had suggested talking to

Tom about it—but how do you talk about the problem *to* the problem? It wouldn't work.

She tried her sister, but at the time Cornelia had been redecorating a faux Italianate *palazzo* in Salt Lake City and had little time to spare, even for family. But that was the problem, for Julia was almost ten years younger than Cornelia, and for that reason they had never been close. Cornelia gave Julia three words of advice: "Talk to Mom."

Shivers ran down her spine. Talk to Mom? She'd never been able to "talk to Mom." Ever. About anything. Yes, others did, all the time. Martha Radcliffe was better than Oprah at that kind of thing if you asked anyone outside the family. But bring it on home and the walls went up. Thing is, you never spoke within the Radcliffe family about anything personal, much less sex. It wasn't done. Problems personal went under the rug. Even in this true "new age" with enlightenment abounding, certain things were never discussed. Especially loss. Loss that had to do with sexuality.

Talk to Mom? Impossible. But that was giving up, and she was a fighter. She was the daughter of the former governor of California, a published author who had turned an M.F.A. in communications into a job as news anchor for the NBC affiliate in San Francisco, overcoming the tabloid title *TV's Sexiest Anchor* by winning a local Emmy award for hard reporting. But, despite the success, her life had fallen apart a little more than a year ago, and the pieces wouldn't fit back together. She needed help with the hardest part of all, the touchiest part, the desperate part; that's why she was now determined to open up to her mother. And to get Martha to open up to her and tell her *what to do*!

Christmas. That would help. Martha would be in— her cups? Well, that too, she thought, but she meant to say a good mood. She might be receptive. "Ma, this is my life we're talking about," she'd rehearsed again and again. She was ready to say it. Tomorrow, maybe on a walk, Cornelia could watch Molly—yes, take Martha for a walk and just say, "Mom, help me!" She would do it. She had to do it. Her entire future as a wife, mother, as a woman, depended on it.

She kicked up the speed. She felt better.

Molly slept on.

After they passed Merced, as they began their ascent up the mountain, up the long stretch of Highway 140 that eventually snaked into Yosemite National Park, the rain did turn to hail, and their speed plummeted along with the temperature. Wind howled through the fabric top of the car. And the road became slippery. "Daddy said this thing has bad tires," Molly offered.

"This thing" was beginning to worry Julia as well, though she wouldn't admit that to her daughter. She could feel the rear wheels hydroplaning just slightly every few feet. "The tires are fine," Julia said defensively. Then she saw *why* they were slipping. "But I don't think they're going to help," she muttered.

"Why?"

"Look." She pointed ahead. Sure enough, in front of the headlights, the raindrops had turned to white crystals now that the temperature, at this altitude, dropped to the low thirties.

"Snow!" Molly exclaimed with wonder.

"I'll say."

"Oh, Mommy, Mommy, it's beautiful! Can we get out?" Molly hadn't seen much of it in her young life. She was enchanted.

Julia felt quite differently. "Shit! Why in God's name did they move up here for anyway?"

"They retired."

"Smart people do that in Palm Spri—" Julia suddenly gripped the wheel so tightly that her hands lost blood. She could feel the entire rear of the car slide to one side. She saw the look on Molly's terrified face. "Everything's under control," Julia whispered, lying. "God, I hate snow!"

"Baby Jesus was born in snow."

"Just 'cause he froze his buns off in that manger doesn't mean we have to."

As Julia said it, an ancient Honda Civic, which looked like a battered Coke can to which someone had fixed go-cart wheels, came careening down the mountain to their left, passing them—they swore—going sideways. Molly nearly strangled her bear. "I'm scared, Mommy."

"It's okay, darling, just don't make me nervous," Julia snapped, feeling a kink in her neck because she was arching her head so far forward just to be able to see. Visibility was nonexistent now. She knew they were at the curve where you could normally see "forever." Not tonight. Tonight it was solid snow with zero visibility but for a few feet in front of your face. The problem now, at this particular curve, was that they were in a car that would become airborne at any moment; thus the TR7 hugged the right side of the road, almost scraping against the rock that formed the inside barrier.

Molly sat in terrified silence as Julia forged on, muttering, "If I just stay in the center of the road . . ." The windshield wipers whined, feebly pushing the heavy, moist snow from the glass. Finally, she could no longer tell where the center of the road *was*.

"On TV yesterday they advertised tire chains," Molly offered suddenly.

"We live in San Francisco," Julia shouted, "not—" Suddenly, the car slid and spun all the way around, doing a terrifying donut that, from inside, looked as though they were hurtling into that wild blue yonder. But Thelma and Louise they were not destined to be, at least not tonight. The car, with a thud, suddenly lodged itself back against the hard rock of the cliff. "—Fairbanks."

Julia took a deep breath. She silently thanked God they hadn't gone over the edge. Then she hugged her daughter and assured her they were okay.

The car died and with it the heater. They sat there a moment. Julia turned the flashers on. Remarkably, they worked. "Someone will come along, honey, don't worry. They'll take us up to Nana and Grandpa's." But she wasn't so sure. Snow continued to fall. No headlights in sight. "Maybe we should sing some carols."

They sat in eerie silence for a long time. Finally Julia said, "It feels like an eternity." She immediately saw the look on her daughter's face, and anticipated her question. "No, not the perfume."

"Why aren't there cars?" Molly asked.

"I'm beginning to believe we are the only fools out here tonight."

And then Julia saw lights in the rearview mirror. "Here comes someone! I've got to flag them down!" She jumped out, but felt her body turn to ice. She was wearing shorts and tennies and had brought only her nylon windbreaker. A pickup truck stopped. The window rolled down. A puff of smoke wafted from it. When the smell of marijuana lifted, an old man with hair to his shoulders barked, "What the heck? Out for a stroll, baby?"

"Yeah, nice night for a walk. My daughter and I are stuck. Can you give us a ride into Mariposa?"

He ran his tongue over his teeth. "Sure thing."

She saw that the passenger seat was occupied by an upside-down rocking chair. "Where will we sit?"

"My lap's empty." He snickered with amusement and embarrassment.

"So's your head."

He stared at her. "Sorry. Didn't mean nothing by it."

"We'll ride in back."

"Snow out there."

"No laps out here," she tossed back, and went and got Molly, who wouldn't leave without her stuffed bear. Julia locked the TR7, taking only their overnight bags, leaving behind the Christmas presents. When Molly objected, Julia promised Santa would guard them, that Grandpa would drive them back in the morning to fetch them. The geezer hit the horn. Julia lifted Molly into the truck, muttering something about beggars not being able to be choosers, and before they were even seated, the aged hippie at the wheel gunned it, the tire chains took hold, and Molly collapsed on top of her mother in a mound of snow, giggling, as the truck continued its ascent up the mountain.

Julia found it compellingly romantic. The flakes fell silently, and they heard absolutely nothing, for the accumulation of snow had already provided a blanket of sound-absorbent insulation under the tires. Julia thought she had gone deaf, or that the volume had suddenly been turned way down, almost as if they were magically propelled into some kind of white, silent movie. As they looked up from where they lay on their backs, their heads on their suitcases, they could see the huge flakes falling around them, and Julia pretended they were in a sleigh in *Doctor Zhivago,* riding through the Urals with the White Army unaware. Molly said it was like the *Frosty the Snowman* special she had seen on TV the day before.

There was magic and wonder in the moment, so unexpected, so stunning, that Julia was struck with a sense of happiness she wanted never to end. This was a moment of pure rapture, just she and her daughter— this is what life was all about. She wanted to prolong it forever so she would not have to revert to feeling the isolation and pain her marriage now brought her, so she would never have to face her mother and do what seemed so impossible.

The truck slowed in Mariposa itself. A small town with only one main road, it looked like some kind of deserted movie set. Nothing moved. You couldn't even see the road. Snow had piled and drifted so that it was hard to tell where entrances to the various gas stations, motels, and side streets were. The truck finally stopped at the north end of town. The driver called out that this was the end of the line. Julia and Molly got out, but before she could even thank the man, the truck was gone.

Mother and daughter stood with their suitcases in

hand, Nell and Little Betsy, orphans in the storm, at the bottom of the slope on the top of which was a bar called the Miner's Inn. They climbed through the snow to the doors, and made their way inside. The bar was filled with about twelve people who looked like they were there for the duration. Julia asked if the phones were working; she wanted to call her parents.

"Workin' awhile ago," Cathy the waitress said with a shrug, "no tellin' what they're doin' now."

"Car went off the road up in Midpines tonight," an unkempt whiskered fellow named Brian warned. Julia, undaunted, took Molly's hand and led her to the phones. When Julia heard a dial tone, she punched in her parents' phone number, her MCI digits, and it rang through. On the fourth ring, she looked at Molly and said she didn't think they were going to answer, but suddenly she heard her mother's voice on the fifth. "Mom? It's Julia."

"Hi, Nana!" Molly shouted on her tiptoes.

"Julia, Molly, where are you? Daddy and I were just talking about you. Beginning to worry. TV says the roads are treacherous."

"We're in Mariposa, Mom."

There was a pause as Martha whispered to her husband that Julia and Molly had made it all the way to town. And to turn the TV down. Julia heard the familiar sound of a glass bumping the receiver. She could almost smell the Dewar's.

"Can Dad come get us?"

"Oh, honey," Martha said with a serious tone, "I don't think so. We're snowed in. Wait, hold the line. I'll put your father on."

Julia turned to Molly. "She's putting Grandpa on."

"I wanna say hi!" Molly said enthusiastically.

Julia heard her father telling his wife to turn down the goddamned TV, and then he said, "Julia?"

"Dad. Hi. I can't believe this."

"Gorgeous, huh?"

"That's a matter of perception. Molly and I are at the—what's this place called—?" She'd completely blanked.

"Miner's Inn," Molly said, grabbing the phone from her mother. "Grandpa, it snowed and we had to leave the car on the highway. We got a ride in a truck. I'm all wet."

Grandpa seemed to find it amusing. "Hitchhiked?"

"Yes!"

Julia pulled the phone back. "Had to abandon the car where the road curves just past Cathey's Valley. It's hell out there, Dad."

"Don't say. Here too. I can't get out, we're completely snowed in, been like this all evening. Best thing I can suggest is find a room in town. Hopefully they'll have Whitlock plowed in the morning, and I'll ask Matt or one of the boys to come get you, someone with a four-wheel drive."

Julia groaned. "Not till morning?"

Then there was a clicking noise on the line that

sounded to Julia like someone picking up an extension. Neither said a word, because, for a second, they both thought they'd lost each other. "Honey," Harry then braved, "you still there?"

"Yeah, Dad. I'm here. Better hang up before the line goes down. It's crackling with static already."

"I heard it too, baby."

The notion of lines down in the dangerous storm gave Julia a slight premonition, a foreboding, that prompted her to ask: "You and Mom okay?"

"Fine. Watching one of those old Christmas movies in the den. Snug as bugs."

"We'll call you in the morning."

"Get a good night's sleep," Harry said. "Tell our granddaughter we love her." As he was about to hang up, he suddenly added, "Honey, wait, your ma wants to say something more."

Julia heard the phone being handed back to her mother. "Julia? I almost forgot, thanks ever so much for the Mangos."

Julia blinked. "What?"

"The candy."

She rolled her eyes. "Frangos, Ma. They're called *Frangos*. When did they come?"

"Today. In fact, we're eating them right now. Can't stop."

"They're my favorites," Julia said. "You only get them from Marshall Field's in Chicago. I had them sent from their catalog."

"There won't be any left by the time you get here."

"Pig out. We got our own."

"Listen, you girls be sure to lock your door tonight, and tell Molly Santa was here, there's lots of things already waiting under the tree for her."

"Mom, yeah, but . . ." Julia's voice drifted as her mind raced. Do it. Say something. Remind her again. Don't be afraid. Don't back down—

"Julia?"

"Mom," she said forcefully, "that talk I mentioned, we really have to. Maybe tomorrow? Okay?"

Her mother's tone was suddenly brittle. "Julia, I—"

Julia didn't give her a chance. "Just promise me, Ma, please."

"Fine. We'll see you in the morning, then."

Julia said good-bye, and she heard her mother hang up the phone.

Then she did too.

As they cautiously made their way down the slope toward the road, Molly griped, "I want Grandpa to get us."

"I told you, there's too much snow. We're going to walk to that motel down there."

The drifts were over Molly's head. "Where?"

"Mariposa Lodge. I see the sign right down the road. If I can tell where the pavement is."

Julia tried to lead—in sneakers soaked and freezing— down what she thought was the highway, but it was

almost impossible. The flakes had stopped falling, but
the snow had drifted enormously during the half hour
they were in the bar. It was getting colder by the minute.
After they had walked about twenty yards, trudging
through the drifts, suddenly, from behind them, roared
an enormous vehicle. Molly clung to her mother as they
turned, hearing the sound, and were momentarily
blinded, finding themselves bathed in what could have
passed for tennis court lights—floodlights illuminating
the area both from bumper level and high above the cab.
It seemed like a moment out of a prison-break movie,
when in reality they were in the path of a huge Sheriff's
Department truck, its four enormous tires digging virtual canyons into the snow. A young, good-looking man
with hair too shaggy to be taken very seriously as a law
enforcement officer stuck his head out the passenger
window. "Need some assistance?"

Nestled in the warmth of the cab, Julia explained
their plight, the abandoned car, the truck-cum-sleigh
adventure, the trek up to the bar and even faster
descent back down, the call to their father, the desire
for a warm bed and a good night's sleep. "I don't suppose there's any way you could take us out to Whitlock Road, near Midpines."

"You kidding?" said the shaggy cop, the one who'd
first called to them. "Car went off the cliff out that way
earlier tonight."

Julia deadpanned, "Same thing almost happened to
the south."

"My mother is trying to be funny," Molly said with obvious embarrassment. "What if we say please?"

Though the driver was clearly charmed by the seven-year-old, he said, "Not for love or money."

They drove a little. They could feel the crunching of the snow under the weight of the enormous tires. Then Molly suddenly said proudly, "My mom's on TV."

"Right," the cop in the passenger seat said. But when he turned and took a good look, he said, "Hey, you're Julia Larsen, aren't you? My girl and I watched you every night for five years!"

The driver hit the brakes so fast they were almost tossed into the front seat. He jerked around, nearly strangling himself in his seat belt. "The guv's daughter. Had no idea. Wow. I never met anyone on TV before."

Julia said she wasn't on TV anymore.

"I don't care, I still want an autograph," the driver gasped. "Just say, 'Love to Gary.'"

Julia took advantage of her celebrity. "Make you a deal: all the autographs you want if you take us out to my parents."

"Hey," Gary said, "we could try, right, Rob?"

Rob shrugged. "Risking my life for an autograph," he muttered. "Jesus."

Julia felt the exact same way.

*   *   *

The Chevy Blazer dug in its four gargantuan wheels and crawled up the long, winding, quarter-mile driveway to the house. Julia jumped out and punched the control box digits, pushing them hard because they were encrusted with ice. The gate swung open, creaking under the weight of the snow, and then the truck fought the slippery hill for traction as it delivered the Radcliffe daughter and grandchild to their desired destination.

The house came into view. Like some shining Christmas ornament beaming into the night, it was set on the top of the mountain, glistening with decorations that reflected off the newly fallen snow. The gigantic fir trees lining the drive were so laden with white that their lower branches dusted the top of the vehicle, causing small avalanches to cascade from the boughs as they passed beneath. The porch floodlight was on. A wreath filled one of the windows in the greenhouse that wrapped around the left side of the structure. Everywhere French glass panes were ablaze with warm light. "They're still up," Molly said with delight.

"But power's out for miles," Gary said.

"I think they have a generator in case the electricity fails," Julia added.

"You hear that?" Rob said to his partner with amazement. "Their own generator."

The truck stopped at the front walk. Gary tapped

the horn. No one stirred. "They're in my father's den," Julia explained, "watching TV. They can't hear anything, the room's a virtual isolation chamber."

"Nana has asthma," Molly explained.

"Purified air," Julia added.

Gary nodded, understanding now. Then he and Rob helped them from the cab. "You want us to wait and make sure you get in okay?"

"Come in for coffee," Julia offered. She told them she was sure her mother—being her mother—had baked enough fruitcakes to brick up a wall, and at least three thousand Christmas cookies by now. They were welcome to enjoy them. The additional temptation of hot chocolate convinced them, but just as they were about to turn off the engine, the radio crackled and they were called to an emergency in El Portal. Julia made them promise to drop in on Christmas Day, for the family's yearly open house. It had become a tradition since they lived in the governor's mansion in Sacramento, for friends as well as family.

"Merry Christmas," Julia called, and she and Molly watched the Blazer make its way down the hill and then disappear into the white night.

They faced the front door. "I wish Nana had been in the kitchen, or at least near a window," Julia said. "She would have died seeing the Sheriff's Department escort us to the door."

"I want to surprise them!" Molly squealed.

They opened the door with the key they found

under the third rock to the right of the terra cotta cat. "Wonder why they left the floodlights on," Julia mused, "knowing we weren't coming after all."

"You said they were watching a movie," Molly reminded her. Julia set the bags down in the foyer. Molly clutched Mr. Tiddleberk as she walked to the shimmering Christmas tree. She immediately started looking at tags, finding her name everywhere. Julia left her there and continued down the hall, past the kitchen, where she immediately spied the near-empty bottle of Dewar's on the counter. Then she glimpsed the yearly line-up of fruitcakes awaiting Saran Wrap and Martha's signature plaid bows. And that was her first inkling that something was wrong.

Not wrong, odd. Her mother never left the fruit-cakes sitting out. Moist was her fruitcake credo, etched in stone in her cookbooks. *Bathe with brandy and wrap immediately.* Julia touched one. It was almost dry on top. Something wasn't right. No, she was being silly. Perhaps her mother had got so involved in that movie that she just forgot. Or she was too drunk. It had happened before.

But a creepy feeling started to flow through Julia's blood, like little invaders swimming amongst the other cells calling out, *Something's wrong here!* "Molly," she said, "you stay there and I'll go tell them we're here." Look what she was doing! Protecting Molly just in case . . . in case something *was* wrong.

Funny, she thought as she walked down the hall

that led to the center of the house where the den was, but she swore she heard the TV. She did. And she stopped dead. It was loud. How strange. She knew you could hear nothing from inside the den. Then she bit her lip a little. She had never known her quirky dad to leave the den door open. Ah, she told herself, there's always a first time. But as she continued down the hall toward her father's inner sanctum, she wondered, if the door was open, why hadn't her parents heard the blast of the sheriff's vehicle? It was as loud as a foghorn. The lights blazing, the fruitcakes drying in the air, and that air, so still, so quiet, it felt smothering, almost creepy . . .

Then she saw them.

Or saw *it*.

The carnage.

What had been two human beings.

What had been, until about forty minutes ago, her parents.

Julia stood frozen with horror, still in the hall, unable to move, as if entering the den would give credence to the unreality she was witnessing. Here in the hall the little invaders in her blood could say, *This isn't happening!* until she closed her eyes and felt herself dying in this moment as well. Then she fainted into the room, her left arm sliding into a puddle of shattered skull and brains.

Outside, the storm had stopped completely. Where the clouds had hung so low, the moon danced on the

new-fallen snow. From somewhere in the distance
you could hear the faint chorus of a Christmas carol:
"Oh, come let us a-dore hi-im, Chri-ist the Lord." From
someone's TV probably.

And on the TV here in the den of the Radcliffe
home, Ingrid Bergman was saying good-bye to Bing
Crosby at the end of *The Bells of St. Mary's*, through a
screen spattered with blood.

And just over the next ridge, a mere five miles from
the Radcliffe house, a man's feet in two frozen slippers positioned themselves directly onto a big garbage bag in the shadow of a house. The man wearing
them lifted his boots from his shoulder and set them
nearby. Then he dropped the snowshoes that were
under his right arm, making sure they were in the
center of the bag. He pulled the knife from his waistband and crouched down. He stabbed the snow
around him, wiping the blood from the blade and
handle as best he could, and then he set the knife
gently down just to the side of the bag.

He then carefully stepped out of the slippers and
continued removing all his clothing. He took off his
jacket, his shirt, his undershirt. He reached into his
pants pocket and withdrew a key, which he tossed
into the boots he'd set down. Then he removed the
blood-soaked corduroys, his socks, and finally even
his undershorts. He stuffed the money he'd been carrying next to his genitals into the boots as well, and

then gently, meticulously, as if walking on a tightrope, stepped off the bag, turning back to pull the sides up over everything he'd discarded, and leaped into the freshly fallen snow as if he were galloping into the crashing waves of the ocean.

He rolled in it, flailed his arms and his legs, he kicked it up and felt it come down on his head, he twisted and turned and froze and shivered, but he was giddy with excitement, like a seal spinning a ball on his nose, or a porpoise breaking water for hundreds of spectators at Sea World. His eyes were wild, his heart raced. He flopped onto his back and created a snow angel, flapping his arms in the white powder, flailing them, moving his feet apart, then together, his egs stiff, taut, creating a skirt in the snow. When he spread them wide, he felt his testicles touch the snow, and an electrical charge seemed to shoot up his spine, arousing him as never before. He got up, looked at his angelic creation so pure in white, and then fell down again on top of it, facing it this time, and then made love to it, his erection stabbing the crotch of the angel form, his buttocks shimmering in the moonlight peeking through the low-hanging clouds. And even though the cold snow had caused his testicles to retreat into the protective warmth of his body, he reached an orgasm that melted hot and wet into the ice, and left him both exhausted and energized. The smell of blood was still in the air.

He finally stood up. The blood—all traces of it—had

been washed from his body by the snow. Still naked, he bent over and picked up the boots with the money and set them just inside the back door. He heard his dog barking inside the cabin. He retrieved the knife from the snow, walked to the side of the house and turned on the hose, which he'd left dripping so it would not freeze as the night got colder. He rinsed the knife thoroughly in the water. The dog was howling now. He sprayed the entire back yard, flushing away the evidence, the red marks in the white turning the color of pink lemonade, until it started to crystallize and the yard looked like a failed attempt at creating an ice rink.

Then he went inside, calmed the dog, made himself that mug of cinnamon hot chocolate laced with rum that Martha Radcliffe had showed him how to prepare, and stepped into the hottest bath he had ever taken in his life.

In the water, his breathing became more regular, his heartbeat slowed, and his balls returned to the sac between his muscular thighs. He had taken the hunting knife into the bubbles with him, and after letting it soak for a while, he took it apart with a screwdriver and scrubbed it again and again with a loofah and the new bar of soap he had got free for buying a bottle of aftershave, eradicating any trace of blood on both the handle and the blade. No one would ever be able to tell that this was a murder weapon. The dog sat at the side of the tub and licked his nose.

When he got out of the tub and opened the drain, he left the two pieces of the knife lying in the water. The wood handle floated and bobbed like a rubber duck. While the water slowly drained away, he dressed again, in loose jeans and a sweatshirt and his still cold boots, and checked to see if the money had dried inside the oven, where he'd placed it. The bills were as crisp as when Mr. Bagett had handed them to Harry. He scooped them up, hid them along with the den key, and folded the newspapers on which the money had dried, carefully putting them near the door. He then put on his dark jacket and his leather gloves, and returned once more to the bathroom and lifted the two pieces of knife from the still sudsy bottom of the tub. He wiped them free of hairs and soap with a towel, and put them in his pocket. He took the damp loofah as well, just in case.

He told the dog to stay, to sit tight, promising he'd be back in a little while. Stuffing the folded newspaper under his arm, and carrying the Liquid Tide bottle he'd filled with kerosene that afternoon, he went back outside. It was nearly three in the morning and the world was still. The yard glistened with waves of ice. He grabbed hold of the cinch-tie handles of the garbage bag, and it crackled as he lifted it from its icy frame, frozen stiff.

When he got to the mine shaft, he lit a match and made sure he was alone in the cave; this was no time for a run-in with a bear or fox. Then he checked the contents of the bag. Gloves, ski mask, shirt, under-shirt, pants, shorts, socks, slippers, snowshoes, every-thing was there. He added the loofah from his pocket. He poured the kerosene into the bag from the plastic Tide bottle, then dropped the bottle in as well. It would melt.

He lit the newspaper on fire and tossed it into the bag. He watched it explode before him, burning, scorching, blazing, until the smoke started to choke him, and he realized he couldn't afford to have the clothes he was wearing reek of creosote. *Better wash them tonight just in case. Didn't think of that.* He hurried from the opening of the shaft, looking back to see black fumes pouring out of the front of the cave, and he smiled, pleased. He'd just destroyed all the evidence.

Or not quite all. He walked to Sherlock Road and looked out over the valley. He reached into his pocket and withdrew the handle of the knife. It still smelled like the soap he'd washed it with. He pitched it into the air, down the incline as far as he could throw, and heard a faint crack as it hit a tree. Then he walked about ten feet, and did the same with the blade. It glinted in the air as he tossed it, catching a moonbeam on its shimmering clean flat side, but it, unlike the handle, made not a sound wherever it landed. Per-haps, he thought, it took flight with an angel.

He looked in the direction of the Radcliffe estate.

Over that hill, he was sure, the flashing lights of sher-
iffs' cars and ambulances were dissecting the night
sky. He grinned. But he thought of Julia making the
discovery, and the profound sadness and shock she
would be feeling right now, and the smile faded from
his face. He began to hurt for her.

He then went home and stripped again, putting his
smoky clothing into the Whirlpool.

He sat down and wrote a poem about this night.

When he was finished, he flopped on his bed, next
to the dog, and slept like a baby, dreaming only of *her*.

2

"**I** know you're all cold, and for that reason I'm going to be brief," the eulogist began in a steady, somber voice, facing the mourners huddled in the tent. "I am honored to have been chosen to say a few words today, for I respected Harry Radcliffe as his business partner, was inspired by him as a politician, enjoyed his and his wife's friendship, and loved them like a son."

Julia looked at the handsome, well-dressed man standing before them and thought not of her pain but of his, for she could see it in his vibrant eyes, and his voice was cracking. "It is most difficult to stand here today and speak of Harry and Martha in the past tense. It is, almost, unthinkable . . ."

Yes, Julia agreed, it *was* unthinkable. Her soft blue eyes were hollow shells now, as if they'd lost their sparkling treasure, oysters without their pearls. With her husband, Tom, seated on one side of her, and their daughter, Molly, on the other, a sadness permeated the face of this girl who had always been, in the recollection of anyone who'd ever known her, happy-go-lucky, always smiling, brimming with life. It was as if someone had stolen her innocence overnight.

"Last evening," the eulogist continued as Julia clutched Tom's hand, "when I tried to prepare this speech, I thought to myself, how to best convey the spirit, the goodness of those wonderful people who were our neighbors, our friends, our former governor and first lady? So, let me tell you a little story about Harry and Martha Radcliffe. Several years ago . . ."

Julia's mind wandered to the howling, icy wind that threatened to blow the tent down the steep hill. It was a bitterly cold day, but it seemed that people were frozen not so much by the temperature as by shock. For four days now, since the morning of December twenty-third, when word first spread through the area that the "Gov" and his wife had died violently at the hand of an intruder, friends, neighbors, government officials, and even people who'd never known the Radcliffes personally felt disbelief and denial. By Christmas Day the sheriff had been calling the murders the work of the "Snowshoe Killer," but he offered no leads. And the press had hounded Julia and her sister with a vengeance.

There were theories, there were whispers, there was fear and there was outrage, but overall there was grief. People had loved Governor Harry, and not only because he'd made California prosperous once again.

He had been their friend, the retired guy down the road who'd pick up a hammer and lend a hand building that new garage. Women had for years delighted their families with the help of Martha Radcliffe's cookbooks—nothing too fancy, nothing too highbrow, just a right combination of good taste and creativity to elevate the routine dinner meal to something a little special. That they could be so savagely murdered—

Julia suddenly realized the eulogist was speaking about her. ". . . like Cornelia and Julia and their husbands—" Everyone looked at Julia and Tom, at her older sister, Cornelia, and her husband, Brad. ". . . like the beautiful grandchild sitting here today—" Julia took Molly's hand. ". . . like my neighbors and friends up here on the mountain, I will find my life less bright now that they are gone.

"One must believe God had a reason for this. Rose Kennedy once said she could not have continued to live her long life had she not had faith. Perhaps we must too. Faith in what we cannot, as mortals, know of God's plan."

Tom bent his head toward Julia's ear. "God's plan," he muttered disparagingly. "Fuck Rose Kennedy and her demented notion of faith—"

"Tom!" Julia whispered in alarm, afraid Molly—or others—would hear him.

"I don't care," the striking blond man responded. "This is horseshit."

The eulogist, aware of the consternation in the first row, was not flustered. He seemed to direct his words to Julia, to comfort especially her. "Pearl S. Buck once wrote, *For Prayer is not only kneeling in a church. Prayer is the soul's intense desire.* Our intense desire today is that we never forget Harry and Martha Radcliffe, and that justice"—his eyes found Tom Larsen, as if he knew what he was thinking—"however long it takes, and by whatever method the Lord deems necessary—be done. If not in this lifetime, certainly in the next."

"This one," Tom commented, loud enough for most people to hear.

"Shut up," Julia whispered emphatically, embarrassed.

"Truth is," the eulogist continued, "Harry'd probably want me to apologize to Jim Benko for missing the poker game next Friday, and to tell us all to stop sniffling and go have a beer. *Life keeps moving*, he always said, and he was right, it will. But for one day, this, our day of mourning, we bring life to a standstill in respect for the souls of our dear friends and neighbors, and to show the world how much we cared." He wiped his eyes, then ran his hand through his shaggy brown hair, composing himself. "Harry and Martha Radcliffe touched us all, and we are better people for it. There is no greater legacy than that."

The man sat down, and tears in the audience flowed freely. Then the minister stood up and with his comforting voice, as softly as it had begun, ended the ceremony with a prayer. *Rest in peace.*

Julia thought, Is that even possible?

Wind gusted under the flaps of the tent. Tears would have frozen on cheeks in tiny icicles had the edifice not protected them. But the bitter cold seemed only fitting on this desolate, unimaginable day. Again and again, as friends and officials made their way past the caskets to say good-bye, people spoke to the girls of their sympathy, of their shock, of their horror, offering sympathy, good wishes, invitations to drop in for coffee or a hot meal, whatever they could think of that might somehow diminish the pain. The reporters covered it all.

Tom stood at Julia's side, and they looked like the perfect couple: a stunningly attractive girl with hair the color of amber nectar clinging to the arm of the tall, well-dressed, young and successful architect. On first sighting one might peg them, with their blond locks and Southern California tans, as characters escaped from the TV screen. But any dumb-blonde notions were put to rest when you witnessed the intelligence of their eyes. Wedgwood blue, Martha used to say: they both had eyes the color of delicate china and New England doors.

But what the mourners today didn't know was that one half of this perfect pair was wondering if Tom would even be part of her future without her parents.

What she hadn't gotten to talk to her mother about would have to be settled some other way. *Damn*, she thought, looking at Martha's flower-covered coffin, *we weren't finished yet! We had so much more to—*

Molly, as if hearing Julia's silent cry for help, squeezed her hand. "Mommy," she said with a burst of emotion, "I love you."

Twenty minutes later, the tent had nearly cleared. Cornelia and Brad told Julia they would see her back at the house. Julia found herself standing alone with Tom and Molly. "Did you say good-bye to Nana and Grandpa?" Tom asked their daughter. Molly's wide eyes filled with apprehension, masking a child's lack of total understanding of what had happened a week ago, what had happened even today. Julia suddenly envied the innocence of children, youthful naivete. She longed to have it back herself. This had been a time when being mature wasn't an advantage, when having grown up wasn't such an accomplishment.

Tom and Molly knelt in front of the coffins for a moment as Julia watched. "Good-bye, Nana. Good-bye, Grandpa." Molly's voice was soft, quavering. "I will miss you very much." Then she and Tom got up, and Tom put his arm around Julia, who felt she could not bear this. Then Tom asked if she was ready to leave.

She shook her head. "No. I need . . . to do the same."

"Sure." He took a step away, toward the flap in the

tent, pulling the collar of his camel overcoat up around his neck. His thick blond hair fell over it. But he turned back. "You know you'll have to say something to the reporters out there."

She nodded. "As soon as I'm done."

"I'll be in the car," he said softly. "Come on, Molly, Mom will meet us there."

Julia cautioned, "Keep the press away from Molly."

Tom nodded, and they left.

Julia turned back and stood in the near-empty tent, facing the caskets. She looked down at her father's. "Dad," she whispered, "he was right, you're probably having a poker game with the angels." She found a smile. "But they know you cheat." She sucked in her breath at the horror that suddenly charged through her mind. That room. The blood. "I hope . . . it didn't hurt. I miss you, Daddy. I'll always miss you." She swallowed to keep from choking. The tears were in her head. She worked hard to keep them there.

She then turned to the casket in which her mother lay. She stared for what seemed an eternity. Then she whispered, "Mama, I need you now. Who else . . . can I ask?" Then, on her knees in front of the cold steel boxes that contained the remains of what had been the bodies of her mother and father, she reached out and touched them for the last time.

When she stood up, a hand was touching *her* shoulder. She turned and recognized the most incredible eyes she'd ever known. She honestly didn't see a face, only the emeralds under his eyebrows, just as she'd done while he was speaking the eulogy. "Julia," the man said softly, "I'm so sorry. I had to tell you personally."

"I looked for you right after the service," she told him, taking his hand warmly. "We wanted to thank you for the beautiful words."

"Your sister already did. I hope I wasn't too self-indulgent."

"You were eloquent."

"I loved them both."

She felt tears brimming again as she gazed at the caskets, and then squeezed his hand tighter. Then she looked back, into the deep pools of his eyes, and whispered, "Oh, Matthew—"

3

Matt Hinson stood transfixed. Before him, just feet from the room in which he'd murdered Harry and Martha Radcliffe in cold blood, a party was in full swing. Neighbors, family friends, cronies, they had come from the cemetery to eat, drink, and make merry. People were recalling the good times with the Radcliffes as they nibbled on Martha's intoxicated fruitcake. Matt shook his head. This was about dead people? Someone started playing Christmas carols on the piano, and the mourners suddenly became the Mormon Tabernacle Choir. You'd never have guessed a slaughter had taken place here just a week before.

But Matt noted that Julia did not join in the festivities. She stood alone, removed from the others, caught in her own grief. He watched her carefully. He was worried about her, worried sick. He knew she was teetering on the edge, having lost so much in this past year, and now this. His heart ached at the thought of the pain she must be going through. He set his champagne glass down and studied her.

He saw her fingers grip the back of the chair as she turned and stared out at the snow-covered drive. He saw her muscles tense and her fingers clench the wicker so tightly it cracked. He sensed the rage inside her. He felt rage too, but a different kind: he looked over at her husband talking to a group near the kitchen, beer in his hand, no doubt dazzling people with the story of his newest architectural accomplishment, paying no attention to her needs. Why in the hell had he ever let her father marry her off to *him*? That was where his anger was born. He stared at Tom Larsen, wishing *he'd* been in the den with them a week ago. . . .

Julia was aware of Matthew watching her. Now that his attention had turned toward the people near the fireplace, she dared look right at him. When she'd found herself listening to his moving eulogy, she could not deny that even now, years later, in the midst of her grief, she felt the way she had the day she met him; she believed him to be the most attractive man she had ever set eyes on.

She remembered that moment, right here, in this very room—though it hadn't been a room yet. Matthew had just finished cementing the last rock in the fireplace when she got out of the car. He was kneeling only feet from where she was now standing, trowel in his hand and—she'd never forget—shirtless, his head covered with a hard hat, looking up at her as if he'd seen a vision. It was summer and it was noon, and she recalled her body breaking into an embarrassing sweat as she told him who she was, not so much from the temperature as from the heat generated by the electricity immediately flowing between them. He took off his hat, and when she saw his eyes she thought she was melting. Nothing—no one—had ever done this to her before. But she had Tom, her boyfriend—no, her lover—no, her possible fiancée— who had designed the very house this gorgeous man was building. The guilt felt like ice water in her veins.

She felt the same sensation now. It had always been this way—passionate, intense—which was why she avoided Matthew Hinson as much as possible. The overriding emotion was guilt, guilt for having run from her feelings for a man who had saved her life. Guilt for experiencing those tingling feelings again every time she saw him. Guilt for realizing she had made the wrong choice, and that she'd let others push her into it.

She suddenly wondered, *What's wrong with me?* Her parents had just been put into the grave, and she was recalling lustful feelings for Dad's business partner? She pulled her eyes away from him. She didn't want anyone to know she was watching him. She walked to the window. Staring out at the drive made her remember the walks she and her father used to take back

when they were first building the place. The walks on
which she hoped she'd see Matthew—

Don't think about it, can't think about it. She stepped
down into the greenhouse porch, and with the change
of humidity and environment, she tried to put all
thoughts of her empty love life out of her head. She
felt unfulfilled and lonely enough without that.

Matthew watched Tom lean against the rock fireplace. He was standing exactly where he'd first set
eyes on Julia. He had been kneeling there waiting for
Harry to examine the finished hearth, and instead his
eyes were rewarded with something heaven had sent.
In a flowing, long white summer dress silhouetted
against the sun, her hair wrapped in a kind of gold
turban that shimmered like a halo, she towered above
him like an apparition. His mouth dropped open, and
the trowel he was holding fell from his fingers. He felt
goose bumps; his chest heaved with a surge of emotion, his nipples actually hardened, and his balls tightened as his heart stopped. Here she was, the girl his
mother had always said would come one day, the girl
from the top of the Christmas tree, the girl he'd wor-
shipped, loved, longed for, lived for . . .

His angel.

Now he saw her standing at the glass wall of the
greenhouse, and she was grieving. It was time to give
her some comfort.

*   *   *

"Julia?"

She turned, startled. It was clear she had been a million miles away. "Yes? Oh, Matt, hi."

"Everyone's putting on a real brave front," he said, gesturing toward the crowd through the wall of French doors.

She nodded somberly, then turned and looked blankly out the window at the yard filled with so many vehicles. "Thank God the sheriff is keeping the mob of reporters down on the road."

"You handled them real well at the cemetery."

She closed her eyes. "If only we'd been a little earlier that night. Two sheriff's officers brought us here—" She stopped abruptly. "I'm sorry."

So that's why a Blazer came up the drive. Talk about timing. "You can talk to me. You know that. You've always known that." He made sure his voice rang of support and strength, the shoulder for her to cry on. He wanted to be there for her now. He needed her to see how important he was to her. He needed her to know that he cared.

He sat down in the very chair she'd been gripping, and motioned for her to sit across from him. When she did, he reached forward and held out his hand. He wanted to probe, be her shrink, her confessor. He wanted to know the secrets of her feelings, past the loss of her parents, to see if there was a chance for him, for *them*. So he said simply, "I'm your friend, Julia."

She took his hand with both of hers and held it for a long moment. Sparks ignited a fire in his soul. He felt a stirring in his groin. His eyes flashed brilliantly, but he had to be careful—just a blink might betray his love for her. On the surface remaining as calm and patient as any good friend would at a time like this. "It must feel like a bad dream, like it's just some kind of awful lie or rumor or someone's idea of a sick joke." He chose his words carefully. He needed to ease himself into her impressionable hand.

"I swear I can hear Mom shouting from the kitchen, *'Julia, where's your father? Inga wants to tell us about the raccoon she rescued.'* I feel like I'm losing my mind."

"You're not. You're still in shock. We all are." He crossed his legs. He could see his words were having the effect he wanted. He was on a roll. "My parents send their condolences, by the way. They live in Wisconsin—"

"I have a friend in Madison," she said with a smile.

But he already knew that. That was precisely why he'd said it. He'd done his homework. He needed to show her they had things in common. He needed to teach her she could feel comfortable with him, the way she had felt that one day at Leucadia. "Mom said your father should have run for president. I sent them one of your mom's fruitcakes last year." None of it was true. He'd never spoken to his parents of the Radcliffes, and certainly never bothered mailing them

Martha's shitty fruitcakes. But it was the right thing to say at this moment.

"Take a few today. My mother never got to—" She paused, swallowing the words. She cast her eyes toward the floor. And there was a lull.

Think of something, Matthew. Don't falter now. Their eyes met, and he knew she felt awkward. So did he. But he had to keep going. "Your daughter is gorgeous," he said. "She's growing so fast."

"Seven already." She sat down.

He did as well. But found himself crushing an already crushed teddy bear.

"Don't mind that," Julia said. "It's Molly's security blanket from age three. Mr. Tiddleberk, she calls him."

"Tiddleberk?"

She shrugged. "She named him. Don't ask."

"I had a lion." He watched her push her honey blond hair back over her ears. Her hair had been much longer—a lion's mane?—until just recently, when she had cut it at her mother's urging. He hated Martha for making her do that. He remembered how it had cascaded over his shoulder that day at Leucadia, how he had run his nose through it, his teeth—

"So, what are your plans?"

"My plans?" It caught him off guard. "Oh, I'm completing two houses right now, pre-construction on another—"

"I never asked you, did you always want to be a builder?"

"Well, I was always good with my hands, so when I made the move to California when I was eighteen, I got a job making wooden drums, of all things, in a Quonset hut in Thousand Oaks. Then a guy asked if I'd build him a deck outside his house. Decks led to hardwood floors, then to kitchen cabinets, then to whole rooms and finally whole houses. What are you going to do?"

She shrugged. "I don't know. Everyone says write another book. I'm not sure. I haven't done that since before my TV stint."

"Why haven't you gone back to television?" He knew the answer but pretended naivete.

She sounded vulnerable suddenly. "I'm . . . just not ready yet."

"Can I ask something personal?"

She froze. Was he going to ask something about her operation?

"How is it you live in San Francisco and still have that gorgeous tan?"

"We were in Puerto Vallarta the first week of December."

He raised his eyebrows. "I saw you coming out that tanning salon in Merced last Friday . . ."

The first grin of the day appeared on her face. They both laughed. The ice was breaking. She was warming up to him. He remembered how hard it had been to talk to her after she rejected him for Tom, to find the time, the courage, the right moment. Not that he'd ever had anything amounting to a real conversation with her after she married the asshole, but on the occasions they had found themselves in a position to speak to each other, he sensed she was still very attracted to him. He thought it strange, though, that they never spoke about Leucadia, about that day she was naked in his arms. Perhaps it had bonded them in a way that they didn't need to.

"I guess I'll sell the house. My sister and I are going to stay and do what has to be done."

"If you need help with anything—"

"Yes," she said, a little too quickly to succeed in masking the attraction. "I'd be happy for the company."

Mission accomplished, but there was more. *Mother, get to the mother.* He took a deep breath and nervously rubbed his chin. "I know this sounds selfish, and I probably don't have a right to ask, but there's a favor I'd like to—" He stopped, as if talking himself out of it, hesitating with an embarrassed look on his face for her benefit. "Never mind."

"No, what?" Julia asked, intrigued.

"Well," Matt said, sounding as humble and apprehensive as he could, "when you take the tree down, there's an ornament I'd like to have. It would mean a lot to me."

Julia looked as if she were asking *why*?

Go for the kill, Matthew. This is your chance. "I want something your mother loved," he said in defense to her silent interrogation, as if he could read her mind. "This was my second home, and Martha was my California mom."

Julia was touched. Joy burst through her sadness. "Of course. Which one? Show me."

He put Mr. Tiddleberk down, and they walked into the living room, made their way through the friends and neighbors, and to the tree.

"This one here." He reached up and lightly touched a beautiful white, shining glass ornament with little cats chasing each other's tails all around it.

"Oh, yes," she said, filled with emotion, remembering. "Mom always said this was her favorite."

"Probably because it came from you."

"You know that?"

"She told me," he said with a tenderness in his voice that he could see melted her. They drifted back toward the greenhouse. *You have her now, Matthew. Good old Mom is her weakness. Martha is your hope.* "We talked about you all the time."

Julia's eyes brightened. "You did?"

"We'd sit over hot chocolate, iced tea in the summer, when my work with your dad was finished. Martha would share things with me. She really was proud of you."

"Proud of me? I won an Emmy and then blew it all. I got fired. It humiliated her."

"She thought you sold out to TV, said you were born to write. I found a copy of *Epiphany* in a used bookstore in Fresno after she bragged about it to me, so I could have one of my own. She sent me to the mall in Merced the day they got your short stories in. Had me get twenty copies for her alone—"

"I never knew that!"

"She wanted to single-handedly put you on the *New York Times* list."

Julia's eyes were brimming with tears now. She tried to say more, but the words would not come, and she asked Matt to please excuse her and she moved to a window that looked out over the very ground he had trekked across not too many nights ago.

After giving her time alone at the window, he went to her and put a strong, steady hand on her shoulder. "I'm sorry," she said, trembling, still trying to hold it in, but she started to cry softly, as if the word *sorry* had been the plug that unleashed the torrent. Yes, he thought, she did cover it better than the others. But now, after he'd pulled her defenses down, she wept.

"I apologize," he said, turning her to him, taking her in his arms, holding her as she cried. *She's in my arms. I'm holding her. It was worth this moment.*

"I miss her. I miss her so much," she cried, clinging to him for the second time in her life. "I . . . need her right now."

Yes, this was only the second time on this earth that he'd held her and comforted her. And though years had passed, because of his dreams it was as if it had happened yesterday. He'd held her every night since that fateful day at Leucadia . . . that afternoon when he had watched her strip off her clothing, dive into the water . . . observing her swimming, playing like a nymph, her breasts floating like lily pads on the surface of the water . . .

Then panic! His heart stopping as he realized she was bobbing in the water, lifeless. Leaping from the rocks, the water engulfing him, pulling her over his shoulder, onto the ground, forcing the water from her lungs. And then holding her. Holding her as she came to, as she realized what had happened, and as she cried, with her head on his chest. He recalled how, when the sun lowered over the hill, her lips had found his, and how they—

He closed his eyes. How they had done what no one had ever known. Their secret. Now, as she clung to him in her parents' house, the memory of that moment surged through him, but today was much more a milestone than that first time. That was the beginning of the divine obsession; this was the start of their life together.

But in holding her, in this moment he'd lived for, with his heartbeat thumping so loudly he could hear it himself, with carols rising and children screaming in the background, Matt suddenly realized, in looking over her shoulder, that there was an event taking place outside. Yes, out on the snow, as far as you could walk on the property behind the house without disappearing down the hillside, a tall man was kicking the snow around with his feet, looking down, crouching, feeling with his hands. "What in the world—?"

"Julia, are you okay?" The voice cracked through the stillness of the room. Matt stiffened and turned. He saw the wimp blond architect had entered. And he heard Tom's voice again, sharper now: "What's going on?" Julia pulled away from Matthew, but her attention was still on the figure out in the yard.

"Thomas," Matt said, offering his hand.

"Nice eulogy," Tom said coolly, shaking hands without enthusiasm, "but total bullshit."

"Pardon me?"

" 'A divine plan.' Get real."

Matt let it go. He could see Tom was angry about catching his wife in his arms, and Matt relished his displeasure. He had always figured that Tom sensed his wife's attraction to him—he loved that he held that ultimate secret about Leucadia—and because of that the prick would never find affection in his soul for him. That was okay. It would make easier what Matthew was planning to do to him.

"What the hell are you looking at?" Tom asked Julia, following her gaze out the window.

"Who *is* that?" she asked him.

Matthew froze. He could see who it was immediately. "Looks like that Crowley guy."

"The investigator?" Tom asked.

Julia squinted and took a better look. Sure enough.

It did look like the detective they'd brought up from the Bay Area. "But what's he *doing* out there?"

Matthew began to sweat. *Yeah, what the fuck* is *he doing out there?*

The official report had deemed the slaughter a "homicide during the course of a robbery," but Julia had repeatedly told the investigators in the days following the deaths that nothing—at least nothing she knew about—had been taken. Julia had felt she could not bear to enter her father's den after her first excursion in which she found the bodies, not that night, the next day, or anytime after that; she had sworn she would never walk into that room again as long as she lived.

But she did what had to be done; she went over everything, through everything, trying to figure out what might have been stolen, for the condition of her father's desk certainly suggested that a robbery had been committed. But she had found nothing. The sheriff concluded that either the killer had got mad because their father refused to open the safe or the killer could not get it open himself, fomenting a murderous rage.

Julia, however, wondered if there wasn't another motive. She found it hard to buy the robbery reasoning because nothing else in the house had been touched, ransacked, pilfered. Gifts remained undisturbed under the tree. Her mother's purse sat open on a kitchen counter. Tom asked what she was getting at. She shared with him the growing creepy feeling that her parents had been murdered for some reason perhaps only they knew. Some *secret*.

And thus help was needed. And the Radcliffe sisters felt Jim Crowley was the right man for the job. Despite the criticism of him—that he was too young (thirty-four), too inexperienced (he had been a detective only four years), and that he was a "foreigner" (imported from San Francisco)—the girls trusted him. They trusted him because their father had trusted him, and liked him as well. Jim Crowley had begun his career, in fact, as an aimless rich kid who had dropped out of college, became a runner in their father's Sacramento office, worked his way through various political jobs until finally deciding he really wanted to be a cop, making detective practically overnight. Harry Radcliffe particularly admired him for successfully and brilliantly solving a sensational Nob Hill murder case just two years before, which gave him statewide recognition. "That guy is *good*," Julia remembered her father saying. That was enough for her and her sister.

And now everyone inside was standing with noses pressed against the glass like royals at Ascot, eyes focused on the towering man who was finally approaching the house. Matthew watched with slightly more intensity than the others as Jim Crowley made his way to the front door. He knew that whatever was going on, it had to do with him.

Julia hurried to open the door as Jim stomped the snow off his boots on the top outside step. "What was going on out there?" she asked with excitement, ushering him in with some hope. Matthew moved as close to them as possible, listening intently.

"Mind your party," Jim said, to Matt's disappointment, and then made his way to the corner of the living room, where he huddled with two of the local sheriff's officers, who proceeded in due time to don their jackets and follow him back outside. Before he left, however, he picked up a small cardboard box in which a neighbor had brought pumpkin and mincemeat pies, and handed it to a deputy to take outside. Then he turned to Matthew and asked, "Where'd Harry keep shovels?"

"Shovels?" Matt asked. *What in the world does he want a shovel for?* "Snow shovels?"

"Digging shovels. Spades."

I dropped something. My God, I dropped something in the yard. "The shed off the pump house."

"Obliged," Jim muttered, and walked back outside.

No, I didn't. Everything was accounted for. No sweat. But sweat beaded on Matthew's brow nonetheless as he watched Julia and Cornelia, hand in hand, peering out, mesmerized, as the two deputies knelt at the spot where Matt had first spied Jim. They seemed to be gently brushing snow away with their hands. Then

Matt saw Jim approach with a spade. He swallowed hard. He heard Cornelia say, "Looks like they're digging up something. They're putting dirt into that box."

"Dirt?" Julia said, curious.

Yes, dirt. The soil that I walked on. Matt stared out another window. He watched as the three law officers, on their hands and knees, dug and cleared and scraped and finally put something into the cardboard box. "Jim Crowley is the best there is," he could hear someone saying. And he feared that what the person was saying was true.

"Jim," Julia exclaimed, pulling open the front door again, "what did you find?" He was holding the cardboard box, but before he entered he placed it next to the moss-encrusted ornamental cat that had stood guard over the front steps since the house was built. He dismissed the two other officers, who eventually drove off down the drive. "Print," Crowley finally said. He never used two words when one would suffice.

Julia said, "What kind of print?"

"Boot."

Matthew stiffened.

"Under the snow," Jim repeated, "ground was still muddy. Got colder, froze solid. Facing the house. Made on his way up, I suspect."

Jesus. The snow protected it. I never imagined . . .

Julia blinked. "He wore boots in and snowshoes out?"

Jim nodded. "Possible."

Smart man.

"He'd be leaving a trail. That's crazy," Julia said.

"So he was," Jim reminded her.

Fuck yourself.

"You sure it wasn't more recent?" Carrie asked. "Your men have been tromping around out there for a week now, all wearing boots—"

"I'll analyze it. May be a clue to his identity."

Matt felt his throat tighten. *No way.*

"How?" Tom asked.

"We figure the make, the model, how old it was, how much use. Trace where it was bought. See if we can't find the buyer."

Tom said, "So if you learn it's Timberland size eleven, you check stores in the area who sell Timberland boots and see if they have a record of someone buying a pair that size?"

"Something like that," Jim said. "Search suspects for the boots themselves."

"Cinderella," Cornelia said.

Matthew smiled. "Gonna try certain Nikes on every redneck in the area?"

Jim looked at Matthew. "Think people up here are gonna have a problem with that?"

Matthew smiled back. "If the boot fits . . ."

* * *

When Jim Crowley took a phone call in the foyer on the very extension Matt himself had eavesdropped on the night of the murders, Matthew grabbed his jacket from the pile on the black leather chair in the corner. He had to get out of the house before Crowley did. He had to, somehow, some way, knock over that box, pretend to fall against it, stomp it, destroy it before it made its way to the sheriff's office.

"Leaving?" Julia asked.

Matt nodded. "Gotta walk my dog. Listen, you need anything, just tell me."

"Thank you."

At that moment Molly walked up. "Nana said you would show me berries this summer." The little girl found a genuine smile.

Matt's smile matched hers as he bent down. The enthusiasm was addictive. "She gave away my secret, huh? Yup, I know where the best wild blackberry bushes are in this county."

Her eyes went wide. "You do?"

He whispered, "I told Mr. Tiddleberk all about it. He wants to go too."

The little girl was filled with wonder. "Really?" She clung to Julia's leg. "I liked my Nana's berry pie."

"Did you pick them for her?"

"Every time."

Molly smiled a gaze of approval at Matthew.

He smiled back. *The way to a mother's heart is through*

her daughter. Then he saw the sister walk up and his expression changed.

"Carrie, Matthew's leaving," Julia said.

Cornelia said nothing. Matthew read her blank face as thinking "good riddance." *Do something, Matthew.* He offered his hand. She was forced to take it. He felt her squirm slightly. He held on. He shook his head in dismay. "In a way I feel like I'm one of the family. But my grief is nothing compared to your loss."

Cornelia curtly said, "You're right."

He could feel her distance. He flashed his most sincere smile, hoping to hook this bitch with his eyes. But they did not have quite the effect as they had on her sister. She was not melting.

Molly went back to her dad as Matt walked to the foyer, Julia right behind him. Crowley was thankfully still on the phone. Matt turned toward the front door. But he didn't get out it, for a fat deputy walked in carrying a plastic bag like the kind you unroll in the supermarket to put lettuce in. Inside was a bloodied, chewed mess of material—no, leather—and what looked like mud.

Crowley got off the phone and said, "What's that?"

"Looks like a slipper of some kind, sir." The deputy handed it to Jim. "Hell getting through the reporters down on Whitlock."

"Where'd they find it?"

"Sherlock Road," the fat man answered. "Guy in a car. Pretty chewed up. Coyote or wolf, I suspect."

Matt knew they were wrong. It was a dog. His dog. *She went back to the cave.* "Pretty stupid for the person not to destroy it," Matt said.

"Nobody called him bright," Jim reminded him.

And you're stupid too, you asshole.

Jim asked the sisters if what was left of the slipper looked like the ones they'd known their father to wear.

"Yes," Cornelia said emphatically. "See the little slit on the outside near the front? He cut that. So his bunion could breathe."

Julia agreed, staring at the plastic bag. "That's Dad's, all right."

Matthew recognized it as well. But what could a stupid moccasin tell them?

Jim explained it was his belief that the killer had put on Harry's slippers because his own feet were covered with the Radcliffes' blood and he didn't want to leave prints on the hardwood floor of the hall. He surmised the killer wore them on the snowshoes till he discarded them somewhere, or hid them or buried them, until an animal sniffed out the blood and dug them up.

Aren't you brilliant? Matt was seething. "Your horoscope must have something to do with feet today."

"What will this tell you?" Julia asked, pointing at the slipper in the bag.

"Fibers, maybe. Hair from his feet. His own blood. Who knows?"

Matt shifted his weight from one foot to another. He was nervous, scared. He was sweating up a storm. He stayed to the back of the group, trying to be unobtrusive, trying not to give his mental state away. This was something he had never planned on. This was imperfect. This was not him.

"Jim," Cornelia said with a very serious tone, "tell us the truth, level with us. Any lead you're not sharing with us? Any real clue? Any names?"

"Suspects?" Tom added.

Matt watched Jim turn to look at the fire burning in the fireplace. He seemed to be thinking, weighing what he should or should not tell them. His lower lip quivered a little. Matthew was nearly on his toes waiting for the answer. *Say something!*

Jim grabbed the plastic bag and held it under one arm as he fished for his car keys. Then he said, "Promise an arrest before New Year's Day. Gonna tell the hungry press down there the same thing. Throw 'em a bone."

They were stunned.

Matt wasn't. "You sound sure, Mr. Crowley," he said with a tone that said he didn't disbelieve him. "And I want you to know that we're all sincerely grateful."

Jim nodded to him. "Obliged," he said as he zipped up his jacket.

Matthew did the same.

But Julia called out again, "Matthew, Jim, wait—"

Matt turned. He shrugged. He knew. The fruitcakes.

What made him stay was Jim Crowley was getting one too.

Jim stood at the center island. Cornelia poured him a cup of coffee as Julia opened the refrigerator door and told Matt to pick a couple. He reached in. *Just like that night.* He poked around, wishing he could tell her he hated them, but finally grabbed two at random. Cornelia said she would wrap them.

"Just put them in a sack," he said, trying to mask his urgency. If he could get out before Crowley—

"They need plastic around them. I have to find a new roll ..." She started rummaging in the pantry. "Where did Mom ... ?"

He was dying. "Cornelia, don't bother, I'll wrap them myself when I get home—"

"Matt left you the chocolate one," Julia said to Jim. "You a chocolate fan?"

Who cares if he's a chocolate fan? Everything I've worked for is ruined if I don't get out of here before the chocolate fan. Damn it, find the Saran Wrap.

She did, and she wrapped them, but she stopped just as she was about to set them into a Pioneer Market bag. "Who—?"

Matt saw why she suddenly sounded so surprised. The chocolate fruitcake had a big hole in it. There was a crater the size of a finger in the top of the loaf.

"Molly," Julia said, knowing how much her daughter loved anything her nana baked.

But Jim was already studying the tray, and he reached out and picked up the fruitcake next to the one with the missing chunk. "Look," he whispered.

Matthew could see that the top of the cake was an impression. Not a gaping hole like on the other one, the one from which he had snatched the cherry. This was the perfect indentation of a finger.

"Someone pushed down there with their finger— index finger, I think—and because the cake was so moist, impression stayed."

Jesus.

Julia looked intrigued. "Like it was pressed into warm clay."

"Like the mud outside," Jim said, his eyes sparkling.

Matthew bit his lip. *Feet. Fingers.* He hadn't thought. He'd been clumsy, amateurish. Imperfect. Matthew slid his left hand into his jacket pocket and squeezed the sack he was holding in his right hand. *None of this is going to prove a thing. Not a fucking thing, you know, lawman?* But he did ask, "Do you think you can get a print?"

"Not from a fruitcake," Crowley laughed. He stared at the cake again as if he were about to inhale it. "But there is a line here"—he pointed carefully along the length of the indentation— "could be the seam of a glove . . ."

Matthew began to feel a sensation of self-loathing that almost consumed him.

When Matt saw Jim zipper up his coat, he knew it was now or never. He couldn't do a thing about the fruitcake in which he'd left his calling card, but he could do something about the frozen footprint sitting just outside the door. While Cornelia slid the fruitcake with the impression in it into a sack, Matt said a final good-bye, and told Julia he'd stop back in a day or so, but he knew in his heart he'd see her sooner than that. She thanked him, walked him to the door, and said, "It was nice talking to you."

He added one last zinger to insure that it happened: "I'd like to tell you about the last conversation I had with your mom."

She melted the way he wished the frozen footprint would have. He knew it was exactly what she needed to hear. And he had made clear that he was the only person she could ever hear it from. She grinned with anticipation from ear to ear. In that moment she was *his*.

Then he opened the door, and she took hold of the handle as he started out. But Jim was right behind him, saying his good-byes over his shoulder. The door closed. They were on the top step together. Matt turned and said, "Have a good evening, Mr. Crowley." Then his foot lifted to descend to the next step down.

Then he faked a turn, as if back to Crowley to say something more, his arm moving wide—

"Matt, careful of—"

Like hell I will. It was too late. Matt's arm smacked the box, knocking it off the cat, into the air—

Where Crowley caught it!

Matt didn't betray his anger, but the shock was honest. "Lucky move, Mr. Crowley."

"If I say so myself," Crowley crowed, proud.

Fuck yourself. It won't mean a thing. Not a damn thing. "You be sure to let us know what you find out."

"Sure thing," Crowley muttered, stepping into his vehicle.

And Matt drove home in a rage.

Inside the house, Julia said to her sister, "He's such a kind man."

"I assume you don't mean Jim," Cornelia muttered.

"Aren't his eyes amazing?" Julia said, covering her mouth as if worried the world could hear her girlish confession. She wondered where she'd seen that color of green before—in marbles when she was a kid? In a jewelry store display case? The writer in her had known those eyes in her dreams. "I've always felt a little guilty."

"What for?"

"For not being nicer. Or more grateful. Or something like that."

"That's ridiculous."

"Matt saved my life!"

"You said thank you."

"I always felt he was hurt because we didn't get closer. I mean, I knew he wanted to be my friend after that, and I never gave him the time of day."

Cornelia shoved the rest of the fruitcakes back into the refrigerator and closed the door. "You had the hots for him then, and you still do now."

"Carrie!"

Cornelia looked her squarely in the eye. "Just don't give in to it, Julia."

"Come on!"

"Julia, I know you and Tom are having troubles. You won't talk about it, but Mom and Dad knew it too."

Julia closed off. And mustered her reticence. "All I said was I think Matt's a sweet and kind man."

"And I think," Cornelia said, "that he's really a creep."

At two o'clock in the morning, Julia heard a soft knock on her door. "Come in."

The door opened. It was Tom, carrying a cup of steaming tea. "Thought it might help you sleep." He handed it to her and sat on the edge of the bed.

She sipped it and her face brightened. "You remembered I like cinnamon."

"It hasn't been that long since I've made you tea."

"Oh, Tom," she said with an empty sigh, "it has."

"Listen," he said, taking her hand, "I know I've been a shit. I know I've had tunnel vision for the firm, I know you feel lonely, I know life has been real tough, and I've been burning the candle at both ends. And now this."

She reached out and touched his leg, running her fingers up and down his muscular calf. The thick blond hairs felt like steel wool on her soft fingers. He was wearing the flannel boxer shorts she'd gotten him for Christmas. And his old Stanford sweatshirt. She thought he looked incredibly sexy. But she had no feelings of sex or desire anymore. Not for over a week now. Feelings had died inside her the day she found her parents. She hardly even remembered their problem now; it seemed trivial at the moment.

He rubbed her knees through the down comforter. "I wish I knew what to do for you."

Another time, another place, she would have said, "Make love to me." Now, instead, she just closed her eyes.

He turned on his stomach and brought his feet up, lying next to her, forcing a pillow under his chest. "I think we should go home tomorrow."

Her eyes opened quickly. "Home?"

"It's over. There's nothing more to do. I can barely sleep here either, knowing what happened downstairs. We need to go back to San Francisco and get on with life."

"We were trying to do that before this happened. It wasn't working." Her voice was suddenly brittle.

And he knew the tone well. "You know I have a lot of problems," Tom said, turning away slightly. He could never look her in the eye when they touched on it. The shame was too great. So she shrugged, then changed the drift. "Let's not fight. Just come back with me in the morning."

She paused a second, the impact of his words hitting her suddenly. "You mean you're going back no matter what?"

"I have a job."

"Most people have this whole week off."

"I don't. Our life has to go on."

"*Your* life has to go on."

He crossed his legs on the bed and grabbed his toes with his hands, bending forward. "What happened to us?" he asked, looking bewildered. "Why can't we talk to each other anymore?"

"You *know* what happened! You—"

"No, Julia, I'm not talking about that. I'm talking about communicating."

"You haven't tried. Every time I attempt to talk about it, you shut me out, just like Mom did. You can go on and on about the new mall you're designing, and the fame it'll bring you—"

"Recognition," he corrected her, "which will get me that promotion, which will benefit *us*."

"I don't care about money," she said, getting off the bed. "I care about our marriage."

"What do you want from me? I have a job, and I'm grateful for that because a lot of fellas I graduated with don't, but I'm only on the middle rung of the ladder and the senior partners aren't going to elevate anyone who doesn't bust their balls, no matter how much talent they have. I am going to make it. For us— *for our marriage*, to use your phrase—not only for me."

She was looking out the window, her back to him. He tried to make her understand. "I'm a dinosaur, the Last Yuppie, okay? I'm driven, I like BMW's. But it doesn't mean I don't love you. I love you more than ever. But it's not a contest between you and Marin Design Group. I just simply have to put my time in there for our future."

She faced him again. "It isn't about any of that, Tom. You *know* what I want from you."

"I'm handling it, Julia. It's just going to take more time."

"But I'm *not* handling it! I don't *have* more time!" She turned back to the window, looking out across the lawn, where the moon cast a bluish tone over the snow. She'd never before realized how many trees dotted her parents' property, gigantic towering pines and firs, ancient oaks, small seedlings gasping for breath through the ice. She felt like that, gasping for breath as a woman with a husband who would not, could not—

She stopped herself. She knew to try to discuss it would be to no avail. If only she could have talked to her mother about it! She was feeling robbed and alone and outraged and betrayed and deprived and cut off— "Damn you!" she screamed suddenly, banging her fist on the glass so hard the entire window rattled. "Damn you to hell!"

Tom jumped up and grabbed her, pulling her away, afraid her hand was going to go through the pane, turning her around, forcing her to face him.

"Bastard!" She hit him on the chest with both fists, so he pulled her to him, telling her it was okay, he understood how she felt about him, he deserved it, but she kept on screaming, shouting, beating on his back with her hands, then digging her fingernails into him as she clung to him, telling him through tears that she was hating not him but *him*, the man with the snowshoes, the man who stuck his finger in the cake, the man who walked down the road squishing in her father's bloodied slippers. "Why did he do it? Why? Why? Why?"

Tom helped Julia to the bed, and then reached out and turned off the light on the bed stand, as Julia cried softly against his cheek in a desolate, unrelenting, and unimaginable pain.

At that same moment, on the other side of the mountain, a man dressed in jeans and a leather flight jacket rolled another boulder into place and then lodged it, packing it in with dirt and snow. There. It was secure now. Matt was positive no other animals would get inside. But, damn, he was mad—at himself. He should have made sure it all burned. That night. When he had his one chance. He'd said he wasn't going to make a mistake, that it was going to be perfect. But he'd fucked up. He hadn't counted on the fact that he had cut off the oxygen to the fire too soon. He'd thought everything on the pyre had fried to a crisp. Leave it to a dog to remember where. Leave it to a dog to drag out that one half-burned, blood-encrusted slipper. That piece of *evidence*.

God, but he hated himself at this moment. Fucking fruitcake. Fucking boot print. It wasn't perfect. He wasn't perfect. Well, he'd never prided himself on that, but he did believe he was clever, perhaps more clever than anyone he'd ever met. Not this time. And that was a bitter pill to swallow. But he was being clever now. He was fixing things. The stuff that hadn't burned was wet with moisture—the moisture he'd created because of the temperature of the fire. It was too risky to take them out of here. Better to leave them. Someday, when the heat died down—he laughed at his own pun—he'd take out what was left and burn it elsewhere.

But for now it was hidden safely, impenetrable to curious dogs, including his own. He was covering his tracks with the perfection he expected from himself. As he should have done at the Radcliffe house, where stepping on Jim Crowley's frozen mud print would have been a step in the right direction. Another pun. He should have been a comic. He slapped his hands together to shake free the mud and snow, and then pulled his collar up and made his way down the hill toward his house. Fuck the footprint, what can they learn from boots everyone buys? The impression of a gloved print? No worry there. Naw, no problem. He started to like himself better already.

And as he walked, he looked up to heaven, to the angels, and could think of nothing but Julia.

4

Julia awoke before anyone else the next morning. She'd slept a restless, agonizing sleep, haunted by dreams of sharing her frustrations with her mother— only to have Martha laugh at her. She feared the demons that lurked inside her. Three times she'd fought the desire to go downstairs and open the liquor cabinet to anesthetize the pain. No, she told herself, it would be too easy, too much like her mother; it had never solved anything for Martha, why would it work for her?

Now, as sunlight streamed in through the window, she tried desperately to find something positive to do, and decided a walk in the brisk air would help clear her mind. She eased herself out from under the covers, pulled the drapes closed so the light would not disturb Tom, and dressed silently in the darkened room. But putting on her bra—the very action of it, which she'd taken for granted all her adult life—meant something now, said something now, and as she looked down at her sleeping husband, the clasp between her fingers, she started to shake with the fury of hopeless insecurity, which rendered her helpless. She rushed out of the room.

Downstairs, she realized the demons were not easily mollified by a change of venue; she had to finish dressing, and that meant resisting what she'd begun to feel. She saw her mother's bottle of Dewar's. She wondered if that would have been Martha's answer— "Darling, I drank the problem away!"—or would her mother have been less facile and really have shared with her the feelings she went through after it had happened to her. She knew the Dewar's numbed her mother's pain, dulled her feelings. As she stared at it, she began to be revolted by it, and brewed a strong pot of Starbucks Colombian instead. She drank a cup with a slice of fruitcake, but the flavor of brandy made her nervous, so she dropped it into the disposal, switching to a single piece of toast. She checked on Molly—still fast asleep—and then, leaving a note so no one would worry, she put on her Reebok high-tops, tied a muffler tightly around her chin, and set off for the road.

The temperature had dipped into the mid-twenties during the night, but as the sun cut through the clouds, she could feel the warming. It was finally going to move above freezing, and she was glad. For she felt an odd sensation that had nothing to do with the physical snap of the cold; she knew from now on she'd associate snow and cold weather with death. It was enough to make her want to book a Caribbean cruise this very morning.

But the walk did her good. As she started to focus on what she was seeing—mounds of plowed snow, early birds, rickety mailboxes, a gorgeous pine cone serving as a nose on a snowman someone had built— and her mind concentrated less on the reason she was here in these mountains, the reality of what she'd left behind in her parents' house faded.

As she walked, she could only think about what Matthew had told her he'd been privy to—her mother's last conversation about her. She was curious. Her mother and father had known she and Tom were having problems ever since the surgery. They had never asked about it, but she knew that her mother knew what was wrong, that history was repeating itself, that nothing was the same after the surgery in a marriage that had been young and fresh and good. Her curiosity was strong, however—how much had her mother assumed? How much had she really known? And could Matt possibly know about that?

No, she was being silly; her mother would never have talked to anyone about it. She couldn't speak to her own husband or daughters about it, how then Matthew? Julia kicked snow with her feet and tried to remember the tone of her mother's voice on the phone that night. Yes, she'd been drinking. But still, what did she communicate? Julia recalled her being warm and kind; she certainly didn't snap at her or make any disparaging remarks. But it was the end of the conversation that bothered her. Martha had turned reticent at Julia's plea that they "really talk." Why? Had she been afraid? Had she anticipated what Julia was going to tell her? God, she would never know. Unless, that is, Matthew could tell her—

Don't think about it, can't think about it.

About a mile farther, in the center of the road, at the far end of a curve, were two deer. A doe, proud and regal, and her fawn, not tiny anymore but still probably less than a year old. He stayed close to his mother, whose ears were perked, ready, alert, even though she seemed to be concentrating more on the berries on the bushes at the edges of the asphalt. Julia watched them for as long as they ate, marveling at their beauty, their innate grace. Then both animals suddenly went rigid, and Julia froze as well, thinking that they heard hunters. But when they bounded off into the gully and galloped down the slope, a car came by, and Julia stepped aside, realizing that's what they'd sensed before her ears even picked it up.

She suddenly thought of a cake she'd seen at the Lucky food store a few weeks back, right around Thanksgiving. It was a sheet cake, beautifully decorated with a blue stream cascading down the center, trees of green standing on either side, and on the right side, three deer grazing, and a little fawn drinking from the stream. But on the left side—and this was what made her recall the cake now—had been plastic figures of two hunters, guns raised and pointed at the deer across the water. It had made her sick.

As she stood here thinking about it, she realized she never could abide the violence of hunting. A gun, the noise, blowing a beautiful duck out of the sky, killing a sleek buck bounding through the trees, exploding the side of a squirrel into bloodied balls of fur. It revolted her, shook her to the core. If only her mother could have run like the doe, she thought, if only her father had perked his ears and sensed danger before the bullets exploded into their bodies and—

Don't think about it, can't think about it.

Dammit! She stood up straight and shook her head. *I'm not going to do this anymore.* She'd promised herself. Last night she had let herself come apart, allowed herself to grieve and be angry, to be filled with hate for an unknown man who deserved to be hated. But not today, today was going to be different—*don't think about it, can't think about it*—that's why she was out here, that's why she had done this. She could have stayed in bed and cried and wallowed in her grief all the way to sunset, as she had so many times since the operation, during the treatments. No. *Not anymore. I licked the big C, I can lick this. March on, girl.*

And she did, literally. She walked all the way to Sherlock Road and turned left, tackling the hill that rounded the mountainside, and when she reached a point where she could see forever, she stopped and untied her muffler and opened her jacket, for she was starting to sweat. The incline was a steep one, and she'd already hiked four miles at a good pace. She looked out at Yosemite National Park in the distance, thinking for the first time how truly spectacular the scenery was up here, how it truly was God's country, most of it still untouched by human hands, and she felt she really understood why her parents had loved it so—

Don't think about it, can't think about it.

She was aware of smoke coming from a house down the hillside, and she realized that's where Paul and Inga lived, two of her parents' closest friends, and she choked up, turning away, screaming silently in her mind about the reminders. *Reminders.* Everywhere she looked, everything she saw, reminded her of what had happened—

Don't think about it, can't think about it.

She saw a dog rushing toward her, a German shepherd and collie mix. At first she was fearful of the big animal, so she stood still and held out her left hand. The dog took a sniff, then a lick, and that did it; in a moment the beast was all over her, wanting to play, putting her muddy footprints on Julia's jacket, excited as could be. Then a man's voice suddenly cut through the air. "*Maggie!* Maggie, come here, girl!"

Julia couldn't see who was saying it, but she took the cue and said, "Yeah, Maggie, honey, down . . ."

But Maggie, hearing her name from the girl, took it

to mean something else, and within seconds she'd knocked Julia into the snow, joining her on her back, kicking all fours into the air right next to her, in a sort of girl-and-dog snow angel party. In the midst of squealing with laughter and trying to push the dog away, Julia saw a man's gloved hand reach out to her and she grabbed it, and felt herself being pulled up. Then, as she got her bearings, she heard him give the dog's butt a good crack, accompanied by, "Maggie, bad girl. What do you think you're doing?"

When Julia wiped the snow from her eyes, she realized it was Matt who had helped her up.

"I'm really sorry," he said apologetically, "but she thinks she's still a puppy. She loves to play."

"No kidding." She brushed herself off and then looked at the dog, who was hanging her head. "Oh, hey," she said to her, bending to pet her, "it's okay, it really is. I was a kid once too, I understand."

Maggie licked Julia's nose. All was forgiven.

Then Matt made the formal introduction. "Maggie, meet Julia. Julia, Maggie. She seldom takes to strangers like that."

"That some kind of compliment?"

He smiled. "Gosh, you look cold."

"I was warm till she came along."

"My place is just down the road. I make a mean hot chocolate, I really do."

"You're on," she replied.

* * *

"This is wonderful," she said, cupping a mug of steaming cocoa in her left hand as she picked up something that intrigued her with her right—a globe upside down on a wooden pedestal, filled with water and bits of snow—and shook it to watch the white flakes float through the liquid. "I've always loved these. What do you call them?"

"Snow globes, or water globes. Your mother gave me that one for Christmas."

She almost dropped it. "She did?"

He nodded. "Last year. I didn't mean to upset you."

"No, it's just that I didn't expect it. Tell me more. Why this?"

As she set it back on the coffee table, he sat on the sofa facing her. He reached out and turned her jacket around in front of the wood-burning stove, where it was drying. Then he twirled the water globe in his hand. The snow billowed around the angel, a virtual blizzard in a bottle. "Last year, when she was decorating for Christmas, she asked me to put the angel atop the tree for her, the cat angel with the silk dress and feather wings."

Julia smiled slightly at the memory it tugged out. "Cornelia made it for her in the fourth grade."

But he already knew that as well. "When I was a kid I made a plaque out of copper for my parents, three angels doing their 'hark' number with trumpets, you know?"

"Molly did almost the same for me for my birthday."

"Angels are great. I told your mom I had a thing about them, and I guess that's what made her think of this for me for Christmas." He picked it up again and held it close to her face so she could see the detail. "It's exquisite. The angel inside is hand-carved from wood, then glazed like ceramic. Probably the nicest thing I own."

"You have very nice things," she said, because she'd been looking around, studying the place. It was simple and unpretentious, a young bachelor's house that felt like a cabin in the woods, but it was tasteful and real; a "Ralph Lauren" spread without anything labeled Ralph Lauren in it. He told her that the living room sofa had spent a former lifetime in the presidential suite in Yosemite's Ahwahnee Hotel, and was now simply covered with an Indian blanket. She saw a needlepoint pillow of an angel, and in the center of the dining table, a ceramic bowl with the faces of cherubs carved all around it. A weathered club chair looked so inviting she wanted to curl up in the buttery leather with a good book for the rest of time. She felt oddly at home here, more comfortable than in her parents' glass and rock edifice. Matt's house had a warmth that appealed to her creative spirit.

And she felt that Matthew himself was like that, down-to-earth and unassuming. His voice was mellow and calming, like the warmth emanating from the iron stove. That he had taste and style was evident from the effect of the room. But Julia knew he was smart too. One glance around his space told her a great deal about him. A framed, Xeroxed flyer from his first political campaign. A photograph of him with her father on the day of Matt's swearing-in. A pile of yellowing *New York Times* sitting near the hearth. The complete works of Shakespeare, which actually looked dog-eared. She stared at the bookshelves that covered three walls of the living room. Then she got up and looked closer. "Great collection of poetry."

"Thanks," he said, pointing out her novel, *Epiphany*, and the collection of short stories, *Musings*, a slimmer volume right next to it. Just as he'd told her.

She saw several shelves lined only with titles on angels. She ran her fingers over a few—*The Angel Carver, Angels in America, Angels & Insects, The Angel in Renaissance Art*. He took one from the shelf and handed it to her. "This one's great."

She was looking at a copy of *Ask Your Angels*. "This sort of started the angel craze, didn't it?"

"You'd like it," Matt said enthusiastically. "Especially since you created that great archangel in *Epiphany*."

"Yeah, but it was the character's fantasy."

"Was it?" he asked with a pixieish twinkle in his eye.

"What's this passion for angels?"

"Oh, it's not just 'cause it's the New Age thing to do.

My mom used to talk about angels all the time when I was a kid. And when something bad happened, I'd close my eyes and think about my guardian angel, and the bad feelings would go away." He laughed suddenly. "I used to want to be an angel, thought it was sexy or something."

"I guess it could be. I'm not much of a New Ager. Listening to Enya and Yanni are about as far as I go."

"But you had a lot of New Age insights in *Epiphany*."

"Two books under my belt, and I switched to television—about as far from crystals and inner peace as you can get."

"Why haven't you gone back?"

She stiffened even though she wanted to remain unflustered. Her hand automatically moved to her chest. "I . . . I just don't know what I want to do."

He saw she was uncomfortable. So he apologized that most of the other books were the kind you send away to the Franklin Mint for, but that had been the easiest way, he explained, before he had money, to collect the classics in hardcover. "I hate paperbacks. A real book has to have cloth on it. It'll last. Gives it immortality."

"Is that what *you* want?" she asked.

It took him by surprise. "Why would you think that?"

"I see you're a writer too." She ran her fingers over a

leather jacket that said: *Matthew Hinson, Collected Poetry, 1982–85.* "I had no idea."

That was just what he wanted her to think. But he looked embarrassed. "I just bought those, had them stamped that way, they're not real books. Here, I'll show you." He stood up and pulled out the "book" she'd touched and opened it. It was a kind of box like a VHS tape case, an empty receptacle that held anything you'd want to put in it. He withdrew many sheets of paper on which were written, in his hand, short poems. "This is my hobby. I'm not looking for immortality, or even for praise. Just gets me through the night sometimes."

She wasn't listening; she was reading:

> *Lingering doubts, shadows of memories*
> *Long tucked into the winter past*
> *When dreams freeze over like*
> *The lake at the top of the world*
> *Still*
> *Silent, guarded,*
> *Protected until the*
> *Spring of new thoughts bursts with magic,*
> *Exploding, green and fresh and alive.*
> *A bird's tendon cracking the last sheet of ice*
> *As something cold and hungry comes*
> *To life!*
> *Jumping*
> *Splashing*

Whirling spiraling, and feverish we
Begin to dream again.

She put the paper down. "That's lovely."

"Thanks," he said too quickly, then pulled the poem from her hand, replaced it with the others in the box, and slipped it back between Rita Dove and Robert Nathan.

"But I'd like to read more," Julia protested. She saw another "book" spine that said *Matthew Hinson, Collected Poetry, 1990–*. She started to reach for it—

But he put his hand on hers, stopping her. "There's nothing in there. Haven't done much lately. That's why I left the date open. Might take me ten years to fill this one."

She knew not to push any harder. But she vowed to read more someday. She'd always tended to put poets on a pedestal, probably out of envy; as she painfully admitted, she'd never been able to write a decent poem in her life. "Didn't you ever want to be a writer?" she asked.

"Not as a profession."

"How about successful businessman, land baron, state senator, *and* poet as well?"

He smiled, and that smile was her confirmation.

She tried to query him more about his writing, did it balance his business side, but she sensed she was pushing too hard too soon. She felt he wanted to talk, but not so openly about himself. It was then that she realized something she hadn't known before: that, despite his success, he was a bit shy.

He finished his own hot chocolate, which was still steaming because he'd set it atop the stove. He put the mug down, wiping the creamy foam from his lips. He sat in a chair with a needlepoint angel pillow. "Your mom told me I should write a Christmas book about angels. If I do, I'll dedicate it to her."

She said nothing, but her face could not hide what his words did to her, the sorrow, the emptiness that was tapped. *Don't think about it, can't think about it*— "I'm sorry, Matt, it's just tough to talk about her. But I want to. I want to hear everything she had to say, but I just can't do it yet."

He nodded gently. "I understand." He shook off the heavy tone. "So, why didn't you bring Molly?"

"Oh, she was still asleep. And her little legs can't power walk yet. Though she gives me a run for my money at—"

For some reason, at this moment, Maggie decided it was time for another lick. She jumped up from her spot near the stove, but this time she missed Julia's face and crashed against the floor lamp next to her, sending it toppling. Julia thought fast, and moved fast, reaching to catch it in midair before it hit the floor. But at the same moment Matt did the very same thing, and together they grabbed it, their hands touching, overlapping. There was a moment, just a tremor, a fleeting connection in their locked eyes before they started laughing, before they nervously covered it, that broke open that dark part of Julia's soul and told her that her sister was right, that there was much more to her interest in this man than his calm voice and mean hot chocolate. She suddenly felt something sizzling in her bloodstream, and perhaps that was why she'd run from him and lost herself in Tom—the heat was just too intense. This moment was confirmation, for despite her grief and madness, even with her husband just miles away at that very moment, she found something in Matthew Hinson that was irresistible.

But she resisted.

He walked her back to the road. It was even sunnier now, much warmer. She turned to him and asked what he was going to do on New Year's Eve.

"Write a couple of poems," he said with a smile. "I'm not much of a party person. My disco days are long over." Then he took her hand in his and said, "I hope you have a new year that is nothing like this one."

"I do too," she said, and she turned, ready to start her trek back to her parents' house, but a familiar face appeared seemingly out of nowhere.

"Howdy," Jim Crowley said to them both.

"Mr. Crowley," Matt said, nodding.

"Morning, Jim," Julia said. "What are you doing out here?"

"This your doggie?" Maggie ran up to Jim and put her paws on his chest.

Julia turned to Matt. "And I thought *I* was special."

Jim was trying to get the dog down. "Hey, boy."

"Might take offense to that," Matt said. "Name's Maggie."

Jim bent down. "Hey, girl. Maggie, what a beauty you are."

"Wasn't when I got her," Matt said. "She'd been abused. Was afraid of her own shadow."

"You'd never know," Julia said.

Jim Crowley rustled her fur, rubbed her head, and then held the upper part of her jaw with one hand and the lower with the other, forcing her mouth open.

"What the hell are you doing?" Matt exclaimed, squatting next to them.

"Playin' dentist," Jim said matter-of-factly. Then he looked into Maggie's mouth. "Broken incisor." He let the poor animal close it.

Maggie ran and cowered behind Matthew. "Thinks you're the vet," Matt explained humorously, rubbing Maggie's head to reassure her. "She'd been the pet of a couple who were squatters down in a trailer in Whiskey Flats. The guy had been beating both his wife and the dog. Story goes that he tossed the dog from their truck one day, broke the tooth hitting the pavement, lacerations as well. Inga Wilson fixed her up."

Julia was transfixed. "Inga gave her to you?"

"No, the dog ran away, back to the trailer. Good thing, though, 'cause she eventually saved the woman's life."

"How so?" Jim asked, staring at the frightened animal.

"Attacked the bastard before he choked the woman to death, chewed him up enough so she could get away and get help."

Julia patted Maggie on the head. "Good girl."

"Who's Inga Wilson?" Jim asked.

"Woman who lives down the hill, right over there." He pointed at a rooftop in the distance. "Loves animals."

Crowley gave a glance.

Maggie was licking Julia's face again. "She's so playful," Julia said, "you must have worked magic on her."

"A little love makes a difference."

"She might be helpful too," Jim said.

"How so?" Matt asked.

"Slipper found yesterday? Had a canine bite mark. Broken tooth."

Julia's eyes went wide. "You mean Maggie found it?"

"My dog found some evidence?" Matt exclaimed.

"Sure wish she could talk," Jim said, looking off up the incline of the mountain. "Wish to heck she'd tell us where she got it."

"I'll ask her," Matt said with a grin.

Julia laughed.

Jim did not. "Wanna let her lead us to where she dug it up?"

Matt didn't blink. "I'd be obliged. Go ahead, girl. Go, Maggie."

They stared at the dog. She sat and lifted her right paw for someone to take hold. Julia did, laughing.

"Oh, well," Jim said, "dumb thought." He tipped his hat and started to walk away.

"Mr. Crowley," Matt called. Jim turned back. "Anything come of that boot print you found?"

"Sears."

"Pardon me?"

"Sears, Roebuck. Size ten. Wear a twelve myself. What about you? Wear a ten, Mr. Hinson?"

"Nine. And I buy my boots at K-Mart."

"Lucky for you."

Back in the house, Matthew went immediately to the bookshelves. He reached up and pulled down the volume he'd stopped Julia from touching, *Matthew Hinson, Collected Poetry, 1990–*. He opened it and stared inside. Then he spilled the contents onto the sofa. Twenty-three hundred dollars in crisp new bloodstained bills lay in front of him. A key. And an unfinished poem. Shoving the money aside, he picked up a pen and continued to work on the verse.

She had given him inspiration.

When Julia returned to the house, everyone was awake, and the calm she'd come to feel at Matthew

Hinson's cozy cabin drained from her pores immediately, for this was like walking into a zoo. Cornelia was fussing over what was wrong with the toaster, Brad was searching for his ski wax, Molly was refusing to eat breakfast—or was it lunch already?—and Tom was begging everyone to please shut up because he was on the phone with his office. Julia suggested he go to another phone, seeing there were about ten extensions in the house, but he only snapped at her, which in turn made her snap back at him, and one thing led to another and soon they all were screaming at one another. She imagined her mother's voice shouting from the kitchen, as she'd done so many times throughout her lifetime, calling, in a shocked voice, "Hush up, everyone!"

But her mother was not there. Would never be there—

Don't think about it, can't think about it.

Julia went to her room and stared out the window. The hundreds of trees she had dwelled on last evening looked less magical in the daylight. Her insides were on fire and her head was throbbing. She didn't want to be here, in this house. She didn't want to be inside her own body—a feeling she'd felt for nine months now. She felt susceptible and frightened. She needed someone strong. She needed support. She needed understanding. She needed help.

When Tom came upstairs and found her sitting there trembling, he must have read the look on her face, for he immediately and lovingly apologized for snapping at her. He kissed her cheek, trying to explain it had been one of the partners on the phone, discussing the presentation for tomorrow morning's meeting. She felt the malaise that had gripped her about three months earlier really getting a lock on her now as he pulled his suitcase from the closet and began to pack. She watched him, listened to him talking about their return to San Francisco, again telling her why it was good for her, but she wasn't hearing him. She was thinking about hot chocolate and angels in water globes and big licky dogs.

Suddenly, she realized Tom had asked her something and was standing, waiting for an answer. "I'm sorry. What?"

"Aren't you going to pack?"

"Is it so important that I go along? You aren't taking me to that meeting." Her eyes brightened with a new plan. "I know, fly back, like you came up. It's only the twenty-seventh, you could drive back on New Year's Eve."

"Jacob invited *us* to the Fairmont. It'll do you good. He adores you, and his wife's a sweetheart."

She put her finger in her mouth as if to induce vomiting.

"Julia, this dinner could be my big break."

"Why does it mean so much?"

"It just does," he shouted.

And she knew she could not reason with that kind of answer. Tom drove himself almost over the edge, burning to get to the top. Why was it always so important? Was it just success he wanted, or did it have more to do with his strict Boston upbringing, something deep in his psyche that meant proving something to himself? But if he didn't see anything wrong, she could not make him look in a mirror. So she forced herself to be less selfish. "All right, I'll go. As long as you do the talking. I just don't know what to say to that woman."

He smiled. "I'll talk my ass off." He kissed her. Warmly, on the lips. "Thanks, honey. I'll get Molly packed and ready."

But she looked sad. And she felt empty. Cold. After he walked out, she felt even more alone. Angry. Frustrated. She'd let him talk her into doing what she didn't want to do. She always hated herself when she gave into anything that didn't suit her at the moment. Life was a compromise, her father had once told her. She knew it was true. But how she hated it.

At four o'clock, they left for San Francisco in the car Tom had rented at the Merced airport when he flew in the night of the murders. As Molly waved from the back window to her Aunt Cornelia and Uncle Brad, who were sympathetic but sorry to see them go, Julia felt tears running down her cheeks again, and Tom reached over and put his hand on hers. But it didn't help. It had, in fact, the opposite effect; it made her resent him more.

This should have brought them closer, she felt. This experience should have made them hold onto each other, support each other, strengthen each other. She needed Tom now. She had indeed lost her innocence and didn't know how to function in a world suddenly so terrifying, so unsteady, so mad. She wanted her youth back, her laughter and her dreams—hell, she wanted her right breast back!—but she knew the only way to redemption was to deal with this cold and steely reality.

She wanted to stay here because her parents had been murdered. He wanted to go because he needed to kiss ass with the boss and his boring wife. She wanted to scream at him that all he cared about was money, that she'd come into this marriage planning to grow together, but all he'd done was let her simmer on the back burner while he devoted his life to—to what? A penthouse apartment in a newer building, a little higher up Nob Hill than the one they had now? A flashier, more expensive BMW than the one he now drove? His name on the cornerstone of a steel and glass edifice everyone would praise for a few weeks, then take potshots at for the rest of time as it aged and appeared less remarkable than it had when new? She wanted to tell him to take his drafting tools and shove them up his Waspy butt. She wanted to tell him she deserved better, someone who cared about *her*, someone who could make love to her! What had happened—or hadn't happened—since the operation was a truth she could not hide from. No, it wasn't trivial, how could she have thought that . . . She wanted to jump from the car, she wanted to strike him, she wanted to—

But she did none of those things. She knew it was crazy, but now she consciously remembered the lamp Maggie had pushed, and the feel of Matt's hand on hers, the way she couldn't breathe, the way she felt her temperature rise, her heart skip. It was wrong— she was married!—but what she needed to know right now was that there was a man on this earth who put her first, who seemed to care about her, a man who liked her, and who thought she was attractive, *still* was attractive, a man who would, just in looking at her, make her feel slightly like a woman again.

And for a brief, fleeting moment she fantasized heresy: that it was Matt driving with her, not Tom.

At the same moment that Julia and Tom were heading west on Highway 152 out of Merced, Matthew Hinson was stretched out on his stomach in the glow of the wood-burning stove on the floor of his living room. He still wore the old sweatshirt he'd had on when he saw Julia, but he'd pulled his boots and pants off and was clad only in his briefs and socks.

Maggie hunched nearby, lapping up the bits of undissolved cocoa powder in his mug.

Matthew didn't notice. He was completing the poem:

> *Starry sky, somewhere aloft, above the clouds*
> *Laden with their gift of snow*
> *Night of silence, night of death*
> *Whisper, for they are beyond the door,*
> *Carved, beautiful, worthless door,*
> *And they should not hear!*
> *Striking fast, silent, deep—*
> *(What is this, a submarine movie?)*
> *Silent, deep, making him*
> *Watch her die . . .*
> *Revenge is sweet, and red*
> *And sweet*
> *And wet, in the snow, in bloodied slippers,*
> *So cold.*
> *Did you find them first,*
> *Pretty Julia, snow angel from God?*
> *You were not meant to suffer,*
> *But born to the fat fuck you*
> *Suffered unimaginable pain—*
> *I will ease it, my snow angel from God*
> *I will help you lose the memory*
> *Calm the nightmare*
> *Erase the incident as I've erased the incident*
> *So many times in my head*
> *Till we make love*

In the snow
In the night
Under the wintery sky, beneath the heavy snow cloud
Just like the night they died.

Matthew stopped. He dropped the pen. The book jacket at which he'd been staring for inspiration looked back at him now. Julia. He felt his penis hardening—

Then he felt a rush of guilt that paralyzed him. This is wrong! Wrong! He closed his eyes. *Think about your angel*, a gentle voice whispered in his head, wiping the guilt away, *your angel will make you happy . . .*

And the slightly faded photograph came alive in front of him. She stepped up, out of the back of the book jacket, and suddenly she was dressed in white, the flowing dress she had worn the day he met her, and her head was aglow with a halo. Then, miraculously, she sprouted wings. Huge, glorious, powerful angelic wings. She flew over him and then descended onto his shoulders. He could feel the prickly indentations of her feet on his skin. Each sensation sent spasms through his loins. She knelt now, on his left shoulder, reaching down to lift his hair with her hands, to tickle his ear, to tease him. He giggled— ticklish as he was—and turned his head the other way, and heard her squeal with delight as she got up again and ran down his strong back, to his butt, where she rolled over and over his ass cheeks, and then

tumbled, as if swallowed up, between his legs as he
spread them.

He could feel her breathing Tinker Bell-like on his
balls, through the soft, washed cotton of his briefs.
Making sure he didn't crush her, he gently turned
over onto his back. She ran over his hip, uphill,
prancing in a marathon along the band of his shorts.
His penis stood erect, peeking above the words *Calvin
Klein*. He looked down and saw her climbing over the
mound in his shorts, crawling on all fours up the hill,
sliding along it like riding down a banister, racing up
again, balancing on it until she reached the naked
head. Her wings fluttered against him, tickling him
into spasms—what exquisite pain!—and then he
gasped for breath as she knelt there and moved her
haloed head toward the tip.

"No," he cried out, the guilt rising, the fears, an
automatic cry for help from—

But the voice in his head soothed him again. *It's
your angel, your angel, your angel . . .*

Then he looked down and indeed it was his angel—
the voice had not lied; his eyes met hers and locked in
sensual heat for a moment, and then she kissed it. He
closed his eyes again. He could feel her tickling it, tor-
menting him, persecuting him—

"Julia!" he shouted. His right hand gripped the
Indian blanket on the sofa, the other flailed wildly.
"Julia, I love you!" He felt the orgasm wet him even
before he could get his hand down to his pulsating

organ. He had never done this without a little help—at least with his hand—before in his life. He shook, his whole body jerking up and down, his buttocks slamming again and again on the floor, and he cried a guttural, deep sigh, and finally he began to relax. He pushed his cock back into his briefs and wiped his stomach with a T-shirt.

Then he looked at the dust jacket again. She was back there. She'd retreated into it, taking up her same pose, without the wings, without the flowing gown, without the halo, in the same yellowed lacquer veneer that had covered it since the day he bought it. Without thinking—or perhaps thinking this was perfect—he folded the poem he'd written and slid it into her book and put it back on the shelf exactly where it had been. In a day or so he'd go back to the mine shaft and put it in there as well. He had to decide when he was going to take the stuff away, when he was going to burn it for good. He should do it soon, he told himself, now that asshole Crowley knew Maggie had found the slipper. His deduction would be that the dog might try again. But what was the prick going to do, put twenty-four-hour surveillance on a dog? Still, he worried. Crowley might think the rest of the stuff was nearby, someplace where another animal would get at it. . . .

No no no. He was getting paranoid. He had lost his senses jacking off. Maggie might go back there, sure, but the opening to the mine was sealed even from her determined digging now. And, more important, from her nose. No animal would find the evidence. It was protected for now. Secure. Just like the key and the bloodied money he'd just buried in an old Folger's can in the frozen earth—no easy feat—of his backyard. He'd dig it up in the spring; for now it was safe.

Safe, as he was. But it was a safety he had created, carved out for himself, for society had no place for people like him, no category, no slot. Oh, the public Matt, sure; he was bright, witty, serious, successful, gregarious, wholesome, and handsome. But the private Matt, the one lying here at this moment, where would they place him? The viper's den at the zoo? Cold, malignant. Cold, poisonous. Cold, fascinating. Cold. He laughed out loud. It was poetic. He was *complicated*, and it tickled him.

He warmed his cold hands with the heat emanating from the cast iron stove just feet from him. When he shoved another log inside, he could still smell the pungent rubber of the Sears boots he'd burned in there. He closed the door. The flames diminished to a soft coral glow with less oxygen. He got up and flopped on the sofa and put one foot up over the back, his hands under his head, posing with a shit-eating grin. He was glowing. He accepted Maggie's lick to his nose, licked her right back, and then, as she settled herself at his feet in front of the sofa and he reached out to rub her head, he found himself looking again at the water globe he'd stolen from Julia's parents' house.

He reached out and shook it and set it on his chest. He watched the snow blizzard around and around, and finally saw the flakes settle on the angel's wing, and then, in time, the water was crystal clear, just like his plan.

It was coming to pass, everything he'd dreamed about, everything he'd planned. In a moment, in a touch, he knew that he loved her, and that destiny had brought them together, and that it would be no good with anyone else, ever; he would have her, would possess her, if it took his lifetime to accomplish it. For with his angel he would attain immortality.

Yes, he would have her. To do so, he would rid himself of the obstacles, of the people who stood in the way. Harry Radcliffe. Martha Radcliffe. Tom Larsen.

Tom Larsen. He was still alive.

Yes, he thought with a smile, shaking the snow angel water globe again, and perhaps he could remain so. The parents were the real obstacle; they had to be the first to go. But Tom, well, Tom was easier to rid himself of . . . and maybe he could do it without having even to harm him.

5

In a faux Italian restaurant deep in the bowels of San Francisco's Fairmont Hotel, Julia felt adrift. A waiter was singing "Di Provenza il Mar" from *La Traviata*, while Jacob Kirshenbaum attempted to tell a story, his voice vying for prominence over the booming lungs of the singer. Mr. Kirshenbaum's wife, a pleasant if somewhat dull lady whose taut face had been lifted one time too many, sat rapt with attention. Tom Larsen looked as if he was eating up every word.

Julia did not. She twirled the ice cubes in her mineral water with her fingers. She was dying here. She'd done this for Tom, donned her finest Ann Taylor suit, fluffed up her hair, put on her best face, and had been sitting here for more than an hour—not even the entrees had arrived as yet—bored and longing to be somewhere else. No specific place, actually. Just *anywhere* but here. What really made her nervous at this table was Tom's boss himself. For Jacob Kirshenbaum had been responsible for bringing Tom into her life.

Tom had joined Jacob's prestigious firm, Marin Architectural Group, straight out of college, where he had graduated at the top of his Stanford class, the brilliant young Boston dynamo deemed most likely to succeed. His first assignment—a team condo project— impressed Jacob and the other partners. Just as it was finished, Jacob's old buddy Harry Radcliffe, the former governor, walked in and told Jacob he wanted somebody to design a retirement "cottage" for himself and his wife in the Sierras. He wanted it big, interesting, unforgettable. As Jacob and Harry discussed which individual architect might be most suited to the project, Tom Larsen brought a roll of blueprints into the office. Jacob introduced him to the Gov as the newest and the brightest, and Harry said, "Why not this guy?" Jacob couldn't think of a good reason, so Tom was awarded his first solo assignment, years earlier than would have happened under normal circumstances.

It was while planning the house that Julia met him. She recalled she had been wearing a floppy sun hat, sandals, and an authentic flower child dress she'd bought in a garage sale on Haight Street, all of which made Tom pronounce her "weird." But she wasn't crazy about him either; too tall, too blond, too Waspish, too arrogant, and too smooth, he seemed everything she didn't want in a man. He hadn't read her novel, hadn't even heard of her book of short stories. He only liked mysteries. She was also a news reporter, and that part tickled him, seeing her on TV. So they got to talking, went out for a drink, and married seven months later. When Molly was born, they—

Julia was suddenly brought back to earth by Jacob's voice. "Tom, superb presentation today. Great stuff. Pacific Rim, that's the future. We meet with the chinks"—the wife must have kicked him, judging from the sudden change of expression on his face— "the, uh, Chinese next week so they can have their goddamned say, those red bastards, 'cause they're taking over."

"Hong Kong," Tom explained to Julia.

"Anyhow," Jacob continued, "once the meeting's out of the way, we head to Kowloon and begin."

Julia looked up. "Who?"

"Your wonderful husband and I," Jacob said proudly, thinking she'd be thrilled.

"What?" Julia asked.

Tom used a condescending tone, as if her memory had just been unplugged. "The bank, honey. Remember?"

Julia said, "You didn't tell me it was in Hong Kong."

"You didn't ask," Tom responded with a little bite.

"You'll *adore* it," the wife gushed to Julia, "such an exciting city. The Star Ferry every day, oh my."

"One big shopping mall," Jacob added, "and all the Peking duck you can eat."

"Beijing," his wife corrected him.

"Peking, Beijing," Jacob cursed, "it's still the same goddamn duck."

"Hong Kong," Julia only said, thinking already of the questions—when? When were they expected? Would she have to spend much time there? How long would they need to be gone? Hong Kong! She couldn't go to Hong Kong. Not *now*. It was on the other side of the globe. It was too far from Mariposa. It was too far from Matthew—She blinked, stunned that she still had him on her mind. No, she told herself, it was the kindness he'd showed her, the understanding . . .

"For me," Jacob said, "I can take it or leave it. Whose cholesterol can handle duck skin anyhow? Tom, we'll put you in the Regent Hotel, you won't believe it."

The wife chimed in, "They fetch you at the airport in a Bentley."

Jacob beamed like a father. "You know, my boy, this will do it for you. The partners meet for review in a couple of months. You can count on something this time around. I mean that."

Tom beamed. "Thank you, sir. Julia, did you hear that?"

She said nothing.

"To Tom and Julia Larsen," Jacob gushed. "To their brilliant future in China!"

"In *China*," Julia shouted, seething, as she threw her coat on the sofa, "to our brilliant future in China!" The baby-sitter got up from her nap on the chaise and blinked. Tom sent her packing with a nice tip. The moment she was out the door, Julia continued. "It was a setup, Tom. The only reason you wanted me there was so you could spring that on me."

"I swear I said Hong Kong before."

She said nothing. She stood rigidly at the sliding glass doors leading to the terrace, looking out on the city. Tom walked up and put his hands on her shoulders. She felt his lips brush her neck; then he was kissing her cheek from behind.

She stopped him. "Don't do this. Don't complicate the issue. This won't lead to anything good."

He took his hands off her.

She moved to the sofa and sat down, taking off her shoes. "So, you're going to live in the Regent Hotel and be driven in Bentleys. And what am I going to do?"

He sat by her. "You're going to be right there in the backseat with me."

"No, I'm not. I'm going to see this through."

"See what through?"

"What happened to Mom and Dad."

He blinked, unsure of what she meant. "It's over."

"No, it's not."

"Julia, people can only die once."

"Nobody's been caught! It's unresolved. I want the guy to pay."

"He will. But it will take time."

"I won't be on the other side of the earth when it does."

"Julia, please."

She had worked herself into a state now. She got up and walked into the bedroom. Tom followed her. "I feel like I'm coming apart at the seams," she said as she started to undress, "and I hear we're going to the Orient, where I get to sit on my ass at tea with the other proper wives—while you *build a bank*? I was in Hong Kong years ago with my family, and I remember the size of buildings there, clear up to heaven, which means a three-year stint easy."

He closed the door. "Honey, it's what I have to do."

"What I have to do is catch the killer. I want to cut his balls off, throw acid in his eyes. I want to laugh at his suffering—that's how angry and how crazy I am and how much hatred I'm filled with!"

Tom's voice was controlled, and he put his arms around her, trying to make her understand. "You *are* crazy talking like that, like you're going to catch this guy yourself." He moved her over to the bed, eased her down to the duvet. "Julia, it's been rough for us since . . . since your surgery . . . and it's rougher now with this. But we'll make it. We have time. We have to make it, for ourselves, for Molly . . ."

She succumbed and let him hold her, caress her. But she kept herself rigid and apprehensive, which was the defense mechanism she'd come to arm herself with over the months when the situation suggested they make love. She needed to keep her guard up, protect herself; she couldn't take more rejection, not now, not when she felt so exposed and defenseless.

But Tom kissed her. His hand moved over her shoulders, down her side, over her hips, and to her thigh. He caressed and he lingered there, kissing her deeply at the same time, moving the skirt of her slip up with his fingers. His lips moved from her mouth to her chin, to her neck, and then down, down—

Julia gasped. She felt her head exploding. It's going to be different this time, she thought, exposing herself more, the defenses falling. Yes! Her hopes rose, soared. This was what she had wanted, this is what she had expected, this was what she had longed for. *He's going to—*

And then it was over. Tom was off the bed, leaning against the dresser, head against his forearm in a kind of shameful pose she knew all too well. "I'm . . . I'm sorry," he said, and walked into the bathroom, closing the door after him.

A moment later, she heard the click that told her he had thought twice and locked it.

She collapsed on the chaise in the living room where the babysitter had been sleeping. It faced the wall of glass, and as she looked out over the sparkling hills of San Francisco some twenty floors below, she felt more miserable than she could ever recall feeling in her life. Face the fact, she told herself. It is never going to be like it was. She was well now, her hair had grown back, she'd suffered and fought and she had made it. She was no different now inside than she had ever been. Better, even. But outside, she was changed, greatly changed. And her husband was a *guy*, and a guy could not deal with that kind of imperfection. He had actually said that. "It's sort of a *guy* thing, Julia." Those exact words, on the day he'd ended their love life. And part of her hated him for it.

But had she been remiss in this marriage as well? Had she been selfish—concentrating exclusively on the disease, obsessed with the chemotherapy, consumed only with *her* problems? But she was unable to answer that because she wasn't herself any longer. Everything had changed forever with the bullets, with the knife. She was someone else now, and she didn't know how to cope with it. Her mother could have helped. And she hated herself for having waited too long to ask her for it.

She got up, checked on Molly, who was clutching Mr. Tiddleberk's left leg in a deep sleep. Funny, Julia thought, bringing her hand down to brush her little girl's hair from her eyes, that was just how she wished she and Tom were sleeping right now.

She went to her office down the hall and sat at her computer and wrote him a letter. She told Tom she was sorry too, but she needed to be where she could be "crazy" without more hurt from his rejection. She wrote that in the morning she was going to fly with Molly to Fresno, that her sister would pick them up. She asked that he drive up from San Francisco and join them on New Year's Eve. A quiet time, as they'd had last year. She told him she loved him and promised she'd be better after two days in the mountains, where she could walk, relax, be with nature, vent her frustration in the snow. She said nothing about Matthew Hinson, even though he was very much on her mind.

She signed it and took it into the bedroom and placed it on the nightstand next to where he was sleeping, and then she returned to the living room and uncapped the Waterford decanter that held the Cragganmore twelve-year-old single malt her mother used to love so much. It was there for guests, and she felt like a guest now, certainly not someone who lived here; the woman who lived here would be snuggled up to her husband in the bedroom. As the whisky slid down her throat, she studied the symmetry of the room—the deep green leather sofa flanked by two matching chairs, all facing the thick, low glass table set on a slate pedestal. It was balanced, planned, perfect in its execution. But why, she wondered, couldn't her life be like that?

She grabbed the afghan from the chaise and curled up around it on the sofa, and was asleep before the ice cubes even began to melt.

At three o'clock in the morning, she dreamed she

was riding on that afghan, sitting on the soft, woolen squares of green and blue, her hair billowing in the wind. She rose through clouds like an airplane shortly after takeoff, and then everything glowed white. Floating above the clouds so effortlessly, it was as if she had wings like an angel.

Then she realized Tom had come in and lifted her in his arms, and was carrying her, half asleep, to bed with him. She heard him whisper that he loved her, that he was sorry, and he hugged her so tightly she felt she would burst, squeezing the demons, the fears, the obsession out of her, till she found herself riding the carpet peacefully again in her dream.

In the morning, when she awoke after he'd already left for the health club, she found *his* note to her, which said only:

> *I understand.*
> *Yes, I'll drive up on New Year's Eve afternoon.*
> *Safe trip. I love you too.*
> *Tom.*

She started packing within minutes.

She first saw Matthew from the dining room. He was outside in the cold, bundled up, standing at the edge of the land past the rear deck, just where the property began to slope down the mountainside. He had a clipboard stuffed under his right armpit, and he was holding a camera, photographing the back of the house. Near him was one of Harry's gardeners, who was removing a gigantic evergreen limb that Julia guessed had snapped from the weight of the snow. A chain saw buzzed through the wet wood, but she could barely hear it through the double-pane glass. She waited until the man set the saw down, and then she waved, but Matt was still intent on photographing a post on the deck and didn't see her.

When he finally looked up, he almost dropped the camera. She could tell he was shocked to see she had returned earlier than expected. Then a smile creased his lips as his surprise turned to delight, and as she waved him to the door, he closed the lens cover and leaped up onto the deck. It was wet—the snow was beginning to melt—and he slid almost all the way to where she stood in the already open door. "Julia, I'm glad you're back."

"Me too," she said, so enthusiastically that she added, "Cornelia really needed me," lest he think she returned just for him.

"Tom with you?"

"No," she simply said, "Molly and I came alone. Tom's got work to do."

"Me too," he said, looking at the clipboard. "Have to recreate this deck for a house I'm finishing. I'm trying to remember exactly how I built it."

"I wondered what you were doing." Then she made

her voice sound as neighborly as possible as she asked, "Care to come in and warm up?"

"Wish I could," he said, begging off, "but I need to get these photos. Another time, though?"

"Maybe I'll take a walk tomorrow morning. Ask Maggie if she wants another brawl in the snow."

Matt beamed. "I know she does." His eyes drilled into hers, stepping over the bounds, making her feel so wanted that she turned red, and thankfully he averted them. "Bring Molly along this time. Got a present for her."

"Really?"

"See you then."

She smiled and nodded, rubbing her arms through her sweater because she was starting to feel damp, chilled. "See you."

Back inside the house, she sat alone at the dining table, drinking an awful herbal tea concoction she had found in one of the kitchen cabinets. Molly came in and asked her to help button her snowsuit. She was determined to make a snowman.

Julia helped her button up, but her mind was on the man she was watching photograph every angle of the deck. She had always found him incredibly attractive. But why now was she allowing the secret, hidden fantasy to have substance, to take on a soul? Why at this time in her life was her tongue hanging out for a man she could have had years ago and walked away from? Why Matthew Hinson *now*?

"Mom, watch me from the window, okay?"

"Don't go past the trees. It's a long way down that incline."

Molly nodded, and Julia opened the door for her. She watched as Matthew met her on the stairs of the deck, and took her hand and helped lead her down to the white-covered yard. Then Julia's sister entered and took her attention away. She was holding a drawer. Julia asked, "What's that from?"

"Mom's vanity. Look, our old report cards. Photos I've not seen in twenty years." Then she glanced out the window. Matt was rolling a ball of snow with Molly. "Him again?"

"Doesn't he remind you of Mel Gibson?"

"You should be so lucky."

"Was he ever married or have a girlfriend that you know of?"

"Why?"

"I mean, a guy as attractive as he is. I didn't get the feeling there was anyone in his life."

Carrie looked up. "How do you know that? When you talked to him after the funeral?"

"I saw him the next morning, when I went walking. Made me cocoa. Great house."

Cornelia watched her sister watch Matthew. "You're just getting all quivery, aren't you?"

"I said he has a nice house, that's all."

Cornelia tossed two outdated insurance policies into the trash can. "I'm being too hard on you. Mom told me she loved his place, actually."

"He and Mom were close."

"Were they?" She looked surprised. "Well, I guess they could have been. I knew she liked him. I don't think Dad was all that nuts about him, but then again, Dad wasn't wild about anyone he ever worked closely with."

"I wouldn't have wanted to work with Dad."

Cornelia pulled out a sealed envelope and looked at it strangely. "Should I open this one?"

"Nothing on the outside?"

Cornelia shook her head and started to tear the envelope open. As she did, Julia looked at Matt through the window again. He and Molly had rolled the bottom part of Mr. Snowman. She saw them laughing together.

"Could be gay," Cornelia said.

Julia looked out at Matt again. He was making Frosty's middle. "He's not."

Cornelia went icy. "I guess you would know."

Julia stared at her. "What's that supposed to mean?"

Cornelia cautioned her. "Just be careful, okay?"

"Carrie, I don't want to sleep with him, but I do think I could be his friend." Julia squeezed the cool tea bag with her fingertips. "He writes poetry."

"And is first chair violin with the symphony. Give me a break."

"Why do you dislike him so?"

"There's something about him," Cornelia said, looking again, "just something about him."

Julia's attention was drawn to the contents of the envelope they'd just opened. She unfolded the two pages. They seemed to be part of something else, a longer letter or perhaps a story, for they started in the middle of a sentence: *and I watched him after Harry had gone to town, watched him take his shirt off as he pored over the blueprints. His muscles rippled in the sunlight. I could nearly taste the drops of sweat on his sweet skin.*

"My God. Talk about purple prose."

Cornelia took it from Julia and read it. "*Mom* wrote that?"

Julia blinked. "Wow."

"I don't think we should be doing this."

"Yes, you do." And Julia read more: *He sat on the grass and spread his legs out. I wanted to go to him to help him off with his boots. I wanted to touch him, feel a real man's flesh again. I wanted to bathe him and caress him, and I wanted him to touch me, to love me, to make me feel like a woman again—*

Julia stopped. But not because she was embarrassed. She stopped because she suddenly had the feeling that she knew who her mother was writing about.

Cornelia took the paper from her and continued the letter, incredulously: *How I long to feel the love of a man again, if perhaps the last time in my life, and if I'm given the chance to choose, I want it to be—*

Julia looked out the window again at Matthew.

—Matthew. My Matty, who has no idea what he does to me, the pleasure he gives me just looking at him, dreaming of what it might be like to feel, at my age, the kind of man I had when I was only twenty. He sipped iced tea at the island, and I wanted to run my hands over his chest. I wanted him to kiss me, to make love to me. I wanted to be Francesca and he my Robert— "Who?" Cornelia asked.

"The Bridges of Madison County," Julia explained. Molly was reaching up, putting pieces of frozen mud into the head of the snowman to form eyes. Matt made a mouth with a couple of sticks. Julia watched them stand back to examine their finished product.

I want only to feel love again, a last wish, a dream I place on my pillow each night. I have a husband and I have my scotch, and I have my daughters, but the love of a man is illusive . . .

"Stop," Julia said.

Cornelia did. She slid the letter back into the envelope and then ripped it to pieces. "I'm sorry I ever opened it. I don't want to know this. It's pathetic."

"It isn't pathetic. She was a woman, Cornelia. We should understand that."

"You may understand that. I guess I'm the only woman in this family who doesn't have hot pants for that creep out there."

Julia's voice was angry now. "Hot pants? Me? I'm

supposed to go out there and try to have an affair?
Me? One-tit Tessie?"

"Julia, I didn't mean—"

"Don't worry, Sis," Julia interjected. "No man wants
me and I know it."

Then Julia saw Matt do the most amazing thing. He
suddenly ran through the deep snow, right to the
middle of the yard, past the wood chips and shattered
pine cones, and tossed himself backward into it. Cornelia gasped, "What in the world—?" They watched
as he spread his legs in the snow, as far as he could,
then brought them back together. Then he did the
same thing with his arms, flailing them to create the
impression of wings floating on white. Then, beaming,
he carefully stood up and stepped back toward the
snowman in the very steps he had originally made.

He brushed the snow from his back, his pants, his
head, his neck, and then he motioned for Molly to do
the same, and she did, taking a child's delight in the
freedom of her creation that was no less enthusiastic
than Matthew's. When she had made her angel, right
beside his, she looked up at the window and Julia
could make out she was calling, "Mommy! Mommy!"

Julia beamed. "It's great, honey!" she called.

But her sister seemed as if she were about to
explode. "I know what happened that day," Cornelia said.

Julia blinked. "What day?"

"Eight years ago. Leucadia. The swimming hole."

"What?"

"I saw it," Cornelia admitted. "I saw you with him. I never told you. That's why I hate him. That's why I pushed Tom to give you a ring when I knew Matt was in Europe. That man might have ruined everything you wanted with Tom."

Julia was stunned. "Why didn't you ever tell me?"

"Because it would only have fueled the fire."

Julia looked out at the snow angels on the lawn.

"See what I mean?" Cornelia said, and hurried from the room.

That night the demons came.

Julia again felt alone, anxious, nervous. Her mother's private thoughts had been disquieting; her sister's revelation that she'd been spying on them the day Matthew rescued her had really upset her. She had fought her desire for Matthew for eight years, since the day she'd met him—but with the kind of honesty that comes with the night, she was losing that battle. Molly had gone to sleep, then her sister, and TV newspeople just didn't offer much in the way of conversation—and made her think of the career she'd screwed up because of her cancer. She could no longer concentrate on the book she was trying to read, so she picked up the phone to call Tom, but instead dialed Matthew. But when she got his answering machine message, which suggested the caller try his office number, she hung up.

She got out of bed, popped bubble gum into her mouth, and walked to the window. She pulled the drapes open and looked out at the tall trees guarding the house. She could see the moon was so bright that the pines looked almost green instead of their normal midnight coal color. But for some reason, tonight the trees frightened her, as if they had eyes and were watching her. The gum tasted bitter, and she spit it into Kleenex and tossed it in the trash. She remembered Molly's voice warning that the Singapore police were coming, and she smiled. If only they could go back to the car, drive up here all over again, rewrite history, change time. If only.

She went into the hall and walked to one of the guest rooms that faced the back of the house. She looked out the French windows onto the yard. Without the protection of the trees, the moon was even brighter here. She found herself staring at the image of the angel Matt had made in the snow. It seemed to sparkle, to glow in the moonlight on the yard, almost to come alive. She heard trumpets sound, and Vivaldi filled her head. She felt the archangel she'd written about in *Epiphany* connect with her, and she was on that magic carpet again, her spirits lifting, soaring. It took away some of the pain.

But not all, and not for long. For she then went downstairs and retrieved the pieces of her mother's private letter from the kitchen trash can. She didn't know what she was going to do with them; she just

wanted to keep them. She wandered over to the
Christmas tree and removed the ornament Matt had
asked for. She found a box from a gift that was the
right size, placed it in it, nesting it with tissue paper.
She then took the gift up to her room and set it on the
dresser.

She found herself looking in the mirror. She confronted her image, locked her eyes on those peering
back at her. She took up the challenge. She was Tom
now; the face—the body—in the mirror was her. She
would see what he saw. She had avoided this
throughout the ordeal. Oh, she'd glimpsed, she'd ven-
tured a peek from all angles, but she never faced it—
herself—full on. Part of the reason was this was how
she'd discovered it nine months ago, that ugly, hard,
foreign lump, by standing in the mirror. Eyes never
moving from her image, she unbuttoned her blouse
and dropped it to the floor, unfastened the prosthetic
brassiere, and looked at herself the way Tom saw her.
One side the voluptuous woman who wore low-cut
dresses on the nightly newscast, the other side the flat-
chested essence of a ten-year-old, no, seven, a chest
like her daughter's! But not quite, for Molly had
nipples . . .

Then she felt her blood stop moving, and a great
ache began to rise up from somewhere deep inside,
and her hand trembled as she brought it up to where
her right breast had been. Touching the scar was too
much for her; she averted her eyes to keep from

crying. But she could feel it, the hard, thin line bisecting the center, where the nipple should be, had been—

God, those doctors! She could hear them now. *We can give you a reconstructed breast that will last a life-time, guaranteed. Silicone? Naw, saline. No problem. No-sag, either. 'Course, it will take several operations, over time. Nipples or not? Just what I said, you want nipples or without? We transplant part of your labia. Or we can do some tissue build-up in the spot where the nipples would normally be, but we tattoo for darker pigmentation. . . .*

She couldn't bear to think about it any longer. She moved from the mirror and stood in the window again for the longest time, in her nightgown, just standing there, feeling the shadowy moonlight on her face. But she did not look out.

It was a mistake.

For had she peered out the window again, she'd have seen the outline of a man nestled in the limbs of the tree nearest her bedroom window. A man who had not answered his phone because he was here. Watching her. Studying her. Adoring her.

She fell asleep with the drapes open, the ripped pieces of Martha's lustful fantasy clenched in her fist, and slept a deep, restless sleep, and dreamed twisted, anguished thoughts of her mother fighting her for Matthew's affection.

* * *

Matthew made his way silently down the trunk, then across the yard.

What amazed him was not what he'd seen in the mirror, for he knew she had lost a breast to cancer nine months ago, but her reaction to herself. He felt panic and fear for her, his heart heavy, for he knew the anguish she was going through. He had to help her. He had to do something. She didn't deserve to be this unhappy. He never wanted to see a look like that on her face again.

He crept down the slope behind the house.

He knew his way.

He had, of course, done this before.

6

"**H**ow much farther?" Julia asked Matt the following morning. They were keeping pace about three feet behind Maggie, who was leading them up a path to the top of a mountain, where Matt promised Molly she could see clear to China. Julia told him China wasn't a good word in her vocabulary right now, so he augmented it to Cowchilla. Molly, holding her mother's hand as they climbed, thought that was a funny name.

Julia asked, "Whose land are we trespassing on?"

"Mine," he said. "Bought it last year. Gonna subdivide and put twenty-two houses here someday."

"And a funicular railway for those with heart trouble?"

They rested against some rocks. While Molly played with the dog, Julia had the sudden urge to blurt out everything to Matthew—everything she had wanted to tell her mother. She wanted to tell him the truth. But her mind asked, *Why him?* Why a man? This was something you spoke only to a woman about. Why not her sister? Well, she knew the answer to that; she and Cornelia had never been that close. Cornelia's attitude about everything was "It'll be okay." But she couldn't help but wonder how much Matt knew. It was no secret she'd lost a breast, but could he sense the emptiness it had brought her? He seemed sensitive enough to perceive that. If he had been close to mom, maybe he— But she was unsure. Better if it was left unsaid. Talk about something else. "When did you move up here?"

"Twelve years ago."

"Why?"

"Why not?"

"You're not a big city boy?"

"I'm no redneck, but I'm not the kind who can pay monthly maintenance and serve on the condo board either. I think that's why people voted for me up here, they know I'm one of them."

"I think they trust you," Julia said.

He just smiled.

She saw a touch of shyness that she found nothing less than charming.

He stood up. "Molly, ready for another hike?"

"If we can make angels again."

"On the way down. Promise." He started climbing again. Julia followed. He said, "I always wanted to live in California."

"Why?"

" 'Cause the gold rush is still on, despite the hell and high water we've been through in the last years. California can still give you everything you want in life."

"It can also," she said softly, "take everything away."

Ten minutes later and half a mile higher he said, "We're here."

She laughed, taking a deep breath of the thin, cool air, and then she let him help her to a tree stump to sit on. She looked around. She could see forever. Mountain peaks and valley vistas and rolling hills. "My God, this is spectacular."

"Molly," Matt said, putting his hand on the girl's shoulder, "that's Yosemite Park over there, and down there's Whiskey Flats, and if you follow that stream at the bottom of the gorge, you get to a swimming hole called Leucadia—" His voice went dead.

Julia felt emotion surge through her. She could not look at him.

"And over that way," he continued, "is the old Diltz Mine. This area came to be settled during the gold rush . . ."

Julia watched him with her daughter as he stood on a promontory, the wind billowing his open jacket like a parachute behind him. She wanted to thank him for being here, because now, with him, she was finally starting to feel relaxed again. Maggie, who'd taken a rest along the way, finally came up the trail with her tongue hanging out of the side of her mouth. She licked Julia's cheek and then sat down, panting. Julia moved her hand over Maggie's strong back, and felt the doldrums retreating even further. It was a clear, sunny, brilliant morning. Molly began to throw sticks for Maggie to fetch. "My kid is going to force your dog to die from exhaustion."

Matt smiled. "Maggie's got an extra battery pack."

"We're going to put the house on the market."

"Does that bother Tom? That house was the big feather in his career cap."

"He's gone on to bigger things," she said snidely.

"Do I get the feeling you don't want to talk about your husband?"

"We had a rough few days in San Francisco." She looked nervous suddenly, and spoke again before Matt could say a word. "I keep thinking if he hadn't designed that damned house, it wouldn't have happened."

"*I* built it. You blame me too?"

"No!"

"Then that's ridiculous."

"I suppose it is. I'm taking my anger out on—" She stopped herself. She didn't want to, but she did. For to tell the story of her problems with Tom would be opening a window onto her soul, too private for a virtual stranger. But who *could* she talk to? That's what was driving her crazy. Who did she know who was a good listener? Her friends in San Francisco? There were many, but none close enough to truly understand—after all, none of them had been disfigured. A therapy group? She'd tried it for one meeting. It was gruesome, depressing—women attacking her for being so young and attractive and famous, as if she didn't have a right to feel the same loss of sex appeal that they did. Her husband couldn't sleep with her, one woman tossed back at her in a bitter voice, but that was nothing compared to a husband who just walked out and left her. She told Julia to be thankful Tom was still around. Another woman accused her of being smug because she'd lost only one breast, telling her she had nothing to bitch about until she lost the other one as well. One girl screaming because her nipples didn't match. Julia fled. And kept running to . . . here? Matthew was here, and it was so effortless speaking to him, so easy. He seemed not to be judgmental. She knew her mother had felt that about him. God, how she wanted to open up to him—

"Julia? Can I ask you something?"

"Yes."

He was balling up a snowball in his hand. Molly saw him and squealed and started running. He got her in the butt as Maggie barked up a storm, chasing the snowball herself. "Does he love you?"

Julia was blank, startled by the question.

"I ask because we built the house together, and you

know we never got along. But all that time I never heard him, well, talk about you as if he really—"

"Tom loves me," she stated emphatically.

"Sure," Matthew said, without a trace of sarcasm.

"He does," she said in defense, as if his words had carried a message of disbelief. "And I him. Very much."

Perhaps, she thought later, as they were making their way down the hill, she wasn't affirming her love for Tom in that statement as much as curtailing any affection Matt might still be feeling for her. Her memories of his flesh against hers that day at Leucadia frightened her, and in fear she was now making it *clear*, letting him know, in a very subtle way, that if he still harbored feelings for her, there was no chance. She loved her *husband*. She would be Matt's *friend*. That was all she could allow herself to be.

Even though something in a dark place in her soul wanted it to be more.

He was thinking about the same statement as he walked in front of her, carrying Molly on his shoulders, piggyback style. But he took it to mean something very different. Tom loved her. That would not do. Only one man could love her, only one man deserved her: him. As far as saying she loved Tom, Matt knew that wasn't true. He'd known that all along, even as he knelt in anguish in that big church and watched her, in her beaded white, angelic gown, vow to be with Tom forever. Matt knew better. No, he wasn't so loony as to think she had loved him then, that would be demented; she had hardly known him. But he knew the animal attraction she felt, the spiritual pull they shared. She *would grow* to love him, he was sure of that. The way the little girl bouncing on his shoulders was starting to do.

He glanced back at Julia ten paces behind him.

She smiled at them warmly.

Wasn't it starting to happen already?

Gary Estep moved the phone receiver from his ear and pressed it against his chest. "Detective Crowley?"

Jim turned from his position leaning over a file cabinet. He was digging through the Sheriff's Department's files, scanning the histories of men with records in the Mariposa County area. "Yeah?"

"Mr. Crowley, there's a woman named Inga Wilson on the phone. Mighty nice lady. She's found something I think you should hear about."

Jim took the phone. "Crowley."

"Yes, well," the voice said, "I can't be sure that what I found has anything to do with the 'Snowshoe Killer,' but—"

"Lady," Jim said, stopping her, "you let me be the judge of that."

"I was chasing an owl," she said. "Broken wing, poor thing, couldn't fly. I tracked her for nearly a mile along the slope from our place. When she rested in a tree, I was able to lure her down with food, and that's when I saw it."

"What?" Jim muttered.

"The blade of a knife, sir. A hunting knife that someone had discarded."

When they neared the bottom of the slope, Matt pointed out an endless meadow frosted with crisp white snow. Like the area back of the Radcliffe house, it had been untouched except for a few dainty and distinct deer tracks. "It's enchanting," Julia said as the early afternoon sun cast a silver glow over the field.

Molly had a devilish look in her eyes when he set her down. "Here?" she asked.

"Looks like heaven to me," Matt said.

Molly squealed and ran into the meadow, flopping on her back, and started forming an angel.

"Come on!" Matt shouted, grabbing Julia's hand, pulling her with him as he ran out into the field, through the snow, kicking his heels high.

Maggie barked and chased them, and Matt let out a cry of abandon. Julia shouted with delight as she tumbled into the snow, pulling him down with her. When she got to her feet, she made the biggest snowball her hands could pack, and hit him squarely on the chest. It exploded into his face. Molly howled and tossed snow at her mom. But as Julia bent to make another, Matt scooped a mound of snow in both hands and tossed it at her, like throwing sand at the beach. She in turn grabbed a handful and ran right up to him and plopped it on his head. He howled with laughter, and then did the same to her. They looked like two kids who'd suddenly broken free of their parents after being cooped up all winter, doing everything they weren't supposed to do, running, falling, getting wet, rubbing each other's faces in it. Maggie barked again and again, rolling over next to them, and finally came to rest on all fours as she watched what had been Matt's objective in the first place; together, Matt and Julia made snow angels.

They took their time. It was nearly dark now. The moon was already casting a bluish tint where just a moment ago it had been brilliant ocher from the setting sun. Molly watched as Julia backed into the snow they'd not disturbed, and then Julia silently, as if in slow motion, allowed herself to roll backward, easing down into a reclining position, looking up into the heavens as she felt the ice in her hair grinding down into the collar of her jacket, down her back, but she didn't care. She moved her arms as if swimming, creating the soft wings, her legs making the angel's flowing skirt, as Matt watched with dreamy eyes.

He joined her a moment later, at her side, so his angel's wing touched hers—their fingers met for a moment—and then they just lay there, both of them, looking straight up into the darkening sky. "I don't know when I've felt so peaceful," Julia finally said.

"I can hear Vivaldi right now," Matt said.

"I was thinking about Vivaldi last night," she said.

And Matt really thought for a moment he could hear music. "I feel so good with you."

"I think you're keeping me breathing."

He couldn't believe he was hearing those words from her. They were what he'd lived for. They're what he'd done all of this for. He sat up. He looked down at his angel, lying so close to him. This was the bond he'd been waiting for. He could see the trust building.

"I'm cold, Mommy."

Julia put an arm around Molly, but before she could say anything, Matthew made them an offer: "Cocoa?"

At that moment, about a half mile from Matthew's cabin, Jim Crowley stood with Gary Estep and three other deputies, and Inga Wilson and her husband, Paul. They were staring at the blade of a hunting knife that Jim had just placed in a plastic evidence bag. Mrs. Wilson had been savvy enough not to handle it with her bare hands; she'd instead picked it up with her thick leather bird gloves, holding it where the handle should have been attached.

"Why's the handle missing?" Paul Wilson asked the investigator. "Doesn't look like it rotted off. No rust."

"Somebody," Jim Crowley said, "took it off." Then he looked up at the road. "Gary, boys, search the mountainside. Get some lights. If he tossed this, he tossed the rest of it."

"Yes, sir," the deputy said.

Jim patted Inga Wilson on the shoulder. "Good work," he said. "Now, let me ask you, see anybody in this area?"

Judging from the expression on her face, Inga didn't understand exactly what he meant. Her husband said, "You mean someone suspicious?"

Jim shook his head. "Anybody. Anytime."

Paul said, "Matt Hinson walks his dog on the road above."

"I know him," Crowley explained. "Anybody else?"

"Matt's the only guy living on that stretch of Sherlock," Paul said. "You should ask him who he's seen."

"Will do," Crowley said.

But Inga could see Jim's wheels turning. "Matt walks Maggie there, we see him all the time," she said, adding an unsolicited character reference in defense of her neighbor, "and Matt's the gentlest soul I know."

"Don't say," Jim just muttered.

"We can't stay long," Julia protested, once inside Matthew's house, as much to Molly as to Matthew. "Aunt Cornelia will worry if—"

He pointed at the phone.

She relented, picked up the receiver, and called her sister. He could tell from her side of the conversation that Cornelia wasn't exactly thrilled about Julia's being there. But he heard her assure her sister that he'd drive her home safely, that there was nothing to worry about. Julia hung up without saying good-bye.

Molly was taken with the house, and the books, and in minutes she found herself staring at the cover of a book that Matthew had strategically placed out on the table for her to find. Her eyes went wide. "Mr. Tiddleberk!" she gasped, and lifted the book to her arms. She looked up at Julia and Matthew.

Julia didn't understand. "What is it?"

Matthew said, "Told you I had a present for Molly."

Molly held the book up to her mother, and together they looked at it. Matthew had taken the pains to create a book about Mr. Tiddleberk, the tattered bear, drawing on each page of a scrapbook, hand-lettering the story underneath, of a little bear who is lost in a snowstorm, separated from his friend Molly—"Mom, look, I'm in it"—only to be reunited by the guidance of the little bear's guardian angel bear.

Molly was entranced, and Julia touched.

And as Molly buried her face in the beautifully illustrated book created especially for her, Julia asked Matthew if she could read some more poetry, and he offered the box he had prevented her from looking into the first time she was there. As he reached for the box, she saw he'd placed the ornament she'd given him before their hike near the angel water globe on the bookshelf. She smiled.

Then she opened the box and withdrew several sheets of paper on which he had hand-written his poems. As she started to read one, standing near him in the kitchen area, he poured the milk into a pan, but realized he was out of cocoa. He opened the door that led to a pantry/laundry room, not realizing she was watching as he pushed aside detergent bottles and his stash of Kraft macaroni and cheese to get to the new tin of Hershey's cocoa. As he turned to step back into the kitchen, he saw Julia recoil.

"What is it?" he asked, alarmed. He could see her hand was suddenly trembling holding the page.

"That," she said. She was looking up, over his shoulder, into the laundry room.

He turned around. And he now saw what she was referring to. "The rifle?" He turned back to her. "Oh," he said, "I understand." He knew it was the fact that her father had been shot so many times. "I'm sorry you had to see that."

"*I'm* sorry," she said as he moved back into the kitchen with her. "You didn't do anything wrong. I'm the one with the fear of guns, and after what happened—"

"I understand, Julia." He closed the door to the laundry room. "But it's a hunting rifle."

There was only one possibly worse thing he could have said at that moment, and that would have been *I blew your parents away with that.* Which, of course, he hadn't. But the admission that he was a hunter was almost as devastating. He saw it turned her blood cold. He could read it on her face. He had to think fast.

He was losing her. In this second, this moment in time, all his hard work was going down the drain, all that he'd accomplished was being ruined because he had a goddamned gun on the wall and he was so stupid as to tell her he was a fucking hunter!

"Mr. Crowley, it's for you," Inga Wilson told Jim as he was just starting to sip the coffee she'd made. He had gone back to the Wilson house to ask questions about the area, the people who lived up there, about their suspicions and impressions of the Radcliffes and whoever might have done them in.

Jim took the phone. "Crowley." He listened for a minute, then put the receiver down, without even saying good-bye. Inga and Paul looked at him, studying his alarm. "Infrared pinpointed digging," Jim said.

Paul said, "Pardon me?"

"Took aerial shots all around. Infrared shows recent digging. Straight line from the knife blade. Across the road."

"Same slope?" Inga asked.

Jim nodded, but this time his eyebrows arched as he said, "Directly up, the sheriff says, from the Hinson place."

"I don't mean to say *I'm* a hunter," Matt continued, sweating. "I mean it's *for* hunting, it's a hunting rifle, but I don't use it for that. I don't use it for anything but target practice sometimes. Basically, it just hangs there." She still had a pale, stunned look on her face. He had to think of something more to bring her around. *Her family, bring it back to her parents, push that button in times of panic.* "Harry talked me into buying it when I first started working for him. He said everyone should have a gun in the house in a rural place like this."

"Daddy hated guns—"

He felt himself dying. *Dying.*

"—but he did believe that."

He breathed easily again.

She swallowed. "I know I overreact. I'm very much for gun control. Some of the stories we did on the news . . . because of guns." She shook her head in dismay. "And hunting is barbaric."

"I can't agree more," he said, trying to lessen the impact. "My father was a hunter. And I hate it too." Right on cue, **Maggie** came up to nose around the counter, to see what was cooking. He hugged her. "I adore animals, I'd never take an animal's life."

Molly suddenly shouted, "Mommy, come read my book with me."

Julia closed her eyes and bent down and petted Maggie as well. "I'm sorry I'm so obsessive about this. But I'm obsessive **about** anything I'm committed to."

Will you become obsessive about me? He smiled. "Now, go read to your daughter and let me make you cocoa, okay?"

"Can I have marshmallows in mine?" Molly asked.

"A handful," Matt promised.

Julia walked into the living room and sat on the sofa, wrapping herself in the Indian blanket because there was a chill in the air. She began to read "The Adventure of Tiddleberk Bear" to Molly in as many animated voices as she could muster.

As the milk heated and Maggie slopped up a can of Mighty Dog in the corner of the kitchen, Matt started a fire in the wood stove. When he finally brought Julia and her daughter the chocolate, he sat next to Julia on the sofa. Molly grinned at the sea of miniature marshmallows he had set on top. "Careful," he warned her, "it was boiling. I wasn't paying attention."

Molly stuck her fingers in the marshmallows and started to lick the melted sugar off. Julia sipped apprehensively. "It's hot, all right. Ummm." She looked curious suddenly. "What do I taste? It's not cinnamon, like last time—"

"Vanilla extract." He saw she was amazed. "Your mother's secret."

Julia melted. "She taught you to cook too?"

"Yes. One of the fringe benefits of working with your father."

"Did she tell you she was disappointed that I never had any interest in things culinary? And that I'm lousy at it?"

"She was very proud of your success." Then he turned to the bookshelf and pulled down a volume.

"That reminds me—" He handed her a book. It was a new copy of *Ask Your Angels*. "Now you have your own."

"Thanks." She took a moment while he and Molly sipped their cocoa to read another poem. "Matt, you really should be published."

"I don't write for that reason." He stood up to stoke the fire. "Ever since I was little, I have found myself wondering about the depth with which people feel. About things that I can't feel. So I write poems that push feelings over the edge—texture and images vibrant and alive—hoping it might take hold in me." He looked at her. "I'm not making myself clear, am I?"

"But your words are so—how to put it?—on the edge of raw. They really make *me* feel something."

"It's not my words, it's your capacity. Feeling that passionately is a gift, Julia. Don't ever take it for granted." He saw her looking at him with a mixture of curiosity and incomprehension on her face, and he knew he was reaching into dangerous territory. He wanted to talk of that void in him that prompted him to mimic other writers, but that would require facing things he could never face.

"I think it's just a lack of self-assurance," Julia said. "If you believed in yourself more, you'd trust how good your poetry is, and you'd admit you feel as deeply as—"

"Enough, okay?"

"I'm sorry." She set the mug down. "It's the twelve-step programmer in me, the psychobabbler. I'm always trying to play therapist and enabler. God, who am I to talk?" She kicked off the blanket and stood up.

Molly looked at her. "Do we have to go?"

"We've overstayed my welcome." She picked up the book he'd given her and put it into her bag. "How about that lift home now?"

He nodded, but he could tell she didn't really want to go.

Jim Crowley stood in the entrance to the abandoned mine and looked around. He guided his flashlight beam over the walls and then entered. The sheriff and two deputies followed him inside. Lanterns eerily illuminated the damp place. "Smell fire," Jim said. His nostrils twinged.

He aimed his light on what seemed to be a mound of dirt in the center of the cave, but when examined in the light he could see the mound had once been aflame. He crouched down and realized it was actually a half-melted plastic bag, the contents of which were scorched and burned, but not completely. He poked at it with a stick and lifted the crotch and partial legs of a pair of pants. His trained eyes told him the dark, crusty blotches on the material were bloodstains. He found a bedroom slipper that, he was sure, matched the chewed one that had turned up in the road. He poked a little more and saw something stick-like, something that looked like rattan under the musty clothing, something that looked like—yes, certainly!—snowshoes. "My, oh, my," he said softly.

"Thanks for driving us," Julia said as Matt piloted his station wagon down Sherlock Road.

"Mommy, can we play a tape?" Molly asked from the backseat, still clutching her book.

Matt smiled at Julia. "She's got the book, now she wants the soundtrack too." Then he turned, calling over his shoulder to Molly, "Sorry, can't do. Tape deck is gone."

Julia saw a gaping hole where the radio was supposed to be. "What happened to it?"

"Somebody busted my window and yanked it out a few weeks back. I'd sing, but—"

Molly said, "Do you know any songs from *Beauty and the Beast*?"

"No, but I do know this one." Then he swallowed hard and went for it. "*Oh, the wayward wind, is a restless wind. A restless wind, that yearns to wander ...*" He stopped himself and let out a hoot. "Gogi Grant and Patsy Cline did it better."

"Imelda Marcos did it better."

"You sound funny," Molly said.

"Molly!"

Matt laughed. "It's okay. Hey, it's true." He glanced over his shoulder. "Molly, in the back somewhere there is a bag of tapes. You can have whatever you want." She climbed over the rear seat and started to look for it.

He turned right onto Whitlock Road. Softly he said, "Julia, could we . . . maybe have dinner tonight?"

She did not say anything.

"I'm sorry. Was that too presumptuous?"

She turned to face him in the seat. "Matt, I don't think—"

He glanced at her as he managed a curve in the road. "What? That it would be appropriate? Julia, you want to talk to me, I feel it."

She put her head back against the restraint. "No. Yes. I mean—"

He pulled over to the side of the road. "Don't go home."

"But, Molly—"

Matt turned to see the girl holding two cassettes. "I can really have them?"

"Sure," Matthew said.

"Mommy, can we listen to them tonight?"

"Yes, Molly. Matt, I have to take her home."

"Your sister can baby-sit. Molly won't mind."

"I won't mind," the voice piped up from behind them.

Then Julia looked Matthew in the eye. "You know what a mess I am, don't you?"

He nodded. "Martha talked to me about it."

She took a deep breath, then her voice sounded desperate. "I would like to have dinner together. I think I need to be with someone."

"Hey, hey," he said, taking her trembling hand, "I understand. I'm your friend. I'm here to listen."

A helpless smile found its way to her face.

He grinned and reached for the shift, but suddenly, seemingly from out of nowhere, a yellow fire engine roared up next to them and stopped. Matt quickly opened his door and got out. A man called to him, shouting over the roar of the huge vehicle. Molly grabbed Julia's shoulder. "What's happening, Mom?"

"I think there may be a fire."

"Can we see it?"

"I don't know." Julia could not make out their words, only the urgency of the gesticulating figure beckoning Matthew to join them.

Matt put his head back in the car. "There's a barn fire at Agua Frea, trees caught too—amazing with all this snow. Houses are threatened. I'm on the volunteer department." He looked into her eyes. "But I don't want to leave you."

"You have to go," she said.

"But—"

Julia had an idea. "Listen. I'll take Molly home, then get some food in town and have dinner ready at your place when you get there."

"I wanna go too," Molly whined.

"Shush."

The horn on the huge fire truck blasted three times. Matt turned and put his hand up, indicating he was coming. He pointed over the steering wheel at the keys in the ignition. "The house key is that big one. Oven's a little erratic, lights with a match. I'll be there soon as I can. Molly, enjoy the tapes, okay?"

"Thank you for my present!"

Julia got out her side of the car, and he met her in front of it, and took her hand for a moment. Their eyes met and connected again, and then he hopped onto the fire truck and Julia watched it disappear over the hill.

She slid behind the wheel and fastened her lap belt. Then she put it in gear and headed toward the house to drop Molly off, already trying to plan the menu in her head, trying to think what she would tell her sister that would not elicit a lecture, trying to anticipate what Tom would say, trying to convince herself this was a good idea. But she felt completely and totally powerless, determined not to be alone again for at least one evening.

Gary Estep rushed into the cave with a piece of wood in a clear evidence pouch. "Sir, we found it."

Jim got up from his crouching position, his face glowing. "The handle?"

Gary nodded. "It was about fifty feet up the road, down the hill from the blade. Interesting thing is, smell it, sir."

"Smell?" Jim said.

"Open the bag and smell it."

Jim Crowley did. "Tuscany," he said, recognizing the scent. His wife gave it to him every Christmas. He was wearing it this very moment. And he looked perplexed.

Julia stood admiring the bottle of aftershave lotion on Matt's dresser. Tuscany. She'd seen it in ads for years. The liquid looked just a little darker than the wine in the glass she was holding. She took a sip and set it down. She uncapped the Tuscany bottle. She put some on her wrist. It was familiar. It smelled like Matthew. Or was it Tom?

The phone rang and she dove for it, jumping onto the bed on her knees. "Hello?"

"Julia?" It was her sister. She'd hoped it was Matthew. "You still there?"

"Carrie, I told you I'm staying for dinner."

"You'll be there for breakfast if it gets any later."

"He's not home yet."

"Mom's neighbor, Helen Campbell, called. Said the fire could go all night."

"So? How's Molly?"

"Talked about her 'Uncle Matt' all evening."

"Cornelia—"

"She's out like a light now. Fell asleep listening to her new tapes on her Walkman. Julia, do you think this is right?"

"What?"

"Leave him a note. I'll come get you. I don't think it's healthy for you to be there."

Julia took another sip of the wine. "Jealous?"

"Julia, you don't sound good."

"Maybe you want him too."

"You're talking nonsense."

"If you're asking am I drunk, no, but on the way."

"Julia!"

"I'm going to hang up because you're starting to sound like Mom."

"And you're drinking like her!"

"Cornelia, don't be such a tight ass. I'm hanging up now."

And she did.

"Forrest Campbell?"

"Howdy. Helen, we got a visitor."

"Jim Crowley, investigator for—"

"Yup, we know. Everybody in these parts knows who you are."

"May I—?"

"Come right in."

"Afraid you'd be off fighting that fire."

"I'm eighty-three, for Christ's sake. Nobody ast me to fight a fire in thirty years."

"Good, 'cause I'd like to pick your brain."

"Nobody ast to do that in thirty years either. So, what do ya need to know about ol' Guv Harry?"

"Actually, I'd like to ask what you know about Matthew Hinson."

As the pickup that drove him home pulled away, Matthew saw the figure of a woman in his driveway, and he first assumed, because it was dark, that it was Julia coming out to greet him. But as she neared him, he saw it wasn't Julia at all, it was Cornelia. He realized her car was parked in the driveway behind his. Inside, just barely visible in the moonlight, was Molly—apparently she'd been ordered to remain there. Cornelia hurried to Matthew.

Alarm shot through him like the fire he'd just fought. "What's going on?" Panic choked his throat like smoke.

"She's inside, locked in, passed out, I think."

"What?"

"I think she had too much to drink. She's been very . . . unstable. She's been through a lot."

"I know. I want to help her."

"She doesn't need your help."

Matthew thought for a moment. The words turned his stomach, this woman trying to protect her sister from him as if he were some kind of monster. He could not bear the idea of Julia in pain, but he had no place for the sister, not here, not tonight. This was an opportunity handed to him from God, and he was not going to have it ruined by Cornelia. "I can handle it. I'll make sure she's okay. Trust me."

Cornelia's alarm was as steely as his resolve. "I'm not leaving."

"You are if you want her to open the door. She obviously doesn't want your help. Give me a chance. I'll call you."

"No!"

He glared at her. He gave her a look that had no soul. And he could see that suddenly, shockingly, she was frightened. He had gone too far, shoved her nearly to the edge. So he softened and put his hand on her shoulder. She winced, but he did not pull away—he rested it there to show her how strong and determined he was. He needed to pull her back in. "I'd never do anything to hurt Julia," he said measuredly, "and I know I can help her tonight. She shared a lot with me today. She's in great pain. I'll help her. I promise you. Take Molly home and trust that it'll be all right."

Cornelia looked at him for the longest time—did he still see a fragment of fear in her eyes?—and then choked up, turned, and ran to her car. He heard it start as he was looking in the kitchen window, trying to see where Julia was. He saw a pot with only about an inch of water left simmering on the stove, waiting for the pasta. The counter was heaped with wilted salad greens and shriveling mushrooms. Place mats and plates and silver were ready on the table, and a candle had burned all the way down, the cold wax now molded around a fork. A wine bottle stood empty in a bowl of what had been ice.

He went around the house to the living room window, but she was not in there either. Neither was Maggie. He thought it odd. Then he went to the bedroom window and had to stand on his wheelbarrow to see inside, but when he did he saw both of them, Julia lying on the bed, on the side where he slept, one hand still clutching the wineglass on the bedstand, the other over Maggie, who was protectively lying next to her.

Not wanting to startle her, Matt went to the back door, lifted the loose shingle, and withdrew the spare key. Once inside, he turned off the burner under the nearly empty pot and the oven—he could smell scorched bread—and hurried into the bedroom. Maggie put her head up, and Matt soothingly whispered, "That's okay, girl, you're doing just fine, taking care of her . . ."

He sat next to Julia, pried her hand from the glass, and pulled her up and against him, into his arms. She was rubbery. He knew she had drunk way too much. He carried her into the kitchen and sat her down at the table. He slapped her face lightly to awaken her. He splashed her with cool water. She blinked, jumped, and then started to fade again. He grabbed her before she toppled over, and shouted her name. She reacted.

Then he saw that she'd made coffee, but from the looks of it it had been sitting on the burner for hours.

Good, he thought, the stronger, the more bitter, the better. He poured her a mug. He started forcing it down her. He saw that he'd gotten soot and ashes on her clean clothes, but he didn't care. All he cared about now was getting her sober, keep her from passing out.

And he could feel nothing but hatred for the man who had made this happen to her. He hated Tom Larsen more than he'd ever hated Harry Radcliffe. No one had the right to do this to a woman so vulnerable. No one.

"Tom, she's not here."

"Not there?"

"She's with him."

"Who?"

"Matt."

"Hinson?"

"He says he's going to help her."

"Help her what?"

"I don't know. With her problems. Tom, can't you come?"

"Not till tomorrow."

"Tom, please!"

"Cornelia, it's nothing. I don't like the guy, but it's not like he's going to try to rape her or something."

"How do you know?"

Silence. Then: "She'll be fine. I'll be there tomorrow."

"Why do I feel that'll be too late?"

* * *

"What time is it?" Julia asked, her eyes flickering to see soft light coming from the wood-burning stove.

"Almost two in the morning," Matt whispered from behind her.

She realized that she was lying in his arms on the sofa. She was wearing a fluffy white bathrobe. He was as well. "My God . . . I don't remember anything."

"I came home, found you nearly passed out. I poured a whole pot of coffee into you, walked you around a bit, even took you outside for some air—you vomited—"

"Oh, no."

"—washed you up, you had soot all over—"

"Soot?"

"From the fire, from me. I took a shower while you slept it off. I came in here and joined you, held you hoping God would give you good thoughts and encouragement, praying when you woke up you'd talk to me because I know that you need someone to talk to."

"I burned the meal."

"Not really, but the bread is a giant crouton. The pasta and salad went back into the fridge."

"I never want to see wine again as long as I live. My head." She sat up and pulled away from him.

"You polished off a whole bottle." He straightened his robe and shook his arm in front of him. "It fell asleep."

"I'm sorry," she said softly. "I'm ashamed of myself."

"Tell me why," he said, forcing her to look at him, not letting her turn away. "We're going to do some serious confronting here, got me? Yes, I *know*. I know everything. There's nothing to be ashamed of. I know and it makes me care about you more."

"But you don't know. You only know what Mom told you."

"Then tell me your side. That's all I care about."

She hesitated, then brought her legs up under her to one side, pulled the robe pieces together over her chest.

Matt said, "Your mom always sat like that, with her legs under her."

"All women who lose a breast automatically do it for balance."

He was shocked at her answer.

She laughed out loud. "I'm sorry, but black humor seemed appropriate."

"Julia, come on. What's so painful?"

"Mom and I were very much alike. That's what this is all about." She took a deep breath. "As I grew up, I worshiped my mother. She was everything I wanted to be—talented, creative, smart, successful. And yet everything I feared—alcoholic and dependent. But I loved her."

"And hated her?"

"A little. I wanted to be her, and I wanted not even

to be related to her. I was so proud to be her daughter to people who didn't know the truth, people who saw her on TV or read her books. But at home I was ashamed because she was this Pat Nixon who lived in the shadow of her husband, and drank like Princess Grace, and whenever I saw myself in her I prayed that God not let me be like her."

"Just because you got a little loaded tonight doesn't mean you're an alcoholic like she was."

"No. That's not what I'm afraid of. It's that I can't get my life together the way she did after her surgery."

"What do you mean?"

She took another deep breath. It was now or never. This was someone to talk to who cared. That it was a man shocked and gave her pause, but she knew this might be the only chance she'd get. So she went for it. "My father . . . he stopped sleeping with her after her mastectomy. It was many years ago, one of the first breast-cancer operations we had ever heard of. Back then it was hardly talked about—Betty Ford was just about to lift the veil on the subject. But Mom could never even really admit to it, much less discuss it."

"Why?"

"Cancer was like leprosy for my mom's generation. And I think because of the shame she felt that my father had no interest in her after that." She folded her arms, thoughtful. "Oh, we knew about it, Cornelia and I. We heard her crying at night—that's when she started to drink—and we knew they switched to separate beds shortly after that, sometimes even separate rooms."

"Is this only about your mother?"

Her eyes met his. She did not answer him. Instead she said, "Do you know how it must have felt for a woman at the peak of her sexuality to suddenly have the man she loved treat her like some kind of freak? To lose interest totally? God, you feel so awful to begin with. You're fighting for your life, you go through the treatments, nuclear cocktails drip into your veins, blasts of radiation turn your mouth dry, and you struggle to hold on to what's left of your self-esteem when your hair falls out and the drugs make you sick, and you crave support and love and you look in a mirror and see only a freak, that ugly scar, that off-balance body that you don't even want to admit is yours, and you need someone to love you . . . to touch you . . . to make you feel whole again." She shuddered. "My mother went through hell."

He took her hand. "Martha was a wonderful woman. She didn't deserve that."

"I was going to finally talk to her about it. I was going to make her talk about it at Christmas. I had found the strength." Tears suddenly formed at the corners of her eyes. "If only I'd done it sooner."

"You didn't know she was going to die."

She closed her eyes for a moment. "What I wanted to know was how she went on with Dad."

"Why she stayed in the marriage?"

"Their sex life ended. And yet she continued to love him as if it had not been important. But it was, we knew the misery she was in, the loneliness. She drowned it in Dewar's, but it never really went away. But how did she live with it? Did she ever confront him about it? Did she just turn her head and accept it? Did she just escape to her fantasies? Because if that's what she did, I can't!"

Their eyes met and locked. It was clear that she was talking about herself and Tom, not only her mother and father. She had wanted to get advice from her mother, who had been through the very thing she was going through. Matthew said, "You're a beautiful woman. It shouldn't make a difference."

She tried to conjure a smile. "That's what the surgeon said. That's what Tom said when we made the decision for a mastectomy instead of a lumpectomy. And a good thing too, because eleven of the twenty lymph nodes they removed from under my arm were cancerous."

"My God."

"That's why the chemo for six months."

"But that's over now."

"And I'm fine. I won."

"I'm glad."

"But I lost everything."

He shook his head. "No, you didn't. You have yourself, and you're as whole and together and beautiful as you ever were. You're a woman, Julia, a courageous and vibrant woman who has everything to live for, and I can't imagine a man not wanting to love you. . . ."

She sat staring into his eyes for what seemed an eternity. She could not believe these words were coming from him. He who hardly knew her—or did he know her better than she knew herself? She wanted to hide in shame, and yet she wanted to kiss him, for what he said made sense, she knew he spoke the truth, and she felt a surge of strength inside her like the spark she had wanted so badly from Tom, feeling for a moment that her disfigurement was only in her mind, that it didn't *matter* one bit.

And yet she could not bear this. She was embarrassed having opened herself so nakedly, admitting her husband could not have sex with her, sharing the most personal nightmare she could imagine. She started crying, crying and crying, sobbing into his arms until he lifted her and carried her to his bed.

He sat on the bed next to her. He looked down into her eyes, gazing lovingly. "You are so beautiful," he whispered.

"I don't feel beautiful."

"That's because Tom makes you feel that way."

"I can't . . . can't even look at myself."

His hand moved to her robe. He started to ease it open. She grasped his wrist. "No," she begged, "please don't."

"Julia, I've seen you."

"That was long ago—"

"No, tonight. When I put the robe on you."

She froze. Her body actually stiffened. Of course, he had to have seen the bra, the prosthesis; he had taken her clothes off when she was so drunk. She closed her eyes in shame. Then she tried to get up, off the bed, out of there, shame chasing her like a wild wind. She wanted to run out of the house, down the cliff, roll down it, become a giant snowball and keep on going for the rest of time.

He grabbed her and pulled her to him. "You're not going anywhere," he said, "not until you know you're still beautiful, that it doesn't make a difference, that it doesn't change your heart, it doesn't change your appeal, it doesn't change you." He pressed his head in the middle of her chest and held her to him.

"Please . . . oh, please don't do this . . ."

But he did. He pushed the robe off her shoulders and reached behind her to unfasten the bra. Gently, almost as if he'd practiced this, he brought his arms back in front of her, held both cups in his hands, and gently eased it away. She stiffened in shame, trying to cover herself again, but he would not allow it. "Relax . . . slow . . . just let yourself feel, don't think . . . trust me."

Slowly, she did. She felt him touch her left breast with his fingertips gently, and the nipple responded, hardening under his touch. She felt him bring his lips to it. She moaned with pleasure and fear and apprehension. Then, as he still had her in his warm mouth, she felt his other hand touch the unsightly scar that had once been the matching right breast. His other hand pulled his robe open—she could feel he was naked underneath, she could feel his penis pressing against her thighs—and then he slowly eased her panties down her legs and pushed them off with one of his feet. All the time, never taking his mouth from her breast or his hand from her scar. Then he lifted his head, kissed her on the chin, and whispered, "Look at me."

She opened her eyes.

"You're the most beautiful woman alive," he whispered with deep intensity. "I want to love you."

"Oh, God," she moaned, and she watched as he moved his head to her right side, his eyes still looking up at her astonished expression, and then he looked down in front of him and kissed where her breast should have been, kissed the flesh, ran his tongue lightly over the scar, and whispered, almost inaudibly, "I love you . . ."

They made love. Tenderly, lovingly, without words, with passion and emotion and respect.

And when it was over, she looked at him with admiration and felt inside her a sense of loyalty that she knew would never die. This was the kind of moment that tied a person to another person for the rest of their lives. This was the kind of connection you could not explain to anyone, when souls bonded and truths joined hearts together forever in time.

She felt whole again. She felt like a woman again. She could look in a mirror now, she could bear to touch herself now, she could even put on a sweater and feel attractive now. He'd done for her what no book could teach her, what no therapy group could accomplish, what Tom could not do. He'd given her the most valuable and meaningful moment of her entire life.

And for that she would be indebted to him for all time.

She closed her eyes and thought about Tom. It should have been him. It was *supposed* to be him. But it hadn't been and would never be. And she knew, in this last breath before sleep overtook her, that she would never forgive him for it. Ever.

Matthew sat watching her. He timed her breathing pattern, and as the hours inched toward morning, she became more restful and finally slept the sleep of angels. He left her side only to allow Maggie out to pee at five. He turned up the heating blanket when he felt the warmth of the fire diminishing. He caught about a half hour's sleep himself, but he did not require more; he was functioning on adrenaline alone now, and happiness. She'd needed to feel whole again, and he had done that. He had shown her support and patience and understanding and strength

and determination. He had made her feel attractive.
He had made her understand it was all in her mind.
He'd done for her what Harry had never done for
Martha. Hell, maybe he'd even rescued Julia from the
path her mother had taken—no, he could never
imagine her as a drunken old hag.

What he was sure of was that she had started to love
him tonight.

Happiness like he'd never before known began to
flow through his bloodstream. This would end her
marriage to Tom Larsen. This was better than murder.

She was his now, forever.

7

She was still in his arms when she woke up.

It was the first time in nine years that she had awakened next to a man other than Tom. She knew people would say it was wrong. Yet she felt more right at this moment than she had for months. Yes, this should have been Tom holding her, should have been Tom who made love to her last night, made her feel whole again, but it simply was not. She kissed this man next to her, kissing awake her savior, her life enhancer, this precious gift from God. No, she felt no guilt; she wouldn't allow it. There was no reason to be ashamed or remorseful. That's why she had stayed the night. Her sister knew where she had spent the night, and she'd never hear the end of it. But it was worth it. Matt pressed his head into her hair. They held each other, the way lovers do, the way husbands and wives *should*, she thought. "You're as beautiful this morning as I remembered last night."

Her head turned away automatically.

"Hey," he cautioned. She turned back. "I thought we were over that."

"I'm not used to it."

He kissed her on the lips and then placed his hand over the right side of her chest. It said more than any words ever could.

At eleven-thirty that same morning, a tall man knocked on Matthew Hinson's door. The dog barked inside, but there was no answer.

Jim Crowley went around back and did the same at the rear door. Still no one answered.

He peeked in the window and saw Maggie growling at him. He called her a nice girl. She stopped barking and licked the window pane. Over her head he could see that Matthew had had company, at least for breakfast. Two places were set, the dirty dishes still sitting there, two coffee cups half empty. He stood up straight and said aloud, "Well, guess you won't mind if I have a look around, then . . ."

As they pulled into the Radcliffe gate, Matthew felt the Subaru automatically engage four-wheel drive to climb the incline. He asked, "Hear anything about the investigation?"

"Nothing. It's New Year's Eve." She shrugged. "Remember he promised an arrest today?"

He shook his head. Then he tried to smile again, pulling to a stop at the front of the house. Cornelia stood in the window, arms folded in front of her. "I'm going to get shit," Julia said. She gave her sister a big smile and a little wave.

"You know how to give it right back," he said, amused.

She turned back to Matthew. "How do I ever thank you?"

"Thank me?"

"What you did for me."

His eyes connected to hers like never before. "What you did for *me*," he said, and then took her hand and squeezed it tightly. "You're the most beautiful creature on earth. There is nothing to feel ashamed of. You've got to remember that."

She looked as if she were about to cry.

And he knew, there, at that moment, she was going to kiss him, or at least she would have had Molly not come running around the side of the house. Covered with snow, one mitten gone, she raced up to the station wagon calling, "Mommy! Mommy!"

Julia opened the car door and held her arms out. "Hi, honey." She embraced her daughter.

"Aunt Cornelia said you left real early, before I got up."

Julia shot Matthew a look of relief. "That I did."

"I wanted to go too."

"I'm taking that as a compliment to me," Matthew teased the girl.

"Hi, Mr. Hinson." Her wide almond eyes glowed.

"Call me Matt."

Molly giggled and blushed. Julia found Molly's other mitten in her pocket and forced it over her hand as Molly asked Matt, "How is Maggie?"

"Misses you. And Mr. Tiddleberk?"

She blushed and cleverly said, "He misses *you*."

Matt whispered to Julia, "Think she's developing a crush on me?"

Julia said, "It runs in the family."

Molly suddenly said, "I know my book by heart. And I'm making snow angels out back, a whole yard full!" And she squealed and raced back around the house.

Matt looked at Julia. "She's a great kid."

"Wanna buy her? Just kidding. But there are times when—"

"I'd bid. Listen, seriously, you two spending New Year's without Tom?"

"No."

The word devastated him.

"He's driving up as planned."

Was he hearing right? After last night, after what had happened, after what he had done, she was still going on with this sham of a marriage?

"He should be here in a couple of hours."

Even though she did not sound thrilled, he felt the pain rising inside him. He could not mask his disappointment. "I guess I won't see you tomorrow, then."

"I guess." She started to get out of the car, but she

suddenly stopped herself and turned back to face him. "Matt," she said with a warmth of emotion in her voice that was unmistakable, "happy New Year, I really mean that." She paused, looking like she could not find the words she really wanted to say. "Matthew, I've always—"

His heart raced. "Yes, Julia?"

"I've felt . . . I feel . . . well, very dear to you. You saved my life twice now." Then she impulsively put her head forward and, despite her sister watching from outside the car, kissed him tenderly on the cheek.

He closed his eyes and said nothing.

As he drove down the hill, his hands trembling at the wheel, Matt's penis was as hard as when it had sprung up the moment her lips touched his cheek. *Matthew, I've always*— Sweat beaded on his brow. *Matthew, I've always*— His blood pressure made him feel his head was going to explode. He thought only of her, the sight of her, the smell of her. He touched the seat where she had sat. He thought of the moment, of her words, of her lips. But in that kiss, in the touch of her lips to his flesh, in the warmth of her breath on his cold, brittle cheek, she had sealed their future forever. *Matthew, I've always*— He knew the words she had not been able to get out: *loved you. Matthew, I've always loved you.* But she didn't need to voice it; he had his proof now.

He turned onto the road and gunned the engine.

The trees whizzed by, he nearly sideswiped mailboxes, for now rage set in. Tom was driving up this
afternoon. She was going back to Tom even after he'd
showed her how precious lovemaking could be.
She was going on with her marriage—just as her
mother had wanted her to do—despite what *they*
shared. How could she do this to him? After what
he'd done for her!

No, wait, don't blame her. It wasn't her fault. She'd
been programmed by her parents, taught to hold onto
her sacred but stupid marriage. No, it wasn't her fault.
It was Tom he had to do something about. God had
appointed her to be his prophet, to give him the sign,
to tell him when and to tell him how. She'd seen the
rifle in the laundry room. He remembered the buck
he'd shot in November, how his sights had taken in
the proud animal's right eye. Would it be as delicious—as easy—with a man's head? He could picture
the blond hair in his telescopic sights now. It would be
exquisite. Tom would be in his beloved BMW. He
would be unaware. There was only one road into
Mariposa that he'd take. There was the tight curve
where he'd have to slow down, the rocks . . .

Julia was right, she *wouldn't* see Matt tomorrow.

And though she didn't know it yet, she wouldn't be
seeing Tom tomorrow either.

Tom Larsen was doing ninety-five m.p.h. out of
Merced while Jim Morrison belted "Light My Fire"

from a CD spinning in the changer in the trunk, and all Tom could think of was how much he loved the Doors and this car. He'd driven a 325i when he was on the bottom rung of the corporate ladder at Marin Design Group, but with his promotion and accompanying pay raise for the success of the Radcliffe house, the dream of something bigger and more powerful came true. Three days after their honeymoon, he told Julia he'd bought "them" a spanking new Iceland green 540i. With wide Pirellis, which now were living up to their potential as he zoomed up Highway 140 toward Mariposa.

Fifth, then down to a redline fourth as the grade steepened. Smooth as silk. What power. God, he thought, Julia's never even driven this. How can she keep that shitty TR7? He downshifted again to third for a tight curve. Silky. Smooth. Sensual. Like slipping into a woman, he thought, with a grin. He chugged the last of his beer. The engine purred. *What a car.*

"You know that it would be untrue . . ."

When he got his next promotion, post-Hong Kong, when he was one step closer to becoming a partner, then it would be time for that 740iL—no, make that an 8 Series, may as well go the whole distance. Christ, what would he drive when he was made a *partner*? Well, no problem, then he'd be *driven*. He laughed out loud. Rolls? No, Bentley, like the Regent had waiting for him at Kai Tak. Bentley Turbo.

He passed the spot where Julia had told him she and Molly had abandoned the Triumph on that fateful night a little more than a week ago. Molly. He couldn't wait to see his daughter. Julia too. Maybe—God, he hoped so!—maybe this time he could manage to over-come his problem. Man, why this thing about the physical? He never knew it was so important to him. He'd not slept many nights wondering why—why did his dick die when his hands felt what was missing? The love wasn't missing, the desire was still there, he wanted to make love to his wife just like before, but every time he tried—

He turned the headlights on. It was starting to get dark. He saw the CD indicator on the dash change from #2 to #3. He was listening to k.d. lang now. Fine by him. This had been a pleasant trip. But he hated himself for what had happened since Julia's surgery. He told himself now that he was determined to change that. Tonight. Ring in the new year the right way.

"Just a kiss, just a kiss, I have lived just for this . . ."

As he approached an even tighter curve just outside Mariposa itself, he downshifted again to third and used the lower gear to slow the muscular land rocket. He'd be within the town limits soon, and he didn't want to get another ticket. This time he'd lose his license. Harry always used to tell him, "Watch that last curve. The bastards like to hide behind the rocks there." He cranked up the volume a little more. "Sing it, girl," he said.

And she did.

At that moment, on the very bend Harry had warned Tom about, just to his left now, behind a large rock and several trees, Matthew raised the barrel of a rifle and looked through the sight. He'd seen the car over his shoulder, rounding the promontory on the other side, the dark green BMW. He'd seen it before, many times, and he knew how fast the driver liked to push it. Sure enough, he was speeding today as well. He was going to have to be quick, precise. He figured it should be rounding the corner, now it should be coming into sight, the sight of his rifle—he lifted his hand from the trigger to the scope, adjusting it, making sure he'd get a clean shot to the head, like he had with that buck, like Lee Harvey Oswald had with—

"*Freeze!*"

"*Drop it!*"

"*You move, you're a dead man!*"

Matt froze. He dropped it. And he didn't move because he didn't want to be dead. No argument. He trusted these voices, which rang out with no-nonsense authority, even though he couldn't as yet see to whom they belonged.

* * *

Tom glanced in the rearview mirror and slammed on his brakes. *Holy shit, they got me.* He saw the flashing lights of a California Highway Patrol car in the distance. *Damn!* And he'd just slowed down. He'd wanted to get to Julia, Cornelia had told him she was in trouble, she needed him—and now this! Where had they been hiding? How in the hell had they—? Harry was right, the bastards hid behind those rocks. He started to pull to the side of the road, shoving the two empty Anchor Steam bottles under the passenger seat. But then he realized the CHP car wasn't moving, wasn't giving chase; it was just sitting there. All of a sudden Tom saw that it was joined by several more, one after another, lights ablaze, descending from the side road, the trees and God-knew-where, to this one spot. He knew then they weren't after him. There was too much manpower back there. What the hell had happened? An accident? A plane crash? He hadn't heard or seen anything. It was eerie. It made his skin crawl.

He was about to turn around and have a look, but his desire to get to his wife got the better of him. Who cared what happened back there? He put the car into first and hit the accelerator, speeding again right through town, feeling safe, smug even as he broke the law with relish, for he knew every police car in the area was far behind him, by those dreaded rocks.

Matthew Hinson felt heavy, brutish hands grabbing both his arms, pulling his hands behind his back, and as they forced him up from his kneeling rifleman's stance, turned him around, and started to cuff him, he saw who had been speaking. He had hoped for one split second that he was being arrested for aiming a gun toward a highway and nothing more. It was cause for arrest on its own, that's for sure. Rabbits. He'd say he was shooting rabbits. No, he thought quickly, Julia might hear about it. Target practice. He'd say he was shooting at targets. But what targets? No, he'd have to risk Julia's wrath that he'd lied to her.

But he knew there was more to this when he realized he was facing half the state police, sheriff's deputies, troopers, and highway patrol in the entire state of California. He'd taken the back road to the spot, and he'd been followed. And he'd had no idea.

But the real confirmation that he was in trouble came when he recognized the man who said, in a rather surprisingly soft voice, "Read him his rights."

It was Jim Crowley.

At precisely 11:48 on the night of December 31, the phone in the Radcliffe house rang. "You get it," Julia called out to her sister. She was eating popcorn and her fingers had butter on them. "I don't want the phone to slide out of my hand."

Cornelia called from the kitchen. "I'm busy in here. Brad, answer it. I don't want any more bad news this year."

"*Tommy'll* get it," Brad said, ribbing him by calling him "Tommy," which he knew he loathed.

"Like hell Tommy will," Tom laughed. He was on his hands and knees, picking up the two hundred poker chips that had fallen to the floor as the card table on which they were playing royal rummy had collapsed. "You heard your wife, answer the phone."

Brad said, "I'm changing the music. Maybe they'll just give up."

But they did not; the phone continued to ring. No one went near it. Cornelia came in from the kitchen with a bottle of champagne. Julia offered to open it. Cornelia went back into the kitchen to get the glasses she had chilled. "Isn't anyone going to answer that thing?" she added. "It'll wake Molly."

"I turned off the extension in her room," Julia said. But the sound was beginning to annoy her. "Oh, all right, I give up," she finally said, trying to wipe her hands quickly on a napkin, grabbing it, saying, "Hello—but if it's bad news, don't even bother." She started to undo the champagne cork.

"Very *good* news," the man said in response. Her expression went blank. This was a familiar voice.

Tom saw her expression and stopped picking up the chips. Brad never did get to put the new cassette in. Cornelia came back in from the kitchen, three champagne flutes in her hands. Julia cupped the receiver and said, "It's Jim Crowley."

"First, happy New Year."

"That's not the good news."

"Cut it close, but kept my promise."

Julia held her breath, her eyes darting back and forth from her sister to Tom. The champagne cork was starting to slide out of the neck of the bottle on its own accord.

"I expect you'll be hearing it on the news in a little while," Jim continued. "Wanted to tell you myself."

Julia felt goose pimples rise all over her body. She gripped the neck of the champagne bottle tighter and looked triumphant now, suddenly realizing what he was saying, suddenly understanding that the waiting was over, they'd gotten him, they'd gotten the bastard, they knew who did it! Exuberantly, she cried out, "Oh God, Jim, did you—?"

"Yes, Julia. A couple hours ago, we took someone into custody for the murder of your mom and dad."

"They arrested him!" she cried to the others.

"Who?" Cornelia breathlessly asked.

"*Who?*" Tom said, louder.

"Do we know him?" Brad shouted.

"Julia," Jim Crowley said somberly, "the man I arrested is Matthew Hinson."

The cork popped out of the bottle. Champagne bubbled up and cascaded down Julia's leg. Then the bottle fell free of her hand and hit the floor as she closed her eyes and felt every last drop of blood drain from her head.

PART II

Matthew

8

San Francisco Times-Herald

BORDEN J. MONROE
President

AUGUST P. MONROE
Proprietor — 1893-1946

"SNOWSHOE KILLER" TRIAL STARTS TODAY

By Tom Davies
OF THE *TIMES-HERALD*
STAFF

SAN FRANCISCO—The trial of Matthew Hinson, accused killer of former Governor and Mrs. Harry Radcliffe, began opening statements today in the courthouse here in San Francisco. The venue had been changed from Mariposa County, where it was ruled the defendant could not get a fair trial.

The family entered the courtroom this morning without speaking to the press, although Julia Larsen, youngest daughter of the deceased, author and Emmy-award winning former Bay Area news anchor, has for the past six months attested to Hinson's innocence in interviews. Accompanying her to the courtroom today was her sister, Cornelia Younger of Salt Lake City, and her husband, Brad Younger. Several residents of Mariposa County, where the brutal killings took place, arrived in vans and automobiles early this morning, eager to get ringside seats in the courtroom.

Jury selection in this trial took two weeks, and there has been a barrage of media interest not seen since the trial of O.J. Simpson in Los Angeles. The prosecution is seeking the death penalty against Hinson in this case, trying both murders as one. The judge, Esther Mae Barnes, began the trial this morning by appealing for order and "restraint" on behalf of all present when speaking to the "voracious" media on the courthouse steps. She has, however, allowed one camera to tape the trial.

Prosecutor Robert Hughes, from Mariposa County, began his opening statement with a cry for justice, promising that the state would prove Hinson did willfully and with careful planning murder the former governor and his wife. Michael Glass, the 27-year-old attorney for the defense, said flatly that the state did not have a case, and that he would show that the case against Hinson is circumstantial, without motive, in his words, "no case at all." Curiously, the prosecution did not suggest a motive other than "greed, jealousy, and hate."

Matthew deliciously watched her every move—the way she touched her forehead with her fingertips, the way she crossed her legs, even the way she breathed. Until yesterday he had not seen her in six months and two weeks and four days. He had longed for this moment, anticipated it impatiently. He was not in the least bit nervous, frightened, or anxious. On the contrary, he had not looked so calm and collected—so *happy*?—since moments before his arrest. This was rhapsodic. He sat thinking he could hear background music, Debussy—no, Telemann, that new Telemann CD he'd bought just before they nabbed him. He'd had time to play it only once. No matter; he'd be out of here soon. This circus would be over and he'd take Julia to his house and they'd listen to it together, and make love.

The trial—*his* trial—for the murder of two beloved, prominent public figures was under way, but he was as concerned as he'd be at a picnic in the park. And that's just how this felt to him. He didn't give a shit about anything but seeing his beloved Julia again. That's why he'd tallied the days pacing his cell, counting down, anxious and thrilled. Yesterday the fat cow on the bench had rapped her gavel, and those two clowns rattled out their stupid opening statements. But he hadn't listened. He'd been looking and concentrating on Julia. His angel. Who still loved him, would not betray him. The only other person in the room who believed him.

And that's all that mattered.

"The prosecution calls Marguerite Del Padre."

COURT TV TRANSCRIPT: PRIME TIME JUSTICE / AIR DATE JULY 22 NYC STUDIO: TERRY MORAN / SAN FRANCISCO LOCATION: CLARA TUMA

MORAN: Clara, what was the most interesting moment of the day for you?

TUMA: I thought it was quite amazing that the prosecutor asked Miss Del Padre point blank if she'd ever slept with Hinson.

MORAN: And that the judge allowed it.

TUMA: She was looking for relevant character testimony—

MORAN: And she got it, didn't she? Let's look now as Miss Del Padre describes being with Matthew Hinson:

COURTROOM CAMERA / WITNESS: MARGUERITE DEL PADRE

WITNESS: He took me back to my apartment, I asked him in, we got to fooling around, and I gave him head.

PROSECUTOR: You performed oral sex on him?

WITNESS: Yes.

PROSECUTOR: Did you have intercourse?

WITNESS: Nope. Wanted to, but he couldn't do it, said he was saving it for someone special.

PROSECUTOR: What happened then?

WITNESS: I got mad. I felt used. I told him so. And he hit me. Yelled at me, threatened me.

PROSECUTION: So you were witness to a side of Matthew Hinson that could be called violent?

WITNESS: He's no lover boy.

COURT TV TRANSCRIPT:

MORAN: But the defense pretty much neutralized her on cross.

TUMA: Yes, Terry. Mike Glass elicited her arrest record, drugs, robbery, and a battery charge for trying to run over a neighbor's fourteen-year-old son with her car after he made an allegedly obscene gesture toward her with his baseball bat.

MORAN: A wash?

TUMA: I'd say.

MORAN: The same happened with the next witness, right?

TUMA: Yes, she also said the defendant had grown violent, but not so violent as to hit her. She said he smashed up the room, ranting on about angels. But the defense again undermined it by proving she had a record of lying.

MORAN: And the man they brought up to prove Hinson had a temper?

TUMA: He claimed he saw Matt Hinson beat up someone the previous Easter Sunday after an argument over the way his car was parked. Again, the defense poked holes in it.

MORAN: How about the neighbor? She cause him any damage?

TUMA: She did him a lot of good, I think.

MORAN: She was rather amusing to watch. Take a look:

COURTROOM CAMERA / WITNESS: INGA WILSON

PROSECUTOR: Mrs. Wilson, do you know the defendant, Matthew Hinson?

WITNESS: Of course I know him. Why would I be here? And I liked him.

PROSECUTOR: Mrs. Wilson, please do not comment, just answer the questions put to you. Is Matthew Hinson in the courtroom today?

WITNESS: Be pretty damn strange if he wasn't. It's his trial, isn't it?

COURT TV TRANSCRIPT:

MORAN: She told it like it was.

TUMA: I wouldn't want to tangle with her.

MORAN: She later told him to ask her something not so stupid, didn't she, Terry?

TUMA: Yes, she kept everyone laughing.

MORAN: What did she accomplish?

TUMA: Not as much as the prosecution wanted. She established the murder weapon, and identified the wooden handle from the knife as smelling of Tuscany cologne, which she buys her husband.

MORAN: And she also bought Matt for Christmas.

TUMA: Yes, she said that, but where's it going?

MORAN: We don't know yet. Did you watch Julia Radcliffe Larsen in the courtroom today?

TUMA: Who can keep their eyes off her? She's the defendant's biggest advocate.

MORAN: I would be too if my wife was the only known advocate of the man accused of shooting her parents.

TUMA: We here in San Francisco hear there is some kind of surprise coming from Mrs. Larsen. Word on the street here is that it's got something to do with publishing.

MORAN: Has she written another book?

TUMA: No one seems to know yet.

MORAN: Keep us informed, Clara.

TUMA: I shall, Terry. We'll be back here at the San Francisco County Courthouse tomorrow morning.... Now back to the studio.

MORAN: This word just in, it has been announced that tomorrow afternoon, Julia Larsen, who was once a news anchor right there in San Francisco, will be doing the *Oprah* Show live from that city, in what is said to be an announcement of the publication of a book by the *defendant*.

Matthew lay on his bunk under the courtroom and replayed the day. That fat ass sister was always looking at Julia looking at him. He watched Julia finally give the bitch a defiant look. It pleased him. For he knew that in the six months while waiting for the trial to begin, Julia's undying belief in him had alienated nearly everyone she knew. He'd read in a tabloid that her sister was barely speaking to her, and the beloved husband hadn't even bothered to show up; Tom evidently preferred to build his bank. He knew she was lost, adrift, and that there was only one person who could keep her from drowning. He had caught her gaze. His eyes spoke silent words, saying he'd protect her, he'd get her through this. Like some kind of guardian angel.

And those idiotic witnesses! Marguerite Del Padre, his ass. Told him her name was Margie Parsons. She had been even fatter then, in that muumuu with that squeaky, saccharine voice. She'd had cats, seemed like twenty of them. Cat hair, cat shit everywhere. How had he ever let her talk him into going home with her to that disgusting little room? Cheap, warm beer she'd served him. Took some pills herself. He should have taken some to destroy the reality that he was with this bovine creature with stringy hair and cow tits and the breath of a frog. And to think he named his dog Maggie. Christ.

But he smiled as he remembered striking her, just as she'd testified, because she wanted him to fuck her. Hell, no, she could go down on him all she wanted, but there was only one woman he was going to make love to and that was his angel. The memory of hitting her surged through him and felt warm and satisfying.

And under what rock did they dig up that other chick? Even he'd forgotten her. Christ, that was ancient history. So what that he tore her precious bedroom apart? She was just another cunt with bad taste in bed linens. He should have known better. He should have saved himself the trouble. He should have realized he was meant to be celibate until he could have his angel again, and his angel alone.

The only person they were wrong about was the

guy who thought he'd seen him pick a fight on the street. No way, not his style. He had a public image to maintain—would a successful pillar of the community risk a street brawl? On Easter Sunday, no less? On Easter Sunday he had been at the same church where years later he would give Harry and Martha's eulogy, in the pew right behind the whole famous family, Martha and Harry, the older daughter—the ugly one—and her husband, and little Molly with Tom and Julia. He missed Molly. He wondered if she still had the book he'd made for her. He wondered if she'd read the poems he sent her.

Julia. He recalled the words of the minister. *And the angel pulled aside the rock, and behold, hallelujah! Christ the Lord is risen today!* No. Not Christ. Julia!

Fuck this trial shit. What a waste of time.

MARIPOSA
"Above the Fog - Below the Snow" - John L. Dexter

30¢ A Copy
Tax Included

Since 1854 THE GAZETTE, YOUR WEEKLY LETTER FROM HOME

Deputy Gary Estep of the Mariposa County Sheriff's Department today testified to finding the murder weapon in proximity to the defendant's house. Drawing a line from where the knife blade was found to where the handle was discovered, and bringing lines from both of them to where the deputy said the knife had to have been thrown, the lines formed a triangle that pointed almost directly toward Matthew Hinson's Sherlock Road residence. He also testified that the scent on the wooden knife handle was indeed the cologne called Tuscany.

The New York Tribune

Founded in 1847

KILLER SCENT?

By Jayne Bialkowski

New York, July 16—Bloomingdale's today reported a surge in sales of the men's cologne called Tuscany. The scent has been in the media of late because of the murder trial in California of Matthew Hinson. Evan Shagrun, spokesman for Aramis, Inc., who manufactures the line, said that seventy percent of buyers surveyed at Bloomingdale's over the past week have wanted to try the cologne because of the connection to the trial. When asked whether or not Aramis is considering Matthew Hinson as a spokesman, Shagrun replied, "I don't think that would be appropriate."

Much has been made of the fragrance in the trial, since the prosecution first tied the scent to the handle of

a knife that has been called
the murder weapon. . . .

*TRANSCRIPT FROM HARPO PRODUCTIONS, INC.
THE OPRAH WINFREY SHOW. TAPE DATE: 7/25
(BROADCAST LIVE). SAN FRANCISCO, CALIFORNIA.
PAGE SEVEN, SEGMENT TWO.*

JULIA: He sent me a poem from jail every week. As I
received them, I faxed them to my publisher. He rushed
the book into print, and it will be in the stores next week.

OPRAH: Why do you think he chose to write so many
poems about angels? I know they're big business now.
We've even done shows on them. But is there a stronger
reason?

JULIA: Matthew deeply believes they protect you from
real danger.

OPRAH: Which is where he is right now.

JULIA: He will be acquitted.

OPRAH: You're positive of that?

JULIA: A man who writes like this [HOLDS UP BOOK]
cannot do what they say he did.

OPRAH: That's what Norman Mailer said about Jack
Abbott. And what did he do when he got out of prison?
Stabbed a waiter in Greenwich Village to death because
he gave him coffee with cream instead of black or something like that.

JULIA: Matt isn't in prison.

OPRAH: Julia, you really, in your heart, believe he
didn't do it?

JULIA: You read his book, Oprah. Can you believe it?

OPRAH: I'll admit . . . it's hard. These are some of the most sensational, sensual, feeling poems I've ever read. The man's sensitivity is astounding, and he captures it in images you can't forget.

JULIA: Angels.

OPRAH: Someone said, "What is Satan but a fallen angel?"

JULIA: I want to see justice done. I want to see the person who did it punished. But that person is not Matthew Hinson.

9

$1.25
Canada
$1.49

JULIA & TOM

MATTHEW & JULIA IN FORMER LOVE TRYST?

Hunk-in-chains Matthew Hinson once saved Julia Larsen's life while swimming in a lagoon called Leucadia near the mountaintop home of deceased Governor Harry Radcliffe and his wife. Sources told the Star that Larsen, who had been swimming nude at the rock-lined natural swimming hole, was rescued by

Shocking untold story behind their marriage

Hinson when she slipped and hit her head against the wall of the canyon. A man from Mariposa, California, who claims to know Hinson well, said he privately boasted of "holding her naked in his arms" that day.

The man also went on to say that it would explain Larsen's unwavering defense of Hinson, against overwhelming public opinion.

ABSENT HUBBY

The fact that Tom Larsen has not yet shown his face in the courtroom in San Francisco gives rise to the rumor that the Larsen marriage may be on the rocks over Julia Larsen's dedication to the innocence of the handsome Hinson. . . .

TOM VOWS JULIA FAITHFUL

Reached in Hong Kong, where he was boarding a Cathay Pacific flight for San

TOM JEALOUS

Francisco, architect Tom
Larsen, husband of Julia
Radcliffe Larsen, who is
said to have had an affair
with the handsome Matt
Hinson, who is accused of
murdering her parents in
cold blood, refused to comment other than to say,
"She's my wife, and she
sleeps only with me."

Matt balled up the Star. Sleeps only with him? The
fuck won't sleep with her! The asshole can't fuck her
because he can't get his little pecker up 'cause she's got
scars. Fuck him! They should keep the asshole in China.
He'd fit right in. Those chinks all have little dicks.

He didn't like what the press was doing to her.
Prying, digging, robbing her of her privacy and her
peace. If only he could be there to help her, to shield
her from them, to protect her. He saw it wearing on
her face each day in court, and how badly he wanted
just to speak to her, to say a few words of comfort and
love. It was wonderful to see her every morning, he
lived for it, but to see her this way was getting him
down. He wanted this thing over already. He wanted
to be free.

He calmed himself and wrote her another poem.

The New York Tribune

Book Review

Up and Coming. . .
(Editors' choices of other recent books of particular interest)

Pleading with the Angels, by Matthew Hinson (Carleton & Jarvis, $21.95). Enthralling poems of the accused killer, now on trial in San Francisco. Engaging images don't seem to jive with the accusations about the writer. Reviews have been good, subject matter is timely, the notoriety doesn't hurt one bit either.

In his cell beneath the courthouse, Matthew Hinson lay on his bunk with a yellow pad and a blunt pencil. He'd been trying to write a poem for hours. Tonight he had the images but not the words. He was restless and couldn't sleep. All he could think of was Julia and how beautiful she had looked today, despite the fact that the husband from hell had joined her.

He was thrilled by the reviews his book had been getting. Already in places—Boston, Chicago, Los Angeles, and San Francisco—it had hit the best-seller lists, the first book of poetry to do so in a very long time. The thought of having become a best-selling author thrilled him, but this damn trial bored him silly. Yet, he had to remember, as long as it continued, as long as they trotted out this idiot and that moron, he'd see Julia tomorrow, and the tomorrow after that, and for as long as it lasted. It was almost as if he wanted his own trial never to end.

He looked at the wall. Previous guests had left their calling cards. *Blow me. Fuck Reagan. Now I lay me down to sleep.* Something in Spanish he didn't understand. A drawing of a penis. One, more detailed, of a woman's body from the neck to the knees. Several dates, many crossed out. And a snowflake. In red marker some-one had drawn a delicate snowflake. He closed his eyes. *Snow.* Falling from the sky. A dark, expansive night. Angels peering down from above the clouds, guarding, protecting. *Angels.*

He lifted his pen and started drawing on the wall, to the left of the glorified vagina and just south of the snowflake, where there was room. He sketched the sweeping lines of a skirt blowing in wind, then the outline of a pair of wings taking flight. Then he added, in front of the figure, a long trumpet, heralding news. He thought of the angels he'd done on copper when he was so young, the one he'd made for his grand-mother. It had looked just like this.

Archangels heralding the news—acquittal? Angels singing of glory to God, gusts of white wind . . . He was inspired to write again, but he left the pad at his side. He continued to work on the angel on the wall, detailing it until the face was as close as he could duplicate, as close as his limited artistic talent was capable of bringing him to sketching *her. Julia*, he said in a whisper, looking up at his masterpiece, seeing her come to life in the snow, *Julia, my angel* . . .

She leaped from the wall, landing on his chest. She teased him, asking him what he wanted her to do. She was coy—she pretended she wasn't quite sure he wanted her to turn around and walk down his stomach, over his navel, onto his dick head, and then to run up and down, up and down . . .

He came with a shout, a guttural cry, the kind an animal makes when its leg has suddenly been bitten by the teeth of an iron trap, a cry of pain as real as if he'd been suddenly struck by a car, or a gasp of realization as a rabbit, sitting innocently near the fence, feels its head shatter into small chunks of fur and blood and brains from the astonishing force of a bullet.

The guard rushed down the corridor and looked in.

Matt just lay there with semen all over his shirt, his penis in his left hand, his pencil still in the other.

And above him, almost as if spotlighted on the wall, the guard observed the most beautiful drawing of an angel he'd ever seen.

TRANSCRIPT EXCERPT: RUSH LIMBAUGH AIR DATE 8/1

RUSH: But haven't we gone too far? Look at the Hinson circus out in California. The man is on trial for two of the most grisly murders since Nicole and Ronald—

remember them?—and his book is number seven on the
N.Y. Times best-seller list! I mean, where's the justice?
Think the jury each got an advance copy from the publisher? Autographed maybe. He's sitting in that courtroom and we're watching him and hearing a lot of stuff
we've heard before—DNA admissibility, circumstantial
evidence, did he have time to make it up that mountain?
etc.—and at the same time they're making a star out of
him. And who's the biggest culprit? The daughter of the
people they say he slaughtered! This Julia Larsen, running around promoting him, telling anyone who will
listen how she believes in him. They're going to call her
as a defense witness but why bother? I'll bet the
Menendez boys wish they'd had her in their corner. Who
needs a defense lawyer when you've got her? She's
single-handedly, outside the courtroom, destroying the
prosecution's case.

*TRANSCRIPT EXCERPT: DATELINE NBC WITH JANE
PAULEY. NBC NEWS DIVISION // GUEST: TOM
LARSEN*

PAULEY: Does it embarrass you?

LARSEN: Sure. She's my wife.

PAULEY: How's your daughter taking all this?

LARSEN: She's a smart girl, and she doesn't watch TV.

PAULEY: Still, it must be hard.

LARSEN: Sure is.

PAULEY: Does it present a strain on your marriage?

LARSEN: (SMILING) Whatever gave you that idea?

PAULEY: Tell me why you decided to come to talk to us today. This is the first interview you've given. Why now?

LARSEN: I'm sick of all these stories about Julia and that—can I say this?—bastard being lovers. She believes in him as a friend, she has a deep regard for talent, and she finds him very talented. Once Julia is committed to something, there's no changing her mind.

PAULEY: In the midst of this media circus surrounding the trial—which is now in its third week—how would you characterize your own feelings about what you've seen thus far?

LARSEN: He's a sick, manipulative monster. I have no doubt he did it.

PAULEY: I don't think I'd like to be sitting at *your* dinner table when you and your wife get home from the courtroom.

LARSEN: Julia has that way about her that's like . . . well, with all these guys, they find someone who says, *"Well, now, I'll tell it plain: Eugene was the nicest, gentlest soul you'd ever want to know. Pinned a blue ribbon on him myself, I did, at the county fair, for one of them beautiful quilts. Very religious boy, never missed Mass on Sunday. When they told me he machine-gunned a whole convent full of nuns, I said that can't be our Eugene. . . ."*

PAULEY: Blind faith?

LARSEN: Sometimes we just don't want to know bad things about the people we like.

PAULEY: What do you see for the future?

LARSEN: Hinson will be put away. Even I don't believe they'll give him the death penalty. He's too good-looking. Says something about our values today, doesn't it?

PAULEY: And you and Julia?

LARSEN: We'll get through it. She's a victim in this. She'll see things more clearly as she gets some distance. And I'll be there for her, despite her belief in Matthew now.

NBC NIGHTLY NEWS TRANSCRIPT, AUGUST 7

TOM BROKAW: *The defense in the Hinson trial suffered a blow today when an expert announced that after weeks of testing, the DNA of the mucus found inside the Radcliffe home matched the defendant's blood and tissue sample taken while he was in jail. It places Hinson in the room where the murder took place. A room, they say, where no one but the family ever entered.*

August 10—

Dear Julia,

I heard today that you went to Stanford to have cancer tests done. I know the paper said it was just a follow-up, routine, but I worry. I worry that you had to do it alone. If I could, I'd be there for you and with you. I'd hold your hand, I'd sweat with you and share that great joy when the doctor tells you everything's okay. As I know it is. You went through enough. You deserve no more pain.

And yet I'm causing you that, and I hate myself for it. If I could do anything to undo what happened, I would. This is one big mistake, we both know that, but if I had to be found guilty just to be put away so you could be happy and get on with your life, I'd gladly accept that.

Please tell Molly I said hello. I hope Tom hasn't taught her to hate me. I just . . . I just want to play in the snow again someday with you both.

Hang in there. It'll be over soon. And we will put it all behind us.

Love,

Matthew

Matthew put the letter into an envelope and called the guard, who took it, promising to mail it.

When the guard was gone, Matthew kicked off his shoes, thinking how tomorrow he'd see ol' shitkicker Crowley ambling up to the witness stand in his cowboy boots. He laughed.

Then he stretched out on his bunk and farted.

COURT TRANSCRIPT / WITNESS: JIM CROWLEY

PROSECUTOR: Mr. Crowley, did you notice anything unusual about the Christmas fruitcakes you were offered?

WITNESS: Yup.

PROSECUTOR: And what was that?

WITNESS: Impression stuck in one.

PROSECUTOR: Like Grauman's Chinese Theater in Hollywood? Where stars put their hands in wet cement?

WITNESS: Yup.

PROSECUTION: Did it look like a naked finger?

WITNESS: Nope.

PROSECUTION: Could you elaborate?

WITNESS: Glove.

PROSECUTION: Pardon me?

WITNESS: Finger had a glove on it.

PROSECUTOR: How did you know that?

WITNESS: Glove fibers stuck in the moist cake.

PROSECUTOR: What did you learn from that?

WITNESS: Sent inquiries to every glove maker in America.

PROSECUTOR: And did you indeed find the manufacturer of the gloves?

WITNESS: Mmm. [UNINTELLIGIBLE]

PROSECUTION: What was that, Mr. Crowley?

Spit it out, Jim. Man of few words, all right, most of them useless. Fruitcakes. Gloves. Matthew picked at a fingernail at the witness table. He thought the idiot they had assigned to defend him smelled today. Mike Glass, stupid nigger yid. What did he sneak for lunch, chitlins and borscht? He chuckled to himself. God, but he was bored. Crowley and his expert opinions, his boots still caked with horseshit, everybody acting like he's some kind of star. What a crock.

Julia caught his eye. He saw her twinkle, as if she was thinking the exact same thing. Then Tom looked over at him. Vapid, Matt thought, uninteresting, dull, vacant, arrogant. What had possessed her to marry him? Well, he knew that, good old Dad. The Deceased, may he rest in hell. Bastard. He wished he could bring him back to life so he could kill him all over again. Julia would be his. The same Julia whose beautiful picture they kept putting in the papers. The same Julia he had kissed, made love to, the Julia whose scarred chest he had licked. The Julia he loved.

He looked up. Someone new was being trotted up there. Who the hell was *this* clown?

Mariposa Gazette

GLOVES TIED TO HINSON

Arthur Beckenstein, vice president for marketing of the Finesse Corporation, testified his company made a line of gloves called Ultrafine. Then the prosecutor produced a blow-up of the fruitcake print, which Mr. Beckenstein compared to a photo of his Ultrafine glove, identifying the weave and the seam, and clearly stated the response his company had sent Jim Crowley: This woman's Ultrafine glove, gray in color, was indeed the glove they

were looking for. Becken-
stein said he informed Jim
Crowley that they sold their
gloves exclusively to the
Macy's chain in California.

Then the prosecution
called Sally Holland, of
Chowchilla, a salesgirl at
Macy's in Fresno. . . .

*COURT TV TRANSCRIPT: PRIME TIME JUSTICE / AIR
DATE JULY 24 NYC STUDIO: TERRY MORAN / SAN
FRANCISCO LOCATION: CLARA TUMA*

MORAN: In the Hinson trial, it was a day about gloves.
Clara Tuma, who has covered this case from the start, is
with us now from San Francisco.

TUMA: Thanks, Terry. Well, the talk of the day was Sally
Holland.

MORAN: She seemed a little starstruck.

TUMA: She admitted that she swooned over Hinson
when he walked up to her counter. She said she was
trying to get a date.

MORAN: Her point about him saying he wanted stretch
gloves because they were for his mother in the Midwest
seemed a bit thin.

TUMA: The parents being there have won him some
sympathy. I think that's why the judge asked Hinson's
mother to approach the bench and compare the size of
her hands to Matt's. It turned out to be the most dramatic
moment of the trial thus far.

MORAN: You don't mean in a sensational way, do you?

TUMA: The sight of mother and son, tears streaming down their faces, it moved everyone. They couldn't pull their upraised hands apart. Even the judge was affected.

MORAN: And Esther Barnes seems like the kind of judge who'd never show emotion.

TUMA: I don't think you could help it. A mother's love for her son, how can you beat that?

MORAN: Before we leave you, Clara, what was all that about wrapping the package for him with a big red bow on the top of a shopping bag?

TUMA: It simply introduced the next witness. . . .

COURTROOM CAMERA / WITNESS: PATROLMAN JERRY PENACOLI

DEFENSE: Officer Penacoli, can you tell me your rank and where you are employed?

WITNESS: I'm a patrolman. I'm with the Merced, California, Police Department.

DEFENSE: And were you on duty there the evening of December 14 of last year?

WITNESS: Yes, sir.

DEFENSE: And did you stop at the Pine Cone Inn, a coffee shop just off the freeway?

WITNESS: Yes. I eat there often. I had dinner there that night.

DEFENSE: While you were having dinner, did anything unusual happen?

WITNESS: A man who had been eating at the counter rushed back in and said someone had broken into his car.

DEFENSE: Is that same man here today?

WITNESS: Yes. Right over there.

DEFENSE: And what did you do then?

WITNESS: I put down my fork and went outside with the gentleman. His car's rear door window on the driver's side was busted. It had been vandalized.

DEFENSE: Was anything stolen?

WITNESS: The tape deck. That's what they always go for. Some tapes too. And the owner said he had Christmas presents behind the front seat. In a shopping bag.

DEFENSE: Why not in the trunk?

WITNESS: It was a station wagon.

DEFENSE: Jerry, here in the police report you filed that night you list several articles which the owner of the vehicle said had been stolen.

WITNESS: Yes, sir. He had his receipts in his shirt pocket. He had been Christmas shopping.

DEFENSE: And was a pair of women's gloves one of the articles he told you were missing?

WITNESS: If they're listed there, yes, sir.

PROSECUTION ON CROSS:

PROSECUTOR: You're suggesting the gloves he bought were stolen and then used to implicate him?

WITNESS: It is possible.

ABC TV "20/20"—TRANSCRIPT—AUGUST 16

BARBARA: *In our follow-up to last week's story of new media star poet and accused killer, Matthew Hinson, whose trial for murder in California is now in the defense phase, I want to ask Hugh, have you ever seen anything like it?*

HUGH: *What amazes me is that it constantly keeps you guessing. Just when you think, ah, he's guilty, it turns and you say, well, I wonder.*

BARBARA: *No hard evidence, no witness, the deceased's own daughter fighting for his innocence—it's hard to believe that public opinion is against this man.*

HUGH: *Is it? It may have started out that way in the small town near Yosemite where the feeling was someone had to be blamed. But now Hinson has been turned into a public figure— and we're partially to blame for that ourselves, Barbara— because he's good-looking and smart—*

BARBARA: *—and talented, successful, no record, never in trouble before. I keep wondering, what's the motive? Why hasn't the prosecution introduced a motive?*

HUGH: *Maybe, Barbara, because there isn't one.*

BARBARA: *Our requests for an interview with Matthew Hinson have, of course, been rejected. But as soon as the trial is over, and no matter what the verdict, I want to talk to this man.*

HUGH: *And I think we'll all want to listen.*

DEAR JULIA,

I'M WRITING THIS AT THE WITNESS TABLE DURING THE ENDLESS ENNUI. I'M GOING TO GIVE IT TO MIKE TO SLIP TO YOU. I HEARD YOU'RE OKAY, THE CANCER CELLS WENT SOUTH AND STAYED THERE, AND NO ONE IS MORE THRILLED FOR YOU THAN I. YOU SHOULD BE SO HAPPY! BUT THEN WHY DO YOU LOOK SO SAD?

LOVE, MATT

NATIONAL WEEKLY EDITION

The Washington Herald

DECEASED GOVERNOR CALLED ABUSIVE

Ever since Barbara Walters and Hugh Downs brought up the question of a motive on the ABC News Show "20/20" two weeks ago, the talk of the Hinson trial has been just that, the motive— or lack thereof. Yesterday, the prosecution tried to introduce one: that former Governor Harry Radcliffe had been "abusive" to his business partner, Matthew Hinson, on several occasions, and that Hinson killed the man to get even. Art Bagett, Harry Radcliffe's banker, testified that the afternoon of the murders, he witnessed Matthew Hinson have a verbal battle with Mr. Radcliffe, one in which Radcliffe severed their business association. Today, the questioning of Mr. Bagett continues.

*COURTROOM TRANSCRIPT / WITNESS: ARTHUR
BAGETT*

DEFENSE: *Mr. Bagett, did you or anyone you know ever take
Harry Radcliffe seriously when he had one of his outbursts and
was abusive with people?*

WITNESS: *No, sir. We took it with a grain of salt. Hell, he
wasn't nice to his banker a lot. (LAUGH) And I have to say, no
one I knew ever held it against him.*

DEFENSE: *No more questions.*

```
internet > sf/GIRLCHAT
girlchat/S.F. COMPUTER BULLETIN BOARD
momcat > All geared up for the trial today,
girls?
marina > I got an invitation to join the
m.hinson fan club.
kari > Send it to me. I'm on Julia's side.
momcat > She gonna testify? My daughter bet
me her hubby wouldn't let her.
et > Screw the husband. She'll do what she
wants. She'll save him.
momcat > Who wants him saved?
kari > Every horny woman in America.
et > Anybody know how to get red wine out of
the rug?
momcat > Club soda.
kari > I think the jury's on his side.
marina > They damn well should be.
```

et > That judge's girdle is too tight.

kari > I just like looking at him. Don't tell my husband I said that. I mean mh is just too humpy for words.

marina > He's gorgeous. She's gorgeous. But the husband is gorgeous too.

kari > I feel sorry for their little girl.

marina > How's it hurting her?

momcat > Hey! Did you just hear that?

kari > I'm signing off. Can't miss a moment of this.

marina > The newscaster is saying it right now, FORMER GOVERNOR'S DAUGHTER CALLED AS DEFENSE WITNESS IN MURDER TRIAL. . . .

COURT TRANSCRIPT / WITNESS: JULIA RADCLIFFE LARSEN

DEFENSE: Mrs. Larsen, was your father abusive?
WITNESS: He—
PROSECUTION: Objection.
JUDGE: Sustained.
DEFENSE: I'll rephrase, Your Honor. Was your father ever abusive to those who worked for him?
WITNESS: Sometimes. He blustered.
DEFENSE: Blustered?
WITNESS: Blew off steam. You paid no attention.
PROSECUTION: Once again, Your Honor, this is shaky ground.

JUDGE: I agree. Rethink your line of questioning, Mr. Glass.

DEFENSE: Mrs. Larsen, in your pretrial deposition, you state that you made a phone call to your parents from the Miner's Inn the night of the murders.

WITNESS: Yes, I did.

DEFENSE: You say, on page sixty-three here, *"And my father said that Matt or one of the boys—someone else with a four-wheel drive—would come out to get us in the morning."* Mrs. Larsen, the first name he mentioned was 'Matt.' Who was he referring to? Matt Hinson?

WITNESS: Yes.

DEFENSE: Why him?

WITNESS: Because Dad knew he would.

DEFENSE: But your father had just severed his association with Matt that afternoon. If Harry Radcliffe had ended his relationship with that 'stupid asshole' Matt Hinson, as Mr. Bagett testified your father called him, would it make sense that he'd tell you he was going to ask Matt Hinson, of all people, to go out and fetch you in a dangerous storm? If your father hated Matt and did not want him to work for him again, would he have trusted this man to come pick up his daughter and granddaughter the next day?

WITNESS: No.

DEFENSE: Mrs. Larsen, do you believe that Matthew Hinson, seated here today, killed your mother and your father.

WITNESS: No, sir. I do not.

10

NATIONAL LARGEST CIRCULATION OF ANY PAPER IN AMERICA

ENQUIRER

$1.25/$1.49 CANADA

JULIA'S SHOCKING TRUTH!

Cornelia Radcliffe Younger said today, "My sister's marriage is happy and healthy. Her belief in Matthew Hinson doesn't have anything to do with her marriage. Husbands and wives often disagree." Easy for her to say! She and her husband are on the same side. But it's becoming more and more obvious that Julia and Tom Larsen's marriage is coming apart over Julia's undying belief in the innocence of Hinson.

Last week, at Jeremiah Tower's playground for the rich and famous, San Francisco's Stars restaurant, Mr. and Mrs. Larsen were overheard arguing about Hinson,

UNTOLD STORY BEHIND SECRET

and about each other. "I need some support," Julia Larsen was quoted as saying.

"I've always been there for you," her husband reportedly said.

"Like you were after my surgery?" Julia barked back. She was referring to her cancer surgery over a year ago. At the time she was a SF news anchor. She lost her left breast to the disease. Her mother suffered through a double mastectomy while the Radcliffes were still in the Governor's mansion. Julia Larsen never returned to her career at the NBC affiliate, saying she was planning to go back to writing books. Sources who know her well say different. They claim that she had such low self-esteem after the surgery, she could not bear the thought of ever appearing on camera again.

Los Angeles Examiner

EXAMINER EDITORIALS

MODEL DEFENDANT

By Lillian Kasparik Chorvat

Yesterday, the moment we'd all been waiting for: Matthew Hinson took the stand in his own defense. If ever a witness appeared before a jury with the right demeanor, it was this man. He had an air about him of utter simplicity, which translated to honesty and credibility as he spoke. He was strong, however, in his body language; he stood straight up, shoulders back as he took the oath, not haughty or proud, but confident, sure of himself. He did not look fearful, or nervous, nor did he avert his eyes from the jury; he faced them head-on. He did not look—in a word—*guilty* of anything. We watched, riveted, to each well-chosen, polite, intelligent response. . . .

COURT TRANSCRIPT / WITNESS: MATTHEW HINSON

DEFENSE: Can you tell us, Matthew, where you are from originally?

WITNESS: I'm from Wisconsin. LaCrosse. I moved to California a few years after high school, lived in various places, and finally settled in the Mariposa area eight years ago.

DEFENSE: How old are you, Matt?

WITNESS: I'm thirty-five.

DEFENSE: What do you do?

WITNESS: I own a construction company and buy and sell property.

DEFENSE: Did you have a partnership with the deceased, Harry Radcliffe?

WITNESS: Yes, sir. I built his home, and from that time on we worked together.

DEFENSE: How long did you know each other?

WITNESS: Almost eight years from the day I met him.

DEFENSE: Were you friends?

WITNESS: Certainly. I spoke the eulogy at the funeral.

DEFENSE: In your working relationship with Harry, did he ever "dissolve" your partnership?

WITNESS: Four or five times that I can recall.

DEFENSE: So he never meant it?

WITNESS: Never. He'd do that, rant and rave a little, but then he'd reach out and help you the next minute. He was a remarkable man that way.

DEFENSE: Describe the nature of your relationship with Harry Radcliffe outside work.

WITNESS: Father and son.

DEFENSE: Come on, Matthew, we heard testimony that your relationship with Harry wasn't all hearts and flowers.

WITNESS: Is any father-son relationship? Yes, Harry was set in his ways and he could treat people harshly, but you took it with a grain of salt. I respected him, is what it amounts to, even though I didn't always agree with him.

DEFENSE: How did you feel about Mrs. Radcliffe?

WITNESS: I loved her. She was a second mother to me.

DEFENSE: Did you have a fight with Harry Radcliffe on the day in question?

WITNESS: A whopper.

DEFENSE: Would you describe what happened?

WITNESS: We had a stupid fight about something ridiculous concerning a property we had just built. I called him petty and arbitrary, he called me all sorts of things I can't say here, and he said we were through.

DEFENSE: Working together?

WITNESS: Yes. But he wasn't serious. I knew that.

DEFENSE: Because this had happened before?

WITNESS: Yes. It's like Martha once told me, "You think you got it bad? Harry tells me he's divorcing me once a week."

PROSECUTOR: Objection! Hearsay.

JUDGE: Sustained.

DEFENSE: Matt, were you in Harry Radcliffe's den the afternoon of the murders?

WITNESS: Yes, sir, I was. And though not many people are aware of it—I guess people think it was some kind of sacred ground or something—I had been in there several times.

DEFENSE: Any witnesses to this?

WITNESS: Martha was probably the only one who'd actually seen me in there.

DEFENSE: Matt, when you were in the den with Harry that afternoon, did you see the money Mr. Bagett told us he brought him?

WITNESS: Yes.

DEFENSE: Was it a substantial amount?

WITNESS: Sir, I don't mean to sound boastful, but I don't know what you mean by a "substantial" amount.

DEFENSE: Why?

WITNESS: Because I make very good money myself.

DEFENSE: You had no reason to steal this money?

WITNESS: It wasn't mine. That's the best reason.

DEFENSE: Did you have words with Harry in there?

WITNESS: Sure, we argued all afternoon. We were always fighting. He was always calling me a—well, he used expletives—

DEFENSE: "Stupid asshole"? As Mr. Bagett said he called you?

WITNESS: Yeah. And I would tell him he was senile. It was all in fun. It was just *what we did.*

DEFENSE: Did you shout at Harry while in the den?

WITNESS: I'm sure I did.

DEFENSE: As you did, could you have spit?

WITNESS: Well, I didn't actually spit. But I might have given a wet yell or two.

DEFENSE: Matt, let me ask you to explain for us, in your own words, just what you did from the time you left the Radcliffe property the afternoon of the murders to the time the next morning when you found out about them.

WITNESS: When I left, it was nearly dark, and the snow was really coming down. The storm had started that afternoon, the worst we'd had in years, and I'd even told Harry that I knew we were going to have to plow early the next morning. Art Bagett stayed in the house for a while, and I left the property when he did. In fact, I remember warning him to be careful driving, this wasn't gonna quit. Then I got into my Subaru and followed him out—I was worried because he didn't have a four-wheel-drive—and I saw that he was sliding. Whitlock had been plowed, so he was okay from there on out.

DEFENSE: Did you proceed directly home?

WITNESS: Yes, I did. Maggie—that's my dog—had been in all day and I knew she would be wanting to get out, and so I walked with her for a bit, but the snow was coming down so hard she soon looked like a polar bear, and we went back inside.

DEFENSE: And did you stay there?

WITNESS: Yes, sir. I was supposed to go to a dinner party, actually. My friends, Mary Jo Kroll, Rick Radecki, and Jack Hodovance were getting together for Christmas—you can check this with them—

DEFENSE: I did, and Your Honor, we have a signed statement as to the above. I'd like this marked as Exhibit 22 and introduced into evidence.

JUDGE: Done, Mr. Glass. Continue, Mr. Hinson.

WITNESS: Well, Mary Jo called to cancel it because of the weather. So I put in a frozen dinner and watched some TV, let Maggie out one more time. She peed too close to the house, so I hosed it down with water, which turned to ice before it even hit ground. Then the hose burst and my whole yard looked like a skating rink. I went to bed early with a good book, and I think I fell asleep before midnight. The next morning, I got a call from Alan Dayhoff, a neighbor, asking if I heard the news. I couldn't believe my ears.

DEFENSE: Matt, do you have a temper?

WITNESS: Sure. Who doesn't?

DEFENSE: Has that temper ever led you to violence?

WITNESS: I hit my dog too hard once training her. I felt guilty for weeks. No, sir, violence isn't in me.

DEFENSE: Have you ever hit a woman?

WITNESS: Never. Raised my voice a time or two. But never struck a woman, no.

DEFENSE: Matt, did you rescue Julia Larsen from drowning?

WITNESS: Yes, sir. I realized she was in trouble. I jumped in and got her out, and forced the water out of her lungs and she was okay.

DEFENSE: You saved her life?

WITNESS: I did what anybody would have done.

DEFENSE: Did you care about Julia Larsen?

WITNESS: I cared about her whole family.

DEFENSE: Matthew, did you kill Harry and Martha Radcliffe?

WITNESS: No, I most certainly did not.

COURT TV TRANSCRIPT: PRIME TIME JUSTICE / AIR DATE AUG 20 NYC STUDIO: TERRY MORAN / SAN FRANCISCO LOCATION: CLARA TUMA

MORAN: If it wasn't real, this guy could teach acting. It was absolutely mesmerizing in its believability.

TUMA: If it was a performance, it was a brilliantly executed one.

MORAN: Like testimony from God, a reporter commented.

TUMA: I wouldn't go that far. But he remained just as calm and cool through the cross-examination.

MORAN: Bob Hughes was relentless. And angry. Let's take a look at the tape. . . .

*COURTROOM CAMERA / WITNESS: MATTHEW
HINSON*

PROSECUTOR: Did you wash a knife handle with Tuscany soap?

WITNESS: No, sir. I use Tuscany aftershave and soap, but only on my body.

PROSECUTOR: Did you toss a knife, separated from its handle, off Sherlock Road sometime after the murders?

WITNESS: Of course not.

PROSECUTOR: Did you buy snowshoes?

WITNESS: No, sir. I don't think I've ever really seen a pair, except in a Sergeant Preston of the Yukon movie.

PROSECUTOR: Very funny.

WITNESS: I'm not trying to be funny, sir.

PROSECUTOR: Did you attempt to burn clothing and snowshoes in an abandoned mine shaft up the slope from your property?

WITNESS: No.

PROSECUTOR: Didn't your dog find a bloody slipper?

WITNESS: That's what Mr. Crowley told me. But she didn't find it because *I* put it somewhere.

PROSECUTOR: Did you burn boots with rubber soles in your wood stove?

WITNESS: No, sir. The remnants the police found were from my dog's rubber chew toy. It was between some wood I shoved in there. Stunk something awful.

PROSECUTOR: Did you break your own car window that night at the Pine Cove Inn and report to the police that a robber did it?

WITNESS: Pine Cone.

PROSECUTOR: What?

WITNESS: Pine Cone. You said Pine Cove. It's the Pine Cone Inn.

PROSECUTOR: Don't get smart with me.

WITNESS: I'm only correcting a name, sir. But no, sir, I did not break into my own car. You flatter me, but I'm just not *that* clever.

PROSECUTOR: Mr. Hinson, the evidence in this trial proves you bought a pair of gloves. The same gloves were proven to be used in poking into a fruitcake the night of—

WITNESS: No! They were the same *kind* of gloves. If I've been hearing things right, no one has proven that the exact pair of gloves that I purchased and then were stolen were the gloves whose impression they found in that fruitcake.

PROSECUTOR: Mr. Hinson, you said you didn't like Harry Radcliffe. Isn't it true you hated Harry Radcliffe? Isn't it true that you hated his wife too? Isn't it true that inside you had a pathological resentment of these people with power and money, greed, a sense of revenge, and perhaps some interest in their daughter that made you feel—?

DEFENSE: I object, Your Honor, strenuously and passionately. This pathetic attempt at tacking on a motive here—something no one has come near doing in this trial—is an outrage to the criminal justice system.

JUDGE: Mr. Glass has a most valid point. Mr. Hughes, please, you should know better. The jury will disregard Mr. Hughes's last question. Mr. Hughes, you may continue.

PROSECUTION: I'm done, Your Honor. I don't ever want to talk to this man again.

Matthew thought, What a silly old queen. Like a fussy lady. This was their prosecutor? Making a fool of himself. From the get-go he had looked like some character Jimmy Stewart would have played, the country bumpkin with his hayseed straw hat, rumpled suit, and sweaty shirt. And that bow tie! *"I don't ever want to talk to this man again."* Probably a prissy old fag.

Matt was proud of himself. What bullshit he'd given them, slapping it on with a palette knife. He had them, every one of them, from the old bag with the white sweater in the first row of the jury to those court junkies who didn't even know him but were there every morning like he was some kind of movie star reporting to the set. He had fans, it suddenly occurred to him. Groupies. He was famous. *Court TV* said he was almost as watched as O.J.

But who gave a rat's ass? All he wanted was to be left alone with Julia. Make a life. Love. Go on book tours together. Raise Molly. Thank God this carnival ride was almost out of steam. Soon he'd get his dream. It was pretty much over. There were no surprises left. He just couldn't wait to surprise the non-believers when he was acquitted.

SAN FRANCISCO

Times-Herald   NATIONAL
EDITION

1 DOLLAR & 50 CENTS

AMAZING TURN IN LAST MOMENTS
OF HINSON TRIAL!

San Francisco—In the final moments of the trial of Matthew Hinson, currently taking place at the county courthouse, the defense surprised everyone by calling back to the stand Mr. Charlie Ross, the expert technician who had testified earlier about DNA. The attorney for the defense, Michael Glass, read from Mr. Ross's report which had been introduced into evidence two weeks prior. *"My findings here,"* Mr. Ross wrote, *"after examining the death site, the deceased, the ballistics reports, after speaking to the coroner, and most important the condition of the room and the placement of Mr. Radcliffe's body as it was found by the examining team, I'd have to say that one conclusion we could come to is that these things are consistent with self-defense."*

The courtroom was at first confused by what the words meant, and the court asked for clarity. In fact, Judge Esther Mae Barnes, who had never given much indication as to what she thought of anything she'd been hearing throughout the trial, strained in the direction of the witness stand and was all ears. Glass asked Mr. Ross if he could explain, in layman's terms, what he meant. "Self-defense?" he said. "Whose?" Mr. Ross's reply was, "The intruder's, of course."

Mr. Ross went on to say that the court could find other examiners and technicians who would refute him, for this was not an exact science, but from the way Harry Radcliffe's body was positioned, and from studying the wounds and comparing the coroner's reports on those wounds, and ballistics reports on the distance the gun was held, which way the knife came at him, he was positive a case could well be made for the fact that Radcliffe was killed in self-defense. "What I mean is," he said when pressed, "it is probable that Harry attacked the intruder first, and that the intruder killed him and Mrs. Radcliffe as he tried to save himself."

It was a phenomenal turn of events, the defense suggesting that the intruder— whether it be Mr. Hinson or someone else—actually killed to save his own life. It almost made Harry Radcliffe the assailant.

The judge seemed fascinated, and asked Mr. Ross why he had not enlightened the court with his findings when he was questioned earlier. Ross replied, "No one asked me, Your Honor."

SAN FRANCISCO

Times-Herald   NATIONAL
EDITION

1 DOLLAR & 50 CENTS

JUDGE SHOCKS JURY WITH INSTRUCTIONS

San Francisco—After the summations of the prosecution and then the defense, in a heartfelt plea that the prosecution had not proven their case within a shadow of a doubt against the defendant, Matthew Hinson, the judge took an unusual step. She addressed the jury directly, saying, "We heard troubling testimony yesterday on the fact that there exists the possibility that this murder—no matter who committed it, that's not the issue in what I'm discussing right now—might have been perpetrated in self-defense. In 1984, in the case of *Oberman* vs *the State of California*, the supreme court of this state found that because the possibility of a self-defense situation on the part of an intruder occurred, the jury in that case was instructed that they could find the defendant guilty of a lesser charge.

"In other words—plain English—I'm so instructing you today that you may, in the case of this trial, if you see fit, find the defendant guilty of first degree murder, as asked for by the prosecution. Or you may find the defendant not guilty of the charges and release him. Or—and this is the reference to Oberman—you may find the defendant guilty on a lesser charge of manslaughter, if you believe the self-defense testimony is warranted and conscionable with your decision."

august 24

dear Matthew

Thank you for the Poems. They are very nice. I KNOW you are still in jail but Mom says you will get out soon. I HOPE SO. Then maybe everyone can feel better. I am sorry that ~~everyone~~ people think your bad. I don't. You were very nice to me. I know you didn't hurt NANA or GRANDPA Mom says when you are free we will go back to Mariposa and play in the snow. Mr. TiddlEBerk says HELLO to you. Could you have a stuffed animal in jail? I'd let you have him for a while if it would help. My Dad doesn't want me to write this, but MOM said I could. I pray for you every night.

Your friend,

Molly Larsen

Matthew held the little girl's letter in his hand and paced his cell long after lights out. Not because he was worried, anxious, or fearful. No. He paced his cell as a tiger might at hearing the sound of the cage being unlocked, knowing freedom is within reach. He was sure of it now; the jury was hopelessly deadlocked. Oh, he much rather would have had a clean and immediate "not guilty" verdict, but he knew that was fantasy; there were too many people on that jury who wanted to fix blame on someone, anyone, too many voters who had worshiped that old son of a bitch Harry like some diehards still revered John Kennedy.

They were stalling. Holding things up. It would take
time, but they'd finally come around. The grand-
mother who adored him would convince the others.
Hero, he'd be called. Hero who had saved Harry's
very own daughter. You don't convict a hero.

He strutted a bit, swaggering in a kind of macho
Errol Flynn swashbuckling way as he passed the bars,
running his right hand over them with his fingernails,
clicketyclicketyclicketyclickety, picturing himself standing on that rock above the water at Leucadia, above
the spot he'd followed her to, watching her strip her
clothes off, lying naked for him for twenty minutes in
the blazing sun, seeing her put her toes into the icy
water, mustering the courage to dive finally. . . .

He let Molly's letter drop to the cement floor as he
brought his left hand down to his pants and took hold
of his crotch. He jumped up on his bunk, standing on
it with both feet, just as he'd stood on that rock, rubbing himself in the exact same way, watching her,
adoring her, loving her—

Then disaster. Blood on the rock. Her hair spreading
on top of the water like a honey-colored jellyfish. But
wait—her head was sinking under the water. Bubbles
rising to the surface. The soft and horrifying image of
her buttocks floating, her head submerged. He
recalled the ice water filling his boots as he jumped in,
his hands grabbing hold of her, lifting her, flipping her
up and over his shoulder, rising into the sun, victo-
rious, Spartacus with the spoils of his courage. On the

rock, breathing life back into her, swallowing the water that erupted from her lungs, lips against lips, pressing down on her chest, touching her breasts, feeling life returning.

He sank to his bunk by crossing his legs, both hands between them. *Julia!* Sun on their bodies, feeling her breath against his mouth, licking her ear, a hand on her forehead and another between her legs, pressing his body to hers, only his wet T-shirt and jeans separating flesh from flesh, and then, when her eyes opened and she saw him and she realized, then ... what she hadn't said about that day in the courtroom.

Matthew felt a wave of warmth fill his pants. He held his hands there, gently manipulating between his legs, like Martha had taught him to knead pizza dough. Then he felt the semen sliding around his testicles and oozing through the cotton of his pants. Soon, he thought, perhaps tomorrow or the next day—the ninth day of deliberations—at the latest, he'd be free again. He'd resume his plan. Julia loved him. So did Molly. He could get her to divorce Tom—that would probably happen even without him. Then it would be only Julia. Julia and Matt. Always. Forever. Soon. *Not guilty!* Soon.

NBC NEWS TRANSCRIPT/PRE-EMPTION OF DAYS OF OUR LIVES/ *SEPT. 2*

LADIES AND GENTLEMEN, WE INTERRUPT THIS PROGRAM TO BRING YOU AN NBC NEWS UPDATE:

SOURCES AT THE SAN FRANCISCO COUNTY
COURTHOUSE HAVE JUST INFORMED US THAT THE
JURY IN THE TRIAL OF MATTHEW HINSON IS ON
ITS WAY BACK TO THE COURTROOM. WE REPEAT,
THE JURY IN THE HINSON TRIAL HAS OBVIOUSLY
REACHED A VERDICT AFTER ALMOST TEN DAYS
OF DELIBERATIONS. . . .

TIME
THE WEEKLY NEWSMAGAZINE

Will He Walk?

Los Angeles Examiner

EXAMINER EDITORIALS

HUNG JURY IN HINSON TRIAL

CYNTHIA MCFADDEN, ABC NEWS:

MCFADDEN: Matthew Hinson had not nearly the same confident, bright look he'd had when the trial began weeks ago. Today he seemed broken and somewhat sad. The jury's deadlock clearly shocked him. Ironically enough, it was the judge's instructions to add the possibility of a manslaughter verdict that might have caused the hung jury. For when interviewed outside the courthouse after they were dismissed, every juror said had it been a clear-cut choice of either guilty in the first degree or acquittal, they would have had to choose acquittal. So what happens now? As with Eric and Lyle Menendez, the prosecution wants to try him again. The D.A. is against bail. The judge has a mind of her own. We'll know on Tuesday.

*THE TONIGHT SHOW WITH JAY LENO /
SEPTEMBER 7*

TRANSCRIPT:

LENO: Do you know that Hinson's book sales doubled the day they announced the jury was deadlocked? I hear Judith Krantz is looking to hire a hit man. . . .

SAN FRANCISCO

Times-Herald

HINSON DECISION TOMORROW

RADCLIFFE DAUGHTER STILL
MAINTAINS HIS INNOCENCE

COURTROOM TRANSCRIPT:

JUDGE: Mr. Hughes, your recommendation?

PROSECUTOR: Your Honor, this man is a menace to society, a danger to everyone, and there is no reason why he should be granted bail. He didn't get it before and he shouldn't get it now. We want him held at the San Francisco County Jail without bail until which time a new trial date can be set.

JUDGE: Mr. Glass?

DEFENSE: Your Honor, the prosecution did not win. Oh, they technically didn't lose, but they didn't win. That means their case has problems. That means there was a great deal of belief on the part of the jury that Matthew Hinson is innocent. Another trial is a waste of time and taxpayers' money. But the prosecution has the right to do just that in our criminal justice system. However this man—a man no one has proven guilty—deserves bail until that time.

JUDGE: Will the defendant please rise?

[DEFENDANT STANDS]

JUDGE: Matthew Hinson.

DEFENDANT: Yes, Your Honor.

JUDGE: This is a difficult decision for the court. The case for bail is well put, but the prosecution's reasoning is sound as well. It is my decision, but it boils down to my belief in innocence or guilt. And for that reason I'm ordering that you be held as the prosecution has asked, until a new trial date can be arranged on the court calendar. Bail is denied.

[GAVEL] Court adjourned.

Matthew felt a bullet pierce his heart. Not because he had lost, not because he hadn't been clever enough, not because he was going to have to do this all over again. The thing that paralyzed him was the time he'd have to spend waiting, the knowledge that he was not sure when he would see his beloved angel again.

As they took him away, he looked over his shoulder one last time with his now diminished emerald beams, at Julia, and saw that she was starting to cry.

PART III

Tom

11

Tom knew she needed time. For whatever the reasons she hung onto and supported Matthew, it was over now as far as he was concerned. It would take a good six months before they could retry the bastard, and hopefully in that time another jailbird would stick a blade into him. Fuck him, Tom thought, he had caused his marriage enough pain. He and Julia'd had terrible troubles before Matt came along, and he felt they needed now to get their lives rolling again, work things out, get past this. Tom felt like shouting, "I'm thirty-three years old, and I don't have all day!" He decided that a few weeks together with Julia and Molly might bring some semblance of order back into their lives. He saw an old movie on cable one night, *Diary of a Mad Housewife* it was called, and figured Julia was just that—mad. But she'd be okay. They would make it yet.

Many times over the years, and recently on the way back from Hong Kong, Tom had stopped for a few days of R&R in Honolulu. The Halekulani Hotel there was his idea of paradise on earth. The staff made him feel pampered and special, and so he booked a suite for the three of them. Julia needed to get away, Molly had never been to Hawaii, and Tom figured a few thousand miles of water between Julia and Hinson could only be good. He came home with the tickets to find Molly and a sitter there, not Julia. "Surprise," he said to his daughter, "we're going to Hawaii."

Her eyes lit up. "When?"

"Tomorrow."

She was thrilled. "Can I go scuba diving?"

"I'll teach you." He turned to the sitter. "Where'd my wife go?" The girl shrugged.

"Dad, is Mom coming with us?"

"Of course."

"What about my school?"

"It'll be fine. It's only for a week."

"Cool." She had taken to saying "cool" a lot. Tom was picking it up himself, perhaps trying to be hip, at least in her eyes.

Molly dragged him into her room to ask excitedly what she should pack, and when he said how strange it was that Julia hadn't told the sitter where she'd gone, Molly suddenly had a guilty look on her face. Tom asked her if she knew. She nodded, her eyes turned down.

He didn't need to hear it from her. *He knew, sensed it*

right away. She was at the San Francisco County jail. Visiting *him*.

Matthew Hinson showered, washed his hair, put on clean underwear and jeans, and the brand-new T-shirt that had been issued to him just this morning. Now he stood dabbing cologne—Tuscany—under each ear. The big black man in the cell directly across from this new one they'd put him in after the trial stared at him and shook his head. "You think you goin' on a fuckin' date?"

Matt said not a word. He checked out his wavy reflection in the piece of stainless steel bolted to the cement block wall that masqueraded as a mirror. He nodded. He'd pass.

The other prisoner forced a prissy "tsk-tsk" sound and laughed. "Think she gonna smell ya through the bulletproof glass?"

"Gimme a break, Scully." Matt turned away.

"Bring your rubbers too?" Scully called out. "Maybe you can poke her through the glass." The man roared with laughter so loud that several voices from other cells in the block called out for him to shut the fuck up.

Then a guard arrived, and Matthew was relieved it was the young one named Walter. Matthew had taken a liking to this gentle, seemingly fair man over the time he'd been here. Walter unlocked Matt's cell door and then led the prisoner down the corridor, through another dark steel door, down another corridor, and onto an elevator.

They arrived at the visitors' area, where Walter ushered him into a small cubicle. On the wall opposite the door was a counter, with a folding chair in front of it, and from the counter clear up to the ceiling was the solid bulletproof glass Scully had referred to. There was a little microphone on the other side. "Pretty lady you got waiting for you," the guard said.

And then he left.

Matt sat on the metal chair. He put his hands between his legs, feeling himself swelling just at the thought of her, and tried to stay calm. But his heart leaped at the knowledge that he would soon be face to face with the object of his desire. He'd not seen her since that last day in the courtroom. He didn't know what she was thinking. That's what he had to find out. He had never counted on this, having to stay in jail, face another trial, go through it all over again. He feared time would change her mind. Tom and all the other bastards who hated him might turn her against him. Would he lose her?

Insecurity raced through his being, and where there had been almost overwhelming, smug confidence, there was now apprehension and fear manifested in the brilliant green eyes of a lost little boy.

He sat still and waited what seemed an eternity.

What the hell was she doing there? What was it about this guy, already? Tom had asked himself that again and again during the trial, when she was making Matthew more famous than he had already become, and never found a satisfying answer. He confronted Julia about it, but the stock response was the same thing she had told Oprah: she *believed* in him. Tom felt he didn't know his own wife anymore. He didn't know her mind. Worse, he didn't know how to break the spell, how to detox her, how to cut the chains. He didn't know because he didn't understand what was at the heart of it. But he didn't blame only her; by his own admission, he hadn't been willing for a long time to open his own selfish eyes.

Matthew never took his eyes off her as she fumbled with her purse, the chair. She looked nervous, just as he was. He drank in her hair, which he saw was shorter now, and his eyes caressed her smooth cheeks and full lips, and he saw she was wearing purple, a color he'd never seen her in, not even in all the times he'd sat in the tree outside her father's house, peering through the window of the guest bedroom she always used, watching her, studying her from so close a vantage point and yet so far.

As Walter explained to her how to use the microphone, he knew she couldn't see what he was doing under the counter, so he unzipped his pants and put his hand inside and grasped it. One hand on top of the counter. One hand below. But his face gave away nothing. He looked—if anything—a little lonely, a little sad. He'd practiced, in that stainless steel mirror in his cell, for days.

When the guard left, she faced him. Her voice was soft, measured. "I'm ... so ... sorry," she said with deep feeling.

"You're here now," he said equally as softly, tightening the grip on his penis. "And that's all I need."

A *book*? Tom was astounded that she had the nerve to tell him that she was seeing him because she'd decided to write a book on the case. She needed to "interview" him. She'd be spending a "substantial amount of time" with him. She couldn't "do" Hawaii, as if it were a meeting he was asking her to attend. Forget Molly's disappointment, her excitement dashed. She was only a little girl who wanted her mother back. Tom's guts burned—how could she treat Molly like that? This wasn't Julia. Christ, he felt he and Molly didn't mean anything anymore. Julia's obsession with that prick was inexplicable.

Tom called his friend Melba DeMello at the Halekulani to cancel. But instead they got to talking, which was easy to do with Melba, who had a soft voice and caring soul. Maybe that was why Tom Larsen, who was usually a very private person, poured out his guts. Sometimes it's easier to talk to someone not too close to you, Melba said in answer to that very question at the end of the two-hour phone call. But in that call she'd gotten closer to Tom than anyone in recent years, including Julia. The problem, she said, was his, not Julia's. Her advice was to come to the island, talk to someone here—she knew a good man, a doctor. Tom laughed, talk to a shrink? Julia's the one who needs that.

But he knew, despite his protestations, he would do it anyway. Go to Hawaii, he told himself, not the shrink. Well, maybe—for his daughter. He didn't want her seeing her mother continuing to make a fool of herself. Or fools of them as well. Denial loomed in his brain, but he knew he was going to take all of Melba's advice, because the bottom line was he loved Julia more than not wanting to face the truth about himself.

Tom and Molly went to Hawaii. Without Julia.

"It's the waiting, Scully, the not knowing. Fucking judge won't give me bail. The prosecutors keep fighting with my lawyers. They want more time to prepare for a second trial, wanna nail me this time. I want it tomorrow so they can't manufacture some kind of new evidence."

"You got a nice butt."

Matt ignored the words, flipped over onto his back on his bed and gloated. "She turned down a trip to Hawaii with her husband just to be with me."

"Be one stupid white bitch."

"She loves me." Matt kicked off his pants, put his hands under his head, stretched back in his underwear.

"I see why."

"What the hell is going on with you?" Tom asked Julia during their first dinner together after he and Molly had returned from Oahu. Molly had been trying to make conversation with her mother all through the meal, but Julia just sat there, wearing the lei Molly had picked out especially for her, but utterly blank.

"I'm a little distant, I know."

"A *little distant*? Your daughter's talking to you."

"I realize that."

"Then pay attention. Like you do at the jail."

"Don't do this to me in front of her, Tom."

"Mommy, do you know how to make popovers for breakfast?"

"Huh?"

"Dad and I had them at the hotel in Hawaii. We ate on the balcony. In our bathrobes." She giggled.

Tom told Molly he'd call Melba and have the hotel send the recipe so they'd be exactly the same, right down to the *poha* jam, then suggested she go do her homework. When she went to her room, Julia got up and started to pace. Tom told her she was being selfish. "Molly shouldn't have to suffer just because you're going through some kind of angst with Gary Gilmore."

"I'm a mess, Tom. I'm not sure about anything, I'm walking a tightrope."

"What kind of tightrope? Between where and where? Ever since you started interviewing that cunning liar—"

"See? We can't even talk about him because when I mention his name, you have to take a shot at him."

"I'm using words. He had a gun."

"That's not true."

"Jesus, Julia." He stood up. "I can't believe you're falling for it all over again."

"What if he's telling the truth? Come on, Tom, I never asked you that. What if I'm *not* wrong?"

He didn't answer. He didn't need to. The question was ridiculous. He opened the door to the balcony and walked outside. Julia followed him and stood beside him at the railing. "Don't see him again, Julia," Tom implored, giving it one last shot. "Forget the stupid book. Forget him." Then he decided to tell her something she didn't know. "I saw this guy in Honolulu. A guy I found who maybe can help me, us."

"What kind of guy?"

"A professional. A psychologist."

She was startled. "You?"

"I'm not as stuck in my ways as you think. He brought up some issues that ... well, that I hadn't thought about." He told her how he thought the problem was her obsession with Matthew, that he never even considered the obstacle was him. "I mean,

I know the trouble we had before last Christmas. I know how you were hurting, but I was too."

Julia said nothing, but he could see she was listening.

"I need to understand something," he said, turning to face her. "Is this really all about your belief in Matthew, or is it more a reaction to what you're not getting from me?"

She shocked him. She said, "Don't flatter yourself, Tom," and went back inside without another word.

"I'm working on a new poem for you," Matt said to Julia, "but I'm having trouble finishing it."

"It's almost December. Make it my Christmas present."

"I have something already ordered for you."

"They let you do that in jail?"

"Walter's my buddy. He's helping." He moved his face closer to the glass partition. "What are you planning for Christmas? I know it's going to be hard this year."

"One whole year later," remembering that horrible night. She cast her eyes down. Then she seemed to pull out of it. "Molly and I are flying to Hawaii to meet Tom. And Cornelia and Brad. We always spent the holidays in the mountains. We need a change. No snow, no mountains, no reminders."

Tom was all he heard, *Tom* was all he could think

about. So he still hadn't shaken her hold on the husband. *Tom Tom Tom*. He needed to do something, make her feel for him, hurt for him, bring her even further under the spell. For there was no telling what might happen in Hawaii, on a romantic beach, with *Tom Tom* filling her head full of ugly thoughts about him. He needed to get her to the point where she'd divorce the putz. And marry *him*. He needed her to be his.

She left one of her cassettes out. Tom saw it on her desk as he was in a rush to get to the airport on the first of December. He was flying into Kai Tak to work on the bank before he met Julia and Molly in Hawaii on the twenty-third—this time Julia had agreed to go, figuring Christmas on the beach was what she needed to eradicate the memories of snow and death. Without even thinking twice, Tom grabbed the cassette and took it with him. He knew it had Matthew's voice on it.

On the plane, he sat staring at it. He figured she'd think she misplaced it—her office was such a mess anyhow. Funny, he thought as well, he didn't feel guilty about it. Just a little queasy about what he was going to hear.

The car they sent for him in Hong Kong had a cassette player in the dash, so he rode up front. The driver thankfully spoke little English, so he didn't feel too embarrassed. There was nothing on the tape about

Julia and him, as he'd feared. But the words he did hear turned his stomach. . . .

J: Nothing's wrong. It's just—

M: What? Come on.

J: Something's always bothered me.

M: Tell me, Julia. We have no secrets.

J: The day you were arrested, Jim Crowley said you claimed you were hunting.

M: I lied.

J: You lied?

M: I was shooting clay targets.

J: Why didn't you say that?

M: 'Cause guys up there think it's a sissy thing. Something the fags in this jail would do. They're all hunters up there. They can relate to that.

J: You said you didn't hunt.

M: I had a bad experience with hunting.

J: What do you mean?

M: Dad was a hunter. He told me I had to learn how to shoot. I didn't want to. I was sort of a sissy when it came to macho shit like that. I could fish, that was okay, but I couldn't hunt. Dad made me go rabbit hunting with him one November. It was cold, the first snow had fallen, and we were wandering around these old cornfields for what seemed like hours, and I was carrying a 4-10 rifle, which felt like it weighed about a thousand pounds.

J: How old were you then?

M: Fourteen or fifteen. Suddenly, I saw something run.

And another behind it. I lifted the rifle without even thinking, just doing what I was supposed to be doing. Both furry things had stopped behind a stub of corn stalk. Then they made a dash for it and I shot, pow, pow. They kicked up into the air. My heart was racing. Dad was shouting, Hey, boy, you did it, you did it! and I dropped the rifle and ran down to where they were. And what I saw there— (BEAT)

J: Go on.

M: Two little bunnies. Not rabbits, these were little Peter Cottontails, you know? Just little baby bunnies, like you see in the pet stores at Easter. The first one was dead, and there was blood all over the snow. The second one was still kicking, its back legs arching out as if it were trying to hop away. But it was on its side and its insides were coming out, and I fell to my knees and lifted it up and unzipped my jacket, my new parka. I put him inside it to keep him warm and I prayed to God that I could make him live. As I felt the blood filling my shirt and coat and long johns, I prayed that he wouldn't die. But he did and I sat there and cried until I was so cold I felt like rigor mortis was setting into me.

J: Oh, Matt—

M: Dad didn't know what to say. He was too embarrassed. I thought he was ashamed of me, but I think he understood because when I finally found the car, he just said he thought it was time to be getting home, and from that day on, we never, ever talked about it.

J: I'm very sorry you had to go through that.

M: They gave me a dog for my next birthday. I think animals started to mean something different to them from that day on. You couldn't blame Dad; everyone in Wisconsin hunted. My first dog was a lot like Maggie. Do you know how she is?

J: No.

M: They told me Inga took her. She's good to animals. Maggie will be happy there.

J: I'm sure she'll be waiting for you when you get out.

M: Will I get out?

"No, you won't," Tom actually said out loud. All the Regent doormen and several guests were staring at him sitting there alone in the Bentley, waiting for him to get out and enter the hotel, but he didn't care. He sat there as if lost in time, thinking, Why doesn't she see through him? Why can't she figure out he's bullshitting her? What bond did they have that he didn't understand, that he couldn't comprehend? Or was it him?

A day later, he was on another plane, retracing his route from the day before, but this time not quite as far as San Francisco. This time he was bound for Hawaii. He was going earlier than planned. He had a doctor to see again.

It was after midnight. Matt lay on his bunk in his shorts and snickered. "I told her a story the other day, Scully. Man, it was incredible. What do they call that kind of thing? Improvisation, that's it."

"Jus' show me that piece," Scully said.

Matt teased him by ignoring him. "Man, oh man, I had her going." And he had himself going, paying no attention to what he was saying, proud of himself, careless. "She bought every word, Scully, every fucking word. Bunnies and blood and how it destroyed me. I was something else."

"You right 'bout that, baby. You right 'bout that."

"She was a little unsure there for a while, Scully, but I haven't lost her yet. I'll give her a poem tomorrow, that'll weaken her for sure."

"Stop teasin' me, man," Scully growled. "Jus' pull those shorts down an' show the governor what ya got."

Matt flipped over on his stomach, grabbed the pencil and the legal pad at his side, and finished the last lines of the poem while Scully feasted his gaze on the curve of his buttocks.

Matt read his poem to himself. Pleased, he tossed the pen across the room, turned onto his back again, and spread his legs. "Got another book coming out soon." He looked proud.

"You gettin' hard, pretty boy," Scully said, the timbre of his voice anxious now. "Thinkin' on her, huh? Show your pal, Scully, jus' show it a little, huh? You get Walt let you come in here, I do you."

Matthew lifted his head. "What the hell do you think this is here, *Kiss of the* Fucking *Spider Woman*?"

"Huh?"

"Stupid nigger, rent the tape." There were bars
and a corridor separating them. He could dish it right
back. Then he gave Scully a wink. "Say please."

"Please."

Matt clicked off his light.

"Shit," the voice across from him said, and then
Scully's light went off as well.

Geoffrey Sjostrum had turned out to be the only
guy Tom had ever been able to really talk to in his
entire life. A big fellow who looked daunting, the
doctor had immediately put Tom at ease with the
sound of his mellow voice, and the way he listened.
Maybe that was the problem with all his male friends
in the past, Tom thought: no one ever wanted to really
listen. And his father never went deeper than baseball
scores. Guys don't do that anyhow, talk about their
feelings. At least not the guys he knew. Geoff's mother
was Hawaiian, Tom learned, and that explained it for
him, for he'd always found a gentleness in Polyne-
sians that he felt comfortable with. This felt very safe.

He spent three weeks in Honolulu before Julia
and Molly arrived. It was his secret. He'd come to the
fact that answers were not going to tumble from
Julia's lips, that his marriage was on the rocks, that his
life was falling apart. Screw the bank in China. He
took a leave of absence from the firm, just for the
month, which didn't sit well in the middle of a project.
He was risking his 850Ci Christmas bonus, but hell,

his future, his marriage, his kid, were more important than any goddamn car.

The more he talked, the more Geoff probed, the more he learned about himself. No, this was no Iron John experience, and he didn't swing from vines searching for the real man inside him either. He just started to take a look at himself and what he'd been taught to believe most of his life. He started to understand that he'd always seen Julia as a person who couldn't think for herself. With Geoff's help he came to realize the trauma of the surgery and the trauma of the murders had intensified that perception of her. And this was a woman he'd been attracted to because she was so forceful, because she was so dynamic. He figured she'd grabbed hold of something floating by to keep her from going under, and that something was Matthew. But Tom agonized over the question why that couldn't be him?

But he came to the answer. And it was simple: because he'd been pushing her head underwater himself by his inability to make love to her after she lost her breast.

It was a "guy" thing, Geoff said, just as Tom had told Julia several times, a pretty stupid statement actually, but not uncommon. Tom assured Geoff that he loved her, desired her, but then when it came time to make love, he just couldn't function. Geoff asked him about his feelings today—did he still desire her? Still love her? Did he want a future with her? Of course he did. Then, the good doctor said, Tom had better get over his "guy" thing real fast. Tom said he had tried, man, had he tried, no one knew how much he hated himself for not being able to get it up, that he'd even tried fantasizing that last time, doing anything to keep an erection, but hadn't succeeded. "Doctor, I hated the emptiness Julia felt, hated seeing her so unfulfilled, hurting so deeply, a despair I'd caused. Before this she'd been vibrant, vivacious, even a little wild. She got that Emmy because she had such an infectious quality of loving life. She exploded on the screen. Now she was a shadow."

He knew she had been going to talk to her mother about it, and then there was no mother to talk to. Tom admitted he'd planned to talk to Harry about it! And then there was no Harry to talk to. He hated fucking Hinson more than he could put into words.

But he finally asked Geoff how. How could he overcome this thing? What would it take? Geoff knew Tom hated the word *therapy*, so he said, "Some hard work."

Tom Larsen said he was ready.

"Matt, what did Mom tell you that last time you spoke?"

His heart stopped. He felt a rush. He'd waited a year for her to ask. He knew he'd melted her down with the bunnies, but this was an opportunity not to be missed. This could be *the turning point for her heart*.

This could make her divorce the dickhead. But he had to choose his words carefully; he could not risk slipping.

First, he played a little hard to get. "Julia," he said, closing his eyes for effect, "it was a long time ago now . . ."

"You must remember."

He opened his eyes to see her begging stare. "She was working on the fruitcake dough and called me in for some coffee. I'd been inspecting the framework of a house out on Triangle Road, and I was freezing. This was the day before she died. We talked some small talk, what I was doing for Christmas, would I see my folks in Wisconsin, that kind of thing. Somehow the conversation turned to you, and she said she was worried about you."

"Worried how?"

"She knew the problems you were having. She was a very unhappy, lonely, unfulfilled woman. She didn't want you to be the same."

"But I was successful!"

"She had been too. But she had a husband who wouldn't sleep with her. Now you did too."

"You knew all that?"

"I surmised it from what she was saying. She'd had a drink. She didn't want you to become what she was, unfulfilled and living in pain." Matthew could see her heart swelling, her eyes bulging with locked tears. He went for the jugular: "She was going to tell you to dump Tom."

Julia gasped, "That's not true! She adored Tom!"

He presented an innocent shrug. "I'm only telling you what she told me."

"But it makes no sense, she and Tom—"

"She knew he was treating you the way Harry treated her. No matter she 'adored' Tom, she wanted to protect you from a lifetime of misery. That's what the powwow at Christmas was going to be about. She was going to tell you to end your marriage, to do what she hadn't done with her own." There. He'd just given her her mother's approval to divorce the bastard.

"God." Her voice was without life.

Matt reached out his hand to the bulletproof partition, whispering her name. She brought her hand up, and their palms met as his had with his mother in the courtroom, only the thick, cold glass separating them. Then he brought his face to her fingertips and kissed the glass ever so lightly.

"Molly?" Tom heard his daughter answer the phone.

"Hi, Dad. Aunt Cornelia and Uncle Brad are here. We're all going on the same plane tomorrow. I added up the frequent-flyer miles I'm gonna get."

Scary how fast they learn, Tom thought. "Put your mother on, will you?"

"Um . . ."

He waited a second, heard a thunk, voices, then expected Julia to pick up. Instead he got her sister. "Tom, this is Cornelia. She's not here."

"Where'd she go? There's something—" He stopped himself because he knew. He knew where she'd gone, where else? "She's with him *again*?"

"Tom, you sounded so enthusiastic, what's up?"

"I'm in Hawaii, Cornelia, been here awhile now. Been getting my head together, really working on some stuff. I just wanted to tell Julia I love her."

"You can tell her yourself tomorrow. There's nothing I want more, Tom, than to see you two work things out."

The next afternoon, Matthew stood like a peacock in his cell, a bright new shirt—a Christmas present from Scully, who hoped it would entice him to pull his pants down—stuffed into his regulation jeans, and a smile on his face from ear to ear. Scully looked him up and down. "My, oh my," he said, "Pretty Boy be the partridge in the fuckin' pear tree today."

"I hope to God Walter got the present through," Matthew said. "I couldn't sleep half the night thinking about it."

"Walter done fine 'cause I tell him it cool."

Matt shook his head. "You're something else, Scully. They're gonna name this hole after you someday."

"Name *your* hole after me, baby."

"When the hell is your trial?"

"Postpone. Again. Okay by me."

Then Matt heard the sound of the door, and Walter's face appeared in the hall and Matt could tell just from looking at him that it had been done, the surprise was ready. Walter held a Christmas gift. "They had to open it and rewrap it, that's regulation," Walter explained.

"It's fine, fine," Matthew replied, taking one last look in the mirror before his journey to the visitors' room.

"She's here," Walter said as he closed the cell door after them.

"I'm ready," Matt said.

And as Matt and the guard walked down the hall, Scully muttered, "Be one stupid white bitch."

Walter led Matt to a different visitors' room from the one in which he usually met Julia. And he was astonished, because he was on the wrong side of the partition. He was on *her* side, and she was standing just inside the door. Matthew froze. This was the first time since their last walk in the snow almost a year ago, before he had been arrested, that she stood in a room where there was nothing separating them. He couldn't believe his eyes. He felt thunderbolts surge through him. His balls tingled. His pulse raced. His brow was sweating, his head getting light.

"Walter arranged it," she said.

"Man," Matthew whispered, a look of sheer gratitude directed Walter's way.

But Walter explained that he was not free to leave them totally alone. Regulations required he would have to remain here. Matthew wanted to slug him in the gut, knock his head to the floor, lock him out. The sexual electricity was so strong that he wanted to fuck her right there. No, this asshole couldn't stand here the whole time. He wanted to kiss her, hold her, bring his lips to that scar again . . .

She handed him her present first. He opened it and found a needlepoint throw pillow with an exquisite gowned angel on it. "My mother made it years ago," she explained, "found it when we were closing up the house."

He pressed it to his chest, then kissed her on the cheek. He saw her flush. Then he indicated the wrapped box sitting on the counter. When she opened it, she found an envelope and another box inside. He told her to open the envelope first. She withdrew manuscript pages, already typed by someone, and the cover page said *OF ANGELS & CHRISTMAS / POEMS BY MATTHEW HINSON / DEDICATED TO THE MEMORY OF MARTHA RADCLIFFE*. He saw tears come to her eyes when she looked up at him. "I don't know what to say."

"Open the box," he suggested, "it'll bring you back to earth."

Julia pulled the wrapping off and found chocolates. Five boxes of them tied together with green ribbon. "Frango mints!" she exclaimed, examining the flavors, "Raspberry, coffee, lemon—"

"Peanut butter too."

"What a kick!"

He could see she was honestly tickled, thrilled. He told her he had ordered them from Marshall Field's catalog. He watched her unwrap the cellophane from the top box. "Had to get you your favorite candy."

"How did you know?" she asked, popping one into her mouth.

"Huh?"

"I never told you."

He hesitated a moment. Panic button. *Never told him? Jesus. Think fast.* Then he remembered. "Your mom did," he said, whispering as if he were revealing a secret.

"Ah, sure," she said. "Well, I'm glad she did."

But then, all of a sudden, something happened. Her expression went blank, and all emotion drained from her.

He panicked again. "Julia? What's the matter?"

She looked paralyzed.

"Julia?"

She let out a deep wheeze. Then she opened her mouth to say something, but no words came. Instead she turned white, and she started to topple forward.

"Julia! Walter, help me—" She seemed to be

fainting, collapsing. Matt and Walter got her into the chair and made her breathe deep, and in a few moments she seemed to recover. "Julia, what happened?"

"I'm sorry," she said.

"What is it? Tell me."

"Tom."

He blinked. Tom? "What about Tom?"

"He . . . he gave me my engagement ring in a box of Frangos."

Matt said, "That warrants this reaction?"

"I've decided to divorce him," she said softly.

He held his breath. "Do you mean it?"

She nodded. And then she stood up, telling him she had to go, some fresh air might do her good. He was filled with joy at hearing the news that she was finally dumping her husband, but he was still worried about her. He took her hand and asked if she was sure she was all right. She nodded. "When will I see you again?" he asked.

"I fly to Honolulu tomorrow."

"Are you back right after Christmas?"

"We were going to stay through New Year's."

His heart sank. "You're going to divorce him, and yet you're spending over a week with him?"

"For Molly's sake."

He looked lost. "I can't go that long without seeing you. Julia, please, come back sooner. Please."

His eyes were pleading. "Say you will, promise me you will."

She finally promised.

And he kissed her passionately, the way he had the night he made love to her.

Then she picked up her Frango mints and left.

But she did not go home.

12

"Tom?"

"Cornelia? Why aren't you on the plane?"

"We don't know what to do. Julia is missing."

His heart did a flip. "Missing?"

Cornelia explained that Julia hadn't come home last night, that the last anyone had seen her was when she drove out of the jail parking structure.

Tom listened and was mystified. Matthew sure as hell didn't have her. She had not been seen anywhere, had not called any friends; she seemed to have vanished. She couldn't be reported missing until twenty-four hours had gone by, and they had six hours to go. A chill came over him when he talked to Molly and assured her Mommy was all right and that everything would be fine. But who was he kidding? He read the papers, he knew what the world was now like. Molly herself had watched in horror on the playground one day as a man tried to abduct the boy who sat next to her in kindergarten. Christ, a man had slaughtered her grandparents. No wonder she was scared for her mother.

So was Tom.

"Oh, my God. Oh, my God. Oh, my God." Matthew repeated the phrase in an endless monotone, pacing the showers like a tiger. He didn't even see Scully walk in.

Scully stared at his naked body. Matt opened his eyes for a moment, startled to find the prisoner in the room with him. Scully told him he had given a guard some crack to let him join Matthew. He knew Matt was hurting. Matthew kept chanting his fear.

"She gonna be okay," Scully said. Then he saw that Matt was crying. "Listen, man, no bitch be worth this—" Scully twisted a tap, and a cold spray stung Matthew's back.

He was jolted, he winced, ducked into the corner of the shower room, closing his eyes, pressing his back into the hard tiles. "I'll kill him. I'll fucking kill him if he hurt her, if he did anything to her . . ."

Scully moved over to him. The ice water hit his bare ass, but he didn't even notice. He grabbed Matt's arms and shook him. "Who? Who hurt her?"

"That fucking husband. The sick fucking bastard. He's jealous of what she's got with me, jealous that he can't fuck her and I can, jealous that she cares about me, that she wants to divorce him, that—"

"Hey, hey," Scully said, "cool, man, chill."

"Fucking bastard."

"You gettin' a fuckin' boner," Scully said.

Matt kept his eyes closed, in his own world. "He doesn't deserve her. She's an angel, an angel, my angel . . ."

Scully sank to his knees.

"He took her somewhere and he's making her hate me, Scully. He abducted her, he's got her hidden, and he's trying to get it up for her. He's making her hate herself again, he's . . . he's . . . angel . . . my angel . . . I'm inside my angel . . ."

He came with anguish, into the warmth that was enveloping his penis, without even realizing what it was.

"Tom?"

"Cornelia! What—?"

"She just called."

"Oh, God." He swallowed. His heart started pumping again.

"Thank God."

"She's okay."

"Where was she?"

"Mariposa."

His heart stopped again. "*Mariposa?* Why?"

"I don't know."

"She go to the house? Jim Crowley bought it. Did she—?"

"She wasn't visiting Crowley. She's driving back right now. We can make the four o'clock flight."

"It's got something to do with him. I know it."

"She wouldn't tell me anything. Said she'd explain when she got here."

Goddamned right, Tom thought.

Walter looked through the bars. "They found her. She's okay."

Matthew jumped to his feet. "How do you know?"

"I told her sister we were concerned when she called to see if we knew where she was. She promised to let me know when they found her."

"Where was she?"

"She didn't say. Just that she's okay."

Matthew sank to his bed again. "I don't understand," he said to himself. "She never went home after she left here. Why didn't she tell me, why didn't she come back, why did she make me worry like that? She wasn't well yesterday. Something was really wrong . . . my God, oh, my God, the cancer, could the cancer have come back? I've got to get out of here. She needs me. She can't go through that without me this time . . ."

Scully looked into his face from his cell. "You be one sick dude, you know that?"

They went for a walk alone, on the lush grounds of the hotel the first night they were there. Tom had never dreamed that Honolulu could feel more Christmas-y than San Francisco, where Christmas is, he admitted, somewhat of a stretch, but it was. The hotel sparkled with elegant decorations. Julia was fascinated by the millions of mosaics forming the brilliant orchid at the bottom of the pool. She seemed relaxed and calm, more sure of herself than he'd seen her in a very long time. He sensed that she knew he was angry. She knew they'd all been startled and curious about what she'd done, wanting to know why she'd put them through such a scare. She finally tried to explain herself.

She told Tom that she "freaked" at the jail that day. She wasn't even sure why, she just found herself driving up to Mariposa, staring at the house for a couple of hours, and then she went to Matthew's place.

Tom felt the breath knocked out of him. *Matthew's place?* Instead of asking why, he made a crack about getting off sleeping in Hinson's bed, which didn't make Julia any more comfortable in telling this. But she continued. She explained that she just needed to go there—don't ask her why, don't probe, don't try to understand, that it was over and done, and she was sorry and she wanted everyone to forget about it.

Tom tried his best. And despite the cloud of Matthew, they had a wonderful Christmas together, almost like old times. Tom knew that Molly could feel the tension easing between her parents, and it gave him reason to believe he and Julia still had a fighting chance. But so much depended on one thing . . .

The bedroom.

And Tom was scared to death.

On Wednesday morning between Christmas and New Year's, Matthew went about his usual routine. He showered, shaved, made sure his hair was in place, put on fresh underwear, socks, a clean white T-shirt, and then slid into his jeans. His heart started ticking faster about an hour before her usual arrival time, and by the time he neared the five-minute mark, his erection was rock hard. Scully watched with amusement. "That boner for me, baby?"

Matthew looked at his watch. Where was Walter? It was time, where was he? He'd never been late before, she'd never been late. It was a ritual, a rite, like eight o'clock Mass. Never a moment late. Matthew began to worry. What had happened? Something had to have *happened.* "Boner on the decline," Scully howled. "Studly get stood up."

"Shut your ugly black face," Matthew growled. He'd gotten to the point where his abuse of Scully wasn't so playful anymore. Now that he'd let the nigger blow him, he treated him with real contempt. But the lifer seemed to thrive on it. Matt teased him every night, sometimes letting him watch when he masturbated thinking of Julia. The truth was, this had nothing to do with sex or sexual pleasure; the man's interest in him simply intrigued him, this adoration from afar similar to what he felt for Julia. The one thing about Scully he came to count on, because it made life in jail less boring, was his tough, incessant, biting, and salacious mouth. And the more Matthew objected, the more the man seemed encouraged. "I do ya again, white boy, jus' say when," Scully hissed through the bars.

"Walter?" Matthew's voice had a ring of anticipation. "You're late."

"Yeah," the guard said, approaching him, "but there's nothing to be late for. She's not coming."

Matthew looked as if someone had just died. "Not coming?" he whispered, wounded.

"Got her old man back," Scully yelled. "Don't need your little weenie no more."

"Muzzle him," Matthew shouted at Walter, his voice out of control.

Walter glanced over his shoulder at Scully. "Knock it off, big man, okay?"

"Why? Why isn't she coming?" Matthew looked distraught. "What happened—she isn't sick, is she? She's not missing again, is she?"

"Jus' wants ta stick her," Scully sang again, "that's all. Gets a big old hard-on every Wednesday 'bout one o'clock, set a watch by his pee-pee."

Matthew grabbed the bars with his hands and pressed his whole body against them in rage, his mouth screaming between two of the heavy pieces of metal. "You shut your fucking goddamned mouth, man!"

Scully just howled an intensely sissified laugh. "Eeeeeowie! Muthafucker come back here, big wet stain in them pants every time. Whip it out and wipe it off. Jack off talkin' ta her, she tell him what she do if she get on the other side a that glass, stick that big pussy in his face!"

"Can it, Scully!" Walter shouted, rapping on his bars with his fist. Walter turned to Matthew. "I wish I knew what to say. She just didn't show. I'm sorry." He left.

Matthew sank to his bunk. "She must have ... stayed in Hawaii after all." He was devastated.

It was New Year's Eve, and Julia and Tom were completely alone for the first time all week. All week long, Tom had made sure that Molly had the suite's living room sofa, just a sliding slatted shutter away from them, so he wouldn't have to face the sexual part of their relationship. It wasn't so conscious, but he knew exactly what he was doing on New Year's Eve. Their last New Year's had been cut short by Jim Crowley's phone call. Tom was determined that this one was going to start the healing.

Brad and Cornelia took Molly with them to Maui for two days, and Julia and Tom had dinner at the Halekulani's La Mer restaurant with Melba, to whom Tom had grown very close. She had recently lost her companion of many years, a wonderful fellow named George, and they warmly reminisced of the man who'd fetched Tom so many times at the airport, told the worst jokes, tried to teach him better golf technique (finally pronouncing him hopeless), and who had a warm, kind heart. They discussed relationships and how hard they were to sustain and how you have to hold on to the few special people who count. Tom was happy to see Julia was really listening, really trying. He felt hope for the first time.

When Melba left them shortly after ringing in the new year, they stood on their balcony together, firecrackers popping in their ears, watching the drunken revelers reeling along the beach walk. The suite faced Diamond Head, but at night it looked more like a charred baked potato, speckled above by stars and fast-moving clouds. The trade winds that pushed them made the coolish air seem balmy. Tom was trembling when he kissed her. It was the first time in months that he had really touched her except to sleep next to her, but that had become about as intimate as standing next to someone on the BART. He kissed her and told her he loved her and that he knew there was still a chance for them. Then he walked her inside and to the bed. And that's where she froze. "I can't go through this again," she said.

"It'll be different," he promised her. He knew she didn't believe him, and he didn't blame her. But he asked her to give him a chance. He sensed she wanted that too. She didn't resist as he kissed her again, this time moving to the massive white bed with her, stretching out on it alongside her.

He did not rush. And he talked to her. He talked to himself. He had been through this with Geoff, with the guys in the group the doctor put him into for a few days. Julia didn't know that he'd spent three weeks in intensive therapy, that he'd done everything he could to turn his fears around, that he was committed to this marriage, that he still loved and wanted her. He had never wanted any other woman, never had any other women since the day they met. He had uncovered an issue with *imperfection* that screwed up his head. And he was determined to overcome it now.

He took it slowly—she took her cues from him— and they savored the moment, whispered gently, luxuriated in the feelings that were being rediscovered. Tom was careful not to attempt to reach some kind of performance level. He kept telling himself that nothing was expected. He also told her how beautiful she was, how he always had to have things perfect, the perfect car and apartment and job and wife and daughter. He knew he always thought of himself as being perfect, so everything had to measure up. He'd been raised that way. Boston upper crust. He had to unlearn things. He had to rethink what was important. He had to dig deeper than surface. He knew that he used to fear that he had no depth as a person; that's why the slick outside meant so much. "Keep up appearances at any cost," his father used to order. He was wrong.

What he prided himself on was the fact that he had been with her, right there at her side, through it all— the lump, the tests, the fearful hours waiting for the biopsy, their incredulous stares when the doctor said cancer, the surgery, the treatments, the chemo that dissipated her, her hair falling out in gobs as she sobbed in his arms, the infection that nearly cost her her life, shopping for bras with ridiculous plastic beanbags in them, the whole hideous experience. And at the root of it all she feared her husband would not want her again, as her father hadn't wanted her mother. And Tom didn't.

But this night was different. Tom did want her, and he proved it. He had come a long way, learned a great deal. He thought that for the first time he knew what it meant to be a man and not a coward. They made love. Julia slept comfortably in his arms.

It was the best night of his life.

And he knew it was good for her as well.

Scully said, "Come on, man. What you doin' this to yourself for? Fucked up all day, man. This New Year's."

"She didn't come," Matthew said in a deep depression. "She stayed in Hawaii with him. Not even a word."

"Fuck her."

"She could have called, something."

"Gonna miss Barry Manilow sing that song. Watched that every year."

"Something's wrong, Scully. Something happened."

"Hey, man, you be in Hawaii, you wanna come back jus ta talk to your pretty ass? Shit."

"She promised. Julia promised." Matthew's voice had never sounded so lifeless. "She *promised* me."

Melba had made them a beautiful quilt for Christmas, and on New Year's Day she sent them off with it and a huge picnic hamper filled with incredible edible pleasures from the Halekulani kitchens. Tom rented a Jeep, and he and Julia traveled out past Diamond Head, up the east side of the island, stopping to spread the quilt at a pristine beach where they drank wine and defied the rays without sunscreen. They had giddy fun, feeling, Tom thought, like Molly must always feel, like kids themselves again.

But every time he wanted to talk about their future, Julia changed the subject or avoided it completely. Her mind wasn't there, Tom could see that, could sense her wheels turning, thinking hard, but he had no clue what about. By mid-afternoon and a terrific ice-cold mango snack, his paranoia had turned to the reality that something really was wrong. But she would not tell him what.

After giving her some space, when she drifted off down the shore, he found her sitting on a hunk of driftwood, crying softly. All she would say was, "Why couldn't you have done that before . . . sooner?" He had a thousand answers, and no answer. He was confused as hell. Was she saying it was too late? Was she just hurting for the time and love they had missed? When he tried to talk to her, she kicked the sand, crying out, "The timing, you don't understand . . . the timing." Then she clammed up again.

When they got back to the hotel, he left her alone. He put on his jogging shorts and ran down Kalakaua Boulevard, through Queen Kapiolani Park. He sat on a rock with his feet in the water for about an hour. He beat himself up, wondering what had turned her so cold after the tender and exciting night they'd spent together. What was this about timing? Didn't she love him anymore? Had he been too late? He couldn't stand it any longer. He had to confront it. He wasn't going to let this happen. Not after they had just come so far. She was going to have to tell him what was wrong.

He almost wished he hadn't asked.

She was packing her suitcase when he returned, even though they weren't supposed to go home for another three days. She said only, "I'm going back to California. I know what I have to do now."

"What do you have to do? What do you mean?"

"Matthew."

It threw him. He'd honestly wiped Hinson out of his mind. "Matthew? What of Matthew?"

"I'm going to destroy any chance he has of getting a fair second trial."

Tom was dumbfounded. He didn't even know what she meant. "What?"

"If they see it's hopeless, they'll give up and release him."

He could barely find the words. "Why . . . why do you want him released?"

"So I can be with him."

He looked at her without words this time. He used to think that "heartbreak" was a silly notion, that nothing ever could really cause such a feeling. He learned differently at that moment. His heart cracked in two. And he didn't even have to say anything, she read his mind. "I'm sorry, Tom. Last night was wonderful for me too. Thank you. But I love Matthew now."

And those were the last words she spoke to him.

13

"Matthew?"

He opened his eyes and found himself looking into the heavens, into the eyes of an angel. Julia was standing over his bedside. He whispered her name, not sure he wasn't hallucinating. But when he felt her hand touch his forehead, wiping the beads of perspiration, he knew she was really there. "I . . . I didn't think you would ever come back," he whispered.

"Matt, why? Because I stayed the rest of the week? Walter told me you went into a depression, stopped eating. He said it was like you gave up on living."

"I thought you were mad at me."

"My God, why would I be mad at you? I love you."

The green eyes suddenly regained life. "Julia . . ." he whispered. He reached up, grasped her fingers as tightly as he could. "Julia, I can't be here anymore—"

"The infirmary is the only place you should be right now."

"I mean jail. I can't do it. I can't go through another trial."

"Shh." She brought his hand to her lips and kissed it. She held it with both her hands, pressing it against her cheek. "You're not going to go to trial. You've suffered enough. I've already got things in motion."

"What do you mean?"

"You'll see soon enough. They're not going to try you again, Matt. I mean it. I'm going to make that happen."

When Tom returned from Hawaii, he found that Julia had already packed most of his things, she'd talked to Molly about their "arrangement," and he simply had no choice but to load the car and drive over the bridge to Sausalito, where he found a small furnished apartment near the office. It wasn't where he ever planned to live; it was a place to camp out until his wife came to her senses, for he couldn't accept what she'd told him in Honolulu. Tom saw she had a dedication and bond with Hinson that defied reason, but he was sure she didn't love him.

In the months that followed, Tom watched—astonished for the most part—as Julia became someone he honestly didn't know. There was a fever in her that he'd never seen before, even when she had busted her butt as a reporter and news anchor. She worked tirelessly on Hinson's behalf. What startled him most was when she announced her drive to get the big guns of the literary establishment behind the psycho poet. Cornelia told Tom that Julia had flown to New York to meet Norman Mailer, who apparently outlined just how he'd gone about taking up the cause of the convict Jack Abbott some years ago. But he gave her a strong warning not to let history repeat itself. She must *know* what she was doing, he cautioned. Fat chance, Tom thought.

And of course Julia claimed this was different. Unlike Abbott, Matthew had not been found guilty of anything, he had not been convicted of any crime, he was not in prison. He was in the county jail awaiting trial for the second time. Postponements kept happening, which gave him the good luck to have his second book released at this time, and Julia jumped on the bandwagon. Tom read the book, thought the verses were puerile at best, but she mailed copies to every name in America possessing power and cachet. From Astor to Hart, Roth to Rockefeller, all the literary lions and politicians, CEO's and their prominent wives, she covered all bases. Tom watched with slight amusement, figuring they'd all think she was nuts. But her plea to each person was in the form of a zinger of a letter, which he finally got hold of. Tough in its logic but touching in its sincerity, he found himself impressed with it, and admitted that had *he* received it cold, it would have been hard to say no to the support she was seeking. Of the letters she sent out, over fifty

percent replied in her—Matthew's?—favor. An astonishing response.

It made Tom crazy.

"She called and said she was meeting with the
prosecutors."

Matthew felt that he couldn't breathe. "Prosecutors?"

Walter nodded. "That's what she said. The D.A."

"Herself? My God, it's only been three months since
she started the petition. Think she'll convince them
this soon?"

"Hell, I sure hope so."

You're not the only one.

Cornelia accompanied Julia to the meeting with the
prosecutors and called Tom the same night to tell him
about it. Julia's sister was as puzzled as her husband.
Julia didn't present a rational case for Matthew, Cornelia said, she positively challenged them. She was on
the defensive and the attack, with a zeal that Cornelia
said "frightened" her. They both agreed that night
that something deep and profound had happened to
the Julia they knew. Tom joked that it was like the evil
twin sister taking the good girl's place on a soap
opera. Who was this person masquerading as the girl
he'd married, the sister Cornelia had grown up with?
What made her tick? They'd thought they knew; now
they hadn't a clue.

Cornelia said Julia first presented a compelling case

for leniency by offering the petitions and letters of
support of Matthew Hinson's talent and contribution
to society. She then told them—without an attorney—
that she'd discovered evidence previously undetected
that would make their jobs extremely difficult, such as
eyewitnesses to Matthew's whereabouts that night.
Cornelia said she was astonished to hear Julia suggest—not admit—that she herself had perjured herself
in the first trial about the night of the murders, teasing
that she might have been having an affair with Hinson
for a long time and that she could have been with him
at the hour of the actual killings.

If Tom really believed she'd had an affair with that
sick bastard, he didn't think he could ever look at her
again. It was preposterous, of course, and Tom knew
she was lying. Witnesses that night could place her on
the road, in the Miner's Inn, in a sheriff's truck. Cornelia was aghast as well. But Julia didn't explain herself
to her sister any more than she'd explained her motives
to Tom in Hawaii. All she said was she'd do anything
to free him. Because she was sure he was innocent, she
said, she wanted to spend the rest of her life with him.

Tom wanted to puke. And to shake her and force her
to admit why. Why did she think she loved this man?
But she wouldn't even take his calls. He saw Molly on
weekends, or when Julia was racing around the
country drumming up support for Matt. It was taking
its toll on their daughter as well. "What happened to

Mommy?" Molly asked one day over a hot dog in Sausalito. Tom, who could always come up with an answer for his little girl, had no answer for that one.

That same day, he picked up a copy of *Newsweek* and read the following:

Newsweek

SOCIETY

THE TRIALS OF MATTHEW HINSON

by Phyllis Crum

At an informal meeting with the judge and prosecutors, Julia Radcliffe Larsen presented her case. She placed into record over a hundred letters, some from the most prominent names in the literary world, attesting to Matthew Hinson's talent and ability. The man has, she stated emphatically, an enormous contribution to make to society. If she could see this—if she, the daughter of the very people he was accused of slaying, could come to this point of belief and support—why couldn't they? "In the time he has been jailed, Matthew Hinson has written some of the finest words ever put to paper by an American poet. Robert Frost, Carl Sandburg, Walt Whitman, were they alive, would have submitted letters today as well. Matthew Hinson writes in their tradition, of this country and the people in it. He chronicles the goodness of the heart, and spirit of optimism, qualities which live and breathe in his own life. We are here to say this is a man who deserves to be free, to give his talent and creative ability to the rest of the world, and to prove that he has grown in his two years of incarceration."

A month ago, Hinson's second volume of poetry, *The Absence of Angels*, found itself midway on most best-seller lists the day it debuted. The literary community warmed to it immediately, and the general public ate it up. It took the country by storm, garnering praise from all reviewers for its biting portrayal of jail as hell. Yes, angels are absent from this one. This is gritty and excruciatingly real. Critics agreed that Matthew captured the despair of a prisoner, of being accused. He put into easy images the overwhelming loneliness, the fear of never getting out and the fear of getting out, the fear of each other. Poems that spoke of men turned into monsters, and monsters into men. Poems zeroing in on sex and AIDS and corruption and longing for women. Interestingly enough, he's not in prison; he's still in the San Francisco County Jail. But then again, cells are cells, and freedom breathes hard behind all bars.

The point of all this? How's this guy gonna get a fair trial? Jury selection is to begin shortly, but a *USA Today* poll taken just last week showed little hope of finding impartial jurors. A whopping 84% of those interviewed said they'd have a hard time being objective in the jury box on this case. So why doesn't the state of California save the considerable expense and just let this man go free? The first jury was hopelessly deadlocked, but jurors interviewed after the trial indicated they would never have, in any case, found him guilty of premeditated murder; manslaughter, as the judge had instructed them as a compromise, would have been the best they could do in several jurors' minds. Won't it just end up the same way this time?

Matthew put the magazine down. He was elated. He asked Julia, "How do you think you'll get the governor to intervene?"

"Dennis Doyle was a close friend of my father's," Julia explained. "He was like an uncle to me and Cornelia. Plus, with the success of the book on our side, and all the media coverage, how can he say no? The pressure is on for the state to just throw in the towel."

They looked at each other for a very long time. "Why are you doing this?" he finally said.

"Because I care about you," she said softly.

"The way you once cared about Tom?"

She nodded slightly. "The way you have always cared about me. You and I fit together so easily, like the last two pieces of a big puzzle, meant to stay together like that forever."

"Was it ever that way with Tom?"

"Tom and I were—" She hesitated and shook her head. "It wasn't meant to be," was all she added.

She was using words he'd before only dreamed he'd hear from her lips. "I adore you, Julia."

"Matt," she said, "I love you too." She put her hand up on the wire mesh. Since her return in January, they'd been allowed to use another visitors' room where they could feel each other's flesh through what looked like chicken wire. He touched her palm, then raised himself slightly, bringing his lips to her hand and kissed it through the mesh. He would have risen farther, to kiss her lips, but then she would have seen his open fly and his penis in his right hand, and it could have wrecked all that he'd been building.

The right time would come for her to see that.

When he was out of here.

Soon.

When Tom arrived at the apartment, Julia was on the Stairmaster. Dressed in old sweats, perspiring to beat hell, he felt he had never seen her look sexier or more appealing. He wanted to kiss her, make love to her right there.

She wasn't in the same head. "You're early. Molly isn't ready yet."

"Yes, I am," the little voice squeaked. Molly ran down the bedroom corridor with her shoes in her hands, excited. She leaped into Tom's arms.

He saw a painful look on Julia's face that he didn't understand. Then he told Molly, "Let's ask Mommy to come with us."

"Yes!" Molly squealed, and ran back to the bedroom for her backpack.

Julia was brittle. "Tom, I'm busy. I've got a lot to prepare this afternoon. Tomorrow I'm going to—"

"I don't much give a shit where you're going tomorrow. It's today that counts. Right now. Time with our daughter. Come on, an hour for old time's sake? We haven't spent time together in months." He took the risk of putting his hand on her shoulder.

She pulled away. "Hawaii was too late, Tom."

"I'm not asking anything more from you than to go for a short drive with us." He took her hand.

She didn't pull away this time. "Where to?"

Encouraged, he said, "Tiburon."

"Tiburon? What for?"

He pulled into the driveway and turned off the engine. Julia said, "What are we doing here?"

Molly, who had been in on this with him all along, gave the first clue. "Mom, look at the mailbox."

Julia looked at the wooden box made of bleached wood that matched the new house exactly and saw the name: *LARSEN*. She looked shocked. And for a moment Tom thought he caught a glimmer of excitement in her eyes, thought her heart soared, but then she sank.

She was polite and attentive all through the tour, trying, Tom thought, to conceal her true feelings. She admitted that she loved the place. It was the kind of house she had always wanted, and he knew that she knew he'd designed it with her in mind. The sun porch, the cozy bedroom with the fireplace and balcony overlooking the bay, the room that would serve as an ideal writer's office—they were right out of her wish book. The carpeting was even a soft rose, her favorite color. He'd even put the Halekulani towels he and Molly had swiped their first time there together in the master bathroom. Julia sat down on the bed. Molly went out to the yard, where Tom had already built her a playhouse all her own.

He explained to Julia that designing the house was his Pacific Rim doodling, how he passed the time on the many flights to and from the Orient. He was going to tell her about it that day on the beach in Hawaii when he'd found her crying and angry. Construction had started in January—even though it seemed he was a bachelor again, he went ahead with it—and now it was ready to move into. Tom felt she was about to admit her enthusiasm for a moment. "It's a remarkable house. Honestly." But then she withdrew again. "You'll be happy here."

He told her he wanted *them* to be happy here. Would she give it a try? Would she move in? Could they attempt making their marriage work one more time, a fresh start in a new place? She said nothing, so Tom kept on talking. It was obvious her plot to free the psycho wasn't working, he told her. They were finally interviewing jurors. He was going to rot in prison—

"Tom—"

He stopped.

She stood up. She walked to the window and looked out over the water. He had no clue what she was thinking. But she made it clear. "It's no good. It won't work."

He was silent for a long time. He had known all along this would be her answer. He'd known it, but still he'd hoped he was wrong. He knew he could never explain to anyone the depth of his hurt. He asked what it was. "Level with me, Julia. What is it about him? The poems? His green eyes? Fantasy of the rugged beast? The danger? A challenge? A cause?"

She drew in a breath but still said nothing.

"Tell me you still feel something for me," he begged her. He knew he sounded pitiful, but his heart was breaking. "Tell me, please."

She turned to face him. And he thought he saw real pain in her eyes as well, as if her heart was breaking as well. "You'll understand everything one day, Tom, I promise you will."

"God *damn* him," he said, as serious as he'd ever been. Then he cracked. Then he let it out, ranting, venting his frustration. "What kind of future can you have together? He's gonna be tried again and locked up for life. No parole board will listen to that crap you keep spouting, how he's a contribution to the literary world. He's a fucking maniac who's controlling you! You wanted a life like you could have here. This is what we dreamed about. You fought cancer and won, I fought my problem and won. It was psychological, it's okay now! You're the most beautiful girl in the world, the one I love, the only person I've ever wanted through this whole—"

She begged him to stop.

"I don't understand! Explain it to me so I understand. Just make me get it this time." He felt the frustration like a hot, live wire loose inside him. Like beating his head against a concrete wall, trying to knock it down to see what was on the other side.

"Will you drive me home now?"

"That's what I hoped this would be," he replied.

He drove her home. Molly cried most of the way.

And Julia said not one word.

Matthew walked into the shower room and stroked his dick. She'd left not more than twenty minutes ago, and he was still hard. He'd taken out his aggression, his sexual frustration, on his own body, doing a hundred pushups that left him dripping with sweat. He pushed himself to the limit doing countless sit-ups, but still Julia remained etched in his brain. He finally collapsed, his heart racing, straddling the bench in front of the lockers. His head back, his arms and feet down at either side, he closed his eyes, knowing that Scully had entered the room. He'd again given Walter some crack.

"You stickin' it in her?" Scully groaned as he walked closer. "Bet you got it up her ass this time, hey, Pretty Boy? Sure, she like it like that."

Matthew whispered, "She's wearing a gown, Scully, a white billowing angelic gown, her beauty is celestial. . . ."

"What you talkin' 'bout?"

"I hear music and she's got those spike heels on, the devilish underside of the angel, and she wants to put her wand on my dick—"

"Gonna put *my* wand—"

"I'm gonna make love to her, Scully."

"Gonna fuck you, Pretty Boy." Then he brought his hands down and under Matthew's buttocks, scooping them up, lifting his pelvis in front of him as he sat on the bench. "Scully gonna show ya what she like."

Matt opened his eyes. "No way, you ugly nigger."

"Come on, baby, spread that butt hole."

"Suck my cock."

Scully did.

Matthew thought he was sliding his penis into Julia's angelic soul. In a moment he felt himself starting to gush. The wet, soft sucking on his penis was the perfect accompaniment to his fantasy. *Yes, Julia, I'm fucking you, fucking you*— Then his eyes opened. He stared at the ceiling and felt the lips free him. Then something occurred to him. He could use this. This would help him be set free.

"You like it, Pretty Boy?"

"Yeah."

Matthew sat up and grabbed Scully by the hair and pulled him off him. Matthew then shoved the man back into the steel lockers with such force that his head dented one of them. Quickly Matt brought his leg up. Then the ball of his foot, with all its force, struck Scully in the jaw, breaking it.

Matt left him there, blood seeping down his chest.

Then Matthew called for a guard.

San Francisco Times-Herald

LARSEN ACCUSES COUNTY OF MISTREATING HINSON

SEXUAL ATTACKS, PHYSICAL HARASS-MENT REVEALED

Julia Larsen today held a press conference at which she revealed a list of charges Matthew Hinson was bringing against San Francisco County Jail. In his time there, she said, he had been the victim of "verbal attacks, beatings, and forced into sexual situations with other convicts while guards—some of whom are crack addicts—turned their heads." She said that Hinson revealed these things to her just last week after trying to hide them for so long. "The criminal justice system in this state is a crime," Larsen told reporters. "Here is a man who is innocent until proven guilty and his life is in danger while the prosecution takes its time deciding how to find a jury who will do it their way. In the meantime, this jail sounds worse than any penal institution, for Matthew has been repeatedly harassed because of his handsome physical appearance, he has been derided for being a poet, and his life has been threatened after refusing the sexual advances of other prisoners."

On Tuesday, Hinson broke the jaw of another man waiting trial for murder, Jerome Scully, who said Hinson attacked him without cause. Larsen refutes that charge. "Scully was injured because Matt fought off his sexual demands."

Julia came to the house to drop Molly off. That in itself was unusual, but when Tom met them at the door, she seemed in no hurry to leave, even nosed around, asked about this and that, told him the sofa he had bought for the living room was all wrong, the drapes should puddle, and that a Bunn coffeemaker would have suited him better. Amused, he asked if he could make her some to prove he could master a Krups quite well. He had some Starbucks beans, the kind she loved. She shocked him by saying yes.

She told him about her book over the New Guinea peaberry. She was writing night and day, she said, and she was exhausted. She was also sorry for the embarrassment all this must be causing him. She was sure it would be over soon. The prosecution was at wit's end; public opinion was dead against them. Jury selection had been a nightmare, taking seven weeks. He told her he had read that even Governor Doyle was on her side. She nodded, reminding him he was an old friend. He said he'd have to be.

It was tense, Tom couldn't deny that, but there was

something about the way she lingered that made him think two things. One, that she might still harbor feelings for him. Two, that there was trouble in paradise. Yet when he probed, she said she and Matt were only looking to get past this, past the publicity and the jail and the charges and all the hell it had caused.

He boldly asked her if she wanted a divorce. She looked at him with startled eyes, which made no sense to him. Didn't she want to marry Matt one day? He asked it more to get a reaction than because he believed it. He found her answer curious: "I don't want to talk about it now."

He watched her from the front window when she left. She stood looking back at the house after she'd opened the car door, just staring—not at him specifically, he could see that, but at the house in general. He swore she was asking herself why she didn't live there. He was sure that, even for that one moment, she wanted not to be driving away. She wanted Tom's beautiful cozy house to be home, her home, with her husband and daughter.

Or, he asked himself as she drove down the street, was he just a dreamer? And a fool?

Walter hurried down the corridor to Matt's solitary confinement cell.

"What?" Matt asked with alarm, reading Walter's face.

"You're going out," Walter said.

Matt just stared at him. "I'm what?"

Walter thrust his hand through the bars and grasped Matt's hand. "They just announced it, heard it on the radio. Prosecution has decided not to retry the case—"

Tom was mesmerized by what he was watching on the TV screen. The reporter was talking about Hinson. *"It was determined that a fair trial would be impossible at this point, and that the evidence was not of overwhelming proportion as to assure the prosecution of a victory. . . ."*

The San Francisco district attorney then read a prepared statement in a bitter voice, saying, *"We feel the state has spent too much time and taxpayers' money on this case already. It's over. Finished. Hinson will be released tomorrow. We have other cases to be concerned with."*

Tom hit the power button on the remote. Molly had seen it too, and now she was staring at her father. "What?" he said.

"I . . ." Usually a girl of many words, she was having trouble here.

Tom could see ambivalence in her eyes, as if she was fighting feelings inside her. He reached out to her, put his arm around her. "Honey, come on, tell me what you're thinking."

"Mom said . . . when Matt gets out . . . we'll make angels in the snow again."

"Why do you sound so troubled?"

"I don't think I'll go." Her wide little eyes were downcast.

Tom blinked, not sure what she meant. "Why?"

"I want to stay here with you." Then she gave her father a heartfelt hug. "I love you, Dad."

The phone rang. It was Cornelia. "Did you hear?" she shouted. Tom told her that he had. "They're releasing the bastard tomorrow." He said he knew. "I'm in Frisco tomorrow," she said, "I want to see you. I think we're going to need each other."

"I think you're right."

"Matt?"

"Julia!"

"Where are you?"

"At the hairdresser."

"You heard?"

"Yes! I was under the dryer, they had CNN on. Melody started screaming at me."

"It's all because of you."

"It was worth it."

"Christ. I'm free. I'm out tomorrow!"

"I'll be there to meet you."

"No more charges. I'm gonna sue those fuckers— false arrest, unlawful imprisonment—"

"Matt, calm down."

"What will we do? Where am I going to—?"

"Stop. I'll take care of it."

"Julia, what we've dreamed about. Now we can have it."

She took a deep breath. And softly she said, "Yes. We certainly can."

PART IV

Julia

14

Cornelia balanced a mound of sliced black olives on the last bit of pizza crust, then dribbled pungent olive oil over it. "'Come on, Tom, talk to me." She gulped it down.

"Damn it," Tom said, getting up from the coffee table, where they were eating, "I still love her. I want her back. Is that crazy? Is there something wrong with me? What am I holding on to?"

"She's sick. She's under his power."

"Yeah, and I helped put her there. Cornelia, she was grasping for someone to hold on to, someone to take an interest, give her some self-esteem."

"Listen, she was being the professional victim for a while, I know. And Matthew was there for her when she wanted you to be there, that's all—and that wasn't entirely your fault. I don't think you could have done anything right in her eyes. You had the same problems Mom and Dad had. Julia was looking for magic to happen, and when it didn't, she looked elsewhere. Matt was the easy way out, her pattern."

"How do you mean her pattern?"

"Her second book didn't do as well as the first. So what did she do? Stopped writing, went into TV. Reporting got her blood rushing, then it got harder, it was wearing her down, so what did she do? Took an anchor job. Breast cancer made her feel unattractive, so she screwed up and got herself fired. She's never going back, she knows there won't be magic there again, despite her damned Emmy."

"Was she always hot for him?"

"Hinson?" She glided over it the best she could. "She was always a little curious, I think. But so was our mother. The guy has that effect on women."

"Not you?"

"My immune system was stronger, thank God. I was born with the anti-Hinson gene." She sipped her wine. "It's amazing how Julia's changed through all this, how she kept getting stronger, more tenacious."

"Christ, she battled the state and won. So what happens now?"

"Like you, I've never believed this bullshit about her loving him, not for a moment." Cornelia poured him the rest of the Santa Christina.

"What are you saying?"

"I'm saying she's never been convincing."

He looked hopeful suddenly. "How do you mean?"

"I know my sister. Something just isn't kosher."

"Yeah," Tom said, enthusiasm gaining, finally hearing what he wanted to hear. "It's like the wires don't connect, something doesn't fit. She was here the other day, stayed for coffee. She was weird. It's as if she didn't want to leave."

"Maybe she didn't."

"If she still cared about me, why would she be doing what she's doing?"

Molly dashed in from the other room. "Dad! Aunt Cornelia! Mom is on television!"

Cornelia said, "Maybe some reporter will tell us."

It was dark outside when Matt and Julia finally pushed through the throng of reporters, confronting a crush of people and mikes and lights, and they realized they'd never get to the car without making some kind of statement. The frenzied reporters were shouting questions about their relationship, his freedom, his personal feelings at the moment, and he shushed them and tried to answer them all at once:

"All I have to say is I feel wonderful. I've put this behind me, the entire experience, and today is the start of the way my life used to be. Simple and good. I have Julia Larsen to thank, and I thank God for her, for her belief in me, and her friendship."

Then they went wild, and they were brutal:

"Gonna marry her?"

"Cornelia Younger said she still believes you're guilty. Julia, you and your sister still speaking?"

"Were you sleeping together before you were caught?"

"Any truth to the rumor you were sleeping with Martha Radcliffe?"

Matt stopped the assholes with one statement. "Julia's writing a book on all this. You'll get your answers then."

"Julia, gonna divorce your husband to marry this guy?"

Tom turned off the set. Molly said nothing. Cornelia tried to ignore what they had just seen by asking if she'd like some dessert. Molly shook her head. It was a tense moment. Tom finally said, "Why don't you go back and finish your homework, and we'll talk about all this later?"

"Okay." She went, unhappily.

Tom put his feet on the coffee table, tossing his head back against the softness of the sofa. "What a circus."

"Channel Four's gonna be knocking at this door any moment."

"I'm not talking to anyone." He closed his eyes, balling up his fists. "I should have looked at those disks. Maybe I could have predicted all this."

"What disks?"

"Her disks."

"What are you talking about?"

"Her book, the one she's writing. Her notes."

"You could have read them?"

"I *have* them."

Cornelia sat up straight, grabbing his knee for attention. "You have her notes, the stuff she's been writing, on disks? My God. How? When? How long have you—?"

Tom pulled his head up. "This is embarrassing, but I swiped them."

"Embarrassing? You should get a medal."

"I brought Molly home one weekend when Julia wasn't there, saw them lying there in a pile on her desk—Matthew #12, Matthew #16—and I copied them all. She never realized."

"But why the hell haven't you looked at them?"

He shrugged. "Too painful."

"Not for me." She stood up. "Where are they?"

"You really want to read them?"

"I know my sister," she said, "and I know what's happening is all bullshit. And now we're going to learn why."

She dragged him to the office, where Tom turned on the IBM while Cornelia shuffled through the disks. She chose one and slid it into the drive. The list of files appeared on screen. "Which one?" Tom asked.

"All of them. And print them. As fast as you can."

Tom did as instructed. The printer started whirring. The first page moved into Cornelia's waiting hand. "Now," she said, "let's find out what we don't know."

They both glanced at the page. Cornelia was faster, seeing at once that it was written after Hawaii at Christmas. "Gushing how she loved that hotel," she said, handing it to Tom.

Tom perused it as other pages shot out of the LaserJet. "Melba would like to see this," he murmured with a smile.

Cornelia was already three pages ahead of him. "Here, she's talking about you."

Tom grabbed it. And read: *It wasn't all Tom's fault, I see that now. My self-worth was nonexistent. Easy to blame him. I cheated my own feelings. After we made love in Hawaii, I thought I was going to come apart at the seams, because I couldn't tell him, I had to keep it secret still—*

"Keep what secret?" Cornelia asked.

"I don't get it."

"Let's start from the top."

It was raining when they arrived at her apartment building. A thick fog had lain over San Francisco all day, and now its heavy load was dropping on the city. Julia drove into the garage, parked in her space near the elevator, and got out of the car. Matt did the same, and as she put her key into the elevator slot, he ran his hand over the small of her back. She turned to face him.

He took hold of her shoulders with each hand, and pulled her to him, kissing her so hard she thought he was taking a bite out of her face. She pulled back slightly, stunned, but once she caught her breath and saw the passionate, hungry, thankful, grateful, overwhelmed look on his face, she kissed him back. Their lips met tenderly this time, their bodies came together, his chest against hers, then the bones of their hips, then the raised, hard lump under his zipper, pressing into the V of the top of her legs—

The elevator arrived. They got in. He held her close to him until the doors opened again. They walked down the corridor hand in hand. "Classy joint," Matthew said. "I knew you'd have the best."

Julia put her key in the lock, and when the dead bolt clicked, she told Matthew to wait there a second, she had a surprise for him, it would just take a moment. She slipped into the apartment, closing the door quickly, and he stood there, trusting, waiting. What the hell was going on? He couldn't imagine she had a surprise party planned; who'd welcome him? A moment later he heard her. "Okay, come on in!"

He did. And suddenly he felt the force hit him, all the weight at once, leaping on him, knocking him off balance. It took him by such surprise, he didn't even realize at first what had hit him. He gasped as he fell backward to the carpet. Then he heard familiar sounds and smelled the smell of fur, and then a tongue lapped his face, his eyes, his nose, his ears, chin, even his mouth. "Maggie, Maggie, Maggie!" He called out her name again and again, and hugged her, rolled over with her, rustled her fur, slapped her on the butt. "Maggie, honey, I missed you too. And you got fat!"

"She's as slim as ever," Julia defended.

Matt hugged the dog, pressing his cheek to hers,

and wouldn't let go. There were tears running down his face. "Man, this feels so good."

"I went up to Inga's awhile back and got her," Julia said, joining him and the dog on the floor of the apartment. She ran her hand over Maggie's back, and then the dog turned over and they both rubbed her belly. "I told her Daddy was coming home, and she was in the car before I could even tell the Wilsons good-bye."

He brought his hand up and touched the side of Julia's face, gently pressing his warm fingers against her cheek. "Thank you," he whispered. "It means so much to me."

Then he started to look around, to see where he was, and as he drank in the room, he was drawn to the wall of glass. He stood up and walked over to it. And he was amazed. Even through the fog he could see Nob Hill, Russian Hill, the lights of Coit Tower, spires and rooftops and colors of the shimmering city below. *Freedom.* It felt powerful.

"This is the tallest condo building in the city," Julia told him. "We took the top floor because it's so quiet."

"It's incredible." He turned around. "I mean, I expected it to be, but this is . . . just something else." His eyes were drawn to the teal green easy chair, and he approached it, touched the buttery leather with his hands, and then sank into it. "Jesus, I never want to get up."

She walked over and sat on the arm of the chair, and he ran his fingers up her right leg, crossed over her left, and rested his whole hand on her thigh. Julia kissed him, then broke it. She stood up and asked, "Hungry?"

"Famished. For *real* food."

"I've got something special coming up. Give me twenty minutes. Want a drink?"

"You know what I've dreamed about since the day they put me in there? A bath. A real bath, with bubbles."

She smiled. "I don't want to overwhelm you, but I have a Jacuzzi tub."

He winked. "Wash my back?"

Cornelia was back in the living room, sitting on the sofa, her feet once again tucked under her, and every so often she reached out, like a blind woman groping in the dark, for the mug of coffee sitting on the antique table on the side. But she never took her eyes off the pages. She was reading Julia's notes on all her meetings with Matt in prison. Fascinated and sickened by her sister's obvious growing feelings for the man, she couldn't get enough of it. What she found odd was that every now and then it seemed Julia had gone back and highlighted passages that she identified as lies.

Tom would finish a page, set it next to her; she'd pick another page from the pile and continue. It had gone on like this for almost two hours. Neither one of them spoke a word except to comment on something they'd just read, some line that affected them. But neither one of them expected to read what they came upon next. Tom saw it first. His tanned body seemed to go white. He looked at Cornelia soberly and shook his head. His voice was like a zombie. "They . . . they slept together."

"Yes." She said it matter-of-factly, not with surprise. "It explains it. That was the night she didn't come home."

It was as if he hadn't heard her. "He fucked her. He fucked my wife. The bastard fucked my wife."

She looked at him, understanding how honestly shocked he was, how deeply hurt. She knew this was the time to tell him even more, for he could not be more wounded than he was at this moment. "It wasn't the first time, Tom."

"What?" He sounded as though he were gasping for breath.

"She slept with him that day he rescued her from the water."

"Leucadia."

"Yes."

"You always knew?"

She nodded. "I hated knowing."

"You never told me."

"She married you. She dropped him. One time, it meant nothing." She paused. "Or so I thought at the time."

"The obsession started back then."

"No. Obsession didn't play a role till he made her feel attractive again."

Tom turned away.

"I'm sorry. But you have to hear the truth."

He drew a deep breath, rage finding its way into his system. "He fucked her and knew she'd believe in him forever. She needed that . . . that—"

"Validation, I think."

"—so bad that nothing would shake her attachment, not even being accused of murder. That was the bond I didn't get."

"No," Cornelia said, looking at the next page, almost gasping, "not forever. Read this."

Tom took the page and started reading it. His eyes moved faster than his brain, reading faster and faster, as if running a race, making a mad dash for the finish line before his breath gave out—or his heart. "Cornelia," he suddenly said, alarmed, his voice changing, speaking up but not looking up, "it's all been a lie."

"Oh, Jesus. Tom—" Cornelia's face was filled with real alarm for the first time. "My God, Tom, what has she done?"

He was stroking his dick under the bubbles when Julia entered the bathroom. Maggie licked her leg as Julia crouched down and poured him a glass of champagne and set the bottle on the floor. He told her she looked sexy in her sweats, sipped a little, and then lifted himself up from the water and kissed her, and dropped back in. "Dinner smells great."

"*Grazie*. But thank Ciao, my favorite restaurant. I'm merely warming it."

"Tonight," he said smoothly, "I'll bring you cocoa in bed. Remember my hot chocolate?"

"With vanilla," she added. "Mom's touch."

"Taught me everything I know." Then he sat up straight and indicated his back. He handed her the sponge that had been floating under the bubbles.

She picked up a loofah from the towel rack instead, and began to scrape his back. He squealed at first— "Arf!" Maggie added—and then succumbed to a kind of exquisite pain as his angel ran her fingernails over his flesh, driving him mad. This is what his dreams were about. And he'd done it even without having to take out her husband. Julia's growing love for him had eliminated Tom; it was as good as murder. No, better. They couldn't try him for this. He was the victor. *He* was sitting, bare-assed, in Tom Larsen's bathtub. That said it all.

He grabbed her hand and moved it around to his chest. "Wash me here too," he said, the sexual tension growing.

Julia teased him. She ran the loofah down his chest, into the bubbles, into the water, and stopped just short of his penis, standing hard under the protective shield of foam. "How does that feel?"

"Yes," he moaned.

She moved down, letting the loofah rise out of her hand in the water, pressing her fingers close to his skin, feeling only the wiry, thick hair between his legs. She ran her fingers through it, saying, "How's *that* feel?"

He put his head back and groaned. "That's ... incredible. Don't stop. Wash me all over, all over ..." At that moment, that gorgeous second as he anticipated her hand encircling his cock, suddenly there was a loud noise, as if a BART train had just arrived in the bathroom.

Julia screamed with laughter, jumping up to watch his reaction. Just as he thought she was going to stroke him, she'd flicked the whirlpool switch with her other hand, and the jets started pumping. Matt howled when he realized what she'd done, and Maggie jumped up, ears low, earthquake warnings in her eyes. But the bubbles started to billow, the force of the jets creating more and more of them, until Julia backed out of the room, blowing Matthew a kiss, laughing until the door closed.

When he opened it ten minutes later, looking water-logged in a soggy towel, bubbles nearly obliterated the entire room. "I can see the headlines now," he called to Julia in the kitchen, *"Hinson, freed today, dies of foam asphyxiation."*

"But he died happy," Julia said, stirring something in a dish she had just taken out of the microwave.

"Very happy." He was behind her now. He kissed the back of her neck.

She licked the spoon and nodded. "Put some clothes on."

"I only have the suit."

"I went to your place and got you a few things. In the bedroom, go see."

He did. He walked down the hall and saw a small room that he realized was her office. Her computer was set atop a desk littered with stacks of papers and books. That's where she'd slaved for almost a year to get him out of jail, where she had written letters begging people to support him, where she had put his poems together into the volumes she'd gotten published. He saw her disks—pieces of plastic filled with *him*. It make him feel important.

The next door opened into the big bedroom, where he saw, laid out on the bed, his favorite pair of jeans. And the shirt he'd been wearing the day he and Julia went for their first walk. Even a pair of his shorts. He dropped the towel and looked at himself in the mirror. Everything would fit; he was in better shape now than when he had gone to jail. He'd had their tongues hanging out. He could have broken a lot of jaws. Oh, he had nothing against Scully, he rather enjoyed his company; it was just that he had to get some sympathy. More icing on the cake that Julia was serving the state. He looked in the mirror. So many inmates had wanted him, but he was still virgin. He hadn't fucked one of them; he'd saved himself for someone special.

And tonight was that special night. He realized he had a hard-on again, and thus he slid into the briefs, positioning his cock to the side under the band. Then he put on the pair of new white socks and wondered where she'd got them. Had she bought them especially for him? Or could they be Tom's? That gave him a thrill all its own. Her husband's socks. Christ, he should be wearing her husband's underwear too. Wouldn't that be the ultimate tickle?

And so he closed the door to the bedroom and rummaged in the drawers. He first found Julia's things, sweaters, purses, drawers of bras and panties and all kinds of delicious undergarments, but they in themselves didn't turn him on; it was only when he reached the bottom drawer that he felt a surge of pleasure, much like the emotion he'd felt in his blood that cold December night almost two years ago. Sure enough, shirts with Polo emblazoned everywhere, and socks—unopened packages, just like the one he'd just unwrapped. So they *were* Tom's! And pay dirt: three pair of boxer shorts, one silk. Silk! Goddamn silk underwear the preppy jerk wore! Hell, Tom's dick was so small it didn't matter that it flopped around in such faggot underwear. He slid them on.

He looked at himself in the mirror. His penis was still half hard. He thought he looked like the opening scene in a dirty video. But wearing Julia's husband's underwear gave him a nastier thrill than any fuck film, and he jumped on the big bed, turned over onto his back, and kicked both feet into the air. He was in *his* bed, Tom's bed, in *his* shorts, and he was going to fuck *his* wife and this was *worth* killing for! He'd kill a thousand more for this.

He slid his right foot under the jeans, kicked them up from the bed and into the air and caught them with his hands. Then he lifted his feet, forced his pelvis up into the air, and pulled them up. They fit like a glove. An Ultrafine? He laughed out loud.

He pushed his dick down to his left and then zipped the fly. Christ, it was good to be in his own pants again. Tom's boxers, *his* pants. But he had his wife! *His wife, his wife, his wife.* Then he put the shirt on, but he didn't tuck it in because he didn't want her to be embarrassed by the outline of his erection, and walked into the living room.

"You look comfy."

"I am." He walked up behind her and kissed her hair. "I'm also starving."

"Dinner is served." She gestured toward the dining room, where he saw an exquisite, romantic table laden with candles and fresh pink roses.

"Allow me," he said, pulling the chair for her.

When Cornelia got to the page Tom had just read, she nodded in agreement—and disbelief, shock. "But if she—?" was all she said, because the next paragraph told her more. At the end of the passage, alarmed, on fire, she turned to Tom and saw that his panic mirrored her own. "Tom—?"

"Read this," he gasped. He handed her the page he was holding.

Cornelia read it. Then she brought her hand to her mouth, in fear and panic, in astonishment and total bewilderment. "Christ, do you think she's really going to—to do this?"

The enormity of what he'd just figured out hit him like a concussion. "I've got to stop her," he said, grabbing his jacket, his car keys.

"Where are you going?"

"To the condo."

"But they could have gone to his place."

"That's not what we just read."

"Don't you think you should call the police?"

"And what if we're wrong? What if she hasn't tried it? They could arrest her on conspiracy or something." He hurried to the door and turned back as he opened it. "I'll phone you from the car. Just don't call anybody else. We don't know anything for sure yet, it's only a book, remember?"

Cornelia just stared at him, and then at the closed door. Molly came out of her room. "Where did Dad go?"

"Um . . . out for some dessert."

"You're lying."

"Yes. Yes, I am. He went to your mother, honey . . . to try to stop her."

"Stop her from what?"

Cornelia put her arms around the girl and held her close. She couldn't say another word.

When dinner was finished, they sat for a time in front of the fireplace, drinking coffee. Maggie was curled next to them, head on paws, sound asleep. "You know," Matt said, "we haven't really talked about our plans."

"The future?"

"Yeah." He was sitting with one arm around her, playing with her hair. "I mean, suddenly what we worked for for so long is here. I'm free and we can be together, and now I'm a little unsure just what we're going to do. What about my business? I wonder if I can ever live up there again. And I don't know what you want to—"

"One day at a time," Julia interrupted. "Let's just spend a few days here, then go to Mariposa and see how we feel about it. Maybe we can keep your place as our 'hideaway' and live somewhere else."

"We're gonna get a lot of flack up there. Won't be easy."

"Yeah, especially with Jim Crowley as our neighbor."

"How could a stupid detective afford to buy your parents' house?"

"He was rich before he became a cop."

Matt suddenly looked at her suspiciously. "You're really divorcing him? Really going through with it? Didn't think you would."

"There's a lot you don't know about me."

He nodded uneasily, not knowing whether or not she was just teasing. "Like what?"

"Like how much I want you right now."

So he kissed her. Lovingly this time, gently. He felt her hands rise up his back and grasp his shoulders; he could feel her trembling with feeling for him. He held her for a moment, but when he was about to kiss her again, the phone rang. She turned her head toward it. "No," he said, still trying to kiss her, "leave it, forget about it."

"But—"

He ran his fingers through her hair, overpowering her with his eyes, and she succumbed. The answering machine picked up after four rings, and they heard the muffled voice of her sister leaving a message in the office. *Julia, this is Cornelia . . . honey, I just wondered if you were there . . . are you there? . . . I wanted to, um, see how you were doing . . . call me as soon as you get this, I'm at Tom's.*

Matt pulled Julia to him, turning her so she would lie flat on the floor, and he moved atop her, kissing her, pressing his body down on hers, feeling his penis moving upward in the slippery silk shorts till the head was straining to get out of the top of his jeans. He knew he couldn't wait any longer. He was going to come, inside her or not—better inside her. *Inside her, one with his angel again, redemption again after all this time . . .*

Suddenly there was a harsh glare of light. It filled the room and then it was gone. It was as if somebody had flashed a strobe. Maggie lifted her head, ears at the ready. Then came the thundering aftermath that seemed to rock the building. The dog howled and ran into the bedroom. Matt knelt straight up, looking at the window, stunned. Julia pulled herself out from under him, turning to watch as well. They saw two more streaks of lightning through the rain-soaked glass. Then they braced themselves. The thunder came like cannon fire. Matthew held her and winced.

But Julia was overjoyed. "God," she cried out, jumping to her feet, "it's a real old-fashioned thunderstorm!"

"Yecch."

"Look, there's more in the distance." She moved to the window and pointed to the east. "See?"

Matt saw crackling lights and put his arms around her. "But we're safe and warm."

"Let's go out there!" she suddenly giggled. He thought she was suddenly herself again, the person she'd been before the death of her parents had robbed her of her innocence; she was goofy, giddy, silly. She pulled open the glass slider. "Come on, I dare you! I love the rain!"

"Yes!" He was into it now. She stepped outside and he followed. The floor was wet, but the canopy protected them from outright rainfall. Matt followed her, delighted to be living her romantic dream, and his feet hit the cold, wet floor of the terrace and he squealed with pleasure.

She leaned over the edge of the railing and felt the cool spray on her face. "Come over here, come by me."

But he hesitated. "I can't."

"What?"

"I'm afraid of heights . . . a little."

She was astonished. "But you took Molly and me to the top of that mountain!"

"I was quaking in my boots. And solid ground is easier to handle than a little terrace. This is too . . . high up."

"Come on," she beckoned. The rain hit her face. "Come back to me."

She did. And he hugged her, and together they looked to the east, but they saw no more lightning, heard no more thunder. But that didn't seem to diminish Julia's delight at being out in the storm. "God, isn't it wonderful?" she asked him in a breathless voice. "To be alive and happy and with the one person you know you were meant to be with?"

He melted, kissing her again. Then he broke it, turned, and did a little kick, reminding her of the day they had made the snow angels, doing a little kind of dance, crying out, whooping for joy, accomplishment.

"Have you ever felt so good before, Matt?" she asked.

"Yes," he replied, "once. No, twice. The first time we made love. And the second one's a secret." He was thinking of that night when he had danced naked in the snow, the night he killed them. This was the same kind of euphoric high. He never dreamed he'd feel it again. Then he saw that she looked curious. He had to stop that. "You're getting wet. I can see through your blouse."

She grinned. "Thank God water doesn't dissolve a prosthesis."

"Baby," he said, and she turned, seeing him with his hands outstretched to her, and she went into his arms. He held her tightly and kissed her.

Then she moved away slightly, and her eyes twinkled. "I have a present for you."

"I've got one for you too." The sexual innuendo was blatant.

"I mean a real present, a gift. It's something I wanted to give you ever since you gave me the candy last Christmas."

"What?"

"Open it."

"Where is it?"

"Right over there." She gestured toward the far end of the balcony.

"Over . . . there?" He wiped water out of his eyes.

"There," she said softly, pointing, "next to the plant."

On a small patio table, next to a potted geranium, just in front of the railing, sat something he could not quite make out. It looked round, like a tin, but he couldn't really tell. He moved toward it. It was a rusted can of some sort—

And at once he stopped breathing. His heart gave out. An overwhelming rush of violent, hot, unbearable hopelessness and shame filtered through his entire being, rendering him totally helpless, putty. He forgot his acrophobia, he forgot where he was, he couldn't even remember his name. He reached out and shakily lifted the can with his fingers and stared at it. A coffee can. A rusted Folgers coffee can. He slowly pried off the top. Yes. It was filled with money, hundred-dollar bills, the money he had buried—

At that moment, directly behind him, planting her feet as securely as she could on the wet floor of the terrace, Julia drew air deeply into her lungs and summoned her own rush of violent, hot adrenaline. With all her might, all her strength, all her guts, she aimed her hands just above his buttocks and shoved him forward.

The can flew from his hand and into the sky as he smashed into the railing, which gave way from the force of his body, just as she'd hoped it would, as she'd planned it would for so very long. Matthew Hinson catapulted head first off the balcony, toppling into the air, disappearing into the dark pit of eternity forever.

She took another deep breath and leaned against the wall.

It was done.

It had worked. She couldn't quite believe it, but she'd done it and it had worked. She had planned his death as meticulously as he must have planned her parents'. She had loosened the screws to the point where they would simply fall out under pressure. When, moments ago, she had gripped it with her hands, trying to entice him to join her at the edge of the balcony, she had actually been slipping the last retaining screw out. But Matt would not come to the edge. She'd known nothing about his fear of heights, but something had told her to plan a contingency move: the coffee can.

It was daring and bold and risky, but she knew it would get him to the edge and render him stunned, powerless just long enough for her to give him one hard push. And that's all it had taken, a bit of ingenuity and one good shove, one good thrust, and she was rid of him forever.

Matthew Hinson was eradicated. Gone. Into the fog. Into the rain. This creature of the night had gone back into the darkness from which he had sprung in the first place, that evening of December 22, the night her parents died.

Julia, standing with her back up against the slider, away from the rail-less side for fear that it might somehow draw her into its death clutches like quicksand for the guilty, caught her breath. In the moment—the eternity—after he fell, she heard the sounds of horns, the screech of brakes, then a loud metallic crunching sound that she was sure was the railing hitting. She envisioned him clinging to it like some kind of grotesque life preserver all the way to the pavement. She heard the crash of an accident—someone must have hit another car when they tried to avoid hitting the body lying in the street. She hoped no one else was hurt. The monster was not to cause innocent people any more pain. He'd done enough of that while he was alive.

But now he was dead.

And that was all that mattered.

She stepped back inside her apartment and slid the door closed.

She had work to do.

15

Julia lit a Marlboro as she sat staring at her computer keyboard. Maggie was curled up beneath her feet, under the desk, hugging Julia's legs. The dog whimpered a little, then set her head sadly on the floor. Funny, Julia thought, even the dog knows he's gone for good. She looked down at the beautiful animal and reached out and rubbed her fur. She felt sorry for her. Even a dog deserved better.

She lifted the burning cigarette and took a drag. If these had caused her breast cancer, she'd take her chances—just this one night. It was the first she'd had in almost three years, and as the smoke burned her lungs, she knew why. She remembered Stephen King's *Misery* where the writer allowed himself one cigarette and a bottle of Dom Perignon when he finished a book. She had decided she'd try it, passing on the champagne still on the bathroom floor. She needed to keep her head clear. She smiled when she thought

she would have loved to tell him what they were
really celebrating.

She put the cigarette down and looked at the angel
water globe she'd taken from his cabin. Once treasured because it symbolized her mother, it now repre-
sented lies and deceit. She picked it up and tossed it
into the metal trash can near the desk. Maggie barked
softly. The answering machine beeped incessantly
until she clicked it off; she would return Cornelia's call
later. Right now she had writing to do.

And she wrote fast, for she knew it was only a
matter of time till the police came knocking at her
door. They were down there. She'd heard shouts, car
horns, commotion, and then sirens just after she had
come back into the apartment, lots of sirens coming
from the surrounding streets below. So they'd found
the body, and now they would be investigating.
Wouldn't be hard to find; hers was, she was quite
sure, the only balcony missing its railing.

And so she wrote the last words of her book, the
book no one knew about, the book she'd decided to
write from the day she figured out he'd done it, the
book that would be her redemption.

*When I told him I knew the truth and that I'd known it
for some time, he just looked at me, as if to say, "I don't
know what you're talking about, Julia." Then I handed him
the coffee can I'd dug up from his yard. And I saw that he
could lie no longer. His face turned ashen, and a look of*

deep, uncontrolled shame filled his being. And then, sud-
denly, he jumped up, anguish pouring from his penetrating
eyes. What happened next took me by complete surprise, but
in thinking about it later, it seems so simple and so clear: he
was so filled with remorse that he ran out onto the terrace,
and before I could even figure out what he was doing, much
less stop him, he leaped to his death from

Wait a minute, she thought to herself. She hit the
CAPS LOCK key and then typed a note to herself:

WOULDN'T HE HAVE ASKED WHY I WORKED TO GET
HIM OUT OF JAIL IF I TOLD HIM I KNEW? NO NO NO, THIS
DOESN'T WORK. EVEN IF I SAID HE DIDN'T ASK, THE
POLICE SURE AS HELL WILL.

It occurred to her for the first time that she could
never tell the truth—that she knew he had done it—
for in giving that away she was admitting her guilt to
murder. If she'd known all along that he killed her
parents, why had she been so determined to free him
if not to kill him? What possible reason would she
have gotten him out of jail and brought him here other
than to shove him off the balcony?

She had not committed the perfect crime.

And, God, the money! It had gone over the side,
fluttering into the air. People would find it. Bloodstained hundred-dollar bills. Wait, no one would
know the dark marks were bloodstains. And it was
raining. And people were greedy. No one was going
to turn in hundred-dollar bills raining from the sky.
Maybe she didn't have to worry.

She took another puff on the cigarette. She blocked everything she'd written and highlighted it. Then she hit DELETE. WordPerfect asked her if she was sure she wanted to delete the block? "Goddamned right," she said aloud, and struck the key. And it was gone.

She thought for a moment, left the cigarette dangling in her lips, and then started again, inspired this time, a new road map coming in her head:

And so I told him I loved him. I told him that his honesty and bravery and courage had overcome any feelings of suspicion I might have had as to his guilt. I told him of the future I dreamed we'd have together, but as I was talking, he seemed to drift off, to fade, to crawl into himself. I kissed him, attempting to show him my desire, to let him know I wanted him, but he started to tremble and fumble, and I saw that his face was masked with an expression I can only describe as shame. He seemed lost, inept, and so clearly frightened. Suddenly, I knew something was very wrong.

Then he looked me in the eye. The look on his face changed to remorse, though I couldn't imagine what for. I had never seen him look this way. The green eyes, always shining like halogen bulbs, had dimmed. He was in shadows suddenly. Something, some demon—guilt, penitence, contrition—was trying to get out, and then he said, "I can't do this, I have to tell you something." The next thing he said was, "I did it."

"Did what?" I asked naively. I honestly didn't know what he was talking about.

"I did it," he said, "I killed your mother and your father."

Julia sucked on the cigarette, let the smoke out, and

laughed out loud. She was getting a kick out of this. This was *working*. This was good. People would believe this shit.

Tom blew his horn along with all the other pissed-off drivers, but it did no good. Traffic on the bridge barely inched along. Goddammit! Why'd he ever leave the city in the first place? Where'd he get the foolish notion that Julia would follow him to Tiburon and play house with him? If he'd stayed in the city, he would be with her now. He might have stopped her from doing what her notes made it look like she was going to do. The note to herself on her Matthew Disk #18 said: *The only way to see him pay for what he did, it is now clear to me, is to take matters into my own hands. I don't want to. I want to be with Tom in Tiburon, seeing if we can't make it work. In that beautiful house, safe, warm. But I can't tell him. I can't tell anyone. Ever.* He would never forget those words, never in his lifetime. That's what this had all been about. She'd known for a very long time that Matthew had killed her parents, and her mission to get him out of jail had been motivated by one reason alone: to see that justice was finally done. All this loving him, believing in him, had been a sham. She knew he'd probably beat the rap if they tried him again, so she couldn't let them do that. She hadn't been obsessed with loving him; she had been obsessed with killing him. The thought of it caused Tom's stomach to tighten. He blew the horn again, but more out of frustration than the hope that it would actually make the car in front of him move.

He sat there for several endless minutes as the rain beat down, and then he punched the telephone buttons. As the phone beeped, dialing his place, he was beginning to wonder if perhaps Cornelia was right in wanting to call the police, but what would they tell them? That his estranged wife was a possible killer? To go and stop her? That she was with a maniac? But the maniac had been legally set free this afternoon, and wouldn't they tell him *he* was nuts? All he heard on the car phone, however, was static, no ring. He tried again. And again. Nothing. He couldn't even dial the fourth time, the speaker merely hissed. "Ninety thousand dollars," he shouted at the BMW rondel at the center of the steering wheel, "and the telephone doesn't work!"

The brake lights on the Toyota ahead of him shut off. It was moving. Slowly, but it was moving. He pressed the accelerator of the 850Ci and heard the big engine whine. Maybe there was still time.

I don't know if my heart stopped, but I know my breathing did. I felt suddenly encased in a vacuum where the words, "I did it! I did it!" echoed and ricocheted off the walls until my head was splitting. I was in such shock, so stunned, in such anguish, that I didn't realize that he'd gone out onto the terrace till I felt a chill. The door was wide open. I saw him standing right in the middle of it, staring vacantly at the city through the fog.

I could tell he was in torment. In a way, I wanted to help him, but at the same time I was suddenly afraid for my own life. No, he hadn't threatened me. He was, in fact, looking the other way at the moment, into the rain, but I was still frightened of him. This was, after all, the man who'd murdered my family. I also felt rage building, the rage I'd never been allowed to direct toward anyone for what had been done to my parents. I screamed something at him like, "Tell me you're kidding, tell me it's not true!" But he brought his hands to his head and seemed to try to tear his hair out, crying out a deep, guttural scream like an animal who'd just been shot. He almost seemed as though he were going into convulsions, that my love for him, my trust for him, my belief in him had shot him through the heart with more precision than a bullet. He screamed again, and then, before I realized what he was doing, he ran with all his might toward the railing. I'm sure he was planning to grab it with both hands to allow his feet to springboard a leap to his death.

But the railing gave way from the force at which he hit it, and in a flash he and the railing both disappeared over the edge. I heard horns, the sound of brakes, and I knew it was over, this whole painful, incredible saga, on the wet street a quarter mile below.

As I sat trembling, his dog near me for comfort, waiting for the authorities to arrive, I thought to myself that no matter how you get there, no matter which twisted road you

*take and what you must suffer and lose on the way, the gain
does come one day. There is justice after all, God's justice. I
guess, in telling him I loved him, I unwittingly gave justice
a little push.*

"Jesus, I can't believe I'm writing this crap," she
said aloud. She blocked the last line and deleted it.
The book now ended with: . . . *there is justice after all,
God's justice.* She was pleased with that. If her publisher didn't like it, let *him* write a better line in the
editing. She hit the Save button, and the screen
blipped and assured her the new ending was now
locked in memory. She mashed the cigarette in the
metal can, wondering what she'd ever liked about
them, and stood up.

And then it hit her. The ambivalent pull between
being at peace with this justice she'd forced and the
moral aspect of having just killed someone. No, she
told herself, not someone. Not a person. Not a human
being. A monster. A creature with no conscience, no
morality. Just a brilliant liar. Yes, that would be the
title. It hit her now, for the first time. *LIAR: The True
Story of the Radcliffe Murder Case,* by Julia Larsen.

Julia Larsen. Still married to Tom. Was it too late for
them? Had she pushed him aside for too long, had she
shoved him too far? The day Matt had unwittingly
given away his secret, she realized she'd have to
push Tom far away to be able to carry out her plan.
She'd realized what a fool she'd been all this time,
how right Tom had been, but she also knew that in

being smart—in getting Matthew herself—she very well might lose the man who really loved her. Still, she had to take that risk.

But now that her eyes were no longer clouded with Matthew's sinister magic, she viewed Tom quite differently. She needed him now, for at this moment she felt she was hovering somewhere between violence and redemption. Now they could go to Hawaii and truly start again, because the person preventing them from being together, from patching up their marriage, the person who had pushed her to that violence that might give her redemption, was now dead. She prayed that Tom would understand, that he'd give her another chance. She'd done that for him, hadn't she? Had he picked up on it, gotten the hint the other day when she lingered at his house? Maybe there was still time to call him right now. She went to the phone and picked up the receiver—

But then she heard the loud knock on the door.

Just like in the movies, she thought. Cops never ring bells, they give this hard macho police knock.

Maggie barked, got up.

Julia called out, "I'm coming," and Maggie followed her to the door. Julia felt herself sweating, wondering just how cool she could pretend to be in front of them. No, she could do it; she'd done it to Matthew for almost a year, hadn't she? Then the dog started barking again. "Shhh, it's all right," Julia said, trying to shush her but couldn't. The dog put her paws up on the door. "Maggie, down, come on—"

Julia unlocked the door and called out, as she was opening it, "The dog won't bite, she's just not used to strangers." Then, holding Maggie back by her collar, she pulled the door open to admit the officers.

But there was only one man there. And he wasn't wearing a uniform.

Maggie pulled away from Julia and leapt on the man in the framework of the doorway, slobbering him with kisses. And Julia felt her heart stop in one cold second as she faced the dog's master.

Matthew's shirt was ripped, his face bruised, his hands scraped clean of skin, and blood ran down the side of his head. But he stood there, very much alive. Julia backed up, disbelieving, whispering, "No . . . no . . . no."

"Yes," he said, kicking the door closed behind him, facing her. "*Yes.*"

When the sleek black BMW turned the corner on Sacramento Street, Tom Larsen's heart skipped a beat. He saw the lights of several police cars and ambulances cutting through the rain. They were right in front of his building. He drove as close as he could get and then jumped out of the car while it was still running. In his panic he didn't even shut the door. A crowd had gathered with umbrellas in hand, watching someone being loaded into one of the ambulances. Tom shoved through them, shouting, "Who is that?"

A cop held him back as he tried to get past the spectators.

"I've got to know what happened here!"

"Accident," the officer said, "funny one."

"Funny?"

"Strange."

"What the fuck *happened*?" Tom demanded, looking up because several people were pointing above him at the building.

"Railing fell. Hit a car on the hood, almost went through the engine. Broke the windshield. Taking the driver to emergency now. They slammed into another car, slight injury there also. That car hit a parked one, a mess."

"A railing? Just a railing?"

"Money. Money too. Hundred-dollar bills, it seems. Neighbors are all waiting for more."

Tom swallowed hard. Harry's money. The coffee can she'd dug up. He'd just read about it. "No *person* fell?"

The cop gave Tom a funny look. "Sorry to disappoint you, buddy. What paper you with?"

"Do you know what apartment it came from?" Tom said, looking up with the others. The raindrops were coming down so hard they hurt his eyes.

"Naw. Can't see above the seventh floor in the rain. We're checkin' 'em one by one."

Tom turned and was about to dash into the building, but the lobby was filled with policemen and residents who were getting off the elevators, curious to see what the excitement was about. He instead dashed through the rain back to his car, slid onto the now soaked leather seat, and threw the gear shift into reverse. He rounded the corner in a direct reversal of his arrival, then burned rubber as he headed around the back of the building, and drove right through the gate that prevented unauthorized entry to the underground parking garage. The sturdy barrier disintegrated like balsa wood under the attack of the twin kidney grilles.

He brought the car to a stop as near the elevator as he could. He saw Julia's car there. He nearly missed it at first, looking at once for the old TR7, then remembering she'd finally gotten rid of that thing. There it was, the new one, the white Honda Prelude, close to the elevator. He turned his car off. And he started to get out, but at that moment the elevator doors opened and out came Julia. With the dog. His heart leaped for a moment—had he been wrong? Yes, she was alone! He was about to call out to her—

When Matthew appeared from the elevator as well. Matthew Hinson. In a bright blue jacket, *his* blue jacket. His eyes darting around. Tom ducked. Came up again a second later to see Matthew shoving Julia into the driver's seat, the dog jumping in the back. Tom saw he was holding something shiny in his hand—a big knife, their chef's knife—and as he hurried around the car to the passenger side, Tom saw that he had white mittens on his hands—no, they weren't mittens, his hands were wrapped in something, small towels? Wash cloths? No, bandages.

He heard the Honda start. He saw the massive backup lights blaze. He ducked, praying Julia would see his car, that she'd recognize it. He heard her change gears. He sat up. She was driving right by him now. He could see her face clearly. She was terrified. She was scared for her life, he could see that, and she was looking only one way—straight ahead. And he could make out, past her nose, the knife pressed just under her chin.

He started the BMW. As Julia and Matthew drove out the exit ramp of the parking structure, he drove out the entrance ramp, retracing his path over the mangled bits of gate lying on the cement. He saw Julia turn right, and he did too, giving them about a block's lead. He followed the Honda to Gough and then onto the freeway. They were taking the Bay Bridge. He prayed it would be as busy as the Golden Gate, so he'd be able to stop and get Hinson, take him by surprise. He didn't have a gun, a knife, any weapon whatsoever, and he didn't know how he'd do it. But he would. He would save her. He would do what *she'd* so stupidly set out to do. He would get Matthew.

So help him God.

*   *   *

Traffic was heavy because of the storm, but it never stopped moving. A couple of times Julia prayed it would slow to a standstill so she could bolt. Quickly open the door and run for it. She'd not put her seat belt on. It wasn't on purpose; in her panic she'd forgotten all about it. But as she drove over the Bay Bridge she realized she wasn't wearing it. It would allow her to escape. She thanked God Matt didn't notice.

But the cars kept moving. And Julia's hope died.

As they headed through the Altamont Pass on 580, she could see huge wind turbines rising from the mist like eerie mechanical monsters. She shuddered. Then she saw a small accident at the side of the road, two cars that had collided in a patch of fog. What if, she thought, she suddenly swerved and slammed into the car next to her? She could make it look like a real accident. She could be careful not to kill herself—if only, she thought, she could kill *him* in the process—and she was tempted when a black BMW, one just like Tom's but for a dented front end, pulled alongside her and remained there for about five minutes. She contemplated it. But she didn't have the guts. And how could she be certain it would save her from this madman anyway? She'd probably cause a tremendous pile-up that would kill innocent people, and Matt would run free.

She drove on. Fearing for her life.

* * *

"It's *me*. Meeeeee! Julia, dammit, look over here!" Tom's neck was aching from straining to the right, but all the time he drove alongside her he prayed and shouted and begged her to look at him, really *look* at him. He could see her through the rain, and yes, she was looking his way, but she seemed to be looking only at the front of the car, not at his face. "Julia, please! Shit! Julia, look at me!"

Then he remembered something. He had tinted windows. Sixty percent. They weren't legal on the front passenger windows, but he'd had them coated anyway; he'd risk the ticket when an overzealous cop realized it one day. But tonight it was his downfall, and he cursed himself for having been so vain. Yeah, he admitted, that's why he'd done it. He wanted to be *intriguing*, wanted people to wonder *who* was driving that expensive sleek car. Damn, his vanity might now cost his wife her life. He hit a button on the console, and the window silently disappeared into the door. Rain gushed in. *Look at me. Look at me. Look . . . at . . . me.*

But she didn't.

And he finally knew he was risking too much. He put the window back up and moved to a position behind them. He didn't want Matt to realize the same car had been next to them for miles now. He had three-quarters of a tank of gas. He punched the computer. Four hundred and fifteen miles left in the tank. That would be enough. Julia never filled up her car with gas; she was always in a hurry, putting in five or ten dollars' worth. He hoped she hadn't changed her habits all that much. They'd have to stop sometime in 415 miles. And when they did, he'd stop as well.

Matthew set the knife down on the floor of the car and held his hands between his legs. She knew he was in pain. He'd forced her to bandage him, and as she did, she admitted she'd never seen a scrape so bad. But those bleeding hands had saved his life. He told her what had happened. He'd felt himself toppling toward the sky as she pushed him, so he grasped the railing, trying desperately to prevent the fall, but he realized he was in midair. The railing struck and scraped the balcony beneath them, and he released his grip. He did a virtual somersault in the air. And as he did, his foot caught on a trellis on the balcony beneath that one, and his head slammed against the railing there, and he grabbed for it—

But his hands slipped off, and he was holding onto nothing but stucco and cement at that point. He was slipping to his death, the skin leaving his palms, flesh being ripped away. All his weight was suspended by his hands. He thought of the times he'd chinned himself in prison, how he'd held his weight by his hands alone. He was determined, focused. No bitch was going to trick him, fool him, kill him. He swung his feet out, and then in, and let go.

That was how he landed on the balcony three below hers.

He then heard the sounds, the same ones she had heard from the street beneath. He knew it was the railing landing, and he guessed automobiles were colliding from the crashes echoing from the unseen ground.

The apartment belonging to the balcony he landed on was empty; no one was living in it. He had to crack the glass with a lawn chair to get the slider open. Once inside, he lifted the lever on the kitchen sink with his elbow, and put his scraped, bleeding hands under cold water. As he did, he looked at his image reflecting off the window above the sink. His head hurt like hell, but the blood hadn't come yet. It wasn't until he walked into Julia's apartment that the gash had opened. But he put his pain aside, because he knew what he had to do.

And now he was doing it. But there was something he had to know. "When did you figure it out? It was impossible for anyone to know. I was brilliant. How the fuck did you know?"

"Frangos."

"What?"

"You gave me Frango mints from Marshall Field's for Christmas last year."

He blinked. "So what?"

"Remember when I asked you how you knew they

were my favorite candy? And you told me that my mother had told you that?"

"She did."

"No, she didn't. There was only one time my mother and I *ever* discussed Frango mints, and that was on the phone about two minutes before she died."

Matt sucked in his breath. There was a long silence, miles of it. It was coming back to him. He remembered picking up the extension near the piano, and the old lady thanked Julia for the candy, and . . . Julia . . . told her—*for the first time*—they were her . . . favorites. He turned red, flushed. He was mortified and embarrassed. His whole being felt humiliated, disgraced. *You stupid fuck. You stupid fucking asshole. One little detail, and you didn't remember where you knew that from. One little gesture—sending candy—and you screwed it all up. You gave yourself away. All you worked for. All you planned. And you were supposed to be smarter than she. Fucking idiot.*

Then rage infected his blood. He grabbed her arm and shook her so hard the car weaved back and forth on the highway. "Bitch, fucking bitch! All this time, lying to me. You worked to free me so you could do this to me. You stood up to the world for me so you could trick me?"

"Yes," she screamed, starting to lose it, emotion bursting out of her, "that's exactly what I did. I alienated everyone, but it was worth it to destroy you."

"But you *believed* in me," he moaned, his voice sounding truly devastated.

"Are you kidding? I got the second collection of your shitty poems published because I knew it was the only way to *get* you and make you pay."

"Fuck you."

"And I called it *The Absence of Angels* because that's what you're all about. You have no soul."

Matthew spit in her right eye.

Tom saw the Honda swerve and felt he was going to burst from frustration. He was so filled with fear for Julia and loathing for Matt and joy that his wife was still alive and guilt at not reading her notes sooner or forcing her to tell him what was really going on that he felt he would lose his mind. Driving in a blinding rainstorm through the San Joaquin Valley in the middle of the night, following his wife, who was being held at knifepoint by a deranged man who had slaughtered her parents, he tried to hold onto his sanity as tightly as he gripped the steering wheel. They'll stop soon, he kept telling himself, they'll *have* to stop soon. *Dear God, don't let anything happen to Julia. Don't let her get hurt.*

"I have to go to the bathroom." Julia could feel her bladder bloating in her abdomen.

"Too bad."

"Please. I have to."

"Fuck yourself."

She saw turmoil inside him. He would seem to relax, then suddenly spasm. He'd kick the fire wall and thrust his head back. It was as though he was carrying on an argument inside his head. Probably, she thought, telling himself what a fool he was. But she really feared him now. She'd seen the wild moment when his anger came to the surface, when he had spit into her face. She knew there was no way out of this but to trick him physically and run. She'd never get him to trust her again. Stopping was her only chance.

"You betrayed me," he said suddenly, sounding on the verge of tears again. "All this time I thought you loved me. Then you betrayed me."

Her mouth opened in astonishment. "I betrayed *you*? You used me! You slept with me so you'd—"

"I slept with you because I loved you!" He stared at her, imploring her to understand with his eyes reflecting the green lights of the dash. "Your parents stood in the way. They were going to fix your marriage at Christmas, I heard them that morning. Your mother told me—"

"You said she was going to tell me I should divorce Tom."

"I told you what you wanted to hear. Martha told Harry he had to have a talk with Tom, set him straight about this 'cancer thing,' as she called it. Hell, I don't know what the bastard was gonna tell him, how to get it up for a woman with one tit?"

"Stop it!"

"*I* fucked you, not the architect with the faggot underwear."

"Tom and I made love in Hawaii. On New Year's Eve."

He was blown away. "I'll never believe that. Never."

"Why didn't you just kill Tom too?"

"I tried."

The words chilled her to the bone. Target practice. Hunting. Tom had been right all along. Matt *was* trying to kill him the day they arrested him. It took her breath away. But she was too numb to speak.

"You caused me a lot of pain over the years, Julia. Yeah, a lot of pain. I had cancer too, only mine was inside my soul, and I had to have it cut out like you did. They took out your diseased breast; I took out the diseased people who were never going to let me have you. Nobody's gonna judge me on this. Not even you."

Tears streamed down her face in response. *My God, you're sicker than I knew.*

"Snow angel," he repeated dreamily, closing his eyes.

In the rearview mirror, Julia noticed that a car had been behind them for some time. It seemed to her that they were the only two vehicles on the road now. The other car appeared to be going about her speed, but she wanted it to pass her. Maybe if she slowed down just slightly, not enough to make Matt realize, more gradual than abrupt, the car would move by them. Then she'd turn the wheel into it. It was less dangerous out here on a four-lane highway. It was also her only hope.

Hope vanished almost immediately. The car, which indeed had been gaining on her since she slowed, suddenly pulled off to the side, and she watched the headlights fade in the rain-swept distance.

Oh, God, now we're all alone.

"Fucking car!" Tom shouted, standing in the pelting rain. "Fucking Nazi bastards!" He balanced a flashlight with difficulty between his shoulder and his chin as he fastened the wrench—from the trunk tool kit, a device that until tonight he had thought super-fluous—over the bolt that held the windshield wiper in place and turned it till it tightened. For five miles or so, he'd heard the wiper in front of him, a massive thing, slam each time it swiped and retreated. Then it had simply stopped, in the up position, hanging over the A-pillar, as rain pelted the glass in front of him. He couldn't see a thing. He rode for a good mile straining to look out the passenger window, but he'd finally given in and pulled over. It was too dangerous to drive that way.

But as he stood there, soaked, freezing, tightening a Germanic bolt that never should have come loose in the first place, despair began to set in. Because he knew they had gained on him, they'd eluded him. His wife was in the hands of a maniac, and here he was, in the middle of nowhere in a diseased luxury coupe with a useless telephone.

He was so anxious to give chase that when he finished, he left the wrench and the plastic cap for the fitting lying on the hood, but in a moment they were gone. They blew off in the wind, as he accelerated to 100 m.p.h. in less seconds than the official BMW manual boasted. At least the Germans do *something* right, he thought.

And he drove through the night, like a Patriot missile searching out its moving target.

Matthew settled down in the next fifty miles. Maggie had gotten up in the backseat and changed position once, going right back to sleep. Julia again said she had to go to the bathroom. Matthew did not respond. So she just kept on driving.

But something was gnawing at him. "Why didn't you just tell the D.A., or even go back to that asshole Crowley?"

She reached up and rubbed her right eye. It was still stinging. "And say what? You were guilty because of candy? What kind of evidence was that? How could I prove it? You lied your way through one trial. You'd do it again."

"So you hatched this clever plot, this sneaky charade."

"And it worked."

"Almost worked," he corrected her. He laughed out loud, moving the lever at the side of his seat so his seat back eased him into a more reclining position. He actually seemed to calm down. He was talking about this without rage, as if they were discussing a case they'd read about in the paper and were intrigued with. "You could never outsmart me."

"I got the idea to do this from you."

"What the fuck are you talking about?"

"I didn't know where to go after I left that day you gave me the Frangos. I was revolted, sickened. I'd fallen for your lies and manipulation. I couldn't go home to Tom and admit it. I couldn't tell my sister, any of my friends. I felt myself coming apart. I wanted to kill you right there and then. But I covered instead and went to your place."

"My place?"

"I found the poem first. Yeah, the poem, Matthew, the one we never put into a book. Jim Crowley said he went over your place with a fine-tooth comb, but he missed that one piece of paper because it was stuck in my novel. I can quote it, I've read it so many times— *Starry night, somewhere aloft, above the clouds,* etc. I've kept it near me ever since, to remind me, every chance I get, what a demented monster you are."

"That poem was brilliant," he said smugly. "My best, I think."

"I hate you."

He just laughed.

"I was a basket case that night. I cried, I screamed, I got it all out. I trashed your place, I murdered your things to keep from murdering you. I tore up those angel poems you had the gall to 'dedicate' to my mother. I thought I was going crazy. I saw your bottle of Tuscany on the dresser, and I threw it through the mirror so hard it nearly went through the wall. I went to sleep, if you can call it that—it was more like a coma from alcohol and exhaustion—but I woke up a changed person."

"How so?"

She was on a roll. "I began to use my head, as you'd done. I knew the only way to get you was to be as clever as you had been, as smart as you, as brilliant. The next morning I drove down to Whitlock Road and left the car and crawled up the mountain just as you had, retracing your steps that night. I sat staring at the house for hours, and still I didn't know what I could do to get you. When I got back to your place, Maggie was waiting for me in the driveway. Inga later told me she'd jumped the fence, that she must have known I was there. It was a happy reunion, and I told Inga I wanted to keep her with me for the night. She slept next to me, and she was oddly comforting."

"How'd you find the money?"

"Remember how warm it was? I let Maggie out and she started digging. I couldn't get her to stop."

He smiled. "Smart dog. Quite a memory."

"I watched her uncover a rusted can. I knew what

was in it before I even opened it. Then I found Jack Abbott's *In the Belly of the Beast* on the bookshelf, and that's when I knew the future. I called my sister and told her I was okay, then I left."

He laughed again. "I gotta hand it to you. I had no idea. No fucking inkling. You're as good as I am. Just not as lucky."

Tears started to pour down her face. *I hate you. God, how I hate you. You were supposed to die. You were supposed to pay.*

"Why didn't you tell Tom?"

Now she wished she had. She'd *wanted* to tell Tom; so many times she had been on the brink of saying it. But how would she have done it? *Hey, Tom, I'm going to murder Matt, then it'll be all right.* She turned and glanced at him again. He was right about one thing: this was something cancerous. Now she knew she *should* have told Tom. Or Carrie, God, Carrie would have applauded her. She might even have shoved him herself.

But it was too late for that now.

"Fuck you," Matt said. Then he screamed it again. "Fuck you!" And he stabbed the dashboard with the knife, poking a gaping hole in it as he twisted the blade around in the plastic and foam. He slashed the dashboard again and again until he finally settled back in the seat and tossed the knife to the floor. "Why do you want to hurt me? What did I do to you?"

She shivered. The dashboard, slashed, cut, ripped,

vandalized, could just as well have been her body. She gave him time to settle down. She knew he was thinking now about what to do with her. "Where are we going?" she finally asked.

He grinned. "For a walk amongst God's natural wonder."

"What? Are we going to Leucadia?"

He laughed. "Leucadia? You wouldn't want to go back there, Julia. You almost died there."

She almost wished she had. She turned the blinkers on. He shot upright. "What the hell are you doing?"

"Stopping." She braked, pulling into an all-night Texaco station. "If I don't, I'm going to be sitting in my own pee, and I'd honestly rather die first."

He looked around the place as she pulled next to a pump. There were several cars, trucks there. Several people. Phones. A mini-mart. "We don't need gas," he said, looking at the gauge. "Don't park here."

"Why not?"

"The sign says the cans are around back. We're not waltzing around out here. Park it there, in the dark." He was also worried that someone might have started looking for her because of her railing—they must have figured out by now that it had come from her balcony—and perhaps there was more urgency because of the blood and the broken window in the apartment below her. What was he going to do about that? Hell, they could never prove anything. He wasn't there. He never was there. *Julia and I spent the night at my place in Mariposa and decided to go hiking in the morning. And that's when she had her unfortunate accident—*

"Drive back by the toilets and park, you hear me?"

She put the car in gear and drove behind the building. She started to get out. "Wait," he said, getting out first. Maggie, whose bladder must have been as full as Julia's, leaped out before he could close the door and immediately squatted down and christened the ground on the right side of the car. Matt walked around and opened Julia's door. He took her by the hand as she got out—and Maggie jumped back in—and walked her to the cement block building. She turned to the women's rest room door, but Matt yanked her the other way. "In here," he said, pushing her toward the men's door.

"What?" she gasped.

"You're not getting outta my sight."

"But I can't—"

"Like hell you can't." He brandished the knife again, just to remind her. He shoved her against the door of the men's room. It opened, and he followed her in. A teenager stood at the urinal and froze when he found himself face to face with a beautiful woman.

"Shake your weenie dry and take a hike," Matt ordered the boy.

The red-faced kid just stared at them. "What?"

"You heard me. My girl's gotta help me piss." Matt

held his bandaged hands up. Julia closed her eyes in embarrassment.

"Okay, sure, man," the kid said, embarrassed, turning away from Julia to zip up. Then he started toward the sink, but Matt grabbed him and shoved him out the door.

And locked it.

Julia went into the stall. He held it open with his leg, half in the door and half out. "Can't you give me privacy for a minute?"

"Take your leak and let's go."

Julia had no choice. She slid her sweat pants down, then her panties, and she moved down to the seat as quickly as possible. The sound of her urine hitting the water embarrassed her, so she flushed, which made Matt laugh. As she sat there, feeling the relief she needed so badly, she realized he was moving into the stall, closer and closer. His crotch was only inches from her face. She could not look up.

"Unbutton me," he said.

"If you can hold a knife," she responded, "you can open your own pants."

"It hurts too much."

"No."

"Open it, I said." He pressed the knife forward, the tip near her neck.

She reached up and hesitatingly unzipped his fly.

"Unfasten the button."

Dear God, don't make me do this. Please don't let him make me do this. She undid the button at the waistband of his jeans and they spread open. And then she was startled. She recognized the shorts he was wearing. The stone-washed silk boxers she'd bought for Tom. The ones she thought were so sexy. She looked up. He was grinning from ear to ear. She felt nauseous.

"Pull them down."

"Please, no," she said softly, begging him.

"You'd pull them down for Tommy, I bet."

"Don't make me do this."

"Down." The tip of the blade was flat against her ear now. She reached up and lowered the shorts in one good yank. Matt's penis stood out just in front of her mouth. She looked away. He was trembling, however; she suddenly realized that, and she thought it was with sexual longing. "You're gonna do what Scully did," he whispered.

"Scully knows," she said.

"What?"

"I met with him. When you made those allegations. I knew they weren't true. I talked to Walter, he let me see Scully. He knows how sick you are. You didn't fight off his advances. You used him just like you used me."

Then anger rose through his words. "Cocksucking bitch," he moaned in a devastated tone, his hands propping himself up against the sides of the stall. "Traitors, you're all traitors. You and Scully, fucking cocksucking traitors. That guard Walter was a god-damned crack addict—"

She was thinking fast. She knew there was no way out of this, but she hoped in the least that she could use the hideous moment to her advantage. She could bite him! She could bite so hard, hurt him so badly, that he'd see stars—perhaps at the same moment she could ball her hand into a fist and bring it up with force into his testicles. Yes, bite his penis, hit him in the balls, he'd double forward, the knife would fall away because of his pain, she'd yank her pants up and run for it, there were people getting gas, the teenager might still be there, she'd seen a clerk in the mini market, there were—

But suddenly Matt was gone. He just walked away. She saw his feet under the stall and heard him urinating into the urinal.

She didn't understand why he'd suddenly stopped, but she didn't have time to think about it now. She wiped and pulled her pants and underpants up in one fast motion. When she stepped out of the stall, he was still peeing, one hand with the knife at his side, one hand resting atop the urinal. His jeans and under-shorts were down under the cheeks of his ass. He wouldn't be able to run fast like that, she surmised, and this time, without planning or thinking it through, she shoved him forward for the second time that night, into the urinal. His face slammed against the wall, and she heard the metallic ping of the blade striking the tile floor.

She dashed for the door, grabbing the handle with her right hand, the lock with her left, but he was on top of her before she could pull the door open. He grabbed her with all his might, swinging her around, slamming her up against the rusted metal door. She felt something warm wetting between her legs, and she realized that he was still urinating and she started to scream in horror, but he cupped her mouth with his, kissing her, shoving his tongue between her lips until she started to choke. Then he pulled his lips away, turned and shook his penis, and then yanked up his pants and painfully buttoned only the waist. He bent over and picked up the knife again and pulled her away from the door. "Bitch," he said as he pulled it open.

But Julia was shaken with horror, her pants wet and stinking, her entire body trembling. He told her to move, but she was incoherent, starting to cry from deep in her soul. He grabbed her by the arm and slapped her hard across the face. Every fiber of her body froze. "Want to die right here?"

She didn't answer. She pulled herself together. He stepped outside the door. She did too.

Maggie was looking at them, licking the side back window.

They returned to the car. She said they needed gas. He told her to start it, and when she did, he checked the gauge. "Like hell we do," he said. Why, she thought, for the first time in her life had she filled up the entire tank this morning?

At that very moment Tom Larsen cried out, "A gas station!" There was no one to hear him, but he announced it as though he were piloting a tour bus. He felt the hair on the back of his neck stand on end as he prayed he'd see her car there. He'd driven like a bat out of hell, and he was surprised and dismayed that he'd not caught up to them by now. But a gas station—maybe!

As he pulled off the road, he checked out the cars. New Chevy. A pickup truck. White Acura Legend that at first glance he thought was her Honda. A beat-up old Pacer just leaving. That was it. *Shit.*

Tom didn't know what to do. It was decision time. Should he stop and call the Highway Patrol and have them start to look for the car? Or should he keep on driving? He knew they had to be just ahead of him. If he lost time in placing a phone call, would the cops ever find them? Yes, at some point, but would that be too late? No. He couldn't risk a phone call eating up precious time. He gunned the car and continued on his quest, missing the white Prelude behind the building.

Moments later, the same Prelude that had been parked in the darkness behind the mini-mart pulled back onto the highway and turned in the same direction as Tom had. Julia started to speed, but Matt warned her she wasn't going to attract the Highway Patrol, not tonight. "Just keep up with that set of lights ahead of us," he said. He didn't want her to be too clever.

She could make out the taillights of a car about a half mile ahead. Good, she thought, she would. Matt didn't look, and apparently he didn't realize it, but in keeping pace with the other car, they were going 85 m.p.h. The guy ahead of her was speeding. Julia loved it. *Please, someone, arrest me!*

And the two cars continued once again, though this time in different formation, in reversed positions, into the cold, wet night. Julia didn't allow herself to get close enough to see that the car she was following was a BMW 850Ci.

Or that her husband was driving it.

16

The car behind him was beginning to annoy Tom. At first he thought it was the CHP, so his natural instinct was to slow down. Then he realized a cop would be a blessing, so he started to speed again. But the other car only sped up as well, keeping roughly the same distance from him as it had kept ever since he'd first seen the headlights. He played a little game. He went fast. It went fast. He slowed. It slowed. Was someone tailing *him*?

This was getting weird.

"What are you doing now?" Matt growled.

"What are you talking about?"

"Why are you slowing down again?"

"You told me to stay behind that car."

"For Christ's sake, we don't have all night. If you have to pass him, pass him."

Julia stepped on the gas, diminishing the distance between her and the big red taillights. She looked to the right. She could see that Matt's seat was reclined again. His waistband was unfastened, and one hand rested inside his open zipper. The knife was on the front floor somewhere.

"I like to beat off," he suddenly said. "They said I was 'obsessed with masturbation' in high school. Teachers used to catch me doing it all the time."

"I don't want to hear it."

He put his left hand on her right leg. Her wet leg. She was driving, chilled to the bone, sitting in his urine.

"I waited for you. I could have had lots of girls in high school, after. My pick. They were all dropping their panties for me. Let them blow me, but never fucked them. I saved it for you . . ."

It went on and on. She said nothing. But the distance between her and the big taillights lessened. It was only drizzling now. Visibility was getting better. The car was coming into view.

It was a BMW. A dark color—blue? Deep green like Tom's last one? No, black like Tom's new one, the one he'd driven her in to Tiburon that heartbreaking day he showed her the house. She was sure this was the same model, the big sporty two-door. How odd that she had seen the same model earlier—there weren't that many of them around. Oh, how she wished some miracle would make it Tom's, make him be the driver, make him see her and—

God! She felt the miracle happening. The license

plate. *TL ARC. Tom Larsen—Architect.* She'd given him those vanity plates for his 325i when they were first engaged. He'd switched them to his 5 Series when he bought that car, and now they resided on the back of his newest automobile—

But it couldn't be. She was seeing things, imagining it because she *wanted* it so badly. Impossible. Out here? Coincidence. Her eyes were playing tricks on her. This was madness. Insanity. It couldn't be Tom, not in *front* of them. Not out here, not tonight. God, had it been Tom earlier, the BMW with the smashed grille?

But she squinted to make out the numbers on the back or the trunk lid. And yes, it was an 850Ci. It *was* Tom's car. Tom was driving in front of them!

"Pass the bastard," Matt ordered, impatient.

Julia flashed the headlights once. Twice. A third time.

"What the hell are you doing?" Matt sat straight up, alarmed.

"Just letting him know I'm gonna pass. This highway is dangerous at night. I drove it many times—"

"Pass the fucking car!"

"—when my parents were *alive*, you know?" She tried to make the words cut into him, hoping the dig would take his mind off the fact of what she was actually doing. She flashed the lights one more long time, and then started to ease her way into the oncoming lane.

* * *

What the hell is going on? Tom wondered what jerk was flashing his brights? Were his taillights out? If the wipers could go, so could the back lights. Or was it just some punk playing games? The cops? No, he couldn't see any sign of it being a police car, even when he clicked the rearview mirror to day. Just the glare of the flashing headlights.

Well, the asshole was coming around him. Thank God. Now he'd see what was going on.

And he did. The sloping white hood of a Honda came into focus, and automatically his hand went up to shield his face. Nonchalantly, as if bored and leaning on his arm. He wanted to take no chances, even though he had such dark windows. But he watched from the space between his fingertips. He saw Matt staring at him, at the car. He saw Julia past Matt's head, leaning forward, her mouth nearly on the steering wheel, looking at him, her expression communicating, through the glass of the Prelude, through the wind, the rain, and the tinted glass of the BMW, that she knew it was him. That's what the flashes had been about. And now—the payoff—he knew it was her.

He let up on his speed, allowing her to get around him. He saw Matt turn around once and look back. He gave them even more distance. But he was pumped. Now he knew what had happened. They'd pulled off somewhere and he'd driven past them. They'd exchanged places. She'd caught up with him.

And he saw that she was all right, and now that she knew he was here, she would feel safer.

Or so he hoped.

Matthew kept talking. "I used to dream about you all the time," he said, rubbing between his legs again. "I have a whole pad of poems I wrote to you. I was going to show them to you when we were married. I was going to show you how I loved you from the day I met you."

Tom . . .

"I never cheated on you, Julia. You've got my word on that."

Tom . . . he's crazy.

"I never cheated, not even in jail. I let that nigger blow me, but I never fucked anyone. Scully knew. Did he tell you?"

Tom . . . help me.

"I saved myself for you. Those girls they dragged into court, Marguerite Del Fatso or whatever her goddamned name was, I'm sorry about that. I got drunk and tempted, but I stopped in time. They weren't you. That's why I hit them. Who'd want cattle like that when you have an angel in your sights?"

In your sights . . . He tried to kill Tom too.

"Harry wouldn't let me court you. Sent me away. Married you off to that asshole."

"That asshole" was her only hope, and he was still behind them, thank God. She stared, praying, into the mirror. *Come on, Tom, think of something.*

"I knew your marriage would fall apart," Matt continued. "He didn't love you. You were beautiful and famous, that's why he married you. He married you for your nice tits. One gone, he's gone. But your parents weren't going to let that happen. That's what irked me. I had to stop them. I hated killing your mom, I really want you to know that."

Please, stop!

"But I had to."

I'm losing my mind.

He giggled. Actually giggled. "I stole the angel water globe from your parents' house. Martha never gave me anything except those crummy fruitcakes. She was on his side."

You bastard.

"But she sucked me off once."

She glared at him.

He laughed again, smugly this time. "Gotcha going, huh? You almost believed that. Hah. I coulda had her anytime I wanted. Used to see her looking at me with my shirt off. Man, she was horny. Don't think the old fart banged her in a good twenty years. Not since she lost her titties!"

She drowned out the sound of his voice by thinking only of Molly, how she had to make it through this for her, how she couldn't desert her now, how Molly had a right to parents, two parents, and she damn well wasn't going to let this madman do to her what he had done to her mother. "Matthew, what are you going to do with me?"

Emotionless, he said, "What do you think I'm going to do with you? Marry you? I have to kill you."

She'd known the words were coming. She'd known it from the moment he appeared in her doorway. She knew it was over for her. She'd tried to turn the tables, and she hadn't succeeded. Nancy Drew, investigative reporter, book writer, had tried to be evil. But she had screwed it up. Had God devised this as her punishment? Was she ultimately no better than he? Did you have to be born without a conscience—was anyone, truly?—to be capable of murder? Yes, he was planning to kill her, just as she'd planned to kill him. Then she asked, "How can you kill me if you love me?"

"Don't play stupid, Julia," he said with steel in his voice. "I hate you now."

When Julia saw the signs for Cathey's Valley, she suddenly felt a sense of déjà vu. She and Molly were in her battered TR7 and they were starting to slip and slide, wondering if they would make it into Mariposa. It wasn't as cold tonight, and thus the rain did not become snow in the higher elevations. She retraced the path she'd driven that night, passing the spot where they had abandoned the car, where they'd been picked up by the hippie, where they had embarked on their sleigh ride into hell. She wondered now what Matthew had been doing at those moments. Had he already been in her parents' house when she and Molly flagged down the pickup truck? Or had he been just crawling up the hill, as she was doing in a car?

Every so often she held her breath, for in rounding a curve, Tom would disappear for a moment or two. But then his headlights would reappear suddenly, and she started breathing again.

"That the same goddamn car we passed an hour ago?" Matt suddenly asked, turning around.

"Of course not."

He looked again, as if he wasn't sure. Then he reached behind him and started to pet Maggie with the back of his hand, and finally settled back in.

Tom couldn't believe that they were sailing right on through Mariposa. He was praying for them to stop for some reason, give him a chance to—

"Get the fuck out of the way!" he shouted at a man stepping off the raised cement platform of a building in the center of town, stepping right in front of him. He braked hard to keep from hitting the asshole. The man was big, and he was wearing cowboy boots, which might have made him less agile, for in trying to avoid the BMW, he toppled against the right front fender. Only then did Tom see that he knew this man. Only then did he feel God was starting to answer tonight's prayers.

"Get in the car," Tom shouted, one foot out the door he'd just opened.

"What the—? Larsen?"

"I'll explain on the road. Just get in the car!"

"Whoa. What's this all—?"

"Get your ass in this car or Julia's going to be dead!"

As Tom caught up to the Honda at the Whitlock Road turn-off, Jim Crowley finally said, "Now, wanna tell me what's going on?"

"Where are we going?" Julia finally asked him.

"Yosemite."

"Yosemite?" She sounded alarmed.

"Ever see Glacier Point?"

"Yes."

"Beautiful, huh?"

She felt the hairs on her arms stand again. "But why are we—"

"Because it can also be very dangerous." And then he laughed a sardonic laugh. "There are times when I actually find heights exciting."

And she now knew *how* he was planning to kill her.

Tom didn't give Crowley a chance to ask one question the whole forty miles to Yosemite. He just talked, trying to explain what had happened, and he made the decision to tell the truth, risked saying that his wife had tried to murder someone. Crowley, never a man of many words, listened attentively and finally muttered, "Don't say."

But where were they headed? Neither man could figure that one. Tom had been sure they were going to Matthew's place, but they'd passed it long ago. He would just have to follow them until they stopped. But where would that be? Where was he forcing her to drive him? And why? If only Tom could hear what they were saying. If only he knew what had happened tonight.

When he saw them pull into the rustic national park entrance at Arch Rock, Tom was at once amazed and relieved. Amazed because he couldn't fathom what the hell they would be going there for. "No idyllic weekend at the Ahwahnee," Jim Crowley said. But Tom was relieved because he knew the park was full of rangers. Which meant that help was close by.

The sky was beginning to cast off the night, and everything was bathed in a misty shade of gray when Tom and Jim saw Julia's car slow in front of the ranger's gate. Crowley would have jumped out and alerted the ranger and tried to nab Matt if he'd had his gun on him, but seeing the only weapon he possessed was the toothpick he'd put in his mouth when he left the diner in Mariposa, he wasn't ready to risk Julia's life. They watched Matthew hold something up to the ranger—Julia's annual pass?—who admitted them. The white car drove on through. But Tom didn't have any such pass and asked Jim bluntly "Do we stop or storm the barricades?"

"Let me out," Jim ordered. "You follow. We'll be right behind you, call ahead for help."

Tom stopped the car at the gatehouse, and Crowley jumped out. Tom hated going on alone, for he knew the park was immense. There were several roads, several different areas she could drive to. How would they find them? Were there enough rangers to scout the whole park? She'd be dead by then—

He had to trust Jim, trust himself. He forged on. And prayed.

When he saw the arrow markers for various areas, he slowed down. It was almost light now. It wasn't raining anymore. It was going to be clear today, even though huge, marvelous dank clouds still hugged Half Dome. Why wasn't Crowley in a ranger vehicle behind him?

He saw Julia's car disappear around a curve. He held back, not wanting to risk Matt seeing him. Then he rounded the same curve and came to a halt at a stop sign. There were several ways to turn. Each had an arrow pointing out a different part of the park. Shit. Which way had she turned?

He'd lost them.

He sat there for a moment, frustrated, not knowing what to do. Then he noticed a vehicle parked around the corner. A ranger was out in the snow near it, holding a long pole of some kind, marking something on a little clipboard. The man had a parka on, but his badge was visible. Tom jumped out of the car and yelled, "Hey, I need your help!"

"Moment, sir," the young man called back. "Checking the depth of the snow here—"

Tom cut him off. "My wife was in the car in front of me. You must have seen it pass. She's being forced to drive a killer who has a knife."

The guy looked at him as if he were insane.

Then the man's radio beeped, and he opened the door and called in. Tom heard the message from Crowley, the alert for all rangers to be on the lookout for a white Honda Prelude . . .

Tom saw the man's eyes connect with his. "Now get the hell out of the snow and help me!"

Julia was so scared she didn't even think about her wet pants. She was winding up toward Glacier Point, and she hadn't seen Tom since the guard gate. Was it just that the road was so twisty? Had he stopped to enlist the guard's help? Would it be too late by the time anyone came to find her? Matthew had painfully buttoned his pants and picked up the knife. This was the end of the road. This was where he was taking her. But what was he going to do? Stab her as he had stabbed her parents and leave her out in the snow to die? Molly, your daughter, needs you!

No. She wasn't going to die. Not here, not because of him. She was thinking on her toes, now, here, in this moment; without a sign of Tom to help her, she had to help herself. She did not have a weapon. There was no gun, knife, nothing she could use against him. Except words. She had words, what she knew best, her work, her forte. She had to keep him talking till Tom showed up. "I went to LaCrosse."

"What?" He was startled.

"Once I knew the truth, there had to be a reason. Psychopaths aren't born, they're made. I figured someone had abused you, your parents beat you, you were an altar boy and the pastor stuck his finger up your ass before Mass, something!"

"So you could get me to get therapy someday?"

"To explain it, to make some kind of sick sense of it. But nothing happened to you. You were the exception. You were born nuts."

"Don't say that."

"Crazy. You're crazy. You have no conscience."

"Fuck you."

Silently unsnapping her seat belt without drawing attention to it, she continued to yell at him. "And that's what is so creepy about you, you sick fucking lunatic, you're just evil for its own sake." She took a quick glance around. Damn it, where was Tom? She was keeping Matt talking to give Tom time. But how long could she pull this off? "You call me an angel. How the hell would you know about something spiritual?"

"You can't talk to me like this, Julia!"

She slowly and carefully moved her hand to grip the door handle. She tensed her muscles, hand ready. She felt the door handle firm in her fingers. She glanced at the terrain outside the car. "It's what you can't have, what you can't attain. That goodness that you see in angels is what you're missing, and all that crap about loving angels and making me one is bullshit—you're a fraud."

"Shut your goddamned mouth!" He put his head in his hands, and she saw she'd maimed him with words. "I'm not bad, I'm not," he cried. "I'm not evil. Angels protect me. I know they're there. That's why I loved you—"

And she was gone.

She didn't even know how she did it exactly. She just knew it was then or never. Matthew was moaning about his angel fixation, and she'd bolted. She couldn't sit there and wait for Tom any longer. She found herself running through snow, directly out the door of the car, as fast as she could, heading uphill, which was probably stupid—why didn't she run down the road, where Tom might be coming?—but all she could think of was to get away from him, to dart, run, go, hide in the trees, disappear. She had a head start on him. She kept running and didn't look back.

Sweating, shaking, her heart racing with fear and exhaustion, she made her way to a clump of pines, disappeared behind one, stopping to get her breath, bending forward, breathing deeply, feeling relief. Thank God.

And then an arm reached out and a hand grabbed her neck. Matthew had been right behind her. Tom's boots had made him sure-footed in the snow, while she, in Reeboks, had kept slipping.

She was taken by surprise, but she was charged with energy. She tried to pull away from him, causing them both to fall into the snow. They rolled over and over, and finally his head struck the base of another tree, startling him for a moment. Julia took advantage of that second to get back on her feet, shaking the snow and pine needles from her face. She was ready to run again, but when she glanced at Matthew's position on the ground, she knew what she had to do first: kick him in the groin. He was lying with his legs spread. She lifted her foot and brought it between his legs with all the force she could muster. She heard the air go out of his lungs, just a kind of whimper, and then she turned and ran again, and this time she didn't stop.

When Matthew got to his knees, she was long gone. The pain was excruciating, but he forced himself to his feet, grasping the tree bark to help steady himself. He drew in a deep, cold breath and looked at her tracks. And he realized she was going in the wrong direction for safety. That was good for him, but she'd disappeared into the forest. Where exactly was she running? He stood still and listened. His incredible hearing wouldn't fail him. Christ, in jail he could hear a guy whispering his prayers on another floor. . . .

He heard her! He turned in the direction of the sound of feet crunching snow. She was heading toward Glacier Point itself. But she was a woman, and she wasn't used to this, no matter how many ski slopes she and her rich bitch sister had ascended. He knew he was in better shape. And she was smaller. Her steps were so much shorter than his, he could take one step for every two of hers. That would give him an advantage. And he knew a way over the incline that would save him time.

And he set out to do just that.

Julia was freezing and yet burning up at the same time. She wiped perspiration from her brow and realized, to her astonishment, that she was running in the snow without a jacket on. She'd been driving without one, and when she had opened the car door, she had just taken off, not even thinking where she was going or where she'd end up—

Not true. She had thought she'd find herself in Tom's arms. She was far from that now. She had no idea where she was. She could hear the wind singing through the pine needles somewhere high above her head. She could feel the dampness of the low-hanging clouds, and yet, now and then, she felt rays of sunlight like lasers cutting through the trees. She heard no one. She listened, stopping several times to catch her breath. Nothing. Just the sounds of nature, as she'd loved to hear them from her parents' deck. Back then they had been comforting. Today they were horrific.

She saw a clearing in the trees, and as she hurried toward it, she realized that the space opened onto the world itself; at the edge of the snow was only sky. She was on the brink of a huge precipice. She knew the details now. He had been going to push her off Glacier Point, going to make it look like an accident. She had been sure of that from the moment in the car when he'd said it was a "dangerous" place. She shivered, not so much from the cold seeping through her sweatshirt, but from the thought that this was where she was to die. She turned and headed away from the drop, back into the trees, and that's when she suddenly found a man standing in front of her. With a rifle in his hand. She screamed.

"It's all right, don't be alarmed," the young, tall stranger in a parka said to her, taking a step toward her.

The first thing she saw was his badge. And that meant he was not Matthew.

"Mrs. Larsen," the man said to her, "you're safe now."

"Dear God," she said, moving toward him with relief, realizing it was over. She ran to his arms, and he seemed startled by the gesture, a little embarrassed by it. "Tom," she said, "where is Tom?"

"Your husband went up the other way, over the ridge there." He pointed. "I called for back-up after I got the alert. A Mr. Crowley said you were being taken hostage."

"Crowley?" she gasped.

He pulled out his radio. "Where's the suspect?"

She shook her head. "I don't know. I kicked him in the balls and ran."

He seemed slightly amused. "Good girl," he said. Then the radio crackled and he talked into it. "I have the girl up on Pine Ridge under Glacier Point. Send a chopper. Suspect still at large in this area."

A voice over the radio said, "What's he wearing?"

"Jeans," Julia said, "and one of my husband's jackets, bright blue."

"Good." He pushed the button on the radio and said, "Suspect wearing bright blue jacket, blue jeans as well, shouldn't be hard to spot from—" His voice suddenly stopped. His eyes lifted to look directly into Julia's. Then the radio dropped from his hand, just before he did.

Julia gasped as the body crumpled before her. Then she saw the knife handle protruding from his back. And then she saw Matthew step out from behind the tree next to where the young ranger had been standing, reach down, and withdraw the bloody knife from the body. "Fucking bitch," he growled, looking at her.

"No . . . no," she whispered.

"Fucking bitch," Matthew repeated, hissing, and reached up and grabbed her wrist. "Fucking bitch that I loved, that I trusted, fucking bitch, what I did for you, what I went through, how I planned and killed and sat in that fucking jail and worked and worked and worked on you, and what do I get for it but to find out you're a fucking traitor!" It was relentless; the tirade continued without pause, without his even taking a breath, as he held tightly to her arm and pulled her through the snow.

She kicked and screamed and tried to grab his leg, tried to bite it, but he kicked her away when she did. He was pulling her toward the ridge again, ranting about how he should have killed her long ago, how she wasn't worth it, how she wasn't to be trusted, how she was no angel at all.

"You won't get away with this!"

He slapped her across the face. "Fucking bitch," he said again, pulling her even closer to the edge. "I'll tell them we went to the Ahwahnee for a kind of honeymoon—no, we're not registered. I'll tell them we went to my place, no one knows we were in San Francisco— Julia slipped and fell—she—"

Julia cried out to him, "You just killed a ranger! A helicopter is coming! They know you were at the apartment. Someone's going to look at my computer—it's all on the disks. Scully knows. Give up, Matt. You can't get out of this."

His eyes looked glazed suddenly, as if someone had pulled a shade. He knew she was right. It sank in. He stopped, as if dazed slightly, looking around. Julia knew he was assessing the situation, seeing he had no way out, and she hoped—prayed—he was going to give up. Instead, he grabbed her and pulled her to her feet. "We couldn't be together here," he said, putting his arm around her, almost gently, almost lovingly, then turned her to face the open sky off the edge of the cliff, "but we can be there."

He wants to go over the edge with me. It was suddenly so clear. All they had to do was walk a few paces and leap. No, not even leap, just continue walking. They'd fall to their deaths, together. Someone would write a book about them.

No way, she thought. She wasn't ready to die. This was *her* book and *her* life, and she was damned well going to live to finish them both herself. She pulled back, resisting. He tugged her, forcing her. She screamed, "No!"

"There's nothing you can do now!" he shouted back at her.

She fell to her knees again, going limp, grasping for something to hold onto, shrubs, sticks, anything to keep him from pulling her over the edge with him. "Noooooooooo!" she cried, her voice reverberating off the hills.

A second later they both heard, "Julia?" It echoed. *Julia Julia Julia . . . Julia . . . Julia . . . Julia.*

"*Tom!*" she screamed as loud as she could.

Tom Larsen, standing over the body of the ranger, perked up his ears. He heard where the echo was coming from. And he leaped over the man and charged in its direction.

Matt pulled her to the edge. She could see Yosemite Valley below. Her right hand was clasped around what had been an evergreen bush, but was now her anchor. This green thing was her last hope—unless Tom came in time. She screamed again, and Matt slapped her and told her to shut up. Then he got to his knees and started to wrench her hand from the bush. But she knew that Tom was on his way, she had to hold out—couldn't she buy more time? Wasn't she smarter than he was? "Matthew, Matt, wait—if this has to be the end, I want you to make love to me first." She held her breath, sure it wouldn't work. Not even he was that stupid.

But he was that needy, that obsessed. "What?"

She saw she could buy more time. She played right into his hand, improvising an emotional speech as if demons were coming out of her now. "That night with you, no matter what I know about you, it was the best night of my life. Why do you think this has been so hard for me? I loved you, I wanted you, I wanted you to make me feel whole again—"

"Bullshit. Bull shit. You're using me. You're lying to me again."

Julia moved to her feet and hugged him. "Please, Matt, do what you have to do, take us over the edge, but make me feel like a woman again just once." He felt her breath on his ear, he shuddered, she kissed him there. "Matt . . . you don't want to kill me, you want to love me. I lied. I didn't sleep with Tom. I only said that to hurt you. He couldn't get it up—"

He pulled away from her, turned his head because tears were coming. He sounded anguished. "Don't do this to me. Please don't do this to me. I can't love you now, not after what you did. Julia—?" He began to sob.

And she turned and tried to run.

But he grabbed her as fast as her foot lifted from the snow. He grasped her tightly, clinging to her, screaming as if there were snakes crawling in his blood. "You're going with me, we're going to be angels together . . ." And he pulled her toward the edge with a mighty yank.

Julia felt herself meeting her own death—

But then something attached itself to her right foot and instead of falling through space, she found herself hitting the snow with a resounding thud. Tom was holding her feet. He'd tackled her. "I've got you, Julia, I've got you," he cried.

Matt had fallen too, but not over the edge. He found himself suspended between earth and sky, holding onto her arm, pulling her, tugging her, dragging her, with all the weight of his body, toward the edge.

Julia slipped inches more toward the precipice. "Tom!" she screamed.

Tom felt himself slipping as well. He had nothing to anchor his weight to. "Bite his fingers," Tom ordered, "get his hands off your arm."

The fingernails of her right hand dug into the snow so deeply that she could feel them rip off. She heard his voice from beneath crying, ". . . with me, coming with me . . ." Her shoulders were at the edge, and she could see Matt clinging to her, hanging there, his feet against the rock, pulling her with him . . .

But she also felt the force holding onto her legs, the clenched hands of a man who loved her and wasn't going to let her go. Tom was strong, stronger than she'd realized, and slowly she felt herself reversing, going in the other direction. Tom was not only pulling her body back from the edge; he was pulling all of Matthew's weight as well. Julia let out a cry of pain as she thought her arm had suddenly been yanked from her body.

"I've got you," Tom said, grasping her feet with all his strength, "I've got you."

"He has my wrist," she moaned, the pain excruciating.

Matt dangled there, over the edge, screaming in

fright, trying to get his feet to lodge against the wet, slippery rock, but no matter where he tried to step, he slid. Each time he did, he put more pressure on Julia's wrist. She screamed in anguish again as he dug his fingernails into her flesh, and as she looked at his hand holding so desperately to hers, she saw her own blood beginning to seep into the snow.

Tom shouted, "Hit his hand with your other one. I've got you, I'm not going to let you go over. Hit him, bite him—" She did, but the only result was his other hand came up and clasped the one already tightly gripping her. Julia screamed again. She could not see Matt's head. She was not aware there was a man attached to those arms. It was as if hands were growing out of the snow. Julia knew it only because she felt his full weight pulling on an arm that she was sure would never work again.

Then Matt found some footing. Julia felt the pressure on her arm lessen, and suddenly Tom saw her body inching toward his, easier suddenly, as the full weight of Matt's body was no longer being suspended by her arm. Matt had found a piece of rock where his toe had taken hold, and he precariously put his head up over the edge and looked into Julia's eyes.

"Fucking lunatic!" Tom shouted at him. "Get away from her!"

"No," Julia moaned, "no, please—" Her fright made her entire body stiffen.

Matt pulled himself up on his elbows, his hands

moving up Julia's sleeve, grasping her arm near the elbow. Tom warned him to get away, to stop, not to come closer, but Matt called his bluff. "You let go of her and we both go over," Matt said, reasonable. Tom was paralyzed; there was nothing he could do but hold onto Julia. But in doing so, he was holding onto Matt as well. Matthew grasped her arm tighter with both his hands, and using his feet as a wedge, he tugged her so that she, and Tom, moved closer to him again. Tom knew that Matthew was right. If he let go, Julia would fly over the edge with Matthew. He held tight, hoping that Matt would finally collapse of exhaustion, but if he didn't, if Julia was going over, he'd damn well go with them.

Then Matthew gave a last, hard tug, and Julia's arm pulled out of its socket.

Julia screamed with such pain it caused even Matthew to shudder.

But then, seemingly from out of nowhere, they heard a growling sound.

Tom's head turned in the direction of the snarl, expecting to find a bear hovering over them. But instead he saw only Maggie, her head down, her fangs bared, eyes intent on her master.

Julia saw her too. And she suddenly remembered something. Matt's words. *She's been abused. Was afraid of her own shadow.* Yes, when he told her how he'd come to get Maggie. *The guy had been beating both his wife and the dog . . . she eventually saved the woman's life* . . . Julia screamed, this time right at Maggie. And she saw Maggie growl even louder.

Matt shouted, "Maggie, stop."

But the dog didn't.

Attacked the bastard before he choked the woman to death, chewed him up enough . . . Julia seized the moment. She commanded the dog now. "Yes, Maggie, get him, get him, Maggie! Help me!"

Matt saw his dog coming toward him, attacking. He let go of Julia and leaped to his feet, saying, "Maggie, no—"

When the dog hit him, fangs bared, it was with such force that both his feet seemed to levitate from the ground. She leaped to his chest with such determination—much the same way she'd jumped on Julia the day they met two years ago—that he coughed out all the air that was in his lungs, and his entire body shot out into the sky.

Julia and Tom watched the moment, and it was etched into their minds forever, as if it were happening in slow motion. Matthew's shocked expression. Maggie's paws striking his chest. Both of them, suspended in midair over Yosemite Valley, the dog directly atop him as he became airborne . . .

Then they disappeared from sight, and it was quiet and still, the deep snow absorbing all the sound, so quiet you'd never have guessed there were even people there, much less what had just happened.

But in a moment, as Tom let go of Julia's legs and

crawled around her in the snow, pulling her into his arms there on the ground, the stillness was invaded by the whirring of blades, and they looked up to see a helicopter hovering directly above them. It seemed to descend from the clouds, and then a voice from a loudspeaker boomed that rangers were on their way.

Julia cried tears of joy and pain. "You're going to be all right. It's over now, he's gone forever," Tom told her, but she kept her eyes closed, waiting for him to pop up over the edge and do it all over again, the man she couldn't kill.

But that didn't happen. Jim Crowley and an armed ranger came from the other direction, guns drawn, but it was all for nothing. Matthew was dead. They were alive. They had made it.

She closed her eyes for a moment and tried to get her senses back. "How did you—?"

"You know I'm a mystery buff," Tom said, mustering a smile. "Only I didn't know you were writing one. I swiped your disks. I read all of it last night, when you were with him. That's why I came to the condo."

"I wasn't pushing you away," Julia said, choking back tears, "but I just couldn't tell you what I was doing—"

"I know," he said gently, cradling her head in his arms. "I think I would have done the same. But no one ever has to know, ever." He looked into her eyes. "Do you understand what I'm saying?"

She swallowed hard. She didn't know what to say.

"Cornelia would have done the same thing," he assured her, "she even said so. She read it too."

Julia looked somewhat relieved. "Really? Honestly?"

Jim Crowley interrupted. "I'd agree." He eyed them both to make his point. "Get my drift?"

Julia closed her eyes. Keeping the secret, Crowley smiled and left them alone. "Tom," she said softly, "do you think there's a chance? I mean, could you call Melba and book a room at the Halekulani?"

He put his fingertips on her lips. "Forget Hawaii. I'm a changed man. It's you, me, and Molly now. We're going to a Motel 6 in the new Hyundai I'm buying tomorrow."

"Sir?" They looked up. A young ranger was standing over them. "The lady all right?"

"My arm," Julia said, "it feels as though it's not there."

"You're bleeding too," Tom said, looking at her mangled wrist and fingers. Blood was dripping from where the nails had been.

"Better let us see to it," the ranger said, helping her up.

"The other ranger," Tom started to explain, "Hinson stabbed him and—"

"Yes, sir," the tall boy said with a heavy nod, "we know, we found the body. He was my buddy."

"I'm sorry," Tom added.

The ranger looked as if he was about to break down, but professionalism won out and he wiped the look off his face. "You walk all right, ma'am?" the ranger asked Julia.

She nodded. Tom supported her left side.

"Right this way," the ranger said, leading them.

But Crowley suddenly muttered, "Well, I'll be."

"What is it?" Tom asked, seeing she was alarmed.

Julia hurried to the edge, where Jim was standing with both hands on his hips, shaking his head. Tom joined her there, putting his arm around her for support, and they looked at what Crowley was looking at.

There Matt was. On a flat promontory only about fifteen feet down, flattened on a mattress of the purest white snow. The dog was lying right next to him, as inert as he was. "Oh, no," Julia cried, "Maggie . . . she's dead."

Tom pulled her to him to comfort her. "She saved your life," he said.

But then, as Tom attempted to lead her away, she said, "Look! Tom, look—" And he did.

And what they saw astonished them. The dog lifted her head. She shook slightly, wobbling, looking dazed, but she was alive. "The snow must have cushioned her fall," Julia said.

"Or Matt broke it," Tom surmised.

Crowley agreed. "Dog probably landed on him."

And then, with great joy, they watched Maggie get to all fours, shake the snow from her coat, and look up. Her tail started wagging like crazy, and Julia called her name and started to cry again.

Then something else on the bluff caught their eye. Matthew was flat on his back, just the way he'd gone over the edge, just as he'd fallen, just as he'd hit. But what astonished Julia was the position he was in. He was lying on his back, his feet slightly spread apart, his arms stretched out from his sides, and if it hadn't been for the telltale blood seeping from his mouth, one would think he was simply sleeping, or lying there with his eyes closed, enjoying the moment. But what was utterly amazing to Julia was the huge arcs of white that hugged him on both sides. He'd hit the rock and his arms had flailed a couple of times before he actually died, causing wings to form in the snow. His right foot must have scissored out from his body, for it had created a skirt of white to match the wings. A perfect angel. An angel in the snow, the kind kids make.

Tom grasped Julia's shoulder as she peered down. Crowley promised they'd have the dog out in an hour, and the ranger said they'd bring her to the park infirmary, where a doctor would look after Julia. Tom started to lead Julia away, but she stopped one more time to take a last look over the side.

And below, on the flat rock jutting out of the mountainside not all that far beneath them, the angel's snow white appearance began to change. Now the pristine image was being dissected by a stream of warm blood coming from Matthew Hinson's head, melting it, flowing down off one side, where a trickle of pink began to drip onto the rocks below.

A shot rings out at the White House.

But the President is not the target.

Now TV's top reporter is on the run.

Find out why . . .

Hidden Agenda

The new page-turner from
Thom Racina

A Dutton Hardcover
Available in January 1998